Praise for the work of Diana Norman:

"Cracking historical novels."

—*Daily Mirror* (London)

"Drama, passion, intrigue and danger, I loved it and didn't want it to end ever."

—*Sunday Times* (London)

"It's all good, dirty fun shot through with more serious insights into the historical treatment of women and perhaps, in its association of sex, sleaze, greed and politics, not so far removed from present realities after all."

—*Independent on Sunday* (London)

"Quite simply, splendid."

—Frank Delaney, author of *At Ruby's*

DIANA NORMAN

A Catch of Consequence

BERKLEY BOOKS, NEW YORK

This is a work of fiction. Names, characters, places, and incidents
either are the product of the author's imagination or are used fictitiously,
and any resemblance to actual persons, living or dead, business
establishments, events, or locales is entirely coincidental.

A Berkley Book
Published by The Berkley Publishing Group
A division of Penguin Group (USA) Inc.
375 Hudson Street
New York, New York 10014

Copyright © 2002 by Diana Norman
Text design by Tiffany Kukec
Cover design by Rita Frangie
Cover photo by George Romney / Corbis

PRINTING HISTORY
Published by HarperCollins UK in 2002
Berkley trade paperback edition / July 2003

Library of Congress Cataloging-in-Publication Data

Norman, Diana.
    A catch of consequence / Diana Norman.
      p. cm.
    ISBN 0-425-19015-3
    1. Boston (Mass.)—History—Revolution, 1775–1783—Fiction. 2. London
(England)—History—18th century—Fiction. 3. Americans—England—London—Fiction.
4. Upper class families—Fiction. I. Title.

PR6064.O73 C3 2003
823'.914—dc21

                                                                              2002038239

PRINTED IN THE UNITED STATES OF AMERICA

10 9 8 7 6 5 4 3 2 1

To my cousin, Aeron

AUTHOR'S NOTE

During the last half of the eighteenth century the words 'Tory' and 'Whig' were in effect meaningless in the Right and Left sense that is recognizable to us today. Grenville, for instance, who imposed the Stamp Tax on the American colonies, could call himself a Whig, and so could the Marquis of Rockingham, who repealed it. Therefore, to keep things unfairly simple, I have used 'Tory' as Charles Fox did, to designate upholders of prerogative power as opposed to those who believed in the liberty of the subject.

The lines spoken by Wullie Fergusson in Chapter Seventeen come from *The Northumborman* (Iron Press, 1999), a collection of verse by the dialect poet Fred Reed. They are his paraphrase of the Twenty-third Psalm as spoken by an old Northumbrian miner, Mr John Davison, who would recite his version of Biblical passages in the darkness of the North Seaton Pit during the First World War.

I should like to thank my friend Sally Adams, Principal of the KUTA College of Writing, for her invaluable assistance with this book.

A Catch of Consequence

Diana Norman

BOOK ONE

Boston

Chapter One

THE woman feathering her boat round the bend of the Charles River into Massachusetts Bay that early morning on August 15 1765 was about to save someone's life and change her own.

Later on, in rare retrospective moments, she would ask herself: 'What if I hadn't?' A useless question, suggesting there'd been a decision—and she made no decision; Makepeace Burke could no more watch a fellow creature drown without trying to help it than she could stop the wind blowing.

That's not to imply that Makepeace was a gentle woman. She wasn't; she just hated waste, and unnecessary death was wasteful.

If her boat was dirty, she was clean in a scrubbed sort of way, or as clean as you can be when you've been hauling in lobster-pots since before dawn. A virgin who, by 1765 American standards, was like her boat in being ancient. At twenty-four years old, she should have been married with children but she'd been both unfortunate and picky.

The gangly figure in faded brown cotton, her skirt pinned up washerwoman style, a leather cap tied tightly under her chin to hide her hair giving her the look of an insect, propelled her boat with the professionalism of a sea-dog. Bobbing along in the sunlight, from far off she resembled a curiously shaped bit of wrack, a piece off a figurehead, something saltily wooden, astray on the glistening water.

About to have her life changed.

To Makepeace Burke, emerging into the great harbour's North End, the damage that she saw had been done to her waterfront overnight was change enough. Some of the damage was old and caused by the English: empty warehouses, wharves sprouting weed. Boats that had once been proud, respected smugglers delivering cheap sugar to willing Bostonian customers lay demasted and up-ended on the hards, killed by the newly efficient, newly incorruptible British Customs and Excise. Only sugar from the English West Indies, the *expensive* English West Indies, could be imported now—and that was unloaded further down.

But last night, in protest against the English and their shite Stamp Tax and Navigations Acts, Boston had gone on the rampage and done damage in return. *Hadn't* they, by Hokey! Even from this distance, she could see the depredations to the Custom House. The bonfires were dying down but the smitch of burning was everywhere, even out here on the water. Papers that had drifted off the bonfires spewed along the quay. And the new warehouse Stamp Master Oliver was having built was now no more than a pile of broken timbers. Serve the old bugger right.

Makepeace Burke disapproved of rioting—not good for trade—but she disapproved of the Stamp Tax, which had been the cause of last night's mayhem, a mighty sight more. The tax fell heavily on taverns and she was a tavern-keeper.

The August heat had been near suffocating for a month, like a volcano grumbling under the town in sympathy with the discontent of its inhabitants. Last night—what triggered it nobody knew—the cone blew off and out rushed lava of white-heat fury against unemployment, the government, its colonial representatives, its damn taxes and interference, its press gangs and its assumption that Bostonians were going to take all these things lying down.

Customs officials, known English-loving Tories, lawmen: all had been hunted through the streets by Sons of Liberty smeared with war-paint and howling like Mohawks, bless 'em. The British garrison had too few soldiers to put down a ladies' sewing circle, let alone an outbreak of these proportions. The town had been streaked with flame and pounded with the beat of drums until it seemed that light was noise and noise was light.

If that was riot, Lord knew what revolution'd be. Well, maybe it *was* revolution. Sam Adams was preaching something suspiciously along the lines of it being time Americans threw off the English yoke. Didn't put it like that but every good Bostonian knew what he meant.

Customers had run into the Roaring Meg to pass on the latest news, down a glass of celebratory flip and rush off again to join in. 'Don't you go outside, now, 'Peace,' Zeobab Fairlee'd said. 'The Sons is lickered up. Got at a few cellars. No place for a respectable female in them streets tonight.'

So she'd stayed with her tavern in case they tried to get at her liquor stock—Sons of Liberty or no Sons of Liberty, she wasn't in the business of free drinks—but, come the revolution, she'd get her father's musket down from the roof and march against the British with the best of 'em. She'd give 'em taxes.

She liked these lovely mornings, collecting lobster-pots. Peaceful. Hot already. Further out, towards the islands, gulls floated against a sky like blue enamel. Two tundra swans passed low over her head as the squadron came from inland, enormous wings held bowed and still, outstretched feet ready to furrow the water, heavy as pieces of masonry hurtling through the air. They were settling, fluting to each other, their size dwarfing the rafts of snow geese and oldsquaws further out.

More peaceful than ever this morning. Usually, down at the business end of the harbour, angular heron-like cranes dipped and straightened with bulging nets in their bills as they emptied incoming merchantmen and filled the holds of those getting ready to set out. Men with bales on their heads were to be seen filing up some gangplanks and down others, looking at a distance like infestations of marcher ants. Sails were taken in, others hoisted, all flapping like pinioned birds; greetings, commands, farewells—sounds of human busyness floating across the water.

But not today. Captains, worried for their cargo, had stood their ships further off where the Sons of Liberty couldn't board them. They were out in the bay now, like a huddle of white-shawled grannies, until it was safe to come back. Deserted quays waited for them, sticking out into the harbour in protruding, wooden teeth.

She had to feather so that, by standing in the prow, she could negotiate between the detritus that had been thrown in the water during the night: pieces of door, window-frames, the lid of a desk, all of it a hazard to little boats like hers as it was carried out to sea on a combination of current and ebb-tide. A waste. Later on, she'd get Tantaquidgeon to see what he could salvage. Dry it out for tinder.

Lord, it was quiet. As she passed Copp's Quay, a couple of painted figures that had been lying on it staggered to their feet and slunk off like dogs who knew they'd been naughty. Don't let the magistrates get thee, boys. From the look of 'em, she'd guess their heads were punishment enough.

And there was Tantaquidgeon waiting for her as he always did, standing on the Roaring Meg's gimcrack jetty and staring out to sea like the statue of a befeathered Roman emperor.

She was heading towards him when a prickle of movement a hundred yards further on caught her eye. A knot of men on Fish Quay, three, maybe four—it was difficult to see against the reflection of sun on water—a suggestion of furious energy and striped faces. Not all the rioters had gone home to sleep it off, then. No sound from them that she could hear above the call of the swans. One was standing still, keeping watch, while the others threw objects into the harbour as if they hadn't slaked their revenge even yet. Something heavy had just splashed in, something else now—a hat. Waste again.

With her free hand she shaded her eyes to see who the men were. The one acting lookout was Sugar Bart, recognizable at once by the crutch that did duty for his missing leg. Would be. Always in trouble against authority, Bart.

Mackintosh? What was that shite doing this far north of town? No mistaking his swagbelly, painted or not; she'd seen it too often parading at the head of the South End mob on Guy Fawkes' Nights.

Mackintosh was leader of one of the gangs which took flaming papal effigies and trouble onto Boston's streets every November 5, indulging in bloody and, sometimes, mortal battles with each other to show their enthusiasm for the Protestant cause.

Couldn't make out the others.

Sugar Bart had seen her; she saw him stiffen and point. She'd be a blur against the sun. She waved to show she was a friend. A good taverner kept in with her customers, whatever hell they were raising.

Now what? She looked behind her. From her vantage point, Makepeace saw what Sugar Bart couldn't.

A patrol of armed redcoats from North End fort was marching down the wharves towards Fish Quay, heading for Bart and the Mohawks who, because of the overhang of warehouses, couldn't see it. The stamp of military boots came crisply to her, carried by the water, but Bart wouldn't hear that either.

Makepeace put two fingers in her mouth and whistled a warning. Bart looked. She nodded towards the redcoats—and saw their muskets being levelled at her. She whistled on: *With a tow, row, row, row, row, row for the British Grenadiers*—signal to Bart there were soldiers coming, desperate advice to the soldiers she was a loyal subject of King George III, the shite.

One of the soldiers advanced to the edge of the wharf, shading his eyes. The sun was in its stride now, fierce enough to bleach colour and form out of the view of those looking into it. 'You. Seen anybody?'

She cupped her ear, wasting time. The Mohawks had legged it; Bart was hobbling off.

'Seen. Any. Body, you deaf bitch.'

She held up one of her pots. 'Lobster. Lob. Ster.' And may you boil in the saucepan with him, thee red-backed bastard.

The soldier gave up, the patrol resumed its advance down the waterfront and there was no time for reaction because, whilst dealing with the problem, she *had* seen a body. An upturned table with broken legs entangled with rags, part of last night's wreckage, twirled on the current. From the corner of her eye she'd noticed it separate, a piece slipping off from the rest. And the new bit of flotsam was a man.

Idly, in case the soldiers turned round, she feathered the boat to where the current would bring the fellow near it. He was alive; a hand moved before he was carried under.

She kept whistling, for continuity's sake in case the redcoats could still hear her, and to let the man know he didn't have far to swim for rescue.

Je*hos*ophat, wouldn't you know it? The fool couldn't swim. He was being sucked under again, only his clawing fingers visible above the surface.

Keep feathering? It was slower than rowing but to take the oar from the bow, find the other and put both in the rowlocks would lose minutes the drowning man couldn't spare.

Makepeace kept standing, waggling her oar through the water like a giant mixing spoon with a friction that took the skin off even her toughened hands. Passing her jetty, where Tantaquidgeon still contemplated the horizon, she shouted: 'Git, will you?' angling her head towards Fish Quay, and saw him start off in the right direction in his infuriatingly unhurried stride.

The current, fierce at this corner of the harbour, was against her and taking the drownder further and further away from the quay. As he rolled, she saw a face white as cod, eyes closed in acceptance of death. Frantically, she feathered harder and closed the gap between them. She yelled: 'Hold up,' unshipped her oar and ran it forward under his left arm, which rose aimlessly to let it slip. She lunged again, this time towards the right arm and the blade was caught between waistcoat and sleeve, held by the pressure of water.

With all her weight, Makepeace pressed down on her end of the oar so that the man's upper body came up, lopsided like a hunchback, hair trailing across the surface, nose and mouth blessedly free.

There was never anything so heavy but if she let go she'd lose him. The boat tilted wickedly. The body began to swing astern where, if it got behind the boat, it would wriggle itself off the oar.

She let the blade dip and then, with a pull that shot pain up her back, jerked her end of the oar into the starboard rowlock. Even so, to bear down against the body's weight demanded almost more than she had.

She cricked her neck, looking for help. Tantaquidgeon was on the quay. 'Boathook. Fast.' He strolled off to find one. They could drift to Portugal by the time he got back. Nothing to be done; she couldn't control the boat and keep this bastard out of the water at the same time; he wasn't helping, just hung there, dipping under, coming up, eyes half closed. 'Wake up,' she screamed, 'wake up, you crap-hound! D'ye want to die?'

The shout jagged through nothingness to the last cognitive area of the drowning man's brain and found a flicker of response.

Not actively die, he thought, and then: But life's not worthy of effort either. His neck hurt. Plummets of glaucous water swam with the image of two naked bodies writhing on a floor, neither of them his own. Wounded long before the sea decided to kill him, he was slowing to languor. Not worth effort, not worth it.

But there were rises when he felt warmth on the back of his head and shoulders and caught glimpses of lacquer-blue and was disturbed by an appalling voice chiselling him awake.

As always when frightened, Makepeace became angry. Fury helped her haul in the oar until the body was against the boat starboard, a process that dipped it under again.

Holding the blade with one hand—buggered if she'd lose a good oar—she grabbed at the man and hooked his jacket over the rowlock so that he hung from it, head lolling. 'An' you *stay* there.'

Somehow, keeping her weight to port, she feathered back to where Tantaquidgeon was kneeling, boathook in hand. She caught the hook's business end and, none too gently, shoved it under the man's coat which wrinkled up to the shoulders. She directed it as the Red Indian pulled. A long, wet body slithered onto her lobster-pots and flopped among waving, reaching claws.

Then she sat down.

After a while she stirred herself and, wincing, dragged at the man's coat so that he was turned onto his back. Using her foot—

it was less painful to her back than bending down to it—she nudged his face to one side then pressed her boot on his breadbasket, released it, pressed again. She pedalled away, as if at an organ, until water began dribbling onto the lobsters from the man's mouth and he coughed.

Makepeace Burke and her catch looked at each other.

Through a wavering veil of nausea, the man saw bone and freckles, a pair of concerned and ferocious blue eyes, all framed by hair the colour of flames that had escaped from its cap and which, with the sun shining through it, made an aureole. It was the head of a saint remembered from a Flemish altarpiece.

Makepeace saw a bloody nuisance.

Here was not, as she'd thought, a lickered Son of Liberty who'd whooped himself into the harbour; the Sons didn't sport clothes that, even when soaked and seaweeded, shouted wealth. Here was gentry.

'Who are you? What happened to you?'

He really couldn't be bothered to remember, let alone answer. He managed: 'Does it matter?'

'Matters to *me*.' She'd expended a lot of effort.

Long time, thought Sir Philip Dapifer. Long time since I mattered to a woman. He drifted off, oddly consoled, into unconsciousness.

Makepeace sat and considered, unaware she was still whistling 'The British Grenadiers' or that her foot tapped in time to it on the drownder's chest.

If the bugger hadn't fallen, he'd been pushed *and she'd seen it done*. Watched by Bart and others, Mackintosh had thrown the poor bastard in like he was rotten fish. And left him—admitted, they couldn't dally—not caring if he drowned or floated. *And* worked on him first from the look of him—his face might be the moon fallen into her boat, so livid and bruised it was.

So he was enemy. Customs, excise, taxman, Tory, British-boot-licker: whatever he was she'd rescued him. 'Should've let you drown,' she grumbled at him, knowing she could not.

What to do? If she handed him over to the authorities right

now he could identify his attackers—and say what you like about Mouse Mackintosh and Sugar Bart, they were at least patriots and she'd be damned if she helped some Tory taxman get 'em hanged. 'Ought to throw you back by rights.'

Well, staying here would surely solve the problem because, from the look of the drownder, he was on his last gasp. And that, thought Makepeace Burke, was pure foolishness—a waste of the trouble she'd taken in the first place.

She looked up at the quay and jerked her head at Tantaquidgeon to get into the boat. 'The Meg. You row.'

She covered the body at her feet with the tarpaulin to keep it warm. There was still nobody about. What had been an event of hours for her had been minutes of everybody else's time. Boston kept the sleep of the hungover. Tantaquidgeon's white eagle feather bobbed hypnotically back and forth as he rowed past the slipways on which stood anchors as big as whale-flukes, past the rope-walks, the cranes, the ships' chandlers, the warehouses and boatyards, all parts of the machine that on normal days serviced the busiest port in America.

Behind him, appearing to stand on an island, though actually on a promontory, was their destination, the Roaring Meg, two storeys of weatherbeaten boarding. Ramshackle maybe, like the rest of the waterfront, but an integral piece of the great ribbon of function which faced the Atlantic and provided incoming ships with their first view of the town. Here was Boston proper, not in its generous parks nor its wide, tree-lined streets and white-spired churches, not in its market places, bourses and pillared houses, but in an untidy, salt-stained, invigorating seaboard generating the wealth that sustained all the rest.

Makepeace was proud that her tavern was part of it. But it was a matter of shame to her, as it was to all right-thinking citizens, that there was yet another Boston. In the maze of lanes behind the waterfront, out of sight like a segment of rot in an otherwise healthy-looking apple, lay gin houses and whoreshops providing different services, where the crab-like click of dice and a tideline of painted women waited for sinners in darkness of soul.

The city fathers attempted to cleanse the area from time to time, but prevent it washing back they could not, nor did they entirely wish to; they were not only the town's moral guardians but entrepreneurs in a port dependent on trade—and sailors from visiting merchant ships didn't necessarily seek after righteousness.

A voyager disembarking at Boston's North End had a choice. If he were heedless of his purse, his health and his hope of salvation, he would disappear into those sinning, acrid alleys. If he were wise, he would make for the coastal beacon that was the Roaring Meg, with its smell of good cooking and hum of decent conversation.

In winter, when light from whale-oil lamps shone through its bottle-bottomed windows to be diffused in snow, the Roaring Meg resembled a Renaissance nativity scene, a sacred stable. Named after the noisy stream that ran alongside it before entering the sea, the tavern deserved its halo. Makepeace kept it free of the Devil's flotsam by perpetual moral sweeping, brushing harlots and their touts from her doorstep, plumping up idlers like pillows, ejecting bullies, vomiters, debtors and those who took the Lord's name in vain.

A little stone bridge led over the stream to its street door above which was displayed the information that John L. Burke was licensed to dispense ales and spirituous liquors. John L. Burke was in the grave these three years, having energetically drunk himself into it, but a man's name above the door inspired more confidence in strangers than would a woman's, so Makepeace kept it there.

North End magistrates conspired in the fiction and, if asked, would say that the licensee was actually Makepeace's young brother Aaron, but they knew, as did everybody else, who was the Roaring Meg's true landlord and privately acknowledged the fact. 'Makepeace Burke,' one justice had been heard to say, 'is a crisp woman.'

An accolade, 'crisp': American recognition of efficiency and good Puritan hard-headedness. Makepeace took pride in it but knew how hard it had been to win and how easily it could be taken away. One word of scandal or complaint to the magistrates, one impatient creditor, one more storm to hole the Meg's creaking roof—there was no money with which to replace it—and she would lose her vaunted crispness *and* her tavern.

And now that she had a calm moment in which to consider the consequences of what she was doing—in Puritan society wise women always considered consequences—suspicion grew that she might be jeopardizing both merely by harbouring the drownder under her roof.

The Cut, the lane at the sea end of which the Meg stood, was as respectable as the tavern itself, a narrow row of houses that passed through the surrounding wickedness like a file of soldiers in hostile Indian forest. Eyes at its windows watched for any falter in its rigid morality and one pair in particular was trained on herself.

'Makepeace Burke's picked up a man.' She could hear the voices now. And, because the Cut was as patriotic as it was respectable, she could also hear the addendum: 'A *Tory* man.'

It hadn't been easy, a woman running a tavern. One of the proudest moments of her life—and the most profitable—had been when, with the imposition of the Stamp Tax, the local lodge of the Sons of Liberty had chosen the Roaring Meg for their secret meetings. Good men most of 'em, like nearly all her customers, but, again like her other regulars, driven to desperation by an unemployment that was the direct result of British government policy.

And among those very Sons was at least one of the group that had thrown the drownder into the harbour. Mighty pleased *they'd* be to find Makepeace Burke succouring the enemy. An enemy, what's more, who'd report them to the magistrates quicker'n ninepence.

'Who done it on us?' Sugar Bart would ask, as he climbed the gallows' steps.

'Makepeace Burke,' the Watch would reply.

After that, no decent patriot—and all her clientele were patriots—would set foot in the Roaring Meg again.

Oh no, she couldn't trust the Watch not to give her away; apart from being as big a collection of incompetents as ever let a rogue slip through its fingers, it was hand in glove with the Sons of Liberty. Last night, when Governor Bernard had called on the Watch to drum the alarm, he'd discovered that its men had joined the mob and were happily destroying property with the rest.

The nearer she got to her tavern, the more perturbed Make-peace became. 'Lord, Lord,' she prayed out loud, 'I did my Chris-tian duty and saved this soul; ain't there to be *no* reward?'

Like most Boston Puritans, Makepeace had a pragmatic rela-tionship with the Lord, regarding Him as a celestial managing di-rector and herself as a valued worker in His company. Until now she'd found no conflict between Christianity and good business. She obeyed the Commandments, most of 'em, and expected ben-efits and an eternal pension in return.

And the Lord answered her plea this bright and hot August morning by skimming the last word of it across the surface of His waters until it hit a wharf wall and bounced it back at her in an echo: *Reward, reward.*

Receiving it, Makepeace became momentarily beautiful because she smiled, a rare thing with her, showing exquisitely white teeth with one crooked canine that emphasized the perfection of the others.

'You surely can hand it to the Lord,' she told Tantaquidgeon. 'He got brains.'

The drownder was in her debt. There was no greater gift than that of life—and she'd just given his back to him. In return, he could reward her with a promise of silence. Least he could do.

She looked down fondly at the richly clad bundle by her feet. 'And maybe some cash with it,' she said.

Having settled on a conclusion she'd actually reached at the moment the drownder opened his eyes, she felt better; she was a woman who liked a business motive.

Also she was intrigued—more than that, *involved*—by the man.

As someone who'd fought for survival all her life, Makepeace was affronted by apathy. Never having accepted defeat herself, this drownder's 'Does it matter?' had excited her contempt but also her curiosity and pity. Look at him: fine boots—well, he'd lost one but the other was excellent leather; gold lacing on his cuffs. A man possessed of money and, therefore, every happiness. So why was he uncaring about his fate?

The boat bumped gently against the Meg's tottering jetty. Makepeace looked around with a surreptitiousness that would have attracted attention had there been onlookers to see it.

Bending low, she climbed the steps and looked into the taproom. Nobody there. She went through and opened the front door to peer into the Cut for signs of activity. Nothing again.

She returned to the boat and told Tantaquidgeon all was clear. She threaded her lobster-pots together and dragged them up and through the sea entrance to her tavern with Tantaquidgeon behind her, the tarpaulined Englishman draped over his forearms like laundry.

Chapter Two

THE Roaring Meg's kitchen doubled as its surgery, and the cook as its doctor, both skills acquired in the house of a Virginian tobacco planter who, when Betty escaped from it, had posted such a reward for her capture that it was met only by her determination not to be caught.

She might have been—most runaway slaves were—if she hadn't encountered John L. Burke leaving Virginia with wife, children, Indian and wagon for the north after another of his unsuccessful attempts at farming. John and Temperance Burke had little in common but neither, particularly Temperance, approved of slavery, and they weren't prepared to hand Betty back to her owner, however big the reward. She'd stayed with the family ever after, even during her late, brief marriage, despite the fact that John Burke's failures at various enterprises often necessitated her working harder than she would have done in the plantation house.

She examined the body on the kitchen table, deftly turning and prodding. 'Collarbone broke.' She enclosed the head in her large, pink-palmed hands, eyes abstracted, her fingers testing it like melon. 'That Mouse Mackintosh,' she said, 'he sure whopped this fella. Lump here big as a love-apple.'

'I thought maybe we could redd him up a piece, then Tanta-quidgeon row him to Castle William after dark,' Makepeace said, hopefully, 'Dump him outside, like.'

Betty pointed to a meat cleaver hanging on the wall. 'You've a mind to kill him, use that,' she said. 'Quicker.'

'Oh . . . oh *piss*.' Makepeace ran her hand round her neck to wipe it and discovered for the first time that her cap was hanging from its strap and her hair was loose. Hastily, she bundled both into place. Respectable women kept their hair hidden—especially when it was a non-Puritan red.

Although the kitchen's high windows faced north, the sun was infiltrating their panes. Steam came from the lobster boilers on a fire that burned permanently in the grate of the kitchen's brick range, and the back door had to be shut not just, as today, to prevent intruders but to keep out the flies from the privy which, with the hen-house, occupied the sand-salted strip of land that was the Meg's back yard.

Makepeace went to the door. Young Josh had been posted as lookout. 'Anybody comes, we're closed. Hear me?'

'Yes 'm, Miss 'Peace.'

She bolted the door, as she had bolted the tavern's other two. Tantaquidgeon was keeping vigil at the front. 'Git to it, then,' she said.

They were reluctant to cut away the patient's coat in order to set his collarbone—it had to be his best; nobody could afford two of that quality—so they stripped him of it, and his shirt, causing him to groan.

'Lucky he keep faintin',' Betty said. She squeezed her eyes shut and ran her fingers along the patient's shoulder: 'Ready?'

Makepeace put a rolled cloth between his teeth and then bore down on his arms. Her back ached. 'Ready.'

There was a jerk and a muffled 'Aaagh'.

'Oh, hush up,' Makepeace told him.

Betty felt the joint. 'Sweet,' she said. 'I'm one sweet sawbones.'

'Will he do?'

'Runnin' a fever. Them Sons give him a mighty larrupin'. Keep findin' new bruises and we ain't got his britches off yet.'

'You can do that upstairs. He's got to stay, I guess.'

'Don't look to me like he's ready to run off.'

Makepeace sighed. It had been inevitable. 'Which room?'

Betty grinned. The Meg was a tavern, not an inn, and took no overnight guests. The bedroom she shared with her son was directly across the lane from the window of the house opposite. Aaron's, too, faced the Cut. The only one overlooking the sea and therefore impregnable to spying eyes was Makepeace's.

'Damn*nation*.' The problem wasn't just the loss of her room but the fact that its door was directly across the corridor from the one serving the meeting-room used by the Sons of Liberty.

Oh well, as her Irish father used to say: 'Let's burn that bridge when we get to it.'

They put the bad arm in a sling of cheese-cloth and Tantaquidg-eon lifted the semi-naked body and carried it up the tiny, winding back stairs, followed by Betty with a basket of salves. 'And take his boot off afore it dirties my coverlet,' Makepeace hissed after them.

Left alone, she looked round the kitchen for tell-tale signs of the catch's presence in it. Nothing, apart from a bloodstain on the table that had seeped from a wound on his head. Je*ho*sophat, they'd cudgelled him hard.

She was still scrubbing when Aaron came in, having rowed back from Cambridge after a night out with friends. 'All hail, weird sister, I expect my breakfast, the Thaneship of Cawdor and a scolding. Why all the smoke in town, by the way? Did Boston catch fire?'

'It surely did.' He looked dark-eyed with what she suspected was a night of dissipation but she was so relieved he'd missed the rioting that he got an explanation, a heavy breakfast and a light scolding.

He was horrified. 'Good God,' he said.

'Aaron!'

'Well . . . the idiots, the weak-brained, scabby, disloyal, bloody—'

'Aaron!'

'—imbeciles. I blame Sam Adams. What's he thinking of to let scum like that loose on respectable people?'

'You stop your cussing,' she said. 'They ain't scum. And Sam's a good man. Respectable people? Respectable lick-spittles, respectable yes-King-Georgers, no-King-Georgers, let me wipe your boots with my necktie, your majesty. I wished I'd been with 'em.'

'It's a reasonable tax, 'Peace.'

'You don't pay it.' Immediately, she was sorry. She didn't want him indebted; she'd gone without shoes and, sometimes, food to raise and educate him and done it gladly. What she hadn't reckoned on was that he'd become an English-loving Tory.

She broke the silence. 'Aaron, there's a man up in my room—'

He grinned. 'About time.'

'You wash your mouth out.' She told him the story of her dawn catch. He thought it amusing and went upstairs to see for himself.

Makepeace turned her attention to the lobsters which, neglected, had begun to tear each other's claws off.

'Reckon he's English,' was Aaron's verdict on his return. 'A lord to judge from his coat. Did you see how they cut the cuffs now? When he marries you out of gratitude, remember your little brother.'

'Sooner marry the Pope,' Makepeace said. Aaron could be trusted on fashion; he made a study of it. An Englishman, by Hokey, worse and worse. 'That important, somebody'll be missing him, so keep your ears open today and maybe we'll find out who he is. But don't ask questions, it'd seem suspicious. And, Aaron . . .'

'Yes, sister?'

'I want you home tonight. But, Aaron . . .'

'Yes, sister?'

'No argifying and no politics. The Sons is getting serious.'

'Ain't they, though?' He kissed her goodbye. 'Just wait 'til I tell 'em you're marrying the Pope.'

She waved him off at the door.

The Cut was awake now, shutters opening, bedclothes over windowsills to be fumigated by the sun, brushes busy on doorsteps, its men coming up it towards the waterfront—even those without jobs spent the day on the docks hoping, like rejected lovers, that they would be taken on again. Only Aaron went against the flow, heading towards the business quarter with an easy swagger.

Few wished him good morning and she suspected he didn't notice those who did. Already he'd be lost in the role of Romeo or Henry V or whatever hero he'd chosen for himself today; he was mad for Shakespeare. The Cut, however, didn't see youthful play-acting, it saw arrogance.

From a doorway further down came a sniff. 'You want to tell that brother of yours to walk more seemly.' Goody Busgutt was watching her watch Aaron.

'Morning, Mistress Busgutt. And why would I do that?'

'Morning, Makepeace. For his own good. He may think he's Duke Muck-a-muck but the Lord don't 'steem him any higher'n the rest of us mortals. A sight lower than many.'

Makepeace returned to her empty kitchen. '*I'll* 'steem you, you bald-headed, bearded, poison-peddling, pious . . .' In place of Mistress Busgutt, two lobsters died in the boiler, screaming. ' . . . you shite-mongering, vicious old hell-hag.'

Cursing was Makepeace's vice, virtually her only one. John L. Burke, master of profanity, lived again in the Irish accent she unconsciously adopted when she indulged it. She allowed no swearing in others but, as with the best sins, committed it secretly to relieve herself of tension, with an invective learned at her father's knee. Today, she reckoned, having sent her both a dangerous, unwanted guest and Goody Busgutt all in one morning, the Lord would forgive her.

It was a busy day, as all days were. With Tantaquidgeon stalking in her wake, she took her basket to Faneuil Market instead of to Ship Street's where she more usually did her buying, partly because the meat in its hall would be kept cooler and freer of flies than that on open stalls and partly to listen in that general meeting place for mention of a missing Englishman. She doubted if she could have heard it if there had been; Faneuil's was always noisy but today's clamour threatened to rock its elegant pillars.

Boston patriotism, simmering for years, had boiled out of its clubs and secret societies into the open. For once a town that prized property and propriety was prepared to sacrifice both for something it valued higher. There was no catharsis from last night's mayhem, no shame at the damage, everybody there had become a patriot overnight. 'We showed 'em.' 'We got 'em running.' She heard it again and again, from street-sellers to wealthy merchants. She found satisfaction in hearing it from a knot of lawyers fresh from the courthouse, as exhilarated as any Son of Liberty at last night's breakdown of order. Deeds, wills, all litigious documents were subject to Stamp Duty; the tax had hit the legal profession hard. But you sharks can afford to pay it, she thought, I can't.

Even newspapers—another taxed item—had increased in price; she could no longer take the *Boston Gazette* for her customers to read as she once had. From the triumphant headlines: 'The Sons of Liberty have shown the Spirit of America', glimpsed as copies were passed hand-to-hand through the market, she gathered that the press was trumpeting revenge.

Indeed, no catharsis. If anything, those who'd taken part were excited into wanting to do it again and gaining recruits who saw their royal Governor taken aback and helpless.

In one corner, a penny whistle was accompanying a group singing 'Rule, Bostonians/ Bostonians rule the waves/ Bostonians never, never, never shall be slaves' with more gusto than scansion. Tory ladies, usually to be seen shopping with a collared negro in tow, were not in evidence, nor were their husbands.

'Mistress Burke.'

'Mistress Godwit.' Wife to the landlord of the Green Dragon in Union Street. They curtsied to each other.

'Reckon we'll see that old Stamp Tax repealed yet,' shrieked Mrs Godwit.

'We will?' shouted Makepeace. 'Hooray to that.'

'Don't approve of riotin' but something's got to be done.'

'Long as it don't affect trade.'

They were joined by Mrs Ellis, Bunch of Grapes, King Street. 'Oh, they won't attack patriotic hostelries. Tories'll suffer though. I heard as how Piggott of the Anchor got tarred and feathered.'

The Anchor was South End and gave itself airs.

'Never liked him,' Makepeace said.

'Sam Adams'll be speechifyin' at the Green Dragon tonight, I expect,' announced Mistress Godwit, loftily.

'And comin' on to the Bunch of Grapes.'

'Always ends up at the Roaring Meg.'

Honours even, the ladies separated.

Despite the ache in her back, but with Tantaquidgeon to carry her basket, Makepeace detoured home via Cornhill so that she might be taunted by fashions she couldn't afford.

Here there was evidence of a new, less violent campaign against the government. At Wentworth's, who specialized in the obligatory black cloth with which American grief swathed itself after the decease of a loved one, a sign had been pasted across the window: 'Show frugality in mourning.' The draper himself was regarding it.

She stopped. 'What's that, then?'

'Funereals come from England, don't they?' he said. 'The Sons say as English goods got to be embargoed.'

Makepeace had never heard the word but she got the gist. 'Very patriotic of you.'

'Wasn't *my* idea,' said Mr Wentworth, resentfully.

The Sons of Liberty had been harsher on Elizabeth Murray, importer of London petticoats, hats and tippets for fifteen successful years. One of her windows was broken, the other carried a crudely penned banner: 'A Enimy to Her Country'.

Men on upturned boxes harangued crowds gathered under the shade of trees to listen. Barefoot urchins ran along the streets, sticking fliers on anything that stood still, or even didn't. Makepeace watched one of them jump on the rear of a moving carriage to dab his paper nimbly on the back of a footman. As the boy leaped back into the dust, she caught him by the shirt and cuffed him.

'And what d'you think *you're* doing?'

'I'm helpin' Sam Adams.'

'He's doing well enough without you, varmint. You come on home.' She took a flier from his hand. 'What's that say?'

Joshua sulked. 'Says we're goin' to cut Master Oliver's head off.'

'It says "No importation" and if you kept to your books like I told you, you'd maybe know what it means.'

She was teaching Betty's son to read; she worried for his literacy, though he'd gone beyond her in the art of drawing and she'd asked Sam Adams if there was someone he could be apprenticed to. So far he'd found no artist willing to take on a black pupil.

He trotted along beside her. 'Don't tell Mammy.'

'I surely will.' But as they approached the Roaring Meg she let him slip away from her to get to the taproom stairs and his room without passing through the kitchen.

'Going to be a long, hot night, Bet. I don't know what about the lobsters. Can the Sons eat *and* riot?'

'Chowder,' said Betty. 'Quicker.'

'How's upstairs?'

'Sleepin'.'

'Ain't you found out who he belongs to?'

'Nope. Ain't you?'

Maybe she could smuggle him to Government House—she had an image of Tantaquidgeon trundling a covered handcart through the streets by night—but information had Governor Bernard holed up, shaking, at Castle William along the coast.

'Sons of Liberty meeting and an English drownder right across the hall. Ain't I lucky?'

When she went up to her room, the drownder was still asleep. She washed and changed while crouching behind her clothes press in case he woke up during the process. Tying on her clean cap, she crossed to the bed to study his face. Wouldn't set the world on fire, that was certain sure. Nose too long, skin too sallow, mouth turned down in almost a parody of melancholia. 'Why?' she complained. '*Why* did thee never learn to swim?'

As she reached the door, a voice said: 'Not a public school requirement, ma'am.'

She whirled round. He hadn't moved, eyes still closed. She went back and prised one of his eyelids up. 'You awake?'

'I'm trying not to be. Where am I?'

'The Roaring Meg. Tavern. Boston.'

'And you are?'

'Tavern-keeper. You foundered in the harbour and I pulled you out.'

'Thank you.'

'You're welcome. How'd ye get there?'

There was a pause. 'Odd, I can't remember.'

'What's your name?'

'Oh God. Philip Dapifer. I don't wish to seem ungrateful, madam, but might you postpone your questions to another time? It's like being trepanned.' He added querulously: 'I am in considerable pain.'

'You're in considerable trouble,' she told him. 'And you get found here, so am I. See, what I'm going to do, I'm a-going to put my . . .' She paused, she never knew how to describe Tantaquidgeon's position in the household; better choose some status a wealthy Englishman would understand, ' . . . my footman here so as nobody comes in and you don't get out. You hear me?'

He groaned.

'Hush up,' she hissed. She'd heard the scrape of the front door. 'No moaning. Not a squeak or my man'll scalp you. Hear me?'

'Oh God. *Yes.*'

'And quit your blaspheming.' She left him and went to find Tantaquidgeon.

The Roaring Meg was a good tavern, popular with its regulars, especially those whose wives liked them to keep safe company. The long taproom was wainscoted and sanded, with a low, pargeted ceiling that years of pipe smoke had rendered the colour of old ivory. In winter, warmth was provided by two hearths, one at each gable end, in which Makepeace always kept a branch of balsam burning among other logs to mix its nose-clearing property with the smell of hams curing in a corner of one chimney and the whale oil of the tavern's lamps, beeswax from the settles, ale, rum and flip.

This evening the door to the jetty stood ajar to encourage a draught between it and the open front door. With the sun's heat blocked as it lowered behind the tavern, the jetty was in blue shade and set with benches for those who wished to contemplate the view.

Few did. The Meg's customers were mostly from maritime trades and wanted relief from the task-mistress they served by day.

The room reflected the aversion. A grandmother clock stood in a nook, but there were no decorations on the walls, no sharks' teeth, no whale skeletons, no floats nor fishnets—such things were for sightseers and inns safely tucked away in town. For the Meg's customers the sea's mementoes were on gravestones in the local churchyards; they needed no others.

'Going rioting again?' she asked, serving the early-comers.

'Ain't riotin', Makepeace,' Zeobab Fairlee said severely. 'It's called protestin' agin bein'—what is it Sam Adams says we are?'

'Miserably burdened an' oppressed with taxes,' Jack Greenleaf told him.

'Ain't nobody more miserably burdened and oppressed'n me,' Makepeace said. 'A pound a year, a *pound a year* I pay King George in Stamp Tax for the privilege of serving you gents good ale, but I ain't out there killing people for it.'

'Terrify King George if you was, though,' Fairlee said.

'Who's killin' people?' Sugar Bart stood in the doorway, his crutch under his armpit.

'I heard as how George Piggott got tarred and feathered down South End last night,' Makepeace said quickly.

'Tarrin' and featherin' ain't killin', Makepeace,' Zeobab said. 'Just a gentle tap on the shoulder, tarrin' is.'

'I'd not've tarred that Tory-lover,' Sugar Bart said, 'I'd've strung the bastard from his eyelids 'n' flayed him.'

He tip-tapped his way awkwardly across the floor to his chair by the grate, turned, balanced, kicked the chair into position and fell into it, his stump in its neatly folded and sewn breech-leg sticking into space. Nobody helped him.

Immediately the injured man upstairs became a presence; Makepeace had to stop herself glancing at the ceiling through which, it seemed to her, he would drop any second, like the descending sword of Damocles. Bart's virulence was convincing; she had no doubt that, should he discover him, he would contrive to have the Englishman killed before he could talk. Unlike most of those who'd indulged in smuggling—a decent occupation—Bart kept contact with the criminal dens of Cable Street and the surrounding alleys, never short of money for rum and tobacco. Whenever he hopped into the Roaring Meg its landlady was reminded that her tavern was a thin flame of civilization in a very dark jungle. And never more so than tonight.

Act normal, she told herself. She said evenly: 'No cussing here, Mr Stubbs, I thank you.' She heated some flip, took it to him, putting a barrel table where he could reach it, and lit him a pipe.

Sugar Bart asked no pity for his condition and received none; instead, metaphorically, he waved his missing leg like an oriflamme in order to rally opposition against those whom he considered had deprived him of it. An excise brig he'd been trying to outrun in his smuggler while bringing in illegal sugar had fired a shot which should have gone across his bows but hit his foremast instead, and a flying splinter from it had severed his knee.

That Bart had survived at all was admirable but Makepeace had long decided he'd only done so out of bile. In all the years he'd patronized the Roaring Meg, she'd never learned to like him.

He didn't like her either, or didn't seem to, was never polite, yet his sneer as he watched her from his chair bespoke some instinct for her character, as if he knew things about her that she didn't. She'd have banned him but, discourtesy apart, there'd never been anything to ban him for.

'*Was* you whistlin' this morning, weren't it?' he asked.

There was no point denying it. 'Saw the redcoats coming.'

'See anything else?' Makepeace hadn't expected thanks or gratitude and didn't get any.

'Lobster-pots. What else was there?' She was an uncomfortable liar so she carried the fight to him: 'And what was *you* doing there so early, Master Stubbs?'

His eyes hooded. 'Sweepin' up, Makepeace, just sweepin' up.'

Jack Greenleaf said: 'I heard as you was at the Custom House with the South End gang, an' doin' the damn place—sorry, Makepeace—a power of no good, neither.'

'Ain't denyin' it.' Sugar Bart was smug. 'There's some of them bastards won't be shootin' men's legs off in a hurry.'

There was a general 'Amen to that' in which Makepeace joined. Since the government cracked down on smuggling sugar, the price of rum, which, with ale, was her customers' staple drink, had almost doubled. This time she excused the use of 'bastards'. As a description of Boston's excisemen it was exact.

'They got Mouse Mackintosh today,' Zeobab said, 'so you be careful, Bart Stubbs.'

Bart sat up. 'They got Mackintosh?'

'Noon it was,' Zeobab said, 'I was near the courthouse an' redcoats was takin' him into the magistrates. He'll be in the bilboes by now.'

'What they get him for?' asked Makepeace. 'Custom House?'

'Don't know, but earlier he was the one broke into Oliver's house,' Zeobab said in awe. 'Led the lads, he did, swearing to lynch the . . . ahem . . . Stamper when he got him.'

'Busy little bee, weren't he?' Makepeace's voice was caustic; in her book Mouse Mackintosh was a South End lout and although Stamp Master Oliver deserved what he got, he *was* an old man.

'A hero in my book,' Bart said.

'Cut the mustard an' all, 'Peace,' Jack Greenleaf pointed out on Mackintosh's behalf, 'they say as Oliver's resigned from Stamp Masterin' already.'

'Still got to pay the tax, though, ain't I?'

'You have.' Sugar Bart's voice grated the air. 'That's a-why we'll be on the streets again tonight, so fetch another flip, woman, and be grateful.'

Conversation ended for her after that; the taproom was filling up with men whose thirst for the coming rampage was only equalled by that for liquor. Hungry, too, wanting to eat in company rather than with their wives who, in any case, were reluctant to light a cooking fire in this heat.

She wished she'd caught more lobsters, but there was the lamb from Faneuil's for lobscouse and there was always plenty of cod and shellfish to chowder.

Aaron came back from work, taking off his coat and donning an apron, catching her eye.

They managed a brief moment together in the kitchen, a savoury-smelling hell where the great hearth's bottle-jacks, cauldrons, kettles and spits, outlined against fire, looked not so much domestic as the engineering of some demonic factory, a resemblance emphasized on the walls where Betty's shadow loomed and diminished like that of a beladled, shape-changing harpy whose sweat, sizzling onto the tiles when she bent over them, formed a contrapuntal percussion with the hit-hit of mutton fat falling into the dripping well and the shriek of another lobster meeting its end.

'Do you know who he is?' Aaron was excited.

'Philip Dapifer,' she said.

'*Sir* Philip Dapifer. They reckon he's a cousin of the Prime Minister. He's staying at the Lieutenant-Governor's house. There's a search on—he ain't been seen since before dawn.'

'Hokey! Is there a reward for him?'

'Don't know, but they reckon if he ain't found soon the British'll send in troops.'

'Holy, *holy* Hokey.'

There was no time to pursue the matter; voices were calling from the taproom for service. With Aaron, she entered a wheeling dance between kitchen, casks and customers, carrying pots of ale, six at a time, balancing trays of trenchers like a plate-twirling acrobat, twisting past the barrel tables. The air grew thick with tobacco smoke, sweat and the aroma of lobscouse and became almost intolerably warm.

Sugar Bart caught at her skirt as she went by. 'Where's Tantaquidgeon tonight?'

'Poorly,' she said. There it was again, that instinct he had. For all the heat, she felt chill.

'Thought I couldn't smell him.'

Conversation was reaching thunder level, pierced by the hiss of flip irons plunging into tankards.

And stopped.

Sam Adams was in the doorway. He stood aside, smiling, threw out a conjuring hand and there, shambling, was the self-conscious figure of Andrew 'Mouse' Mackintosh.

Little as North Enders had reason to love the South End and its gang, Mackintosh had become an instant and universal hero with them. The taproom erupted, boots stamped planking, fists hammered table-tops, cheering brought flakes of plaster from the ceiling. Even Makepeace was pleased; it was a bad precedent for Sons of Liberty to be in jail, and anyway, she *loved* Sam Adams.

Everyone loved Sam Adams, Whig Boston's favourite son, who'd run through his own and his father's money—mainly through mismanagement and generosity—who could spout Greek and Latin but preferred the speech of common Bostonians and the conversation of cordwainers, wharfingers and sailors, and who frequented their taverns talking of Liberty as if she were sitting on his knee.

Ludicrously, in the election before last he'd been voted in as a tax collector, a job for which he was unfitted and at which he'd failed so badly—mainly because he was sorry for the taxed poor—that there'd been a serious shortfall in his accounts. The authorities had wanted him summoned for peculation but, since everybody else knew he hadn't collected the taxes in the first place, he'd been voted in again.

He marched to the carver Makepeace always kept for him by the grate, his arm round Mackintosh's shoulders, shouting for 'a platter of my Betty's lobscouse'.

'How'd ye do it, Sam? How'd ye get Mouse out?'

Aaron took his hat, Betty came tilting from the kitchen with his food, Makepeace tied a napkin tenderly round his neck—though Lord knew his shirt-front was hardly worth saving—and, less willingly, offered the same service to Mackintosh. As she did it, she saw one of his hands had a grubby bandage that disappeared up his sleeve and seeped blood. 'You hurt, Mr Mackintosh?'

'Rat bit me.' It was a squeak. Large as he was, Andrew Mackintosh's voice was so high that when he spoke cats looked up with interest.

An English rat, she thought. Her drownder hadn't gone down without a fight.

The room was silent, waiting for Adams's answer.

'Told 'em,' he said, spraying lobscouse, 'I told the sheriff if Andrew wasn't released, there'd be general pillage and I wouldn't be able to stop it.'

'That'd do it, Sam,' somebody called out.

'It did.' He stood and clambered up on his chair to see and be seen. 'That did it, all right, didn't it, *General* Mackintosh?' He looked around. 'Yes, there must be no more North End versus South End. We're an army now, my Liberty boys, a *disciplined* army. By displaying ourselves on the streets like regular troops, we'll show those black-hearted conspirators at Government House—'

' 'Scuse me, Sam.' It was Sugar Bart, struggling up on his crutch. 'Seems to me you're talkin' strategics.'

'Yes, Bart, I am.'

'Then I reckon as how you should do it upstairs so's we shan't be overheard.' The man was looking straight at Aaron.

Sam Adams regarded the packed taproom. 'Looks like there's too many of us for the meeting-room, Bart.'

'And it'll be hot,' Makepeace put in desperately. Visions of the Englishman moaning, a passing hand lifting the latch of her door to find that it was bolted from the inside . . .

'Maybe,' Sugar Bart said, not taking his eyes off Aaron, 'but there's some as don't seem so bent on liberty as the rest of us.'

Now Sam got the implication. He crossed to Aaron and put his arm round the young man's shoulders. 'I've known this lad since he was in small clothes and a good lad he is. We're *all* good patriots here, ain't we, boys?'

The room was silent.

It was Aaron, with a grace even his sister hadn't suspected, who resolved the situation. 'We're all patriots right enough, Sam, but this one's going to bed early.' He bowed to Sam, to Sugar Bart, to the company, and went upstairs.

'That's as may be,' Bart said, 'but how d'we know he ain't listenin' through the floorboards?'

Makepeace was in front of him. 'You take that back, Bart Stubbs, or you heave your carcase out of this tavern and stay out.'

'I ain't sayin' anything against you, Makepeace Burke, but your brother ain't one of us and you know it. Is he, Mouse?'

The appeal to his ally was a mistake; Mackintosh was a new-comer not *au fait* with the personal interrelationships of the Roaring Meg and its neighbours; indeed would have been resented by those very neighbours if he'd pretended that he was. Wisely, he kept silent.

Bart, finding himself isolated, surrendered and began the process of sitting down again. 'I ain't sayin' anythin' about anybody be-trayin' anybody, I'm just saying we got to be careful.'

'Not about my brother, you don't.'

Sam Adams stepped between them. 'We *are* going to be careful, gentlemen, careful we don't quarrel among ourselves and spoil this happy day when Liberty arose from her long slumber . . .'

While he calmed the room down, Makepeace went angrily back to her barrels and resumed serving. Wish as I could betray *you*, you one-legged crap-hound.

She wondered if she could solicit Sam's help in the matter of the Englishman. Obviously, he was in ignorance of the assault on the man by his new 'general'. Wouldn't countenance violence, would Sam.

With that in mind, in between dashes to the kitchen, she lis-tened carefully to what Bart had called the 'strategics'. Sam and Andrew Mackintosh were playing the company between them.

Sam's rhetoric was careful, reiterating the need for caution in case the British government reacted by sending an army to quell its American colony.

'No,' agreed Mackintosh, 'we ain't ready for war agin' the red-coats.' And then: 'Not yet,' an addendum which brought a howl of approval.

Sam: 'On the other hand, we can achieve the act's repeal peace-fully through the embargo on British goods.'

Mackintosh: 'Peacefully break the windows of them as disobeys.'

Sam: 'See that Crown officials, stamp-holders, customs officers are made aware of our discontent.'

'Break their windows an' all,' Mackintosh said. 'Keep 'em awake at nights with our drummin'.'

In other words, thought Makepeace, Sam was going to play pretty to the British and let Mackintosh and his mobs stir the pot.

Even had there been an opportunity for her to have a secret word with Adams, she decided, in view of these 'strategics', that it would be unwise. He was advocating reason yet allowing Mackintosh to inflame his audience for another night of rioting. Maybe he was out for revolution but, whether he was or wasn't, he'd got a tiger by the tail; even if he'd be prepared to understand why she sheltered a representative of British tyranny, his tiger sure wouldn't. Word would inevitably get out. Broken windows, lost custom: that'd be the least of it. Did they tar and feather women? She didn't know.

She didn't, she realized, know *what* men were capable of when they got into this state. She was watching the customers of years, ordinary decent grumblers, become unrecognizable with focused hatred.

For the first time, she wished Sam Adams would leave. She nearly said to him: Ain't you got other taverns to go speechifyin' in? But it appeared that he had anyway. She saw him and Mackintosh to the door, curtsied, received a kiss of thanks from Adams, a grunt from his companion and watched them go with relief.

But it was as if they'd lit a fuse that gave them just time to get out before it reached the gunpowder. Makepeace turned back to a taproom that, without the restraint of Sam Adams's presence, was exploding.

Was that old Zeobab climbing up on a table? 'Let's drub 'em, boys,' he was shouting. 'Let's scrag them sugar-suckers.' An exhortation causing stool-legs to be broken off for weapons, perfectly good pipes to be smashed against the grate like Russian toast glasses, and rousing Jake Mallum into trying to grab her for a kiss.

And Tantaquidgeon, her chucker-out, was upstairs.

Makepeace cooled Mallum's passion by bringing her knee up into his unmentionables, yelled for Betty and, with her cook, managed to snatch back two stool-legs with which to belabour heads and generally restore order. Betty lifted Zeobab off the table and planted him firmly on the jetty.

Makepeace went to the door, holding it wide: 'Git to your rampage, gents,' she called, 'but not here.'

She saw them out, some shamefaced and apologizing, most not even saying goodnight as they rushed past her to begin another night of liberty-wreaking. Already flames flared on Beacon Hill and Boston was beginning to reverberate with the beat of drums.

Sugar Bart was in front of her. 'That redskin were healthy enough earlier,' he said. 'Saw him with you in town. Where's he gone?'

Sure as eggs, he knew she'd seen what he and the others had done to the man on Fish Quay this morning and found Tantaquidgeon's unusual absence from her side suspicious. He couldn't think she'd betray him but he knew something was up.

She loathed the man; he frightened her. 'You ain't welcome at the Meg any more, Mr Stubbs,' she told him stiffly, 'not after what you said about Aaron.'

He rubbed his chin, staring straight into her eyes. 'The Sons is at war now,' he said. 'Know what they do to informers in war, Makepeace Burke?'

'Yes,' she said. 'And you still ain't welcome.'

She watched him hop away, ravenlike, into the darkness, then quickly bolted every shutter and door.

Chapter Three

TANTAQUIDGEON opened the door at her rap; he'd been in darkness, she realized, she'd forgotten to leave him a rushlight, and Betty, who didn't believe in fresh air for her patients, had closed the shutters. She opened them. The room was an oven that, from the smell of it, had been cooking Tantaquidgeon and vomit. 'Dammit, what'd you let him do that for?'

The Englishman had been sick on his pillow, his head nestled in it. He was still asleep.

She pushed Tantaquidgeon from the room, fetched a basin of water and a cloth, dragged the pillow from under, propped the Englishman's head while she sponged his hair and face clean, and found a fresh pillow. He slept all through, with no care for the extra washing he was giving her, let alone that someone—she—must now sit up with him all night in case he be sick again and choke on it.

Her eyes pricked with tears of fatigue and self-pity. Night was precious, an escape from seventeen daily hours on a treadmill of work. 'And now you,' she said to the bed. 'Ain't I lucky?'

The wharves were quiet tonight—the rioting was centred on the middle of the town and its noise reached her room reduced and compacted, like the buzzing of an exceptionally angry hive.

She lit a lamp—the oil in it was insufficient but damned if she'd pour in more; he was costing her enough already—put out the rushlight, snatched up her bible and sat on a stool beside the bed, opening the book at Matthew 25 for some encouragement from the Mount of Olives.

'For I was hungred, and ye gave me meat: I was thirsty, and ye gave me drink: I was a stranger, and ye took me in: Naked, and ye clothed me: I was sick'—all over your pillow—'and ye visited me: I was in prison, and ye came unto me.'

As always, it calmed her. She fell asleep.

She woke up in darkness to find the top half of her body slewed on the bed, her head resting sideways on something hard. It came to her that she had been asleep across the drownder's body, her cheek against his knee. Knee? *Christ have mercy.* She jumped up as if on springs.

'Pity,' a voice said, sadly, 'I was enjoying that.'

Shocked, disgusted, Makepeace walked to the window. Her cheeks were hot with embarrassment, so was her ear where it had lain on his . . .

A view of the jetty's mooring post down below, sheeny in the moonlight, did little to restore her composure, but for her own sake she must pretend she didn't realize what his pleasure had consisted of. Her fault for lying on it. Sick as he was, he was a man. 'Still in Boston, am I?' the voice asked.

'Yes.'

'Still your tavern?'

'Yes.'

'And to whom am I indebted for my delivery from Boston's waters?'

'Name's Makepeace Burke.'

'Thank you again, Miss Burke.'

His voice was a pleasing tenor and, despite his questions, suggested an intimacy she found unsettling, as if he'd met her before. Her answers came like a crow's caw in contrast.

'It's been a curious day, Miss Burke . . . has it been a day?'

'Fished you out early this morning.'

'Difficult to distinguish fact from dreams. Did I at some point gather that my presence in your hostelry is a cause for concern?'

She said: 'English ain't welcome here.'

'Ah.'

She was ready for him now. She turned round, went back to the bed and sat on the stool, leaning forward and positioning the lamp so that she could see him. 'How'd you come to fall in the harbour?'

'I was set on, belaboured and, presumably, thrown in while unconscious.' He squinted in order to read her frown carefully. 'Or did I imagine it?'

He was no fool. 'You imagined it,' she said. There was no point in pit-patting around. 'That's my price for pulling you out.'

'Ah.' He thought about it for a minute. 'Do the imaginary ruffians who hypothetically threw me in know that you pulled me out?'

'Not ruffians,' she said, 'patriots. Like me. No, they don't.'

'And would not rejoice that you did?'

'No,' she said, 'they wouldn't.'

'Presumably they are not aware that I am at this moment, ah, in residence in . . . what's the name of your tavern?'

'The Roaring Meg,' she said. 'No, they ain't.' She added: 'And mustn't.'

'Why *did* you pull me out, Miss Burke?'

She frowned again, surprised at the question. 'You was drowning.'

'I see.'

Awake, his eyes, which were brown, took away from the plainness of his face. She saw they were studying both her room and her person. A rectangular attic of lumpy whitewashed plaster cushioned between oak stanchions, bare floorboards supporting a chest, a three-legged washstand with a canvas bowl, a candlestick, a set of drawers on which were placed a small but select pile of books. A sparse woman of twenty-four years.

Makepeace saw no reason to be ashamed of either, both were homely, clean, serviceable and free of fleas. Indeed, in that she had the bedroom to herself and didn't share it with siblings or servants, here was Puritan luxury but, for sure, this man would prefer his rooms painted. Like his women.

He was silent for a minute, then said plaintively: 'I've got a hellish imaginary headache.'

Makepeace lit a rushlight from the lamp and went downstairs to the kitchen. The inn was silent except for the rip of Betty's snores and the occasional creak as beams contracted from a barely perceptible cooling of the air. Aaron's room was quiet—he'd slept through the ruckus before closing time; he'd sleep through the Last Trump. There was neither sign nor sound of Tantaquidgeon; he chose odd corners for a bed. Come to that, she'd never caught him asleep at all, as if some memory of the forest made it necessary for him to be seen only with his eyes open.

She poured a dose of physick into a beaker, ladled still-warm chowder into a bowl and pumped up a jug of water. Before she went back upstairs, she made sure no tendril of hair escaped her cap and smoothed down her apron.

She slipped an arm under the Englishman's neck to lift his head for his dosing. 'Betty's Specific against pain and bruises,' she told him when he made a face. 'Also kills worms.'

He swallowed. 'I don't wonder.'

She gave him some water, then the chowder, spooning it into his mouth for him.

'You've got children,' he said.

'Ain't married yet,' she said. 'You got childer?'

'No.'

'Used to feed my brother like this when he was little,' she said. 'Our ma died when he was born.'

'Where is your brother now?'

'Works in marine insurance,' she told him. 'He's educated.'

'Who set my collarbone? You?'

'Betty.'

'A large black lady?'

She nodded.

'And was there, or did I dream him, an even larger, red gentleman?'

'Tantaquidgeon.'

'His pomade is . . . unusual.'

She grinned. 'Bear's grease.'

The lamp guttered and went out and Dapifer was left with the memory of an astonishing smile. Her arm was instantly withdrawn from his neck and he heard the stool scrape back. She was retreating, as if physical contact with him was improper in the dark.

He saw her go to the window, her head in its dreadful cap outlined against the moonlight, like a carapace. He recalled from the kaleidoscope of the day's feverish images that she had equally astonishing hair.

Out of habit, he began a seduction. He sighed. 'No,' he said, 'it was a saint in that boat. She had a halo round her head—like an autumn bonfire. I distinctly remember a saint rescuing me from the harbour.'

Instead of going into a flutter, she snapped: 'Don't I wish it had been.'

So much for seduction.

He said gravely: 'It appears, Makepeace Burke, that I over-indulged last night. With great carelessness I stumbled into a ditch thereby breaking my collarbone.' Well, he owed her—not merely for his life, which was hardly worth the asking price—but because, just then, she'd made him want to laugh, something he'd not been inclined to do for a long time.

'That's what you'll tell 'em?'

'Lieutenant-Governor Hutchinson, who is my host in this town, will be so informed. The matter will proceed no further.'

'Swear on the Book?' She turned swiftly, picked up her bible and placed it on the counterpane.

He took it, swore, then, since it seemed expected, kissed its battered leather.

She was holding out her hand. Moonlight showed wet on the palm. God, she'd spat on it. He held out his good hand and they shook on it, making him wince.

She went to the door, carrying the dirty plate and spoons. 'Go to sleep now,' she said.

He heard the stairs creak as she went down them.

Resisting the pain in his head, his shoulder, everywhere, he tried to take stock. No need for oaths on the bible; if Mistress Burke thought he was about to broadcast the ridiculous position he found himself in she was much mistaken. He didn't know which was the more embarrassing: Sir Philip Dapifer thrown into Boston harbour by colonial bullies or Sir Philip Dapifer fished out again, like a halibut, by a tavern wench. He imagined the laughter if they heard of it at Almack's. Another humiliation, his least and latest, for the delectation of London society.

A waterfront? At night? In a town already in turmoil? What had he been thinking of, walking it, exposing himself to such risk?

What he always thought of, he supposed: two entwined naked bodies, one of them his wife's, the other—its arse bobbing up and down like a ball bounced by an invisible hand—his friend's.

Ludicrous image, all the more ludicrous that it was set against his own drawing-room carpet; he'd almost laughed. But it had hooked itself into his brain like some flesh-burrowing insect and festered so that it pounded there with the energy of an abscess, debilitating him, making him careless of life in general, his own in particular . . .

Gritting his teeth against pain actual and mental, Dapifer concentrated. What had he done *before* venturing along the waterfront? That's right, that's right, he'd been saying goodbye to Ffoulkes. Dear, good Ffoulkes. They'd gone aboard the *Aurora* as she readied herself to sail and Ffoulkes had tried to persuade him to make the voyage as well.

'For God's sake, Pip, come back home with me. Don't let her infect all England for you, old fellow. Nor him; they're neither of them worth it.'

Looking back on it now, Dapifer saw the restraint their upbringing—where insouciance was the order of the day—imposed on them. In all the weeks the two of them had spent in Massachusetts, that had been the first time either had broached with emotion the matter that had brought them there. Even then, Dapifer remembered, it had been difficult for him to respond to overt concern. He'd said lightly: 'Odd, isn't it? One almost regrets his defection above hers, friends being more difficult to acquire than wives.'

The safety lantern had swung in its cradle, not from the movement of the sea, which was pressed flat by the heat, but from preparations on deck for embarkation. Bare feet had pattered overhead like heavy raindrops; there were commands to the rowers of the sweeps that would pull *Aurora* out of the quays to the open sea. They could hear the bosun rousting out the crew's women from their rats' nests below. 'All ashore as is going ashore.'

But in Ffoulkes's cabin a silence had been enjoined by the ghost of Sidney Conyers demanding recognition of a past that went back to schooldays and the age of eight, which was when they'd acquired him or, more truly, he had acquired them. Not quite of their birth nor wealth but qualifying as a friend by his eagerness to be one and by the orphaned state they all shared, he'd joined them like a frisking, abandoned puppy until, puppylike, his escapades got them into trouble and they found themselves to be a trio in the eyes of their fellow Etonians.

Debetur fundo reverentia: Conyers had adapted the Juvenal quotation for them, translating it into a battle-cry against such schoolmasters and older boys who wanted to beat or bugger their poor little backsides. '*Respect is owed to our arses*'.

At university they'd drunk, gambled and whored together as befitted young gentlemen, gone on the Grand Tour together—on Ffoulkes and Dapifer money—cementing a friendship that had survived Conyers's entry into the army.

It was a ghost, a past, due some sort of salute and Dapifer had found himself honouring it. 'Despite it all, you know, I believe he loved us.'

'He loved what we were,' Ffoulkes had said, less forgiving. 'He always wanted what we had—and you were the first to marry.'

'Well, he had her. On my own bloody carpet.'

Ffoulkes hadn't smiled. 'Come back with me, Pip.'

'Shall, old fellow,' he'd said. 'Intend to. Back in a year or less. But if you'd be good enough to lodge the papers or whatever it is you have to do and see she's out of the place by the time I return. Embrace that boy of yours for me.'

'He's the only reason I'm leaving you now.'

'Of course he is, you've got to go.' His own marriage, thank God, had been childless. 'Just thought, now I'm here, might as well squint at what lies beyond the Alleghenies.'

'Scalping knives probably.'

'More likely to be scalped in Boston. When they hear my accent nearly every Puritan looks at me as if I'd raped his mother.'

'Exactly. A sullen and uncouth continent. And God knows it's cost enough, why it should balk at a not unreasonable tax . . . Listen to it.'

What had begun as confused and discordant noise in the centre of town, whistles, horns, war-whoops, was now rising into an orchestration of pandemonium with a relentless, underlying beat.

'Will you be safe on the streets?'

'Hutchinson's sent an escort.'

The *Aurora*'s captain had appeared in the doorway. 'Sir Philip, I don't wish to hurry you but we mustn't miss the tide.'

They'd said goodbye at the taffrail. He'd tried to thank this best of friends. 'All you've done, Ffoulkes . . . over and above the call of.'

They embraced stiffly, like true Englishmen, patting each other on the back.

He'd stood on the quay, watching water widen between them, watched as the ship had suddenly flared out all sail to catch what breeze there was, kept on watching her until, in the distance, she resembled a cluster of shells. A slightest lightening of the sky beyond her had suggested the beginning of dawn.

By that time the town had developed a patchy flush as if it had become feverish, which it had. A copse of white church spires, usually just silvered by the moon, were orange in the reflected glow of flames from the streets below them. Beacon Hill twinkled with a necklace of torches. Boston was burning to the beat of drums.

And yet, knowing the danger, he'd dismissed the Lieutenant-Governor's escort, told him he'd walk back alone and, against his advice, turned along the quays, meandering away from the bonfires along a waterfront that grew meaner and quieter as he passed empty warehouses, their open interiors smelling of guano and urine. The depression at this end of the harbour equalled his own.

Good God, he thought now, it was suicide. He'd been gambling, casting his life over those dirty stones like dice, baring his neck to a cut-purse's knife as surely as to an executioner's axe.

The thought shocked him. Had she brought him to this? That he *wanted* to die? How hideously gothick, how very *Castle of Otranto*—not that he'd read the damn book—how . . . commonplace.

Bloody nearly succeeded, too.

Yet he remembered fighting the bastards who'd set on him. Illogical, that. Fought like a madman. Wounded a couple at least. After that . . . nothing.

Yes, yes, remembered clinging to the wreckage in the water and wondering if survival was worth it and deciding it wasn't.

And then the God he didn't believe in had sent a boat and a red-haired, interfering tavern harpy to whom, it seemed, his life had mattered.

Couldn't argue with God . . . Christ, his damn head hurt . . . couldn't argue with harpies . . .

Sir Philip Dapifer fell asleep.

Downstairs, Makepeace lay down on one of the taproom settles, closed her eyes, opened them, got up, went to the jetty door, flung it wide and went out, breathing like a creature deprived of air.

The tide was on its way in, creeping up the little beach of silt that had formed under and around the jetty piers. She climbed down the steps until it reached her bare feet and let it cool them while she looked out to sea.

She was not a fanciful woman. Her father had provided enough fancy to stuff a crocodile: some of it had rubbed off on Aaron, none on her. 'D'ye not hear the mermaids singing, daughter?' Standing on this very jetty, staring out at the islands. 'Like the sirens of Odysseus. I hear them, I hear them.'

In the bad times he'd also seen pink spiders coming for him through the walls.

But tonight, on such a night, his daughter too was hearing a siren voice and it wasn't included in the noise of the town and it didn't come from the sea and it disturbed her. 'Stop it, Lord,' she begged. 'Stop this.'

When she finally fell asleep on the settle, she dreamed that a creature with spider legs was clawing its way into Aaron's room. She heard a thump and sat up, rigid, looking at the ceiling. Movement again; her room, not Aaron's. She snatched up the rushlight and raced upstairs.

The Englishman was on the floor, trying to get up. 'Shaky on the pins,' he said. 'Where's the bloody receptacle?'

She got the chamber pot from under the bed and steadied him while he pissed into it; she'd done the same for her father at the last.

He clambered back, querulously. 'Who constructed this bed, Procrustes? And where are my damn clothes?'

She fetched his clothes, dry now but wrinkled, and his one surviving boot. He fumbled through the coat, grumbling. 'Good boots, those; purse gone, of course; where's the time-piece, wedding present so they can have that—oh, they've got it, how charming. Didn't save my sword, I suppose?'

She recognized this stage: irritability, full realization, frightened by their weakness. She said, consolingly: 'Them imaginary men. You pinked one of 'em.'

He seemed gratified, as far as his moroseness could show gratification. 'And the others?'

'Ain't seen 'em.'

He nodded sadly.

She sat down on the stool. Get 'em to talk about themselves: first rule of tavern-keeping. 'And why was you on Fish Quay, Philip Dapifer?'

'I'd been bidding farewell to a good friend, Makepeace Burke. He was sailing back to England on the *Aurora*.'

'Why'd you come to Massachusetts Bay in the first place?'

Gloomily, he said: 'To divorce my wife.'

There was an appalled silence.

He wondered why he'd told her. Apart from Hutchinson, who'd expedited the matter for him and managed to ensure its privacy, the judges—granters of the decree—were the only Americans who knew. In England, just Catty and, presumably, Conyers. Why blurt it out to a tavern wench?

'What do you want to do that for?' It was a rhetorical question, not asking for marital detail but expressing amazement, as if he'd confessed to piracy.

Being a Puritan, for whom marriage was a civil contract, Makepeace did not regard divorce, like a Roman Catholic would do, as an abomination of the sacred, but she was nevertheless horrified; the only person she knew of who'd committed it was Henry VIII. She said: 'Is she American then?'

'No, she's English. In England.' He wished he hadn't started this. 'I wanted to save her the publicity.'

She didn't understand. Publicity, whatever that was when it was at home, couldn't surely be as bad as losing a husband. 'Does she know?'

He smiled. 'She knows. She knows that's why I came. She agreed before I set out. I sent her a letter some days ago, to say the deed was done.'

Makepeace thought: You been saved, Makepeace Burke. He's nothing but a heathen, a Mohammedan, turn round three times and be rid of the poor lady. In disapproving silence, she picked up the bible and began reading.

Dapifer thought: Whom was I actually sparing? Her or myself?

Was it that he couldn't have borne the public vindication of those who'd warned him not to marry her? A swathe through your fortune, they'd said, a scandal to your house, viciousness and charm handed down through the blood of dissolute generations.

And they'd been right. If she'd ever stopped menstruating, which she hadn't, he'd have had to count to be sure the child was his.

His passion for her had cooled into guilt; her father had forced the match on her, though she'd seemed willing enough and, probably, would have been no happier with anyone else. But indulgence had infuriated her. 'Why do you let me? You let me. Why don't you beat me?'

> *A spaniel, a woman and a walnut tree,*
> *The harder you beat them the better they be.*

He wasn't the beating sort; she could only cure herself. Tormented, she'd cast about for more exquisite ways to hurt him until it lighted on the most obvious objects by which to turn the screw, his friends. Ffoulkes had refused her, Conyers had not.

Pink-flushed, she'd smiled up at him from the carpet under the plunging body of Conyers when he and Ffoulkes had walked in on them, bringing down the tree of his remembered past, all his schooldays, Cambridge, with an ease that proved one of its roots had been rotten all along.

She'd engineered it, he saw that now, waited until he was due home, deliberately confronting him with a situation that, this time, he couldn't ignore. Even then, in the midst of disgust, he'd experienced pity at her craze for self-destruction.

No, he'd had to spare her; the world shouldn't know what she was. And in doing so he'd had to spare Conyers; a duel would have been the delight of the gossip rags. Instead, he'd carried his cuckold horns quietly to America to be rid of her, with Ffoulkes along to give evidence. Very gentlemanly, Dapifer, very *noblesse oblige*. You should have shot the bastard.

Christ, it rankled. He hadn't realized how much. *My own bloody carpet.* Was that, in essence, what had taken him along the waterfront last night? Throwing out a challenge to the low-life of Boston that he hadn't issued to the adulterer?

Introspection brought him full circle. No point in going round again, it merely increased his headache. And the silence from his companion was becoming too pointed to ignore. He was aware he'd lost ground with her and must make it up; whatever else, he was dependent on the female to get him out of this place without being lynched. After a moment, he said: 'And what of you, Miss Burke? Is there a lover on the horizon?'

She wanted to maintain her silence in order to show her disapproval. Then she thought: He'll think nobody's asked. So she said: 'I'm handfasted. To Captain Busgutt.' The name blasted the trumpet of the Lord into the quietness.

'Busgutt,' he said.

She took a breath. '*Captain* Busgutt. Has his own ship. Merchantman, the *Gideon*. A hundred and eighty tons. With an improved mizen.'

'And where is Captain Busgutt and his improved mizen now?'

She said: 'Sailed for England six months gone. Should've been back in three.'

'I'm sorry.'

'No need,' she said. 'The Lord has him in His keeping.' It was more a matter, she sometimes thought, that the Lord was in Captain Busgutt's keeping; drowning that thunderous, righteous man would be more than even God could be prepared to do. Captain Busgutt was alive, she was assured; there were a thousand things other than disaster to account for the delay. Even Goody Busgutt was not overly perturbed by it. Both of them expected that one of the ships from England, now anchored out in the Bay until it was safe to come in, might have news of the *Gideon*.

She said, viciously: 'It's your fault I'm still waiting.'

He blinked. 'Never met the gentleman.'

'Your government, then.' She was wagging her finger now, reproving this representative of the tyrant while he was at her mercy. 'Captain Busgutt must go back and forth to London 'stead of trading where he'd wish—and the Atlantic passage is fraught with dangers.'

'Ah,' Dapifer said. 'Carries enumerated goods, does he?'

'Captain Busgutt,' she said, 'trades in tar and pitch.' He always smelled of them, one of the things she liked about him; other men smelled of sweat. 'And has to sell to the Royal Navy—at a lower price'n elsewhere.'

'Not a smuggler, then, our Captain Busgutt?' He seemed to relish the name; on his tongue it gained tonnage.

So he'd learned something in New England. Indeed, Captain

Busgutt *had* been prepared to sell his tar to the French, even when they'd been the mother country's official enemy during the Seven Years' War. As he'd said, 'They are both sacrilegious peoples and the Lord does not distinguish between them.' But the Royal Navy's patrols had grown as vigilant as the shite Customs and Excise, and Captain Busgutt had bowed to the inevitable.

'Captain Busgutt's an honourable man,' she said, shortly.

'What age is Captain Busgutt?' he asked.

She picked up the bible again. None of his business.

There was a mutter from the bed, as if its occupant were speaking to himself. 'I'll lay he's an old man.'

'Captain Busgutt,' said Makepeace, clearly, 'is fifty years old and a man of vigour, a lay preacher famed throughout the Bay for his zeal. Let me tell you, *Mister* Dapifer, Captain Busgutt's sermon on the Lord's scourging of the Amorites caused some in the congregation to cry out and others to fall down in a fit.'

'Pity I missed it.'

Makepeace had not encountered this form of ridicule before but she was getting its measure. This Dapifer would go back to his painted palaces to present Captain Busgutt and herself to his painted women as figures from a freak show. She knew one thing: Captain Busgutt was the better man.

When she'd told Aaron that Captain Busgutt had asked for her, he'd said with the coarseness he'd picked up from his Tory friends, 'That old pulpit-beater? He wants to bed a virgin, the hot old salt. Really, 'Peace, you're not bad-looking, you know. You can do better. What d'you want to marry him for?'

The answer was that Captain Busgutt's was the best offer. There'd been other suitors but none had been a good economic proposition and the only one who'd made her heart race a little had, in any case, drowned before she could come to a decision. She wasn't getting any younger and keeping the Roaring Meg's shaky roof over all their heads was becoming a losing battle—a heightened pulse rate was no longer a factor in her deliberations.

Captain Busgutt was that unique phenomenon, a rich man—or what passed for rich in Makepeace's world—who was also a good man. She thought now: Captain Busgutt didn't divorce his wife, though she was sickly and gave him no children. At her death he'd been left with no one on whom to bestow his riches and goodness, except his mother. He'd promised Makepeace a house, a brick house, near the Common, with an orchard and, most importantly, a place in it for Betty, young Josh and Tantaquidgeon. It was a considerable offer—the prospect of ending up a childless old maid and a burden on Aaron had given Makepeace sleepless nights—and she had accepted it.

True, he was twice her age and didn't set the mermaids singing but Makepeace had seen the unwisdom of her parents' union—Temperance Burke had been made old before her time by her husband's shiftlessness—and did not consider passion a good foundation for marriage.

Captain Busgutt, above all, was admired in the community. The drunken reputation of Makepeace's father, her trade, the colour of her hair, the dislike accorded her brother: all these had kept her clinging onto the edge of social acceptance by her fingertips. Captain Busgutt would cloak all of them in his own respectability and Makepeace, after a lifetime of the unusual, longed for the mundane with the desire of a vampire for blood.

'For a man of his age, Captain Busgutt seems to believe in long engagements,' said the voice from the bed. 'Why are you still waiting, Miss Burke?'

'None of your business.' Then, because, despite everything, conversation with this man was curiously luxurious, she said, 'Goody Busgutt.'

'Another of the Captain's wives?'

'His mother.'

Goody Busgutt had strongly objected to the marriage, pointing out its disadvantages to a man with a position to maintain and, like the good son he was, Captain Busgutt had agreed to delay the wedding until his return from England—the hiatus to be a term of trial during which his mother could assess Makepeace's fitness for the position of Mrs Busgutt.

Makepeace did not tell the Englishman this. She said, 'Goody

Busgutt is a woman of righteous character and forceful opinions. She thinks Captain Busgutt could make a safer choice of wife. Maybe he could.'

Makepeace had forceful opinions of her own and at first the thought of being tested by Goody Busgutt had very nearly led her to break off the engagement. Then she'd thought: Why let that canting, lip-sucking old sepulchre ruin your future, Makepeace Burke? She can't last for ever.

Plums like Captain Busgutt didn't drop from the tree every day.

Suddenly, Makepeace was angry and frightened by the intimacy being established between her and the man in the bed. 'And if she hears of it . . . if Goody Busgutt knew you was here . . .'

'She wouldn't look kindly on the wedding?'

'She would not.'

'What *would* she think we'd got up to?' he said mournfully.

Unsettled, she got up and went to the window. The moon was setting; it would be dawn soon. The shadows of ribbed hulls in Thompson's boatyard across the slipway reminded her of Captain Busgutt's creased, liver-spotted hands, their nails misshapen by a hundred shipboard accidents.

Dapifer, watching her from his bed, smelled air fresher than any of the night and whatever hideous line of soap she used. She was . . . unusual, he thought, with her unexpected answers in flat 'a's; like this damn continent, new and disrespectful. Too good for Captain Busgutt, he knew that.

He saw her stiffen. 'What . . . ?' he began but she hissed at him to keep quiet.

Carefully, Makepeace eased the shutter further forward so that she could peer out under its cover. An unaccountable shadow had moved in Thompson's boatyard. She gestured behind her for the Englishman to snuff the rushlight.

Dapifer pinched out the flame, struggled out of bed and limped across the floor to her. 'What is it?' He kept his voice low.

She shook her head and pointed, at the same time putting a hand out to stop his access to the window. He caught hold of her shoulder to steady himself and felt the tension in there, the skin of it only separated from his hand by a thin layer of material which stopped at the curve of her neck. All at once they were conspirators, allies against whatever was out there threatening them both.

After a while they both heard the tip-tap of movement, like a raven's hopping, receding from the quay down an alley. She let out a breath and the muscle of her shoulder under his hand relaxed as tension went out of her—to be replaced by the awareness of how close he was. She stood still for another second and then turned. He didn't move. 'Are they watching us?' he asked.

She nodded.

Us.

He was taller than she was, her nose was level with his chin, the tip of her breasts almost against his ribs; Makepeace could smell his skin and Betty's Specific. She knew he'd said something, his mouth had moved, but there was another conversation in progress between their bodies and she found difficulty in attending to anything else.

'What you say?'

'Is it trouble?'

Trouble.

She pushed past him. 'We got to get you away,' she said. Away from me. But the damage was done, there'd been an acknowledgement, something had been established.

He used her as a crutch to climb back into bed, his arm a yoke across the back of her neck. He didn't need to lean that heavily, they both knew it.

'I'm still a sick man,' he said.

'What?'

'I said, my dear Procrustes, I am too ill to move.'

'Sabbath,' she said. 'It's the Sabbath today. The Sons won't be on the streets tonight. We'll smuggle you away then. Now get your sleep and let me get mine.' Determinedly, she plumped herself on her stool, crossed her arms and leaned her back on the wall. She should leave, she knew, go down to the taproom and its settle, but the weird enchantment of the night insisted she stay out its last moments.

Dapifer closed his eyes obediently, wondering at a rioting mob which left off rioting on Sundays—and at a shared moment in a window with a tavern-keeper that had proved as erotic as any in his life.

Two hours went by.

Downstairs there was a rap on the door. A yawning Josh, readying himself to escape the boredom of a Boston Sabbath by going on an illegal fishing trip with friends, unguardedly opened it. A squall of camphor and propriety swept by him and up the stairs to Makepeace's bedroom, awakening the two sleepers in it with a voice that could have clipped hedges.

'And what is this?' asked Goody Busgutt.

Chapter Four

CHURCH. Oh God, God, I should've been in church.

Behind Goody Busgutt was Goody Saltonstall; they hunted as a pair. Saltonstall being exceptionally fat and Busgutt thin, they resembled an egg and its timer in petticoats. In fact, they were the area's moral police.

As Goody Busgutt was saying, still from the doorway: 'I knew, I *knew*. Moment you wasn't in church, Makepeace Burke, I smelled licentiousness. 'Twas my duty to sniff it out, even if you wasn't my son's intended.'

And it was. Though innocent, Makepeace did not question Goody Busgutt's right, either as a future mother-in-law or as society's licentiousness-sniffer, to invade her house. The goodwives might be an anachronism elsewhere but in this Puritan part of Boston they had the community's authority to see that its women behaved like Puritans. They had the ear of the magistrates and could ensure that fornicators and adulterers received a public whipping, or at least a heavy fine—and had.

She was ruined. She'd been caught alone in a bedroom with a man—*in flagrante delicto* as far as the Goodies were concerned. No marriage to Captain Busgutt now. Waves of images battered her, one after another: herself standing before the congregation with Parson Mather's castigations roaring from the pulpit; in front of the magistrates' bench, condemned as a trull; the Roaring Meg closed by official seal as a house of ill repute . . .

Dapifer, glancing at her, saw her face age with defeat and became angry.

Goody Busgutt had no interest in him. Her lips distended and narrowed, spouting shame—all of it at Makepeace. Who hung her head. She deserved it. Bringing him here, sending Betty to bed instead of making her sit with him . . . worrying, even now, about what he thought of her humiliation. She was sick; she wanted to fall down.

He was sitting up, looking comically prim with the bedspread clutched to his neck. Uttering something unbelievable.

'Thank the Lord,' he was saying, and he was saying it to Goody Busgutt. 'Thank the Lord for you, mistress. Rescue, rescue.'

Goody Busgutt's mouth paused in a quirk. 'Eh? Who are you?'

'Madam, my name is Philip Dapifer. I was thrown into the harbour yesterday by rioters for being an Englishman. This woman and her Indian dragged me out and, since there was nowhere else, brought me here. Most unwillingly, I may add. You look a kindly soul, will you get me food?'

'Eh?'

'Mistress,' said Sir Philip Dapifer, 'I have been here all night and this female has done nothing but lecture me on my politics and my soul. She has read to me from the Good Book without ceasing . . .' He pointed to the bible lying open on the little table. 'Mistress, I am as eager for the Lord's word as anyone but did not our Lord minister to the sick as well as preach? Not a morsel has she given me, not a sip.'

'Not a sip?' Goody Saltonstall's wattle quivered sympathetically.

'And my head aches most damnably. I'm ill.'

Saltonstall was already won; Goody Busgutt was holding out. 'Thee talks fast enough for a sick 'un, Englishman.'

'There you have it,' Dapifer said, as if the two of them had struck agreement. 'She holds it against me that I am from England. For some reason, she blames me that her fiancé has not yet married her. Since she learned that I have connections at the Admiralty, she has been on at me to find out what happened to his ship. I suspect he has sailed to the Tortugas to get away from her. I tell you, mistress, were I her fiancé, I wouldn't marry her either.' He fell back on his pillow and closed his eyes.

Goody Busgutt walked round the bed like a woman searching corners for cockroaches. In the morning light, Dapifer's pallor looked deathly, a man without enough energy to raise his eyelids, let alone any other part of his anatomy.

'Thee *could* have fed him some broth, miss,' she said.

Makepeace's wits were coming back. ' 'Tis the Sabbath,' she sulked.

'When did the Sabbath stop the Lord's work? I tell thee, Goody Saltonstall and I should wish to be at our prayers instead of here, saving thy reputation. What were thee thinking of? Thee could have been the talk of the neighbourhood. Now fetch this poor soul some broth.'

'An' us,' said Goody Saltonstall, 'I'm moithered.'

Makepeace got up, still astounded. He'd rescued her as surely as she'd rescued him. He'd worked the oracle on the two flintiest women in Boston.

'Get to it, then,' Saltonstall told her, sharply. 'We're seeing to 'un now.'

Makepeace got to it, carefully clicking her teeth and muttering resentfully about free broth for the undeserving. Downstairs she fell into Betty's arms, babbling.

'Never believed you was jus' talkin', did they?' asked Betty.

'They believed *him*. And it was true,' Makepeace said. She sat down, puffing, and ran her fingers round her neck, still feeling the noose. 'In a way.'

'Oh-ah.'

'Don't you start. And get that fire going. Pop in a couple of lobster and I'll run up some pastry for patties.' She was exhilarated by escape.

'On the Sabbath? What'll *they* say?'

'Betty, Sabbath or no, we could set up a maypole and caper round it. I tell you, he charmed 'em.'

'They ain't the only ones, I reckon.'

When the trays were ready, Betty stopped Makepeace from carrying them up. 'I'll take 'em, gal.'

She was right, of course; she usually was. The Goodies might be spellbound but they'd be watchful; she could hardly maintain a hostile front towards the Englishman by seeking his presence every few minutes. With a sense of loss, Makepeace watched Betty's backside sway upstairs. The enchanted night was over.

She sobered. If he'd rescued her from one danger, another loomed for them both. Goody Busgutt had no interest in politics, her concern was righteousness, as was Saltonstall's, but you could as well prevent either from gossiping as alter the weather. The Sons of Liberty and everybody else in the Cut would be aware of the Englishman's presence in the Meg as soon as the Goodies left it; her marriage was saved but her custom was ruined.

Makepeace went upstairs and woke Aaron. He was to take Tantaquidgeon with him and go to Hutchinson's house and tell the Lieutenant-Governor to send a sedan chair for Dapifer with an escort. 'He ain't fit for walking yet.'

'A chair *and* escort? Why not trumpeters while they're about it?'

Makepeace shrugged. 'Might as well, there'll be a crowd whatever we do. I want him safe through it.'

Aaron winked, as had Betty. 'Ooh-er.'

She said wearily, 'There wasn't no ooh-er.' She suspected that her exchanges in the dark with the magical fish she'd caught would be all she had to sustain her from now on. Were they worth it? They'd have to be.

For the rest of the day, he was the Goodies' catch. Every so often one of them would come down to berate her for her neglect of him and command some recipe for his improvement. 'Did thee not see how poorly he be? Now he's coughing. Where's the aniseed? And a plaster for his head.'

She gave them what they asked for, along with some of her best Jamaican rum for themselves, anxious to keep them *in situ* for as long as possible until she could form some plan for counteracting the damage they would necessarily inflict on the Roaring Meg when they departed.

The lobsters and patties had gone down well, the Goodies having included themselves in the Sabbath dispensation of hot food for the sick. Betty came down with trays on which no scrap was left. She frightened Makepeace with a high keening as she flopped onto the kitchen settle and put her apron over her head.

'What is it? What is it? What did they say to you?'

The apron moved from side to side. 'They's snorin'. But he ain't. He . . .' Betty's voice failed. Her hand pantomime indicated that the Englishman had called her over to the bed, putting a finger to his lips.

'What did he want?'

Makepeace waited a full minute before Betty was able to answer. 'Ladder.'

'He wanted a ladder?'

Betty's apron nodded. 'Fetch a ladder for . . .'

Makepeace waited again, her own laughter on the simmer despite everything.

'A ladder and not to tell nobody . . . for him and Goody Saltonstall is plannin' to elope.'

Makepeace sat down beside her friend and wailed with her.

Aaron came back while they were both sweating over the next collation, lobscouse and flummery. His news lacked amusement; what he'd found in town had shaken him.

It was Sunday. Boston, as ever, was a ghost town, frozen under a boiling sun, gone into its smokeless, street-empty, curtain-drawn, diurnal hibernation, only a murmur of prayers through church windows and the clucking of neglected poultry breaking the silence. Sabbath Boston was always eerie, an echoing, hurrying footfall suggesting emergency—its perpetrator having to make explanation to the magistrates if there was none.

Today, to Aaron who had missed both riots, it was shocking, haunted by the daubed, shrieking poltergeists who had rampaged through it the night before, the wounds they'd inflicted pointed up by the stillness, as if a fine face had turned slack and dribbling in open-mouthed sleep. Because no work should be done on the Lord's Day, avenues were still littered with the black scatterings of bonfires. Fences and flowerbeds lay trampled; broken glass winked in the gutters.

In Hanover Square the huge, hundred-year-old oak tree that stood in its middle had sprouted new fruit. A figure was hanging from one of its branches.

Close to, it turned out to be an effigy of Andrew Oliver, the Stamp Master of Massachusetts Bay. Last night the old man had been made to stand before it and apologize for his offence of administering the Stamp Act.

Where Lieutenant-Governor Hutchinson's white, pillared mansion had stood among trees there was no mansion. An empty shell gaped in its place surrounded by wreckage as if it had vomited semi-digested furniture onto the lawns. Birdsong from the motionless trees seemed out of place in the devastation. A statue was headless, urns broken. Over everything, like demented snow, lay paper and, here and there, the leather binding it had been ripped from—Hutchinson had owned the best library in New England.

'Will you look here?' Aaron held out the torn frontispiece of a hand-written manuscript to Makepeace. 'He was writing this, that good man, and they tore it up. Look.' The title was in beautiful copperplate: *A History of the Province of Massachusetts Bay*.

Makepeace's only interest was the present; Lieutenant-Governor Hutchinson's virtues and omissions were ground she and her brother had fought over too often. 'Well, where is he now?'

Aaron shrugged. 'Maybe he's taken refuge with Governor Bernard out at Castle William.'

'Run, run, fast as you can,' said Makepeace nastily. If there was no authority left in town, what safety was there for Dapifer? Or herself, for that matter?

'Stay and be killed, is that it?' Aaron was equally upset. 'They got at his cellars, I tell you. Drunken madmen they must have been.'

'They was patriots,' she yelled at him, hitting out because she was frightened. 'Hutchinson and his yes King George, no King

George, let me lick your boots, King George . . . don't matter if good Americans is starving and all his relatives is living in palaces paid for out of poor people's taxes.'

'Hutchinson advised against the Stamp Tax, you know he did, you stupid female.'

And they were back on their ancient battlefield, made more bitter by the knowledge that both had truth on their side. Sir Thomas Hutchinson's love of English upper-class mores and his nepotism were notorious—Stamp Master Oliver was his brother-in-law and between them the two families monopolized most of the Bay's government offices—but he was also erudite and for over twenty years had devoted himself to the betterment of the colony into which he'd been born.

Aaron was right—Hutchinson was a good man. Makepeace was right—Hutchinson wasn't a good American.

Betty stepped between them. 'This ain't buyin' baby a new bonnet. What we goin' to do with him upstairs?'

'Get him away by boat,' said Aaron. 'I'll row to Castle William and get them to send an escort for him tonight.'

'Take him with you,' Betty said. 'Save time.'

Aaron shook his head. 'Too risky. The Sons ain't observing the Sabbath that religiously. Looks like they're in charge. One of them stopped me and Tantaquidgeon coming home and asked what we were doing. I said we had sickness in the house and had gone for a doctor. If they're patrolling the water like they're patrolling the streets, your fella'll get tipped back in the harbour—and me with him.'

Makepeace groaned. Her brother, usually incautious, was showing common-sense, an indication of how seriously he'd been scared by the situation. Nobody would question him alone in a boat—watchers who knew him would assume he was making another of his visits to Harvard friends across the river—but if Sugar Bart saw him with Dapifer . . .

What Aaron didn't realize, because even now his fingers couldn't take the pulse of the neighbourhood like hers, was how disastrous it was going to be for the Roaring Meg's local reputation when a bunch of redcoats, *invited* redcoats from the loathed garrison at Castle William, turned up to rescue an Englishman from its midst. As well run up the Union Jack and be done with it. The Sons would never drink here again. Probably nobody else either, she thought. But what else to do? Nothing.

She smoothed down her apron. That bridge would have to be burned when she got to it. 'Go up and tell the Goodies we got lobscouse and brandy for their supper in the taproom,' she said to Aaron. 'You can tell the English your plan while they're down.'

Free lobscouse and brandy. She shook her head at her own open-handedness. 'This rate,' she said to Betty, 'we'll be ruined before we're ruined.'

While the Goodies gorged in the taproom, Zeobab Fairlee came to the kitchen door asking for them. Makepeace pounced on him, he was her oldest customer and friend, sat him down and began gabbling her tale of wounded, rescued Englishmen—'What else could a Christian body do, Zeobab? Eh? Eh? Couldn't let 'un drown, could I?'—and, having done it, how could she appease the Sons?

He was preoccupied and barely listened to her. 'There's news, 'Peace,' he said, 'I come to tell Goody Busgutt.'

His brown nut of a face showed no expression—a bad sign; imparting and receiving disastrous news was done in this community with a stoicism that bordered on the comatose. 'It's the *Gideon*.'

Betty paused over the fire, Makepeace sat down, gripping the knife with which she'd been cutting bread until her knuckles showed white. Her own face was impassive. Don't let him be drowned, Lord, she prayed, don't let Captain Busgutt be drowned. Batting your eyelashes at Englishmen and your fiancé drowns—it's the Lord's punishment. 'Dead?'

Zeobab shook his head. 'Pressed.' The word tolled through the kitchen like a passing bell. It was almost as dreadful, it was almost the same.

Among the incoming ships piling up in the Bay, unwilling to risk their cargo and passengers while there was rioting in town and, in any case, last night barred from docking by Boston's laws against Sunday working, was a pursuit boat from the *Moses*, a whaler recently returned to Nantucket full of blubber. Commanding the boat was the *Moses'* first mate, Oh-Be-Joyful Brown, anxious to renew his acquaintance with the young Boston woman he'd been courting now that he had money enough to marry her. Impatient of the delay, Oh-Be-Joyful had irreligiously rowed ashore early this morning though, being nevertheless a dutiful man, he had not gone straight to his lady but had first sought out Goody Busgutt. 'Couldn't find her, see,' Zeobab said, 'so he comes to me.'

'Will you get to it?' snapped Betty.

What Oh-Be-Joyful wanted to tell Goody Busgutt was that while hunting on the Grand Banks, the *Moses* had met another whaler, a homeward-bound Greenlander. Since neither was in competition at that stage of their voyages, they had stopped to chat in the middle of the Atlantic like two housewives over a fence.

'An' the Greenlander,' said Zeobab, 'she says three months previous she come across the *Gideon* sinkin', rammed by a whale, see, and takes off the crew. But she was bound for Liverpool to discharge her oil, so that's where she takes 'em. And at Liverpool, so her master told Oh-Be, the press comes on board an' takes Cap'n Busgutt and his men for the navy.'

'They *can't.*' Makepeace was standing. 'They can't press him. He's protected.'

In order for Britain's trade to flourish, certain classes of seafarers necessary for its success had to be kept safe from the Royal Navy's press gangs, always greedy for sailors to man its ships, and were therefore granted 'protection' in certificates of exemption. Captain Busgutt and his crew, providing the navy with essential tar, came into this category.

Zeobab shook his head. 'He don't have a ship no more, 'Peace. The *Gideon*'d went down, see.'

She saw. With the *Gideon* sunk, Captain Busgutt's certificate was useless. The English press gang had found valuable booty, a crew of trained men without protection, and thought it was its lucky day.

The knife in Makepeace's hand stabbed into the loaf and stabbed it again. She was so angry. How dare they, how *dare* they? King

George and his shite Admiralty. Kidnap your own men but you leave ours alone. Here it was again—British tyranny. Stab. It was an old grievance, another of the reasons for Boston's disaffection and a better one even than the Stamp Tax for tearing down Lieutenant-Governor Hutchinson's house. Stab. Pity he weren't in it.

That the Royal Navy was even-handed and took any nationality it could lay its hands on did nothing to mollify an American seaboard which suffered badly from its predation. Men went missing with dreary regularity. Women and children were left waiting for husbands and fathers who'd been trawled like fish. Most never returned. Having been legally kidnapped, the few who escaped were hunted as deserters.

Makepeace's knife cut the Board of Admiralty's brains into breadcrumbs. Betty leaned over and took it away from her. 'Did Oh-Be say if they was all saved?' Most of *Gideon*'s crew consisted of local men.

'He di'n't know.'

Silence closed in on the kitchen with another question. Eventually Betty asked it. 'Who's goin' to tell her?'

'I ain't,' Makepeace said. Guilty of attraction to another man, she couldn't look Captain Busgutt's mother in the face.

But in the end she accompanied Zeobab into the taproom and held Goody Busgutt's hand while he told her. The old woman diminished before her eyes; there was none of the anger that consumed Makepeace, not yet at any rate, though Saltonstall, on behalf of her friend, supplied enough for all of them. Goody Busgutt kept pleading for reassurance—'I'll not see my boy again, will I?'—a question to which, terribly, she knew the answer as well as they did.

They helped her back to her house.

The evening was giving a rare mellowness to the Cut; to the left, the tide lapped softly at the cobbles of its ramp and along its narrow, north-east facing terrace houses were soft-hued shadows, but there was still ferocity in the light that turned the walls and windows of the Roaring Meg's side into amber.

Oh-Be-Joyful's news had spread and further down the lane was a large cluster of women which hurried towards Zeobab and surrounded him with anxious questions. 'Was my man pressed along of the others?' 'Did the press take Matthew?' 'Pressed.' 'Pressed.'

'Ask *her*.' Saltonstall established herself on Goody Busgutt's steps and her voice rose above the clamour. She was pointing. 'Ask Makepeace Burke. She'll know. She's took in a English lord as is a friend to them as steals our poor lads. Ask her what she's a-doin' with him in her bedroom.'

Unbelieving faces in unison turned towards Makepeace, the women's go-to-meeting caps like the frill of spume on an advancing wave. She began gabbling as she had to Zeobab: *Drowning. What else to do? Where else to take 'un?* Every hurried word an apology and admission of guilt—and unheard. It seemed to her the wave was coming at her and she backed defensively into the Meg's doorway.

But it was still absorbing shock. Almost the whole of the Cut was involved with the *Gideon* in one way or another; the men's loss was not only personal grief but rents that now couldn't be met, unpaid debts, little businesses that had been planned and wouldn't transpire.

Mary Bell from Number 25 shifted her baby more firmly onto her hip. She came up so that she stood on one side of the little bridge that led to the tavern, Makepeace, with her back to the door, faced her on the other. They were friends. Mary's young husband was second mate on *Gideon* and had sailed before his child was born. 'What's she sayin', Makepeace?' Her face crumpled. 'Where's my Matthew?'

Wordless, Makepeace stared at her. Useless, useless to say she'd saved a man from drowning not knowing who he was; her actions had no relevance to this woman.

Had *Gideon* gone down with all hands, Mary could have grieved and recovered. She came of a coastal people; the sea gave, the sea took away, she understood it, her church had prayers to rejoice or mourn the caprice of its profit and loss. But there was no formula for putting to rest the victim that disappeared into the jaws of His

Majesty's authorized monster. Though he didn't come back, he remained the man who might or might not be dead, the husband of a wife who couldn't remarry; he was a disembodied scream that went on and on.

These things had to be comprehended; Makepeace knew it because she too had to come to terms with an altered future.

But once they were—and Makepeace saw this too—somebody would have to pay for them, pain must be subsumed in revenge, a shriek of protest go up against the distant, arrogant, little island that inflicted such suffering.

And this time, there was a scapegoat to hand, trailing blood. Not a governor, not a stamp master—hirelings who took their orders from three thousand miles away—but a real, live Englishman who, on his own admission, had connections with the Admiralty, the same Admiralty that commanded the stealing of men. And he was here on their doorstep.

Helplessly, Makepeace went into the Roaring Meg, shut the door, bolted it and began preparations for a siege.

Chapter Five

'NOTHING much to do,' she said casually to Betty. 'Why don't you take Josh and go visit Hannah?' Hannah was Betty's close friend and lived along the waterfront.

'You expectin' trouble?'

'No.'

'Always could tell when you was lyin'.'

'It's just . . .' It was difficult to clarify even to herself why she felt dread but she knew it wasn't baseless. The nights of riot had created a palimpsest on which further havoc could be written, a ground for old and new scores to be settled in a way that Boston's conformity had previously kept in check. Violence was in the air and she could smell it waiting outside her door. ' . . . just if there's trouble, *if* there's trouble . . .'

'Me and Josh family or not?'

'You know you are, you old besom.'

' 'N' so do every other soul 'round here. Want me 'n' Josh caught strollin' back from Hannah's an' chucked in the harbour? Thank you kindly, we's stayin' indoors an' don't nobody else ought to go visitin' neither.'

'It's me they're mad with.'

'When people's mad they ain't picky.'

As an ex-slave Betty knew what she was talking about, but Makepeace was aware that she was just finding a good excuse to stay. How good an excuse was it, though? Would Aaron be safe going to Castle William?

Yes, she decided, he would, as long as he set out immediately. She was tempted to send the Englishman with him and then rejected the idea; there were people milling about the Cut who'd see them go; a crisis would be precipitated. Better for them all if the man made his escape under cover of darkness and with a force to protect him.

When Aaron came down from upstairs she apprised him of the situation. 'You tell them soldiers to lie out from the jetty an' keep quiet,' she said. 'We'll row him to their boat.'

She accompanied her brother to the jetty. Aaron, too, had been enchanted by Dapifer who had offered to introduce him to the playhouses should he ever come to London. 'Now there's a true English gentleman.'

'Ain't he though,' she said flatly, but her brother's enthusiasm reminded her of how young he was and she became nervous for him. A few of the crowd from the Cut had ambled onto the spillway and were watching them. 'Hold up,' she said. 'You can take Tantaquidgeon with you.'

He refused indignantly, affronted that she thought he couldn't manage on his own. 'Anyway, if there's trouble, you'll need him here.'

Quarrelling would have attracted more attention so she let him go. She called Tantaquidgeon and put him on guard at the jetty, then went upstairs to take out her anger and discomfort on a true English gentleman.

He was sitting by the window, looking tireder and gloomier than ever; a day with the Goodies could do that.

'Well,' she said, storming in, 'you cost me my marriage. You gone and got Captain Busgutt pressed. Ain't I lucky?'

He turned his head, blinking. 'He's been ironed?'

'Pressed, *pressed*. Taken for the navy.'

'I did that?'

'Thy government, then.' She was waving her fist. She'd give him press gang.

He had the sense to listen, giving a nod from time to time.

When she finally ran out of breath, he said, 'I can get him out, you know.'

The sheer omnipotence of the statement made her angrier. 'And what about Matthew Bell and the rest of the crew?'

'I'll get them out as well.'

'Oh.' She paused. 'Do it then.' She still didn't want to be placated. 'But how long'll that take? They could be aboard an East Indiaman by now. Or sailed to China. I'll be in my grave before I'm a bride.'

'Believe me, my dear Procrustes, marriage isn't all it's cracked up to be.' Then he said: 'Does Mrs Busgutt know?'

Makepeace sighed. 'She knows.'

'Ah. Yes. Poor soul. I thought I heard the voice of Mrs Saltonstall. She was using the words "English lord" in tones that suggested a blight on our former intimacy. She's blaming me.' He looked at her. '*And* you.'

He's quick, Makepeace thought. She hadn't meant him to know how much trouble she was in; that was her business. She said, more gently: 'They got to blame somebody. It'll pass.'

'Will it?' He shook his head at her. 'You really should have let me drown, shouldn't you, Makepeace Burke?'

'You wanted to, di'n't you? I saw.' She advanced on him with another grievance. 'You was letting slip. I saw you. You was letting it beat you.'

He shrugged and turned back to the window. 'As I remember, my situation appeared unpropitious.'

'There's *always* propitions—whatever they are. You struggle 'til the Lord sounds the last trump. See him?' She pointed out of the window to where Tantaquidgeon stood on the jetty below them. 'He'd be dead now if he'd thought like you.'

She told him the story, partly so that he could profit from Tantaquidgeon's example and partly because, when things were bad, as now, she encouraged herself with this triumph of Christian survival.

At the time John L. Burke had been playing at frontiersman, attempting to earn a living for himself, his wife and his small daughter—it was before Aaron was born—by trapping along the fur-rich edges of the Great Lakes. Another failure; the family's only gain from that particular enterprise had been Tantaquidgeon. Makepeace, then four and a half years old, had found him lapping from the stream to which she'd gone for water. The wound in his skull was horrific.

The Burkes discovered later, from other sources, that an Iroquois war party had raided his settlement—he was a Huron—massacring everybody in it, including his wife and son, and as near as spit killing Tantaquidgeon himself. To reach the stream where Makepeace found him he'd crawled several miles. She'd run to fetch her mother.

'His brains was coming out, Pa said he was a-dying, so did the other trappers' families. But Ma said he di'n't need to less'n he had a mind to it.' Temperance Burke had prayed over him as she nursed him and become heartened by his repetition of 'Jesus', his only word.

She'd named him Tantaquidgeon after an Indian familiar to the early Puritan settlers. 'He was a praying Indian, see,' Makepeace told Dapifer, triumphantly. 'The Lord hadn't sounded the trump for him yet and he knew it and he fought to stay living, spite of everything. He wouldn't be beat.'

'And you've kept him ever since?'

Makepeace was as surprised at the question as she had been when Dapifer had asked her why she'd saved him from drowning. 'Couldn't manage on his own, could he?' The Indian's devotion to her mother had been absolute; after Temperance's death it had been transferred to herself. 'He's family.'

'Can he say anything at all?'

'He says "Jesus." Ma said that was enough.' Makepeace felt heartened, as she always did by recounting the story. 'Ma was a remarkable woman and Tantaquidgeon's a remarkable man. You want to be more like him.'

She means it, thought Dapifer. That overgrown doorstop down there is being held up as an example to me. He said, meekly: 'I'll try.'

There was that ravishing grin again; she was extraordinary. He said: 'They're going to punish you, aren't they, Procrustes?'

The smile went. 'It'll pass.'

'I'd better stay.'

'That'd rile 'em more.'

'What then?'

With hideous honesty, she said: 'I was minded there'd be a reward.'

'Good God.' He'd been fooled by the relationship that had grown between them; he'd intended to send her some extravagant memento, a piece of furniture, a jewel; he'd forgotten she was a member of a class that grubbed everywhere for money. 'And what are you *minded* my life's worth?' He added, with assumed calculation: 'And don't forget I saved you from the Goodies.'

'Not for long, you didn't.' She pushed an errant red ringlet back into her cap as she reckoned the cost of him. There was the expenditure on the Goodies' food and drink, there was undoubtedly the loss of her custom, she might be forced to close the Meg and open a tavern somewhere else, and the loss of Captain Busgutt. *And*—here she doubled the figure she'd first thought of—there was the cost of falling in love with an Englishman who was about to leave her, who *must* leave her, who would have left her whatever the circumstances—she had no illusions about that—the memory of whom would keep her incapable of loving another man for the rest of the days. That was worth something.

She took a deep breath. 'Forty pounds?'

Sir Philip Dapifer, born to an income of fifteen thousand pounds per annum, appeared to consider. 'Cheaper to marry you,' he said. 'Will a draft on my Boston bank be acceptable?'

'Cash,' she said.

'Cash.'

She spat and they shook on it. He would have held onto her hand but she dragged it out of his and went abruptly out of the room.

He returned to the view. A cormorant slouched on the prow

of a boat, holding out its wings to dry in an attitude of crucifixion, as still and as blue-black as the top of the Indian's head below.

The pain inflicted by his drubbing was beginning to recede, though his shoulder still ached and he could hear the wheezing in his ears which tormented him when his heart skipped and then redoubled its beat as it often did nowadays.

The moon was rising like a transparent disk in a sky still retaining some light. It was losing its perfect roundness as if a coiner had clipped it on one side, bringing with it a lessening of the heat and giving a sheen to the little islands in the Bay so that they looked like a school of curved dolphins arrested and pewtered in the act of diving.

The view almost gave the lie to the violence enacted against it, as if the rioters were merely actors who had mistaken their lines and were capering cloddishly before a backdrop belonging to an altogether more elegant and peaceful play. It was difficult to believe they meant it.

And in London, Dapifer thought, they don't believe it.

Before setting out for America he'd gone to Prime Minister Grenville, suggesting he take soundings of the situation in New England. George Grenville had been courteous—the two were friends—but dismissive, assured that he had complete understanding of the trouble already. 'Mere grousing,' he'd said. 'That's your Boston Whig for you. He may grumble against the Stamp Tax— he *is* grumbling—yet be assured, *au fond* he'll do nothing to jeopardize his God, his King and his business.'

But he will, George. He is.

Dapifer had listened to many wealthy New Englanders in these past weeks and heard more than mere grousing. The painted, dancing figures who'd set the town's fires might not be businessmen but they had the businessmen's sympathy. The whole colony, perhaps the entire continent, was angry. This beautiful scene held danger: immediately for himself, as his broken head and bruises could testify, but, more importantly and in the longer term, for England.

From here he was vouchsafed a view of the government as the

Americans saw it: complacent, arrogant, demanding obedience and taxes, snatching Captain Busgutts from their rightful employment as if they were of no account.

And here, again as he could witness, was a nation that wouldn't stand for it. These, its lesser people, had an energy, a newness he hadn't encountered before. The fat, black cook, the two grotesque old women, even the stage-struck boy Aaron, had addressed him with a directness and familiarity that nobody but an equal would have done in England, as if they were his equal.

Most extraordinary of all was Makepeace Burke, dominating not only this stage but, now, the one he had left behind in England, bustling irreverently onto it, provincial, unpolished, brave, smelling of fresh air, and with a validity that made the painted scenery of London Society appear stale in contrast.

You struggle 'til the Lord sounds the last trump.

What was amazing was that she'd invested him with the will to do it. The lassitude induced by sickliness and, later, his marriage, left him when she entered the room. Life, purpose, bustled in with her.

Even more surprisingly, God knew how, that gawky body of hers had revived the old Adam in his. Just as he'd begun to think he'd lost the lust for women, a tavern-keeper in appalling clothes was concentrating his mind on what lay underneath.

Dapifer gritted his teeth. The best return for what she'd done for him was to leave her alone. The lemans introduced to Society by some of his fellow bucks embarrassed themselves and everybody else; unfair to do that to her.

What *could* he do for her? More a matter, he supposed, of what she would allow him to do. Wait and see what transpired; he wasn't returning to England yet, he could stay on in Boston for a while, keep an eye on her, make sure . . .

The feather on the Indian's headband, livid in the twilight, had suddenly twitched. The fellow was growling softly, looking to his right across the slipway to the neighbouring quay, to where a shape had waited and listened in last night's shadows. Somebody was there again.

Dapifer lost his temper. He leaned out of the window. 'I'm going. D'you hear me? In the name of God, leave her alone!'

Two boatloads of soldiers arrived at the jetty just before midnight, packed upright and rigid, like bottles in a crate, until an officer's shouted order set up a clatter of disembarkation that could have been heard at Cape Cod.

Makepeace moaned; there went secrecy. She met them on the jetty, looking for Aaron. A graceful civilian in a feathered hat was being bowed up the steps; the Lieutenant-Governor himself had come to recover his errant guest. For a man whose gubernatorial estate, like his own house, was in ruins, he retained a statuesque calm.

She tried to waylay him: 'Excuse me, sir . . .' but was pushed aside by a soldier's musket. The men were tense at having to land on what the last couple of nights had proved to be hostile territory. Nor did Makepeace's face—which suggested she was welcoming the Mongol hordes—reassure them.

She stood back until the last man had tramped past her. There was no sign of Aaron. She went inside, pushing her way through a taproom used to natural dyes and comfortable conversation and now ablaze with red and blue and metalled with gun barrels and iron-tipped boots. There was a new and harsher smell, gilt braiding, sweat, the wax they used on their belts and the sausage rolls of hair above each ear. Sir Thomas Hutchinson was embracing Dapifer like a returned prodigal son, 'Sir Philip, we have been most concerned,' and behind him, shifting from foot to foot, impatiently waiting to do some greeting of his own, was a sinuous little man clutching a hamper of clothes.

She managed to struggle through the soldiery. 'Excuse *me*. Where's my brother?'

The Lieutenant-Governor looked down. 'Ale for these men, my good woman.'

'Sir Thomas,' Dapifer said, 'I should like to present my saviour and our hostess, Miss Burke.'

Instantly there was a bow. 'Miss Burke, we owe you a debt of—'

'Yes,' said Makepeace. 'Where's my brother?'

Dapifer explained. Sir Thomas declared himself at a loss; so did the officer in charge. A sergeant eventually said, 'The lad as fetched us? Still rowing, I reckon. Came back in his own boat. We passed him.'

Makepeace was comforted; it would take Aaron longer to cover the stretch of water from Castle William than for the swift launches of the army.

'*May* the company be provided with the wherewithal to drink your health, Miss Burke?' Sir Thomas was all charm.

'Who's paying?'

He blinked. 'I suppose I am.'

While she, she supposed, ran a public house and was obliged to serve paying customers. Grumbling, she called Betty and the two of them went to the barrels.

The writhing little man with the hamper saw his chance. '*Now* then, Sir Pip, we managed to rescue some of our habiliments from the *ruin* those *savages* made of poor Sir Thomas's house. What a night, I thought our last hour . . . The whole town turned into cyclopses and swine! The language, my dear, and the nastiness . . . *How* I saved our things I'll never know . . . and what *have* we been doing to our poor arm? And that coat? *Never* mind, I've brought—'

'Not now, Robert,' Dapifer said.

Sir Thomas was explaining the size of the contingent he'd brought with him. 'I'm deploying armed men round the town but if trouble breaks out again tonight, I shall have to ask London for troops. The *Lord Percy* is standing by to take my dispatches to England tomorrow. The first I sent went down with the *Aurora*, of course, but—'

'*What did you say?*'

Makepeace, glimpsing Dapifer's face from the other side of the room, shoved a tankard into a waiting hand, and elbowed her way towards him.

' . . . tactless and unthinking,' Sir Thomas was saying. 'My dear fellow, I'm so sorry. I should have told you at once. Yes, I fear she went down almost as soon as she got out of the bay—heat causes unexpected squalls in this part of the ocean and they say she was over-canvassed. They've found only wreckage, I fear, no survivors . . .'

'Leave him alone,' Makepeace said, moving in, but the man Robert was before her.

'This way, Sir Pip.' He looked round for an escape route, nodded as Makepeace pointed to the kitchen and guided his master to it.

Sir Thomas, elegantly sad, watched them go. 'Such a loss, Lord Ffoulkes. They were great friends, great friends.'

'Broke it to him gentle, though, di'n't you?' snapped Makepeace and returned to the task of drawing and handing out ale pots, seriously considering the possibility that she and the Roaring Meg had been magicked into Hell. The last normality she could remember was pulling up lobster from the waters of the Bay forty-odd hours ago, as if her subsequent action had caused the earth to jump and shake disasters down on her head like rocks from an eruption. Day before yesterday her life had been neatly patterned, not happy perhaps—whose was?—but bearable, useful. Tonight, because she'd acted the Good Samaritan, she stood stripped of everything she'd previously counted good.

And what in exchange? An ecstasy so acute that she suffered for the man who'd just been stricken as if they were twinned.

'And now having to serve you buggers,' she said, slopping another tankard into another fist. 'Ain't I lucky?'

'I hope you are, miss,' the redcoat said, fervently. 'We was goddam thirsty.'

'Don't you swear in this house,' she snapped at him.

As soon as she could she made for the kitchen. He'd managed to get himself in hand and was putting his good arm into a coat that angels had tailored. Robert stood by, holding a sword and its belt. 'I'm taking ship for England right away,' Dapifer said, briskly. 'Robert, give us a moment and then fetch Sir Thomas in here.'

Robert minced back to the taproom, eyebrows working.

They faced each other in the firelight. Tension had replaced Dapifer's normal assumption of dejection, making him appear better looking and less familiar to her. 'There you have it,' he said after a moment. 'I have to go back. Ffoulkes's wife is dead and he has . . . had a young son. I'm the boy's guardian, I'm responsible.' There was a cleaver on the table and he lifted it and drove it deep into the pine. 'I'm responsible for every bloody thing—Ffoulkes's death. You. All this.'

'Not me,' she said. 'I'm responsible for me.'

'But I'll wager you don't fish any more men out of the harbour.'

'No,' she said. 'They can stay there.'

He nodded. He pointed to a purse on the mantel. 'The reward,' he said. 'Forty pounds as agreed, and a bit extra.'

'Thank you.'

'Thank *you*.'

There wasn't much else to say. She busied herself trying to pull the cleaver out of the table. It was still quivering. 'Look what you done.'

'Look what I've done. Would you do me a favour before I go?'

'What?'

'Take that bloody cap off your head.'

She thought about it for a moment, then pulled the strings at her chin and took the cap off, knowing it was the most sensual and abandoned thing she had ever done or would ever do.

The curls came warm onto her neck. His arm reached for her and the Meg's kitchen twirled into a vortex that centred on the two of them, bodies absorbing into each other in its centrifugal force.

Somebody from another dimension was coughing. Robert in the doorway was a-hem, a-hemming. Behind him, the Lieutenant-Governor of Massachusetts Bay watched them with the benignity of a man used to seeing gentlemen kissing tavern-maids.

Dapifer was unconcerned. He kept his arm round her. 'I want this woman protected, Tom. An armed guard, if you please. For as long as may be necessary.'

'I don't want a guard.' But neither of the men paid attention to her.

'Of course,' said Sir Thomas.

'And I shall need a passage on the *Lord Percy*. I have urgent business in England.'

'Certainly. One of the boats can take you out to the ship. My dear fellow, I feel this has been a most inauspicious visit but I trust . . .'

Makepeace wrenched herself free and Dapifer strolled away from her to the taproom, chatting.

She began bundling her hair back into her cap, wondering what string connected lips to labia that both those parts of her were twanging. She sat down to calm herself, then sat up. The man Robert was still in the doorway. *'What?'*

'Nothing. Absolutely nothing.' He quirked a hand towards the mantelshelf, his little face twisted. 'There's a hundred guineas in gold in that purse, did you know?'

She was suddenly very tired. 'Is there?'

'There is. What *did* you do to earn it?'

The taproom was emptying as soldiers left to take up guard duty at points around town likely to be attacked once the Sabbath lull was over; other reinforcements were being sent from the garrison at South End. The Cut vibrated from the stamp of marching boots.

Two men were being detailed to stay at the Roaring Meg, one of them the soldier who'd said he was thirsty. She saw them have a last swig of ale, shoulder their muskets and take up position on the bridge outside the front door. 'They can't stay there.' She went up to their sergeant as he ordered the last contingent out. 'I don't want those redcoats there.'

He shrugged. 'Orders, miss.'

'But . . .' She looked for Hutchinson; he was talking to an officer: She went up to him and tugged his sleeve. 'I don't want men guarding this place.'

He smiled vaguely; he had other things to think of. 'Sir Philip is worried for you, my dear. He thinks his presence may have made this inn unpopular with the rabble.'

'Will be if it's got lobster-backs outside the door.' But he'd already gone to make final arrangements with the officer in charge.

And it's tavern, not inn, and they ain't *rabble*. No doubt he thought he was protecting her. He didn't understand; a guard on her door put her on the same footing as the Tories, as Stamp Master Oliver and the Lieutenant-Governor—and look what happened to them. She'd be lucky if it was only her effigy the Sons of Liberty strung up.

She could have appealed to Dapifer but she didn't; they'd said their goodbyes.

She and Betty stood hand in hand on the jetty to watch the embarkation. Dapifer's boat was to head south along the waterfront to the *Lord Percy*, the Lieutenant-Governor's north to Castle William. Besides the navy's rowers, each had a guard with them.

As Dapifer went down the steps with Hutchinson behind him a drum began to beat somewhere on Beacon Hill. At first the two women thought it some military signal but the reaction of the men told them it was not. Each sailor's head went up and they readied their oars. Hutchinson flinched for a moment, like a man who'd been punched.

The beat was answered by another in the east, then west, then south, then others joined in, more, until Boston palpitated as if infested by a thousand giant, deep-toned, stridulating crickets. They could hear whistling now, and the crackle of fire. The Sabbath was over.

Hutchinson managed an admirable shrug. 'These Bostonians,' he said.

Makepeace didn't look at Dapifer as he was rowed away, nor he at her; she kept her head turned in the direction Sir Thomas's boat was taking, watching for Aaron. Behind her the silence that had fallen over the Roaring Meg was filled by the distant roar of the town where the glow of bonfires matched the tangerine of an extraordinary moon.

'Boat out there,' Betty said. Her deep shout carried across the water: 'That you, Aaron?'

No reply, but she was right. Makepeace could see a light floating on the sea directly opposite, impossible to judge its distance from the jetty; somebody appeared to be fishing with the use of a fire-pot—a dangerous and, she thought, futile activity at this time of the year.

'Ain't Aaron,' she said.

The projectile came at them almost lazily, not seeming so much to get nearer as to grow in size, a bit of comet spinning out of control with fire at its centre, getting bigger and bigger.

There was a splatter against the end of the jetty and little trills of flame began running along the grooves of planking, so incomprehensibly that Makepeace stepped back a little, no more than she would have done to keep her skirt hem away from a burning log falling from the grate.

Another point of light from the darkness widened into a ball, a plate, then into a cartwheel of fire spinning towards them. Another splatter, this time from above them and sparks came down in a shower.

Batting at her head and shoulders, Makepeace looked up. There was no fire, just the open shutters of her unlighted bedroom breaking the plain gable end of the Meg's upper storey. It was all right.

It wasn't. Now there was a pale glow and a movement of shadows in the bedroom where none had been before, as if someone were dancing in it with a candle. 'Fire,' she said gently to herself and then shrieked, 'JOSH!'

Betty was already lumbering into the inn; Makepeace passed her. 'I'll get him.' She'd be faster up the stairs. 'You get them bloody redcoats.'

It'll go up, the Meg'll go up. In this heat . . .

The boy was asleep on his small bed. She could hear crackling through the partition between this room and hers. As she snatched the child up and took him downstairs she tried to think. What to do? What to do? The end of the jetty was burning but the immediate danger was inside. Water from the kitchen to upstairs? From the harbour and throw it in by a ladder? She carried Josh through the kitchen and dropped him outside in the garden. 'Stay out the way.'

For a moment she stood where she was, rocking with indecision, but the sight of Tantaquidgeon, stalking past her from the jetty to fetch the ladder and bucket by the privy wall, brought back her senses. She went to the corner of the house and yelled that Josh was safe. One of the soldiers was trying to stamp out the flames on the jetty, she could hear the other, the thirsty one, in the kitchen and found him looking for buckets. She showed him where they were and fell on the pump. He disappeared upstairs with one bucketful, she followed him with another.

Her bed was already a burning ghat. Flames licked the rest of the furniture and ran along the ceiling beams. The room was a copse of fire with new trees springing up every minute. She aimed the water at the bed which gave a futile sizzle and went on burning. Through the blaze she saw Tantaquidgeon at the window, looking down as he waited for another bucket, his face and bare chest glistening tawny against the intense light.

Useless. They needed more buckets, more people.

There was a whumph as another fire-tree exploded into being. She and the soldier ran down for more water, ran up, down, up, getting in each other's way.

They had to surrender the bedroom and shut its door, trying to stop the flames spreading, but wicked little red hydra-heads came flickering from under it and the corridor began to burn.

In the midst of her panic, she still remembered to pluck the purse off the kitchen mantelshelf as she passed it. Fire wasn't going to get *that*.

There were people around now, through smoke and panic she saw faces, some of them dear to her, one very dear, but couldn't have put a name to any of them. Down to the kitchen again, crowded now, Josh was on the pump, puffing, hanging on the handle to bring it down and reaching up on his little bare toes as it rose again. The bottom of her petticoat was smouldering, somebody picked her up, smothered the skirt against his coat and carried her out to the slipway to dump her in the shallow water at its bottom. 'Thank you,' she said.

'Not at all,' said Dapifer and went back to the battle.

The sea was cool on her blistered feet and an odd remoteness allowed her to stand in it for a few seconds longer. Very organized, she thought, looking at the Meg. There were figures on the part of the roof ridge that wasn't burning, a rope had been slung round a chimney to take up buckets provided for it by a chain of people that led down to the slipway beside her. Half the Cut was here: Zeobab, Jack Greenleaf, Mr and Goody Saltonstall, Goody Busgutt, the Baler brothers ... Very organized. And—she saw it quite clearly—hopeless as hell.

The most immediate danger to the Meg's downstairs was the jetty, already half consumed. Tantaquidgeon was attacking the end of it nearest the taproom door with an axe. He freed it and she went to help him push it away with a boathook. It came floating back on the incoming tide, aiming at them and the tavern like an attacking fire-ship.

She pulled the coil of rope that always hung on a hook by the door and between them, she and Tantaquidgeon tied each of its ends round two spars of the jetty, then jumped into the water and towed the juggernaut out a few yards before dragging it sideways so that it was caught in a static corner between the slipway and the next-door wharf with only stone to burn against.

She didn't wonder how the Indian, with barely any mind of his own, managed to read hers in an emergency; she'd got used to that years ago.

She joined the chain, finding herself next to Dapifer's Robert on one side and Goody Saltonstall on the other.

Praying Bostonians passed buckets to godamming English soldiers who passed them up to swearing, scorching British sailors who threw their contents on to the common enemy howling back at them. The Roaring Meg herself was on their side: her oak beams had weathered to virtual iron over the years; although fire ran along them, it couldn't gain purchase, and her passages upstairs were narrow enough and crooked enough to seal off the section above the kitchen from draught so that, while the three bedrooms and meeting-room went up, much of the taproom's ceiling held, allow-ing people below to stamp out such roof-shingle as came through in flames.

God was on their side as well; He allowed no wind to fan the fire.

So was poverty; there were no curtains, flounces or stuffed fur-niture to act as extra tinder, no tapestries, no oil paintings along the passages to become fire-fodder.

A Cockney voice shrieked from a perch on the kitchen chimney: 'She's going out, we're winnin', the fucker's going out.'

Next to Makepeace, Goody Saltonstall merely sighed. 'Never knew a sailor so much as pull on a rope without swearin'.'

Makepeace stared at her, emerging from a tunnel of smoke and noise and bucket-passing that had been without future, an end in itself. She looked up at the sailor on the chimney, then at her misshapen tavern with its black, skeletal, smoking upper ribcage and was washed by a terrible gratitude, not so much for the miracle of its deliverance as for the even greater miracle of human grace by which the deliverance had been effected. She joined the other Puritans on their knees while Mr Saltonstall trumpeted a prayer of thanksgiving before she hobbled to the barrels to dole out ale and rum to her various saviours.

At which point the miracle faded. The people from the Cut melted away; even Goody Saltonstall whose figure was not melting material, disappeared before she could be thanked. Makepeace called, pleading, to Zeobab Fairlee and Jack Greenleaf as they were going out of the door together: 'It's on the house.'

Greenleaf shook his head; old Zeobab looked sadly at the rum glass in Makepeace's hand. 'Cain't drink here no more, 'Peace,' he said. 'You let us down.'

She poured bumpers for the servicemen of the British army and navy who sat slumped among the detritus of her taproom. Moon-light, coming through gaps in the ceiling, no longer found reflection in their uniform or even skin: both were dulled to matt black by smoke. Only eyeballs and teeth were white.

She realized the tears trickling down her cheeks would be clearing little paths through the soot on her own face and she smeared them away.

'Didn't need to light a fire to welcome us, miss,' one of the men said. 'We was warm enough.'

She peered at him. He was holding his hands away from his body. 'Was that you up on the chimney? Could have killed your fool self.'

He raised scorched eyebrows. 'Was that a chimbley? Gor damn, thought I was back up the crow's nest.'

They ain't so different from us, Makepeace thought as she kissed him. She led them into the kitchen to give them some food and treat their burns. Dapifer was already there. Betty was resetting the collarbone which had been dislocated once more by, he said, 'carrying lumps of women around'. Robert was moaning and ineffectually trying to brush soot off his breeches but he brightened as the sailors came in.

'Back again, then,' Makepeace said to Dapifer, pumping cold water into bowls to cool the chimney sailor's hands.

'I was passing. Thought I'd drop in.' He'd seen the flames and made the rowers turn the boat round.

Betty heaped the table with what food she could find and Makepeace added her largest jug filled with best Jamaican. One of the soldiers raised his beaker to Tantaquidgeon standing in the shadows. 'Give him some rum an' all, poor bastard. He's worked hard enough tonight.'

'No, and don't you go givin' him any.' She was too weary to go into the explanation about Indians and spirituous liquor. 'He drinks ale.' The few occasions on which the unwary or malicious had plied Tantaquidgeon with rum had scarred the tavern as well as her memory.

Dapifer took her into the taproom. 'Don't get them drunk either. When they've rested I want those sailors searching the Bay in case the boat that did this is still out there.'

'What boat? Did what?' In all the confusion and fear of the last hours, it hadn't occurred to her that the fire had been deliberately started. The missiles she'd seen heading towards her, would always see, were too unearthly to connect with human agency; they were more the unfocused malevolence of Nature, pieces from the tail of a comet or a shooting star. But of course they were not. 'Meteors,' she said dully. 'I thought they was meteors.'

'There was a boat,' he said. 'We saw it as we turned back. It had some sort of catapult rigged up in it, like a siege engine.'

'God have mercy.' Only five years before Boston had been devastated by one of the worst town fires in colonial history but Sugar Bart—she *knew* it was Bart—had risked starting just such another in his haste to injure one small tavern and its keeper.

She realized something else. 'Aaron,' she said. '*Aaron.*' They'd got her brother, her little brother, the responsibility her mother had left her; she'd sent him out to face the enemy on his own.

'We'll look for him,' said Dapifer gently, 'but there's no reason yet to believe he's come to harm. Isn't he a Harvard man? He could have gone to see friends in Cambridge.'

Yes, he'd gone to Harvard—she'd slaved to send him there. No, he wouldn't have gone tonight without letting her know.

There was no comfort he could give her so he left her standing in the doorway looking rigidly out to sea as if by mind and body she could will her brother home, and went to organize the boat party. The hands of the sailor who'd fought the fire from the chimney were too burned to handle an oar without pain and he was replaced by one of the soldiers.

However, as the men were clambering down into the boat from the stump of the jetty that remained, Makepeace reached for Dapifer's sleeve. 'Not you,' she said, 'I ain't losing you both.' She was shaking.

One of the oarsmen said: 'Best leave it to the navy, me lord. We'll find the lad.'

The sailor who was staying behind said: 'And them fire-slinging bastards, you find them an' all. Give 'em my regards, the fuckers.'

When the boat had gone, the remaining soldier resumed his sentry duty, Betty cleared rubble off one of the settles for the sailor to sleep on and came to the doorway to inspect Makepeace; the soles of her feet were blistered where the slippers had burned through. 'Want to lie down or fall down?' Betty asked.

'Leave me alone.'

The cook shrugged and fetched a chair for Makepeace to sit in while she did some salving and bandaging. 'Best talk to her,' she said to Dapifer. 'Keep her mind off it.'

'Take some rest yourself,' Dapifer said. 'You deserve it.'

Betty shook her head. 'Reckon I'll wait 'til he come home. His mamma, she said to me when she lay dyin', she said: "You guard him, Bet, you guard 'em both." An' I'm guardin'.' She went indoors and soon Dapifer heard the sound of a brush sweeping up debris.

Tantaquidgeon established himself in the doorway behind them, his arms crossed, like a dowager chaperone.

'What will you and your brother do about the Roaring Meg? Rebuild?' Assume the boy was coming back in one piece, keep her diverted. He had to ask twice.

She tried to concentrate. 'Sell,' she said. 'We'll move on.'

'You'll get your customers back,' he reassured her. 'One insane arsonist can't stand for a community. The neighbourliness tonight was heartening. And people forget.'

'Not round here.' The insanity of Sugar Bart was not the issue; if he stood for anything it was for those who enjoyed hatred and joined a cause in order to find a conduit for it. It was Zeobab Fairlee who was spokesman for the common, decent Bostonians suffering under the British crown and it was Zeobab who'd condemned her. *You let us down.*

So she had. While they'd been discussing protest, thinking they were in a safe house, she'd concealed a representative of the very rule against which they were to take action. Tonight an English soldier had stood outside her door, musket at the ready. Others had left here to occupy the town.

To Zeobab and his ilk, reliability was everything, from the oak they shaped into ships' hulls, to the cordage they twisted to face arctic ice and tropical hurricanes, and to the anchors they forged to hold off raging leeshores: all these things must be true or they were useless.

Such men were as demanding of their leisure. They had to know their tavern wouldn't bilk them and their blurted secrets would be kept. The trust between the Roaring Meg and its regulars had to be absolute and any betrayal of that trust on Makepeace's part was to betray it absolutely. They wouldn't drink here again.

Ain't that punishment enough, Lord? Don't take Aaron as well.

The Englishman was talking; the sound of his slow, rueful voice was a comfort but she could not attend to what he was saying.

Dapifer was thinking of his wife and wondering how she would have borne the afflictions being visited on the woman by his side. 'A spaniel, a woman and a walnut tree' . . . Makepeace Burke was being beaten if any woman was, and with every buffet showed more quality.

Perhaps, he thought, it was Catty's affliction that she had never loved anybody or anything sufficiently to be wounded by its loss. Had he loved *her*? He supposed so—until she'd run through his affection as carelessly as she wasted everything else and the only emotion she'd left to him was pity.

'I should have divorced her in England,' he said, 'but the process is akin to a public hanging—I couldn't inflict that on her, though, God knows, Ffoulkes urged me to. He was with me when we walked in on them both. I think he was more shocked than I was. Conyers, the man, was his friend as well as mine, you see. I could have told him Conyers was by no means the first. But obviously there was going to be no end unless I finished it. Better for everybody, I thought, if it were done discreetly three thousand miles away—and the Massachusetts courts are more pliable in these matters. She signed her consent readily enough; she's set her sights on Conyers to be her next husband, poor devil. So Ffoulkes came with me to New England to give the necessary evidence—because I decided it was easier. *Easier*, by Christ.'

Makepeace was aware he was stripping his soul for her sake; such a marriage was beyond her social experience, she couldn't identify with it. But when it came to his friend, she could imagine what he imagined and hear, as he must be hearing, the voices of men calling on God to save them from an empty sea. She could hear Aaron's.

She turned to him. 'A squall's quick,' she said. 'Chaos, they say. No time to think, everything blotted out. It would've been all over for him in seconds.'

It wasn't much, all she could offer, but he was grateful for it; he'd been haunted by the image of Ffoulkes clinging to a wreck for hours, praying for help until his strength failed. There'd been no Makepeace Burke to lift Ffoulkes from the sea.

'I ain't losing you both,' she'd said. He felt the same; he mustn't lose her as well.

'I think you should come to England with me,' he said.

'What for?'

'You know what for.' Her own appalling honesty deserved better than the taffeta phrases he used on other women. After all, he thought, when he'd scrupled at making her his mistress he hadn't known how important she'd become to him, nor what disaster his presence would bring to her life in Boston.

'A kept woman?'

'It's about time somebody kept you,' he said, 'and I don't think marriage to Captain Busgutt is going to come off.'

'Holy Hokey,' she said, 'a kept woman.' It took her breath away. If Jack Greenleaf or one of the Baler brothers had made the suggestion, she'd have slapped his face. That this man, who set her blood fizzing, had made it was, in his terms, the greatest compliment he could pay her. He wanted her.

Makepeace was no democrat; she believed in justice, but the precept that men, much less women, were equal one to another outside of Heaven was not one she'd ever heard seriously voiced— nor would she have believed it if she had. That he could marry her didn't occur to Makepeace any more than it occurred to Dapifer. As it was, she understood this offer from a scion of the ruling class to be Olympian; she'd cherish it for the rest of her life.

But she'd be damned if she accepted it. Not from prudery; the Puritan corseting of years had been shaken loose during the last two days. If, earlier, when they'd kissed, they'd been alone in the house, she would have let him take her, whimpered for him to take her, copulated with him on the floor like an animal in heat.

That was one thing; to be *kept* was another. To be kept, by however exalted a protector, was prostitution. She thought better of herself—and him—than that.

'I know you mean well—' she began.

'No, I don't,' he said.

She almost smiled. 'Wouldn't be right. Got to keep my independence.'

'Oh Jesus. Very well, I'll set you up in the biggest inn in England, Betty, the boy, Aaron, the Indian, all of you. You can work until you drop. Just come with me.' England would be a lonely place for him now.

She'd felt England's contempt for its colonials from three thousand miles away; she could imagine how it would treat the ignorant Yankee mistress of a favoured son, the derision she'd attract from his friends . . .

'Wouldn't they just love me,' she said. Here, she was confident on her own territory; there, he'd be ashamed of her within the week.

'I've got to go, Procrustes. Ffoulkes's boy inherits the title, the lands—vultures will be gathering. Ffoulkes would expect me to look out for him.'

'Then go,' she said.

'You realize you're driving me back into the arms of Goody Saltonstall?'

He was sitting on the doorway sill, elbows on knees, chin in hands, morose. *Lord*, she loved him. 'I know,' she said.

The noise of riot from the town had become part of the night. It fretted nerves even while they'd become accustomed to it, occasionally breaking into a clash that had the effect of a curry-comb scraped over a wound, now and then pierced by a scream—always Aaron's.

She clutched at her head suddenly. 'Where is he? Where d'you think he is?'

He put his arm round her and felt the surface of her hair scorched and frizzy against his cheek; at some point during the fire she'd taken her cap off to beat at the flames.

The moon was seeping colour now and hung like a huge, Chinese lantern over an empty sea.

There was a grunt from Tantaquidgeon and they heard a call. It was nearer than the horn-blowing, howling, drumming component of the air, but not from the immediate vicinity. Somewhere in Cable Lane, perhaps. Clear, though.

'*Makepeace Burke.*'

High, fluting, strange, not human. Birdlike, as if the name issued with difficulty from a beak. So frightening that, when Makepeace opened her mouth to answer, she couldn't make any sound.

'Inside.' Dapifer pushed her into the taproom, then Tantaquidgeon. He drew his sword. Betty hurried to shut the doors behind them. Robert came running in from the kitchen; the sailor sat up. For a moment they stayed where they were. The chirruping awoke ancient terrors of bird-headed things in shadow; it hung on the air and had no right to be there.

From under its dust and cinders the grandmother clock whirred and began to chime five o'clock. In the blackness they waited for the strokes to die away. Dapifer opened the door to the Cut and stepped out. 'What was that, corporal?'

'Don't know, sir. Can't tell where it came from.' The soldier had levelled his musket and was moving it in an arc that went from the slipway on his left and then right, down the silent lane.

Dapifer crossed the bridge to join him. The brook behind him gurgled cleanly towards the sea which was beginning to reflect a pearl-grey suggestion of dawn. The overhanging roofs at the far end of the Cut formed an archway of light from a bonfire beyond it.

Whatever it was, it came again.

'*Makepeace Burke.*'

The soldier's musket swung in the direction of the alley that ran into the Cut further down. Dapifer touched his arm. 'No shooting yet.'

In the taproom Tantaquidgeon had begun a soft, incomprehensible chant. Robert was squeaking. Makepeace heard Betty hissing at him to hold steady. The sailor made an attempt at a joke. 'He'll be sorry when he's sober, whoever he is.'

Was it a man, or a woman? Or neither?

'Here's your brother, Makepeace Burke.'

Somehow her legs walked her to the door and outside. Tantaquidgeon was behind her, still chanting, with a knife in his hand, and then Betty, gripping John L. Burke's old blackthorn like a cudgel.

The Cut was empty of everything except an impression that it was watching her; shadows in the corner of Cable Lane could have been people but if they were they didn't move; open shutters had only blackness between them.

She looked to the right; again, difficult to see but, yes, figures passing and repassing against the glow of a bonfire in the square beyond, carrying something on a rail, an effigy. As she squinted, trying to make them out, they tipped the rail so that the scarecrow they'd made slid off onto the ground.

Gone now. The effigy made an untidy heap in the mouth of the Cut against the bonfire's aureole.

Dapifer was telling her to get back inside.

Makepeace kept her eyes on the effigy. They'd made it of hay, untidily; there were bits sticking out all over it, black hay that gleamed when it caught the light. She watched it rise to its feet and start stumbling up the Cut. She didn't move.

The tarred and feathered thing was bowed so that the prickles along its back curved, like a hedgehog's, and it zigzagged as it came, lumbering from one side of the lane to the other, mewing when it bumped into a wall.

I must go to it, she thought, it's blind. And stood there. She heard Betty scream and the soldier say: 'Oh Christ, dear Christ.'

In the end it was Tantaquidgeon who strode down the lane and carried Aaron home.

Chapter Six

THE landlady of the Roaring Meg, her brother and staff sailed for England aboard the *Lord Percy* on the evening tide.

Dapifer, finding himself in charge, had reasoned that a surgeon on a ship, where tar was used extensively, would be more used to treating its burns and therefore better qualified to help Aaron than a land-based doctor. In any case, Makepeace had to be taken out of danger; there was no guarantee that the assault on her brother didn't presage another on her, and he could think of no safer refuge than a warship of His Majesty's navy. Furthermore, the *Percy* was the only vessel on the quays with a surgeon—other large craft still lay further off in the harbour, waiting out the rioting—and her captain, charged with speeding Sir Thomas Hutchinson's dispatches to London, would not delay sailing.

His own imperative was still to serve the memory of his drowned friend and support Ffoulkes's son, a duty he couldn't put off any longer. Neither could he desert Makepeace in her trouble.

Ergo: they must sail with *Lord Percy* together—and today.

This was explained to Makepeace who merely nodded—anything, anything, Dapifer had turned to Betty. 'She can return later if she wants to but I'm not leaving her in Boston,' he said. It didn't seem strange to him that Betty accepted his right to arrange matters, nor that he was consulting an elderly, black, female cook. 'The thing is, are you prepared to come with us?' To separate the two women was unthinkable.

'Ain't leavin' me behind in this place. Nor my boy neither.' Betty's face was drawn, though she was taking the horror of what had happened to Aaron better than his sister.

Makepeace, dry-eyed but oblivious of everything else, clutched a pan of butter as their boat was rowed along the wharves to King's Quay and kept dabbing handfuls from it on the form that lay on the stretcher between its thwarts.

Tantaquidgeon was not consulted but strode up the *Percy*'s gangplank anyway with his usual impregnable serenity.

The ship's doctor was youngish, Scottish, irritable and attributed blame for his patient's condition on those who'd brought him aboard. 'Will ye see this? Have ye revairted to savagery on this continent?' He was examining Aaron as he spoke, prodding and peering in the light of a lantern that hung in a cradle from the bulkhead. 'Why not scalp the lad and be done?'

Aaron lay face down on the cot in the surgeon's own cabin on the *Percy*'s orlop deck, semi-conscious and moaning. He'd been naked and in a foetal position when the hot tar had been poured on him so that most of it had been retained by his upper back, head and arms. His thin young legs sticking out from under his carapace emphasized the resemblance to a helpless porcupine. Makepeace hung over him, still trying to smear the monstrosity with butter and coming between the doctor and the lantern.

An open door in the cabin's thin partition led to a dispensary where the surgeon's 'boy', a crewman considerably older than himself, was responding to clicks from his master's fingers to reach for bottles from a cupboard. Dr Baines glanced up. 'Will ye remove this female?'

Dapifer, who'd already tried, shook his head. 'Can you help him?'

'How can I tell? It's depaindent on the depth of the burns and that I'll not know until they're uncovered. And on how many useless questions I'm paistered by in the meantime.'

The man's rudeness was oddly reassuring and some measure of his competence penetrated Makepeace's brain enough for them to get her outside to the companionway, though she refused to go further.

Dapifer went up on deck to make arrangements for the passage with the captain.

The *Percy* was one of the navy's new frigates, small for a man-of-war, carrying an armament of only thirty-six guns, but fast. Most of her time was spent shuttling between London and Boston, carrying dispatches and, occasionally, a passenger or two on official business. This trip her captain was stretching the point and obliging the Governor of Massachusetts Bay by giving passage to England to one of his female relatives and her maid.

Captain Strang was happy to stretch the point even further and oblige Dapifer and his connections in the Admiralty, despite that gentleman's curious and multi-coloured entourage. He was prepared to relinquish his own quarters as well as that of his lieutenant in order to do so. 'I can't offer you comfort, Sir Philip, but I can guarantee speed. With a following wind we should make England in six weeks, perhaps less.'

The conversation was shouted over the scurry to revictual the *Percy*. Cows bellowed as they were lowered in their slings into the hold, goats roamed the quarterdeck in front of Strang's cabin door and fowls clucked miserably from the coops stacked behind the wheel.

Dapifer went below to report. Makepeace hadn't moved; her eyes were on the surgeon's door. When he told her it was settled they should sail for England that evening, she made no comment. He asked Betty: 'Does she know what's happening?'

'She don't care,' Betty said. 'What we goin' to do about the Meg?'

'I'll write a note now to Hutchinson. He'll keep an eye on it for you.'

Makepeace looked round at that and spoke for the first time. 'Sam Adams.'

Betty nodded. 'Yep. She trust Sam's eye more'n Hutchinson's.'

'Very well.'

In the event Dapifer wrote an explanatory note to both gentlemen and left them, along with two shillings, with the harbour master to be delivered.

A net of lemons was being slung aboard. Captain Strang nodded at it. 'Pray God that satisfies Baines; he demands lemons against the scurvy.'

'He seems a good man.'

'I doubt he'd go down well in London Society but I've never had so few men in the sick bay as since he joined us.'

Satisfied, Dapifer left the captain to his preparations and waited on deck for the doctor to report. Apart from the activity centred on this ship, King's Quay was quiet and the wide street that extended from it into the centre of town quieter yet. With the coming of day, Boston had once again sunk into an abashed calm. Along the waterfront, warehouses lay in ruins as silent as Pompeii's, providing new perches for seagulls.

'Wail,' said a voice at his side, 'we can thank the Almighty it's not as extensive as might be and it was his back rather than his front which received the brunt. I'd not have liked those burns too near the vital organs.'

'He'll live?'

'I'll not say that. My worry is infection, there's penetration of the skin here and there . . . but, aye, we were fortunate the lad was unclothed at the time and the quills didn't take cloth in with them.'

'A full recovery?'

The Scotsman shook his head. 'The scarring will torment him the days of his life, nor will he aiver grow hair on the back of his haid. And I did not tell the lady . . . his sister, is it? . . . the genitals received tairrible bruising from the rail they carried him on. I ask ye, what sort of people? Medieval, so it is, used in the Crusades, so they tell me, Richard the Lionheart ait cetera. Much beloved of London mobs. Aye, well, that's the English for ye but Amairicans I'd thought better of.'

The smitch of dying bonfires was giving way to the fresh air of morning. The doctor drew in a breath of it. 'Is there a reason they punished the boy?'

'His sister happened to save me from attack by so-called Boston patriots the day before yesterday. She and her brother paid the price.'

'A spirited young lady,' Dr Baines said, thoughtfully. 'Were ye acquainted afore this?'

'No.'

They went down to the cabin to see the patient. The surgeon had taken the tar off but it had pigmented areas of Aaron's scalp and skin so that they lay in black petals on raw flesh which showed pinkly through the gauze Baines had put over it. The tiny cabin smelled of tar and laudanum and the boy slept on his front, breathing loudly, his head turned to one side, his arms hanging over the cot edge. Makepeace sat on a stool beside him, basketing his one uninjured hand in her own. She didn't take her eyes off her brother when Dapifer came in. He glanced at Betty, who shook her head. They went up on deck together.

'Is she blaming me?'

'Herself more like,' Betty said. 'No reason for neither.'

'I should have stayed in England.'

'Didn't, though. You just treat her right, is all.'

An entranced Josh joined them. 'Think they'll let me up that riggin'?'

'If they kill me first,' Betty said.

As the ship drew out into the Bay, the sun glistened on the prim, white-painted steeples of Boston's churches, accentuating the messy, blackened tideline of its waterfront. It shone through the bared beams of the Roaring Meg's roof and the open door of its taproom. The watchers on the *Lord Percy* saw her wash dislodge the remnant of jetty floating against the slipway so that it came bobbing after them on the tide like an abandoned dog trying to catch up with its master. Betty sobbed then. Makepeace remained below with her brother and didn't see it.

Since Makepeace refused to leave Aaron, her food was taken to the surgeon's cabin. Betty stayed with her. Josh and Robert—to their mutual but different delight—were to eat with the crew on the gundeck on tables slung on ropes from the deckhead. Tantaquid-geon, who disliked eating in company, was given a plate and dis-appeared with it.

Dapifer was invited to dine with the officers in the wardroom, a coffin-shaped space which he had to enter at a stoop. There'd been no time to light the galley's fires and that first evening's dinner was a cold collation, but it was cheered by the presence of Susan Brewer, the niece of Elizabeth Murray, owner of Boston's smartest ladies' outfitters, who was on her way to study metropolitan shop-keeping and send back the latest London fashions to her aunt's establishment.

A lively young thing, Miss Brewer, of bouncing laugh and bosom, excited by this, her first voyage, and the presence of so many eligible men—though, for propriety's sake she had asked that her black maid, Jubilee, be allowed to join her for meals—and she entertained the company with a second-hand account of the rioting.

'Aunt Bess does not live above the shop, of course, so she was spared, but one shudders to think what might have happened if she did—every window in Cornhill was broken and rifled. Auntie cried buckets, but after a bit we made ourselves amused to imagine those Mohucks dressed in sprigged hoop petticoats. Why they think Auntie is an enemy to her country just because she brings in fashion from London, though, sakes, when you consider, where else can fashion come from? Auntie says it's a political laugh but it's forced her to think of moving the shop to Queen Street where there is more tone.'

After the meal there was a rush to invite the young woman to promenade with the officers on the quarterdeck. Dapifer, tired, ex-cused himself. Miss Brewer was disappointed and on the way up to the deck she turned to whisper: 'Sir Philip, I hope you ain't offended that Jubilee is eating with us? She ain't my maid as such, she's going into service with some friends of Auntie's when we get to England.'

'Not at all.'

'Because I wondered if you did not approve. I saw the other two maids on board are having to eat below and—'

'Two maids?'

'White one and another black one, and I wondered—'

Gently, Dapifer explained Makepeace's situation and Miss Brewer was momentarily silenced with embarrassment.

New England heat extended far into the Atlantic and there was less a prevailing wind than a prevailing draught on which, despite the wetting of her sails, the *Lord Percy* bobbed in a laziness which threatened to extend the crossing from six weeks to at least seven.

Tarpaulins were slung for the passengers to sit under and watch the frisking of porpoises in a sapphire sea, but Makepeace still sat by Aaron's side in near darkness, a single candle in the safety lantern above her head contributing to the cabin's heat, fanning her patient until her arms ached with strain. She relinquished her place only to Betty and only then when she had to.

Dapifer called every morning to enquire after the patient but Makepeace kept her eyes averted from his and did not talk to him.

Aaron's pain was kept at bay for the first two weeks by laudanum but it came snarling in as the doses were gradually reduced.

'Give him more,' Makepeace demanded.

'Now, now, ye'll not want the lad depaindent on it?'

There was an argument, not their first. Aaron's agony lacerated Makepeace as if it was her flesh that lay in open strips; she prowled a jungle of pain, prepared to rend those who threatened more hurt on the wounded creature in it. Baines used his prim, Edinburgh accent to soothe her as he would a defensive dog until she saw sense. That she made trouble did not exasperate him, it seemed to increase his admiration. 'A strong-willed lassie,' he reported to Dapifer, 'but from true concairn for her brother.'

He was her only concern. She was vaguely aware that home, acquaintances, occupation, the lichened stone marking her parents' grave in North End churchyard, all the things that had anchored her life were being left behind. And it didn't matter.

Even if the choice hadn't been made for her, she would have left Boston anyway. Overnight every memory it held for her had become smirched with tar. People she knew had disfigured a seventeen-year-old boy, people she knew.

Because of me.

She thought of the times when she and Betty had sat at Aaron's bedside during his childhood illnesses, of money expended, time spent and sacrifice made to keep this young body whole and healthy. Of the pain that still awaited it.

Because of me.

The orlop was the quietest place on board. Air circulated along its passage from open gun ports; the only sound by day was the slap of sea against the side of the ship and the occasional murmur from the doctor's dispensary next door.

'No good torturin' yourself.' Betty sat down beside her. 'I know you. It weren't your fault.'

'Yes it was.'

'Held him down whilst they poured the pitch, did you? No, an' you didn't cut off Sugar Bart's spare leg neither. Nor you di'n't sell the Sons down the river. There wasn't anythin' you did as asked for this. It's them'll boil in Hell, not you.'

'I brought the Englishman to the Meg.'

That was it, the one needless action. She should have landed him along the quays and sent for the magistrates to fetch him. At the time there had seemed good reason to take him back to the tavern: she'd wanted to ensure that he didn't inform the authorities of his attackers; she'd seen the chance of reward. But now, tracing the causes of her brother's suffering, these motives looked suspect. Had she been attracted to Dapifer from the first? Had her sin of lusting after him fallen on Aaron?

She said: 'Clear enough, ain't it? I should've handed him over. The Lord's punished me through Aaron. Aaron's the lamb in the thicket.'

'That'd do it,' Betty said. 'That's the Lord for you.'

'Oh, go away.' She was irritated. It was her fault. Aaron had lost his youth, would carry scars for ever. Her fault.

Betty left her to her self-flagellation.

Shock had left Aaron with little recall. Rowing back alone from Castle William, he had decided to tie up for a while at White's Wharf, some four or five hundred yards north of the Roaring Meg.

After all, he'd accomplished his task, soldiers were on their way to safeguard the tavern, he could afford a few minutes before he followed them.

There'd been another boat tied up to the wharf with an unusual structure arranged between its thwarts; he'd registered its peculiarity but, with his mind on other things, had remained incurious.

'It'd only been throwing fireballs at us,' Makepeace told him. 'The Meg was burning. Holy Hokey, you must've seen the flames.'

He hadn't. 'There were bonfires all over.'

After that his memory of events was fragmentary—a sack over his head, the smell of cordage as if he were in a rope-walk, a glimpse of whooping, painted men as they stripped him, searing pain. He'd heard screams, whether his own or of someone else subjected to the same treatment, he didn't know.

No, he hadn't recognized any of the men's voices—an omission that seemed to comfort him slightly. Random assault, perhaps because he resembled an Englishman, was less terrible to him than if it had been inflicted by people he knew.

He had his own guilt.

'What for did you stop off at White's?' Makepeace asked him. 'You knew I'd be worrying.'

He turned his head away. Answering took time. 'There was a girl.'

At first she didn't understand and then she did and she was angry. 'All those nights you said you was at Cambridge . . . ?' She stood up to bend over and look into his face. Tears were squeezing from beneath his eyelids.

'I'm sorry, 'Peace, I'm sorry. Wages of sin.'

She sat back, suddenly appalled that she'd been cross with him. He'd only done with a girl what she so nearly had with a man. Betty was right; it would be a poor God who punished his creatures for being natural to the flesh He'd made for them.

This, then, was the atrocity of atrocity; its victims looked for guilt in themselves, seeing some involvement of their own in the crime against them—and it was nonsense.

'Wages of *what?*' she said. 'Wages of being young? Being human?' By absolving Aaron, she was able to absolve herself. 'I tell you this, Aaron Burke, there's only one man owed the wages of sin and that's Sugar Bart and one day I'm a-going to see he's paid 'em.' She hung Bart above a vat of boiling tar by his one leg and dipped him in it like a toffee apple. 'That's all we got to blame ourselves for—letting that shite stay free.'

Aaron almost smiled. 'I don't think it was Bart with the tar,' he said.

'It was Bart with the fire.' She knew that much.

She felt cleaner after that; they both did. It was not enough, though, to help Aaron through the next stage of his hurt. While in delirium and pain, her brother had displayed considerable courage but as both lessened and he absorbed the extent of the permanent damage done to him, he declined into grief. It was mainly for his hair. He kept touching the back of his head to see if the chafed, helmet-like skin on it was producing anything to keep pace with the growth on his chin. It wasn't.

'I'm piebald.' It was a howl of despair.

'It'll grow,' soothed his sister.

'No,' Dr Baines told him, 'it won't.'

Makepeace dragged the Scotsman outside. 'Ain't you got no pity?'

'That I have, mistress, and may I say it's greater than yours that's accustoming the lad to pap.'

Dr Baines went back into the cabin. Makepeace heard him say: 'Young man, there's bravery in battle and bravery for every day which, in my opinion and that of the Lord God, is the higher of the two. Now then, ye can throw the rest of your life to yon savages who tried to take it, or ye can bless yourself with walking, talking, using your wits and partaking of the Almighty's many blessings—among them the love of a devoted sister. Which is it to be?'

A mumble from Aaron.

'Och, b-barley-cakes,' shouted the doctor, exasperated, 'for why do ye think the Lord invented wigs?'

It was almost terrible to see Aaron's response. He summoned up a fortitude he didn't know he had. Before his sister's eyes he changed into a different soul, pitifully determined not to utter a word that wasn't optimistic.

She knew him, knew he saw himself playing a part as much as he had played at soldiers when he was little or, later, at being the complete young-Tory-around-town, but this was the finer role and if he wanted admiration for his portrayal he certainly had hers. There were dreadful relapses but the progress towards mending himself was made by him alone and had nothing to do with her. Baines was right; she hadn't helped him, he had grown beyond her. She drew in a deep breath and let him go.

The wig was a success. Robert, who had been almost tearfully attentive throughout, produced it from Dapifer's wardrobe. 'We don't wear it except when we're going powdered but I've washed it and brushed it and, oh, *won't* we look lovely.'

Aaron was dejected. 'Now it's fashionable to wear one's own hair, I must lose mine.'

'Master Aaron, time I've finished, they won't know this ain't yours.' They would if they'd been acquainted with red-headed Aaron before the tarring because the wig was the exact, sad colour of Dapifer's hair, but it was well wrought. 'See,' Robert said, 'we tie it at the back with a bow and the queue is nice and loose to cover our poor neck.'

Once Makepeace had lined its hessian interior with a silk handkerchief so that it would not rub the still-raw flesh, Aaron put it on and was transformed. Robert clasped his hands: 'Oh, *yes*. Pale and interesting, *just* like Hamlet after he's seen his poor pa.'

A shirt of softest linen, a cor de soie coat and breeches were selected for the patient's first sortie to the quarterdeck. Aaron was helped up the companionway but he shrugged off assistance when he reached the deck, walking stiffly, his arms bent and unmoving like an old man's, to the chair set for him under the tarpaulin next to Miss Susan Brewer.

Dapifer set another for Makepeace on her opposite side, then strolled away unthanked.

Susan Brewer began a pleasant but determined questioning.

Aaron's replies were revealing. 'It flares up from time to time but is much improved now, I thankee. An Indian attack, best left unmentioned . . . and you, Miss Brewer, why do you go to England? . . . Oh, a mere actor off to seek my fortune in London's theatres.'

Makepeace's horror at the tarring and feathering had overlooked its humiliation yet, obviously, Aaron felt it deeply. Since the men who'd perpetrated it had been attired as Mohucks, he wasn't departing far from the truth in calling it an Indian attack. Oh, bless him. But an *actor?* In *London?*

One of the Rev Mather's better sermons had pronounced actors as 'the very filth and off-scouring, the very lewdest, basest, worst and most perniciously evil sons of men'. While Makepeace didn't go as far as that, her Puritan upbringing had nevertheless trained her to regard the theatre as a form of whoring and she had prayed that Aaron's fascination with it would be something he'd grow out of, like pimples.

For a second, his glance met hers with a challenge.

She nodded back. If that particular ambition returned the spark to her brother's eye, then amen to it. Boston prejudices must remain in Boston. But she was overcome by a wave of depression; she controlled nothing any more. She was being sailed to a country she didn't know, didn't like and had little idea what to do when she got to it.

Furthermore, she had fallen out of love with the man taking her there. She didn't blame him but, innocent or not, Dapifer was the cause of her disasters.

It was as if the cataclysm that had overwhelmed her household had swept away with it such feeling as she'd once had for him. Mainly, she wasn't used to powerlessness; she had become his dependent and resented it.

He needn't think I'll be his doxy just because there ain't any other living for me.

Being Makepeace, she had to tell him so right away. She found him in the stern, gloomily watching the ship's wake cream away behind them.

'Thank you for what you've done for Aaron, Sir Philip,' she said, 'but matters ain't changed. I still won't be your mistress.'

She had his hundred guineas. Maybe she'd buy an English tavern with it, get her own boat, trade with the natives, *something*.

He seemed reluctant to leave his contemplation of the waters, but eventually looked at her. 'Mistress Burke, believe me, the situation you mention will not arise.'

'It won't?'

He shook his head. 'I am your servant in everything. That particular offer, however, has been withdrawn.'

'Oh,' she said. 'That's all right then.'

He turned to watch her walk away. She'd bound her hair in a piece of sailcloth and topped it with a ragged straw hat more suitable for keeping flies out of a horse's eyes. Small wonder Susan Brewer had taken her for one of the lower orders. Well, so she was.

Dapifer shook his head. He'd suffered his own revulsion. Her hostility to him since coming aboard had been unreasonable, not to say unattractive. God dammit, he hadn't asked to be thrown into her bloody harbour. Nor that she should fish him out of it. Yet here he was, burdened with sole responsibility for a bad-tempered American scarecrow and her entire entourage.

He returned to watching the wake. He'd set her up, of course, and the family, but it was a relief to find she was holding him to nothing more.

Betty, who was plucking a chicken while sitting on the hen coop—she'd formed an alliance with the ship's cook—saw them part, two people leeched by life's unkindness. Give 'em time, she thought.

Aaron, tired from his first outing, had been taken back to his cabin by Robert. Makepeace sat herself down in his chair. Miss Brewer turned to her. 'I hope you will forgive that I mistook you, Miss Burke. Auntie always says, "Susan, your tongue's too long for your teeth," and I didn't know 'til Sir Pip told me you'd lost all your clothes in the riots but I said to your brother, "Sakes, she can borrow some of mine, I've brought plenty." A proper cloth market Auntie calls me . . .'

'Mistook me for what?'

Susan reddened. 'Well . . . but Sir Pip says you're a business-woman, like Auntie, and it's terrible that these savages can reduce such to rags.'

Susan Brewer's own rags were of glossy white lace-edged lute-string over which rampaged pink and green flowers. She could have attracted butterflies. She had certainly attracted Aaron; Makepeace had seen her brother reanimated by the girl's interest.

Makepeace glanced down. Her clothes had been laundered and her skirt darned by Betty; the hat she had borrowed from Boocock, Dr Baines's assistant, to keep the sun off. In Puritan eyes she ful-filled the requirement of cleanliness and decency. In Miss Brewer's she was a fright. And another thing—with only a difference of perhaps four years in their ages, this miss beside her was addressing her as if she were a much older woman.

Abruptly she excused herself and went off in search of a looking-glass. A pocket mirror was supplied eventually by the invaluable Robert. She took it to the cabin she now shared with Betty and Josh, a space known as the 'coach' that led out onto the quarter-deck. Putting herself full in a shaft of afternoon sun coming through the door, she held the thing up.

After a while she put it down again. Of *course* he'd been relieved by her rejection. Amazing he hadn't run away and hid when he saw her coming. The way she looked now would stop clocks.

She was suddenly frightened. Aaron didn't need her any more, Betty had found congenial company in the galley. Young Josh had been adopted as ship's mascot and was being introduced to the nautical mysteries of rigging-climbing and swinging the lead. Tan-taquidgeon had become a living and appreciated figurehead, spend-ing his hours in the prow contentedly watching the curl of the *Percy*'s bow wave.

Unwanted by anyone, what was she? Ballast. *Ageing* ballast.

Before dinner that evening there was a tap on Miss Brewer's cabin door . . .

'*Aagh*. Are you sure?'

'Certain,' puffed Susan, her foot on Makepeace's backside. 'I can't think how you went without one.'

'Wore my, ow, mother's. Can't breathe.'

'You're not supposed to.'

Miss Susan had accepted the challenge with the enthusiasm of a matador out to win a bull's ears. Makepeace had been immersed in a canvas bath of tepid sea water, scrubbed with soap and unguents and her head held out of the porthole to dry her hair. Now, with a nineteen-inch waist and her arms crossed in embarrassment over her breasts, she was hooped into a contraption like a fruit cage while Susan Brewer considered the next stage. 'It should be green of course but it'll have to be blue. Green curdles my complexion and I shun it like the plague. Now then—this blue or this blue?'

'Anything.'

'That, if I may say so, is your error; you should *care*.' Susan was circling. 'Look at you: Aphrodite up from the waves of wherever. Such hair . . . sakes, I have to wear curlpapers for a month for that effect and you've hidden it like a miser.'

The dress decided on was of deep blue and its décolletage even deeper. 'You sure?' Makepeace asked again, hoisting the front so that her feet nearly left the ground.

'Trust me.' Susan yanked it down. 'Are we or are we not out to catch the eye of a certain gentleman?'

'We ain't.'

But Miss Brewer wasn't listening. 'Only a *little* set of the cap should do it, I think, the good doctor already spends his time singing your praises, it'll but take a—'

'Dr *Baines*?'

'Certainly Dr Baines. Sir Pip apart, he's the most eligible creature on board, your dear brother being too young and in any case your brother and he was telling me only last night he intends to find a wife and settle on land as soon as may be and brilliant as he is he'll soon have patients a-flocking . . .'

Makepeace was distressed; Alexander Baines was an angel of healing from Heaven but, for her, he had the sexual appeal of a bottle of physic. And she prayed, for his sake, that he did not love her.

She noticed that Susan did not suggest she set her cap at

Dapifer—an omission she found irritating. Presumably he was excluded as too aristocratic for her or because Miss Brewer was setting her own pretty headgear at him. Makepeace, having no idea of the gradations of class above her own, instantly decided she was being laced into a bodice by a suitable candidate for the post of the second Lady Dapifer and felt a constriction round her ribs that wasn't caused by the corset.

Good luck to you, she thought, grimly. It was impossible to dislike the kindly Miss Brewer, but at that moment Makepeace was seized by an inclination to knock her down.

They had a difference of opinion over the matter of rouge. 'I ain't trying for a husband,' Makepeace insisted, appalled.

'*Every* woman's trying for a husband,' Miss Brewer said, dabbing anyway.

'Your auntie's done well enough single.' Elizabeth Murray had famously attracted—and refused—proposals from male Bostonians assured that both she and her successful business needed the guiding hand of a man.

'Auntie's a widow, which is the proper thing to be. Now the cap.' This was a mere headband of lace that allowed Susan to trick Makepeace's curls around it in what she called 'wink-a-peeps'.

'There.' Miss Brewer handed over a fan. 'Ye-es, if we could walk a *little* less like we were bringing the cows home, we should blow this boat out of the water.'

Arm-in-arm they stepped out of the cabin onto the deck and Captain Strang, emerging from his, rushed to open the door of the wardroom for them, just beating his lieutenant to it. The purser, who had formerly eaten with the non-commissioned officers, changed his usual practice and followed them in.

Makepeace found the meal unnerving. Her opinion on his ship was sought by Captain Strang, on the weather by Lieutenant Horrocks. Was she comfortable in her cabin? Was her poor brother—Aaron was dining in bed—on the mend? Her plate was piled higher with pickled beef than anyone else's by a steward who tenderly apologized for the lack of fresh vegetables. Dr Baines directed the conversation so that it could display his familiarity with her.

This, then, was what curls and a dab of rouge could do; men responded to the wrapping, not the content.

Only Dapifer, his attention monopolized by Susan Brewer, remained aloof, though Dr Baines's tenderness did not escape his attention. He thought: Wants her, does he? And an excellent match for them both. *Dammit.*

The warm, indigo current of the Gulf Stream pushed the *Lord Percy* lazily eastwards towards the coast of Europe and the heat followed it. At night the sea was illuminated by phosphorescence, sometimes glittering with a thousand pinpricks of light, like a swarm of fireflies, sometimes causing accompanying fish and dolphins to be clothed in it so that they appeared as racing flames through the water.

It was a phenomenon of such beauty that the inclination was to stay late on deck to watch it but Makepeace would sense Dr Baines, moved by its romance, edging towards her with a proposal on his lips and was forced back to her cabin before he could make it.

'But he's so worthy, poor man,' protested Susan Brewer.

'You have him then.'

Susan shook her head in apparent sadness. 'In Dr Baines's opinion and therefore, of course, that of the Lord God, I am too giddy.'

Makepeace grinned. Her life until now had lacked the friendship of a congenial young woman and, Aaron's recovery apart, she saw it as her one profit on this benighted voyage that she had gained Susan Brewer's. They were by no means like-minded; Susan was high Tory and had been brought up with a regard for etiquette that Makepeace lacked and without the angular Puritanism that Temperance Burke had instilled into her daughter. She had no patience with the view of men like Sam Adams.

What they shared was not only an appreciation of female independence but a rare knowledge—Susan's from her enterprising aunt, Makepeace's from her own experience—that it was achievable. They occasionally shocked each other but that only added a zest to their relationship.

It was extraordinarily pleasant and did a good deal to recover

Makepeace's equilibrium merely to indulge in female gossip—
something she'd never had opportunity to do before—to exchange
life stories, to discuss men and manners. Of the latter, Susan knew
a good deal more than Makepeace, being an avid reader of novels
imported from England, especially those of Mr Richardson.

'You saved him from *drowning*? Sakes, he's *bound* to marry you.'

'Oh, very likely.'

'But he *is*. King Cophetua and the beggar-maid. Forgive me,
dear, I know tavern-keeping isn't beggary but compared with *his*
elevation . . . he's practically a peer you know, Captain Strang said
he turned down the King's offer of a dukedom as too vulgar but
is mightily well connected with half the cabinet.' Susan dropped
her voice. 'Captain Strang says he only came to Boston so that he
might quietly divorce his wife. I wonder what she *did*? I've never
known anyone divorced, and you can tell he has a secret sorrow,
so gothick yet with it all so amusing.' She gave a sacrificial sigh. 'I
suppose I must yield him to you now, you having saved his life
and all, and creep off to fade away of unrequited passion.'

'Have him,' said Makepeace, generously, 'I don't want him.'

But, after all, she found that she did. It wasn't just that her
interest had been requickened by Susan's admiration for the man
but that her health was returning with rest and sea air and, with
it, the realization that the two days during which he'd been closeted
at the Roaring Meg had been on the one hand the most terrible
yet at the same time the most wonderful of her life. At nights she
would pick over the conversations they'd held in her poor room
as over emeralds and rubies in a jewel box.

She saw quite clearly that their relationship was now alienated
beyond repair; she was a burden to him. It wasn't her fault; it
wasn't really his. There was nothing to be done except keep her
pride intact by being as remote towards him as he was to her.

Makepeace allowed Susan's rants against Sam Adams and his
cohorts to go unrefuted. The very words 'Sons of Liberty' stank of
tar and echoed with Aaron's screams.

She'd listened in silence when the wardroom, too, denounced
the Boston rioters, but, as the Western Approaches came nearer,

talk turned to the question of what the English government should do about them when it received the news the *Percy* carried—and that was a different matter.

' "No taxation without representation", the saucy rogues,' said Captain Strang, who had aspirations as a landowner. 'Why, your common Englishman is not represented in Parliament yet submits to being taxed and do you hear him complain?'

'I rather think I do,' Dapifer pointed out.

'That's beside the point, Sir Pip, if I may say so. The point is that the plantations must obey the will of their King and his government. Concede the vote to any agitating colonist with straw in his hair who asks for it and your ploughman and cowherd at home will be demanding it too. And there you are—revolution.'

'Reform, certainly,' Dapifer said.

Dr Baines said: 'Captain, ye're surely not advocating sending an army to enforce the Stamp Tax?'

'Why not?'

'If I can judge the taimper of the Amairicans, ye'd have war on your hands.'

'Why not just repeal it?' said Makepeace.

The interjection of a soprano voice into an opus for basso profundo brought only a deliberate silence in which it was supposed to consider its temerity and withdraw.

She didn't care; these men weren't American, they didn't have to scrape and shift to pay for the damn stamps, it was none of their business. 'Colonist with straw in his hair . . .', she'd give him straw in his hair. 'We don't *want* it,' she said.

Even Dr Baines changed his position in order to repel female boarders. 'Aye, well, Miss Burke, we can't always have what we want.'

Only Dapifer met her as an equal. 'It was wrongly applied, I grant you, but it wasn't an unfair tax.'

'You didn't have to pay it.'

'The war with France had to be paid for and not just by England.'

'It wasn't our war.'

'Forgive me, I thought it was a war for all Protestants. Had the French won it, their Roman Catholic compatriots in Canada would even now be swarming over the New England border. Imagine yourself under a Canadian pope—raccoon mitre and bear claws. Doesn't bear thinking of.'

She imagined it and grinned—and the men at the table forgave her on the instant. Two of them made up their minds.

Dr Baines said: 'We'll not bore the young ladies with our political havering. Miss Burke, will ye give me the privilege of your company on deck?'

He proffered his arm but Dapifer had beaten him to it and already proffered his. 'Tonight, sir, that privilege is mine.'

Outside, Makepeace found herself hustled into the captain's—now Dapifer's—cabin, through it and out onto the open stern gallery. 'What are you doing?'

'Saving our good doctor from a fate worse than death. He was about to propose.'

She'd known that he was and had dreaded the moment. Should she marry Alexander Baines out of gratitude for his treatment of Aaron? She should not; it wouldn't be fair to him, let alone to her.

The Boston moon she'd shared with Dapifer had been replaced by another, which, in its turn, was waning, a frail thing like the curve on a capital D. It was the ship's sternlight which lit the path of the wake running white behind them. She felt an anguish for the time they had stood together in another place looking out on this sea, his voice coming out of the shadows. Why doesn't he leave me alone? I'd be all right if he left me alone.

She said dully: 'None of your business.'

'Don't tell me you were going to accept,' Dapifer said, gloomily. 'But I suppose a Dr Baines in the hand is worth two Captain Busgutts in the bush.'

Captain Busgutt, she thought. What a time ago. Before I met you.

'None of your business,' she said again.

'I rather think it is. I want you to marry me.'

Her jaw dropped and then she was so angry that she attacked

him before she could stop herself, giving him a push that sent him staggering. He had to hold onto the rail to avoid falling. 'You dare. Don't you dare. You . . . you shite-poke, you crap-hound, you—'

'Ow!' He retreated along the gallery. 'A simple "No, thank you" would be—'

'I don't need your pity and your marriages,' she hissed at him. 'Don't you *dare*.'

She was appalled that he should offer her charity. For charity was what it was. He'd made it clear that he no longer desired her body when he'd withdrawn his offer to make her his mistress. Now, out of some dreary sense of obligation, he was suggesting a marriage that he didn't want and that was totally unsuited to his station in life. Conscious of being the unwitting cause of all her disasters, the twisted chivalry of an aristocrat was forcing him to sacrifice himself.

Did he think she'd be grateful? That she was so stricken and dependent she'd wed a man to whom such an alliance would be social disaster? She thought better of herself than that, even if he didn't. She must be a prize to the man she married, not a millstone.

Thank you for your patronage, kind sir, I'm beholden to you?

Beholden be buggered. She was Makepeace Burke, American. She had one hundred guineas. She could stand on her own feet.

The pent-up anger at the loss of her home, the sore that the men who'd caused Aaron's pain were walking free, all these things were exacerbated by disgust he should think her so weak and so mercenary . . . that he should stoop . . . think *she'd* stoop . . .

She turned to go.

'I can't help feeling,' he said, holding her back, 'I can't help feeling—stay still, woman—that we are at cross-purposes.'

'No, we ain't. You think you're beholden. Well, you ain't. I can manage. Marry you? I'd sooner marry Boocock.'

'Boocock? Is he the one with the squint?' He had hold of her fists now. 'Calm *down*.' He uncurled her hands and recurled them round the balustrade, then held them there. 'Are you calm?'

'Leave me alone.'

'Take a deep breath.'

She took one, and another. The rail was cool against her palms.

'Now then,' he said. 'Do I understand that you believe my offer to be made out of gratitude and condescension?'

Condescension. That was the word. At the sound of it, she tried to pull away but his right hand clamped both of hers against the iron rail.

'You are an extraordinary female,' he said. 'Most women would at least have pondered the proposal. I admit my looks may not measure up to Able Seaman Boocock's but I'm certainly richer than he is.'

'I don't want your stinking money.'

'So I gather.'

He let go of her hands and moved away to put his forearms on the rail so that his head was directed towards the sea at a level with hers. 'I married within my station once,' he said, reflectively. 'It was a union that pleased all Society except my wife and, as it turned out, me. What I'd thought to be love transpired to be a form of sickness and I came to America in disgust at women, Society and, most of all, at myself. There I was plucked from the briny deep by a female who was . . . well, I can only describe it as *healthy* in both mind and body. So much so that she managed to imbue me with a vigour I haven't felt for years.'

'Makes me sound like a patent medicine.' But she was coming round. After all, that she now considered herself a prize for any man was due to him in the first place; he'd made her think better of herself, realize she was attractive—something Captain Busgutt had never done.

'More a tonic,' he said. 'In fact, Mistress Burke, if I may say so without offence, you give new meaning to the term "rude health". Of course, had I understood your passion for Mr Boocock I would not have offered, but I thought your inclination might lie in the direction of poor Dr Baines.'

'And what's wrong with Dr Baines?' Blast it, he always managed to amuse her.

'Nothing, nothing. An admirable consort for you—could dress

his own wounds and everything. It's just that I thought you might accept him and I wanted to get in first.'

'Oh Hell,' she said, defeated, 'what d'you want to marry me for?'

'Not out of gratitude or pity, I can tell you that. The man who pities you, Makepeace Burke, will have to wear chain-mail.'

'What, then?' She was beginning to fill up with an unbidden, rapturous happiness. It was true she was good for him; despite his sorrow for the death of his friend, he'd clearly lost the pervading despair that had led him to want to drown. She'd done that.

'Because I was wrong in asking you to be my mistress, I see that now. There's little point in making a dishonest woman out of one of the most honest females I've ever met. You're not mistress material, Makepeace Burke. I don't know how you'd go down with London Society and I don't care, you go down with me. I need you. I need you as a permanent fixture. To forgo that privilege merely because of the outworn shibboleths of prejudice would be the act of a fool.'

She said nothing, thinking of the consequences for him and for her, the launch into uncharted difficulties and whether they could survive them.

The ship's bell struck seven—it was nearly the end of this watch.

Her silence unnerved him. '*Please*, Procrustes.'

Until then he'd been assured, amusing, but there was that in his voice now which echoed with the loneliness of the abyss he was going back to. Holy Hokey . . . She closed her eyes. She really was his necessity. 'Oh well,' she said, 'if it's a matter of doing you a favour . . .'

'I'd be obliged,' he assured her, catching her tone. 'Since making you my mistress is out of the question, marriage is the only way I can think of to get your clothes off.'

'Oh,' she said, and took in a deep, glorious breath. 'I see. Why didn't you say so? In that case, I accept.'

Captain Strang, who was authorized to perform weddings, married them the next day.

Chapter Seven

IMMEDIATELY they'd anchored in the Thames, Robert was sent ahead to prepare the staff of the London house for its master's arrival. He was rowed ashore with Captain Strang and the dispatches.

For the rest of the party the goodbyes took some time; it had been a safe and friendly voyage and Makepeace in particular was grateful to the tarry little Eden that had mended Aaron as well as he could be mended and where she had been made happy.

After she'd thanked the crew and while her husband distributed largesse, she and Aaron stood at the taffrail with Susan Brewer to be introduced to the landmarks by Lieutenant Horrocks.

Ahead, the great span of London Bridge was outlined against a dusty, lowering sun. Opposite, a modern Custom House gleamed and the mouth of Traitors' Gate yawned at the water's edge of William the Conqueror's Tower. All around loomed a bespired, cupolaed, multi-roofed skyline of such history, complexity and loftiness that it demanded obeisance from those looking on it for the first time.

'Shakespeare,' Aaron said, 'Dryden.'

'Gloriana,' Susan breathed.

'They ought to do something about these docks,' said Makepeace.

The hurry of wharfingers; squawking, scavenging seagulls; the hit-hit of halyard against mast; a smell of weed and sewage; the bluster of sails; boats ferrying back and forth between the ships, commands and cries issuing over the water: these were Boston again. But in a comparison of the two ports, the Pool of London, main artery of the trading world, came off worse.

Where Boston's forty or more quays provided ease of access to shipping, London itself had twenty and these were crowded side by side together between the Bridge and the Tower. All the way up from Woolwich, merchantmen had congested the river, waiting three or four abreast for lighters to unload them.

'Wait for weeks, some of 'em,' Lieutenant Horrocks said, 'by which time they can lose a quarter of their cargo from pilfering. Oh yes, you've got to keep your goods and your purse battened down in London.' He offered the information as if both his capital's beauty and its criminality were a matter of national pride. 'But don't be afraid, ladies.'

Susan, who wasn't, rewarded him with a tremulous, 'Oh my.'

Makepeace wasn't either, although she knew she should be. She was entering this ancient city as Lady Dapifer and had no idea how to fill the space encompassed by those two words. Already some of the difficulty she would encounter had been exemplified by, of all people, Dapifer's manservant.

Robert had shown much kindness to her and Aaron during the bad weeks of the voyage, raiding the galley and pestering the cook for little treats to tempt their appetites, finding a silk pillow for Aaron's head, bestrawing the passageway outside their door to quieten the footfalls of passers-by. Even during Makepeace's and Dapifer's estrangement she had been aware of his benevolent, if somewhat gloating, sympathy.

But the marriage brought a change. His 'And what does Lady Dapifer require of us today?' and 'Certainly, Lady Dapifer, of course, Lady Dapifer', were issued, out of his master's hearing, with a deliberate grotesquerie of subservience which made it clear that, in his eyes, she couldn't fulfil the role and never would.

She'd actually heard him say with apparent sadness to Susan: 'Of course, the first Lady Dapifer was *such* an exquisite dresser.'

She didn't complain to Dapifer—this was a straight fight between the man and herself. She took him aside: 'I ain't the first Lady Dapifer, I'm the *present* Lady Dapifer, so what's grumbling in your gizzard, Robert?' but she couldn't pin him down; he slipped from confrontation in a flutter of spurious apology.

'What can your ladyship mean? *Mea culpa*, have I offended your ladyship?' She recognized jealousy, pure and simple, and was sorry about it, very sorry, but there was nothing to be done.

It was, she knew, a mere foretaste of the hostility and mockery awaiting her from the society her husband moved in: she didn't walk right, couldn't talk right; the presence of the first Lady Dapifer, that exquisite dresser, would forever triumphantly stalk her shadow.

As if to point up the complications ahead, the weather had changed immediately as they entered the Western Approaches and the marriage ceremony on the quarterdeck had been performed under blustering clouds, with a warm wind whipping away Captain Strang's words and fluttering the petticoats of the women and the ribbons on the sailors' hats. They'd scampered through spots of rain to the wardroom for the wedding breakfast.

'Think the weather's trying to tell us something?' she'd whispered to Dapifer during the speeches.

'Too late, dammit,' he'd muttered back, 'it should have mentioned it last night.' She closed her eyes and he'd dug her in the ribs. 'Stop swooning, woman. It's not Puritan.'

They had consummated the marriage ahead of time. One consensual, unstoppable, liquid move had taken them from his proposal in the stern gallery to his bed and what was officially, deliciously, still a sin. No preparation, no bridal rites, no waiting, nothing to make her tense, just an unthinking swoop into passion.

When, later, in post-climactic quiet, he'd asked her what her experience of losing her virginity had been, she said: 'I enjoyed myself.'

He groaned. 'You sound as if you'd been out to tea.'

But she *had* enjoyed herself and continued to do so, more and more. Perhaps, if she'd been brought up by Temperance Burke in the Puritan tradition of thinking all enjoyment suspect, she'd have been less receptive to lovemaking, but her confidante in sexual matters had been Betty, the former slave, whose attitude was considerably less prohibitive.

She'd nudged her husband-to-be in his bare ribs. 'And so did you.'

If there'd been a lingering suspicion that he'd married her from a sense of obligation, that night and all the subsequent nights swept it away. He loved her; she made him laugh, she made him happy; there'd been a great need in him and she fulfilled it. Whatever Rubicon he'd had to face in deciding to marry her, she could sense his relief that he'd crossed it.

They were becoming very close, not just sexually. She was discovering that he was an extremely kind man. This had been oddly surprising, as if his ability to excite her could not co-exist with niceness, but already, for Aaron's sake, he'd offered to set Dr Baines up in a London practice and, for Makepeace's, had invited Susan Brewer to stay with them, suggesting he buy her a year's pupillage with Mme Angloss who, he said, was the most influential adviser on fashion in England.

Both had accepted.

In one way this easy disposal of people, generous as it was, had been daunting. It brought home to Makepeace how powerful a position Sir Philip Dapifer held and how unfitted she was as his consort. She was used to the command of a small, bourgeois world; she had no guidelines to the society she was about to join now. He didn't give her any, either.

In bed in their cabin, she'd said: 'What are you going to do with me?'

'This.'

All very pleasant but later she returned to the problem. 'Ain't you worried?'

'No.'

'But what do you want me to be? What do you want me to *do*?'

'That.'

'In public?'

In the end she'd got out of bed, put on a wrap, and pursued

the matter out of his physical reach. 'What I mean is, you'll be entertaining royalty and such. I can pour the King a good tankard, but when it comes to—'

'We won't be entertaining royalty.'

'Because of me?'

'Because I'm divorced. The King and Queen are straitlaced about these things.'

'Oh.' That was a relief. Her respect for King George went up at the same time; she'd imagined a court of Nero-like depravity. 'But you got Society friends . . .'

'And we'll be able to tell whether they're friends or not, won't we?'

'But there's fish knives and how to address a duke . . .'

'Fish knives are definitely a problem.'

'I mean it, Pip.' For the first time she approached the nub of the business. 'Your first wife knew all this taradiddle and I don't.'

'The first Lady Dapifer was an excellent hostess, marvellous with fish knives and, while I don't like to speak ill of the divorced, she was also vicious and had the morals of an alley cat.' He sat up and shook his head at her. 'Procrustes, I don't care. I don't *care.*'

She crawled across the bed to hold him.

Afterwards, he said: 'Ffoulkes's opinion was the only one worth a damn and, if it's any consolation, he'd have proposed to you quicker.'

So that was all right. By the time she viewed London from the deck of the *Lord Percy* that morning, she was so armoured by love she was prepared to knock the lights out of any ogre it sent against her.

Lieutenant Horrocks went about his business, Susan hurried off to finish her packing and brother and sister were left alone. 'You ain't scared, Aaron, are you?' she asked.

He shook his head. 'Always wanted to be here.'

'Good.' She took in a deep breath. 'I ain't either, not now. What's the bit about that woman answering her husband's call? You know, from the play, you used to quote it about me and poor Captain Busgutt?'

' "Husband, I come: Now to that name my courage prove my title!' "

'Got it right, didn't she?'

'Actually, Cleopatra was about to commit suicide.'

Instantly, she felt ill-omened and took a precaution against bad luck.

'I don't think Lady Dapifer should spit over her shoulder,' Aaron said. Like her marriage, her title impressed him but he also found it an inexhaustible source of amusement.

'Who else's am I going to spit over?'

Dr Baines joined them to say goodbye. He was going home to Edinburgh before returning to London and the Harley Street practice Dapifer had promised him. His farewell to Aaron was affectionate—on Aaron's part almost tearful—and larded with medical do's and don'ts. To Makepeace he was courteous, if re-proachful. 'May ye prosper in your chosen path, Lady Dapifer.' She was afraid she'd hurt him but there was something else to him . . . a touch of relief? She was irresistibly reminded of Pentecost Pringle, one of the Meg's customers, who'd constantly and mournfully ex-cused his bachelorhood 'acause her I loved married another', while enjoying every minute of it.

Dapifer came up to say it was time to go. Soberly, he offered her his arm. Soberly, she took it. Knowing what she knew of their nights, the enforced propriety of their behaviour in company still enchanted her like a secret naughtiness.

The gangplank remained obdurately stable beneath feet expect-ing it to roll.

Robert had been told to send carriages to the quayside but none were in evidence so a coach had to be hired. Luggage and Tanta-quidgeon were placed on top, the rest of the party squashed inside.

It was a measure of London's extraordinariness that the sight of a large Red Indian, complete with feather, sitting atop a vehicle did not attract more attention than it did. There were a few stares, occasionally rude boys ran alongside shouting unintelligible Cock-ney things, but the circus provided effortlessly by their streets seemed to have sated most Londoners' ability to be surprised at anything.

It didn't sate the Americans'. An elephant was being taken for a walk on Tower Hill and in the course of the City's mile Makepeace, peering over the head of Josh, who sat on her knee, saw pigtailed Chinese, gaberdined Jews, astrakhan-hatted Russians, an Indian robed like a maharajah and another in a loincloth. Countrywomen sold apples to the occupants of gilded carriages; wraithlike women shouted out the price of their bodies. Negroes with slave collars, dressed like princes; free negroes in patches; beadles in tricorns; aldermen in scarlet; running footmen in wigs; two dancing bears; a snake-charmer; lawyers clutching briefs: all of them bustling about their business and expecting others to be about theirs.

There was no comparison with Boston here: poverty was too deep, riches too extravagant, thoroughfares too dirty, too grand, too narrow, churches horrifyingly old and astonishingly beautiful crammed about by stalls. Trades came in blocks, with their stench and noises: Smithfield mooed and baaed and ran with blood; Poultry held them up to let by a flock of turkeys with their feet tarred into boots. One street seemed entirely given over to the melting of metal, another ticked with clocks.

When they reached Temple Bar, Makepeace sat back to rest from astonishment. Dapifer paused in his commentary: 'Will it suit?'

Aaron spoke for them all. ' "Behold, the half was not told me." '

Once out of the twists of the Middle Ages, the going became straighter and more genteel but just as congested, this time with shoppers, playgoers and carriages delivering well-dressed men and women to their clubs. In the hot evening Piccadilly smelled like a stable from its thickening carpet of horse manure.

The coach turned north into gridlike squares of restrained elegance, where the tall houses, still too new to be polluted by the rest of the city's grime, commanded unperturbed views of trees and flowers.

'Grosvenor Square,' Dapifer said, 'and this is Dapifer House.'

The mansion they had stopped at dominated the row on this side of the great square with a pediment and six-columned façade.

Robert had been looking for them and came down the steps at a flurried run. He and Dapifer held a whispered conversation at the coach door. Not invited to descend, the rest of the party kept their seats, querying each other with their eyebrows.

A woman appeared in the doorway, smiling, holding out her arms. 'Husband,' she called. 'Welcome home.'

It was a pretty sound and it carried. For Grosvenor Square it promised interest; heads appeared in some of the windows. For those who'd been in the Roaring Meg on the night of Boston's bonfires and heard the fluting cry of Makepeace's name it was a reminder of something else.

She came down the steps as prettily, holding her skirt up over little tripping feet and stood on tiptoe in an effort to kiss Dapifer's cheek. He moved back out of the way so she continued forward to the coach and stood on its step to look in, extending a hand as frail as a frond.

Bemused, Aaron shook it.

'I wasn't expecting so many Americans,' she said, 'but how delightful that you've brought your own totem pole with you. Robert's told me about *you*, my dear . . .' This was to Makepeace. '*What* an interesting style of dress—and a little piccaninny on your lap, how free-*thinking*.'

'Exquisite' was the *mot juste*, pinning her delicacy and petiteness; cloudy dark hair was set off by a primrose gown and her scent had the fleeting sweetness of bluebells. She had animal quickness with a smile of tiny, white, backward-sloping teeth.

Makepeace knew she'd been born to hate her. It wasn't for the insults or because this little weasel had shared Dapifer's bed. If they'd merely passed in the street, each would have sniffed the other out—they were the other's antithesis.

Drums smeared with blood and howling for sacrifice coughed along the square's frontages. Small shapes hunted with stone-tipped spears through the bushes of the central garden. The two warriors from opposed tribes watched each other's eyes for the opportunity to kill.

'Oops. Sorry.' Makepeace had opened the carriage door so that her enemy was forced to cling onto it like a monkey, and be swung ridiculously outwards.

Makepeace descended. 'Want some help?' But Robert had run forward to lift his former mistress down.

'I told you to leave the house,' Dapifer said, quietly.

'What?' The first Lady Dapifer was brushing herself down, her eyes still on Makepeace.

'My letter with the divorce decree told you to leave this house. I hope you received it.'

'I believe I did, dearest, but I must have got bored before I reached that bit.'

'Leave now.'

'Very well, my darling. Where to?'

'Great Russell Street. I've given you Great Russell Street.'

'Thank you, dearest. Robert, run and tell Maria that Lady Dapifer wants her things packed. I'll sit here and wait. Oh, and have the carriage brought round. May I have the carriage, Pippy dear? Or should I carry the trunks on my head, like your Red Indian friends?'

She returned to the steps and sat on them, arranging her skirt.

Dapifer addressed the coach: 'I apologize. I'm afraid I must ask you to wait here.' He didn't look at Makepeace who retreated back into the coach.

A weeping maid with hatboxes put them on the steps, followed by a train of footmen with luggage. She was already packed, Makepeace thought.

Every window in the row now had heads peering out of it. Residents came out of the houses. The square had spawned people, chimney sweeps, footmen, maids. Passers-by stopped; carriages drew up so that their occupants could ask why a so-obviously forlorn and delicious little creature was being evicted. Robert ran back and forth, windmilling signals of distress and loving it.

A female neighbour, somewhat untidily dressed for a ball, hurried solicitously round to the figure on the steps—'My dear, my dear'—and was waved away. The first Lady Dapifer needed no help; she was managing nicely. It was the man standing and watching, arms folded, by the hired coach and those inside it, who appeared boorish.

Makepeace felt larger and lumpier than at any time in her life. I look stupid. Tantaquidgeon on the roof looks stupid, we all look stupid. The *bitch*.

It was an exercise in humiliating that touched genius.

The neighbour ran to Dapifer. 'Sir Philip, will you let this happen? Your own wife?'

'Go away, Lady Judd.' He said it softly but Lady Judd backed away.

Tell her, tell her that hag's not your wife any more. Perhaps he couldn't, perhaps if he said anything he'd lose the control that was reining his fury in. Makepeace could feel it radiating from him and loathed the woman who was hurting him, resenting that she *could* hurt him—even hatred argued intimacy.

After nearly half an hour a coach with a gold emblazon on its doors drew up. It was directed to move along a little so that it did not obstruct the crowd's view of a pathetic farewell between erstwhile mistress and staff.

As it left the square, the two Lady Dapifers were level with each other for a moment. The first smiled.

When they were all going into the house, somebody in the crowd threw a lump of horse manure which hit Dapifer on the back of his coat.

The entrance hall was chillingly beautiful and as high as the house itself. It was lit through a glass dome roof from which hung a great glass and filigree lantern. An oval staircase, cantilevered and in marble with a wrought-iron balustrade rose to a gallery of rooms.

Susan Brewer opened her mouth to express wonder but after the first 'Oh my', shut it again. This was not the moment.

An incredibly old, powdered footman, looking as if he'd collapse under the weight, relieved them of their wraps. Another comforted a maid on the verge of hysterics. A large and severe woman came forward. 'Welcome home, Sir Philip.'

'Makepeace, may I introduce Mrs Peplow, my housekeeper. Peplow, this is Lady Dapifer.'

'How de do, Mrs Peplow. Hope we ain't a bother to you.'

The housekeeper addressed Dapifer: 'With such little notice, I fear there is nothing in for dinner, Sir Philip. *Madame* was going out.'

He didn't notice the snub to Makepeace, he was struggling out of his manured coat, helped by a footman. 'Serve whatever you're having.'

'Yes, Sir Philip. Do I assume that the darker persons in your party will be eating in the basement?'

'Tonight they will dine with us.'

'The feathered gentleman too?'

'For God's sake, Peplow. *Yes.*'

Hot water and towels were provided in a small room off the hall so that they could wash their hands before proceeding to the dining room, a vast place of maroon and gold.

It was a gruesome meal. Dapifer barely spoke. The effect of whatever he was thinking clenched his face into straighter lines than his usual mock dejection allowed and had the effect of rendering him conventionally handsome. Susan was the only one to rise to the occasion with chatter that became more maniacal as nobody joined in.

It was the first time Tantaquidgeon had eaten in any other formal company than his tribe's and he refused to do it sitting down; his plate had to be served to him in a corner of the massive room by a footman who wanted to press napiery and cutlery upon him until Dapifer sharply told the man to desist.

The array of cutlery was, in any case, as bewildering as Makepeace had feared it would be. She took the bit between her teeth, a fork in her hand and followed Betty's example of using it for everything.

The only person at the table enjoying himself was young Joshua who was staring around him with the disbelieving joy of a creature returned to the wild after incarceration. He kept squeaking and drawing Makepeace's and his mother's attention to details of the room that caught his attention: the superb coffered plaster ceiling, painted panels on the walls, the gilt-backed chairs, the statuary in their niches at the far end.

Makepeace had no knowledge of design; the room oppressed her and she found the paintings and statues somewhat shocking, but she was aware that it was magnificent. It was the only heart-warming thing of the evening that this child of Betty's, never having been exposed to interior architecture more elaborate than North Street's plastered church (*well, I ain't either*) reverberated from the room's beauty like glass to a high note.

There was nothing wrong with the food. Smoked fish, pâtés, oysters, buttered shrimp, roast beef, capons, broiled mutton, pastries, flummeries . . . Makepeace caught Betty's eye: if this was what the servants ordered for themselves they were living high off the hog's haunch. She and her cook watched how much was taken away; they could have fed half Boston on it, let alone a household.

If I was running this here establishment . . . It occurred to her that, as the new Lady Dapifer, she was.

Since everybody was tired, the housekeeper was ordered to show them to their rooms. Makepeace went with them, leaving Dapifer still at the table.

Portraits of past Dapifers lining the staircase wall looked down their noses as she and the others followed Mrs Peplow to the gallery. Makepeace took against them. Her own pilgrim ancestors had defied bullying by men and women of this species and, by God, so would she. If the English were trying to intimidate her—and they were—they'd chosen the wrong American. Any sauce from you lot and I'll spit in your eye, she thought.

She glowered at the housekeeper's ample backside ahead of her. Yours an' all.

Actually, Peplow had done well by them. Betty and Josh had

an attic room considerably better furnished than the Roaring Meg's, and so did Tantaquidgeon, though whether he'd stay in it was a different matter.

Joshua, hopping from foot to foot, tugged at Makepeace's sleeve. 'Where can I piss?'

She'd been wondering the same herself. Was there a privy in the yard? If so, where was the yard? During the meal she'd been shocked when a footman opened one of the dining-room cupboards to see a chamber pot in it—a most insanitary arrangement in her view.

Mrs Peplow pointed grimly to the underside of the bed. 'Unless, madam, you wish your people to share the use of your water closet.'

What's a water closet? 'Oh, piss in the pot, Josh.'

They left him to it and went down to the next floor where Susan had been allocated a guest bedroom panelled in powder-blue flock matching the coroneted tester and coverlet of the bed. A maidservant was unpacking Susan's boxes and traps that had been piled neatly in the middle of a silk Persian carpet.

Miss Brewer winked at Makepeace and gave a die-away sigh. 'I guess this will have to do,' she said. Makepeace winked back. *Good girl.*

Aaron was being accommodated in equal luxury. He bade his sister goodnight, went into his room and then reopened the door to utter an Indian war-whoop at Mrs Peplow's retreating back that sent chandeliers tinkling and stiffened the housekeeper in her corsets. Makepeace grinned, her brother was back to form.

A corridor ran off the gallery to a wing of the house. 'The family apartments, madam,' said Mrs Peplow. She hesitated by a door and then opened it. 'The Yellow Room.'

Makepeace looked in. Yellow was too crude a word for the first suggestion of dawn, neither acidic nor honey, that some Chinese dyer had transformed into wallpaper and which an artist had then brought alive with flowers and long-legged birds. Apart from Makepeace's stained and battered holdall on the golden carpet, every piece of furniture, every hanging complemented the surrounding paradise. It was like stepping into spring; it smelled elusively of bluebells; it was exquisite.

'No,' Makepeace said.

'It's your room now, madam.' The woman was smirking.

'No.'

'Then I don't know where, madam. There's only the master's room further along.'

Hadn't they slept together? Or did this class keep separate beds?

'Show me.'

Dapifer's apartment had a Roman motif and could have housed the Praetorian Guard. Makepeace settled herself and her holdall in its ante-chamber which served as a dressing room and contained a divan. 'This'll do.'

'Very well, madam. Should you need anything more, there is a bell pull in the corner. And a bagnio through that door.' Mrs Peplow twitched her nose. 'Perhaps madam would wish to take a bath?'

The inference was she needed one. Which she did, but damned if she'd take it at this woman's instigation. 'No, I thank you.'

'As you please, madam. Shall I send your maid to assist you in undressing?'

'What maid? Oh, Betty. She ain't my maid.' Makepeace smiled at the woman—a last attempt at rapport. 'I take my own clothes off.'

'I'm sure you do, madam,' said Mrs Peplow with meaning, and went.

You sailed into that one, Makepeace Burke. Was this how it'd be? A battle of broadsides?

To cheer herself up, she explored, stroking materials, sniffing, opening cupboards and doors. This, then, was a water closet, a little room with marble pavement and walls, glided plaster ceiling and a painting of disporting nymphs to look at while you sat. What you sat on was a mahogany seat over a marble bowl with a hinged metal pan in its base.

Makepeace studied it, then tentatively pulled at a handle which stuck out from an arrangement at the contraption's top. Immediately the pan tilted downwards; she glimpsed a water-filled tank below before it tilted back into its place. So that's how it worked. She saw no advantage to it—some poor soul would still have to clean the pan and empty the tank below.

And this door . . . here, oh Lord, here was the bagnio. She'd expected it to be improper, associating it with 'seraglio', a word much used by Rev Mather in the condemnation of sin.

It *was* improper. Marble again. A tiny double staircase led to a plinth on which stood the statue of a naked youth and from which another flight led down to a plunge bath big enough to swim in. Coloured towels—she'd thought they only came in white—rested in piles on glass shelves decorated with bottles of Eastern allure and mystery.

It was a long way from a tin tub on the occasional Sunday morning in the Roaring Meg's kitchen.

As in a trance, Makepeace retreated to the dressing room and tugged the bell pull. 'I *will* bathe, Mrs Peplow, iffen you'd fetch the water.'

After all, there was no need to cut off her nose to spite her face and it would be some gain to see the woman carrying buckets, she was hefty enough.

Instead there was a smile. Like the Sphinx, Mrs Peplow held all the answers. She crossed to the bagnio, bent over the bath and did something that resulted in a rush of water and steam. 'We call it *plumbing*, madam.'

Makepeace called it the eighth wonder of the world. She was awestruck and couldn't pretend she wasn't. When the housekeeper had gone she rushed to spreadeagle herself over the side of the bath to see how it was done. Underneath each of two cunning caps shaped like dolphins was a cock, one permitting a flow of blisteringly hot water, the other cold.

They'd raised water to first-floor level and heated it.

The system wasn't perfect; by the time there was enough water to reach her middle, both cocks were running cold but long before that Makepeace had covered the statue's eyes with her petticoat and was floundering naked in soapsuds, unguents and the future.

However, once she'd closed off the magical water, the present flowed back in. She leaned back in the steam to consider it.

A sour place, England. 'Better is a dinner of herbs where love is, than a stalled ox and hatred therewith.' For all the marble and gold herewith, hatred was what she'd encountered so far.

Oddly enough, the fracas with the previous wife outside the house had upset her less than the reception she'd received inside it—she'd relish the picture of that bloody little marmoset swinging helpless on the coach door for the rest of her days.

What she hadn't reckoned on was the servants' attitude. She couldn't understand it; she'd always got on well with those she'd employed at the Roaring Meg. She'd expected to be looked down on by the society Dapifer moved in but her rebuff by the house-keeper, and the behaviour of the footmen at dinner and of Robert, showed she had no friends among his staff either.

The first Lady Dapifer, she thought, must have been an exqui-site employer along with all her other exquisiteries for her people so to resent her successor.

To hell with her. She hadn't been an exquisite wife.

But it was going to be a desolate business and she was suddenly racked with longing for the Roaring Meg, racked again that it didn't exist any more. Hatred there, hatred here. Lord, why d'you allow so much hatred?

The water was growing cold. Makepeace wiped the tears from her eyes with one of the beautiful towels and wrapped it round her. Dapifer's room was still empty. She found one of his robes, enveloped herself in it and went downstairs to find him. Her bare feet on the cold stairs were as noiseless as the rest of the house. The servants had gone to bed.

He was still sitting in the dining room, a decanter of port and a glass in front of him. He had a document in his hand and was slowly tapping the table with it. She took a chair beside him.

He didn't look up. 'Where have you been?'

'Bathing. There's this bagnio upstairs, it's a wonder.'

'Yes,' he said. 'The first Lady Dapifer had it installed. Very far-sighted, the first Lady Dapifer.'

You're drunk. She wondered how she knew; his voice and eyes were as steady as the hand which kept up its regular beat with the document, but he was drunk.

'What's her name?' she asked.

'Who?'

'First Lady Dapifer. What's she called?'

'Her name,' he said, 'is Catherine. They call her Catty. Everybody calls her Catty.'

Not surprising, Makepeace thought. 'Servants and all?'

'They addressed her as Lady Dapifer.'

'Not madam?'

'Lady Dapifer.'

So that was cleared up. 'What's the matter?'

He held out the letter. 'This is from her. She's had it sent round by messenger. Quick work. She says she will be petitioning for divorce on the grounds of my bigamy.'

She tried to take it in. '*Bigamy?*'

'With you. Maintaining that she's still married to me.' He wouldn't look at her. Paper hit-hit against wood in a slow, regular rhythm that attacked the nerves.

'But you divorced her.'

'Always a gamble. Legal opinion's divided on whether an American divorce pertains in this country. Fact is, my solicitor wasn't happy about it.' He was speaking with careful and remote judiciousness, like a judge delivering an opinion with which he was not overly concerned. 'Took the risk. Didn't want our dirty laundry hung out before great English public. More a nominal gesture— had no intention of marrying again.'

'She agreed to it, though.'

'Oh yes. Signed her permission, confessed to adultery, would comply with the decree.' His fist crashed down on the table, making its epergne and Makepeace jump. 'Should have known. Never kept her word. Should've known.'

'Can she do this?'

'Ah yes.' He nodded, still without looking at her. 'That'll be interesting. Whether an English court upholds a New England decision, whether *Parliament* upholds it. Got to be done through Parliament. Private bill. House of Commons'll be full that day. Spectator sport, that'll be. Better than bear-baiting.'

The statues in their niches at the end of the room were staring at her. Didn't they ever get dressed in mythology? Very cold, mythology must have been. I'm cold.

He wasn't looking at her; he didn't want her to look at him. She thought: He's ashamed because he's been a fool. Well, he has. She said: 'She wants money, doesn't she?'

'For dropping the case? I imagine so.' The tap of the letter against the table redoubled for a moment and then resumed its steady beat. 'Given her a bloody great settlement already but she's profligate with money. In effect, this bit of paper's a demand for what I imagine will be a ruinous sum.'

'Stand and deliver.'

He nodded. 'Pay or publicity. Good case she's got now. Even if I counter petition it's only my word against hers. No reliable evidence of her adultery any more, y'see. Ffoulkes is dead, the only other witness is dead.' Dapifer's mouth twisted; she assumed he was smiling. He said: 'I've been talking to Robert. He commiserated with her on Ffoulkes's death. She laughed.'

Makepeace leaned across the table, took the letter away from him and put it out of his reach.

'She laughed,' he said.

'Yes.'

' "A spaniel, a woman and a walnut tree . . ." Should have beaten her but tried to spare her, y'see. Ffoulkes warned me. "She wouldn't spare you, old man. Don't turn your back on her fangs, Pip, that's a snake needs killing, not scotching." Wouldn't listen. Made him go to America with me to give evidence. Killed him.'

She put her hands round his face and turned it to her. His eyes were appalled and appalling. He said: 'Drowning again, Procrustes. And this time dragging you under with me.'

'Oh no, you ain't. We're going to fight her. Pay her off and she'll only ask more. I'm your legal wife and we're going to prove it.'

'Didn't want this for you.'

She said what he'd once said to her: 'I don't care. Pip, I don't *care*. We got each other, we're going to fight her and we're going to win.'

Somehow she got him to his feet and up the staircase. After she'd put him to bed she sat beside him until he went to sleep. She sat on, listening to his breathing, as she'd done in her room at the Roaring Meg.

Ain't fair, it ain't fair. He's a good man. What did he do except marry the wrong woman?

It was a sad moment of realization, too, that he was vulnerable in being so naïve in this matter. Sailing off to America to procure a divorce that might or might not be valid in his own country . . . that was something she herself, so less sophisticated than he was, would not have done. *I'd have made sure, by Hokey.* Protecting the name of his undeserving wife was one thing, carelessness another. But, as he'd said, he'd not expected to marry again.

She got cross. *Adultery was adultery. Divorce was divorce.* The marriage had ended; effectively when Catty had been caught copulating with her husband's friend, officially in New England. If English courts didn't recognize a legal American decree, it was another example of the mother country's scorn for its colonies.

It was beyond her comprehension that a wife would wish to insist on a marriage the husband didn't want and which she had already betrayed. Without understanding the talk of courts and procedures, Makepeace's practicality told her money was at the bottom of it. *Catty Dapifer was demanding Danegeld. Pay me and I'll go away.* But the Danes hadn't gone away until King Alfred—the Rev Mather's history lessons had been admiring of Alfred—fought them. Why *should* Dapifer pay that corrupt little besom for sleeping with another man?

Fight, yes. She could say that, but she couldn't help him do it. She was out of her depth in this world of his, even a liability. If it came to a judgement between the two of them, what sort of image would she herself present, a tavern-keeper, compared to the exquisite Catty?

Makepeace was settling her mind to the assumption that, in the end, what it came down to was a duel between herself and her predecessor. It was all she could cope with; it made her feel better.

Puritan upbringing had its faults but it imbued its children with the knowledge that the survival of their forebears in the wilderness was proof that they were Jehovah's favoured people. They grew up assured that in His sight neither riches nor titles prevailed against godliness. Such knowledge buttressed Makepeace now. God was on her side; she was the better woman.

After all, Catty's challenge had been issued in Grosvenor Square—England's age-old sneer against the colonial. All the impotent fury of her countrymen returned to Makepeace as the contempt in which they were held came to be personified in the beautifully dressed figure of one woman.

By *God*, I'll show her I'm her equal.

Not just her, either.

Since she'd set foot in this damn country, she'd been shown no respect by anyone, high or low. Well, they could start now.

Carefully, so as not to wake him, she kissed her husband's forehead, then she went out, closing the door behind her. In the dressing room, she crossed to the bell pull and rang it. Rang it again, and went on ringing it.

After a while, she heard angry feet thumping along the corridor.

'Yes, madam? What now?' Mrs Peplow was in a flannel nightgown and curlpapers.

'Yes, Lady Dapifer,' Makepeace said.

'Eh?'

'Say it.'

Mumble.

'Bit louder.'

'Yes, Lady Dapifer.'

'You remember it. That's all, Mrs Peplow. Goodnight.'

The second Lady Dapifer had gone to war.

BOOK TWO

∽∾

London

∽∾

Chapter Eight

O N entering the salon, Mme Angloss gave a dramatic stagger. 'Mon dieu, quelle rousse. Qu'est qu'on peut faire?' She walked round Makepeace as if assessing horseflesh.

'I thought green,' Makepeace ventured.

'Indeed? I do not.' It had become fashionable for an expert to be rude and Angloss was all three. At least, it was fashionable to call her in; she herself was as modish as a chimney brush which, with her untidy black hair, olive skin and thin body, she nearly resembled. She was the first woman Makepeace had seen since arriving in England not wearing hoops, favouring instead what looked like a black silk sack and knobbly jewellery.

Left to herself, Makepeace would have given the job of choosing her wardrobe to Susan Brewer but Dapifer had said no. 'Too provincial yet. Give her a year with Mme Angloss and then we'll see.'

Susan's pupillage had already begun and her obsequiousness to Mme Angloss suggested she was happy to give herself up to what, as far as Makepeace could tell, was black slavery.

'Sakes, she's the tsarina of *haute couture*,' Susan said when Makepeace had wondered whether she did not object to being called 'Brewer' and ordered about like a dog. 'She's even famous in Boston. Wait 'til Auntie hears I'm her 'prentice.'

Susan and a depressed-looking seamstress were now running back and forth to the entrance hall where hat boxes, dress boxes, shoe boxes, boot boxes, wicker hoop cages, swathes of materials, cards of buttons, ribbons, lace, were being delivered by manufacturers anxious to comply with Mme Angloss's wishes and gain Dapifer custom.

The matter was urgent. Makepeace could not appear in public until she was suitably dressed.

It had been a bone of contention between her and her husband that she should appear at all. 'I ain't a public person.'

'What are you going to do? Rattle in a closet like a skeleton? I don't happen to be ashamed of you.' He'd recovered his self-possession though the prospect of the publicity attached to fighting his first wife through the courts was horrific to him.

'But ain't we *persona non* whatsit?'

'That's at Court. But the Court is not Society, in fact the two are inimical; Their Majesties being undoubtedly worthy but undoubtedly dull. I think you'll discover that there are still some among the powerful eager to make your acquaintance.'

'Glad to hear it.' It had been established between them that in the forthcoming divorce battle they would need all the allies they could muster, especially in Parliament. But privately she thought: They ain't falling over themselves. (So far not one invitation had been delivered to Dapifer House.) Even next-door don't talk to me.

Accustomed to a community that chatted over the yard fence, the silence of her neighbours was thunderous in Makepeace's ears. At least, it was silence only as it extended to her; actually, the Judds on her left were a noisy family with an apparently inexhaustible supply of leather-lunged children. To hear their play over the other side of the wall dividing the two properties accentuated her own exclusion and it broke her heart to watch Josh listening to it as he wandered alone among the neat parterres of the Dapifer back garden.

She doubted it would help him even if she and Lady Judd were intimates. This wasn't Boston where children of the two races played together—at least, until the approach of adolescence brought down the shutter between black and white.

Mrs Peplow had suggested to Dapifer in Makepeace's presence that Josh be dressed in the costume and jewelled turban inflicted on other little black boys to be seen dancing attendance on their mistresses in the square. 'It would make use of the child and add tone to Lady Dapifer's equipage.' Tone, her voice suggested, was otherwise lacking. In saying 'no' Makepeace's tone suggested that what Mrs Peplow lacked was a kick up the arse. Later she asked Dapifer what became of those garish little boys when they grew up. He didn't know.

On the matter of the Judds, Dapifer said that Sir Benjamin Judd was too unsure of his own social position to risk bolstering Makepeace's. He was a Birmingham manufacturer made rich by the Seven Years' War and had outlayed some of his money on a wife from the minor aristocracy, a baronetcy and a seat in the House of Commons.

Makepeace was drawn to Lady Judd because she didn't conform to the rigid elegance of the rest of Grosvenor Square. A harassed-looking woman, she was invariably late emerging from her house to take her place in a carriage where Sir Benjamin impatiently awaited her, and when she did her appearance was never tidy. According to Fanny Cobb, Makepeace's personal maid, the Judd household was unmitigated chaos.

But such warming inefficiency had to be regarded at a distance. Makepeace tried speaking on the one occasion when she had been on her doorstep at the same time Lady Judd had been on hers, but was ignored. Whether the un-neighbourliness was due to Sir Benjamin's instructions, Lady Judd's light blue noble blood or her loyalty to the first Lady Dapifer, Makepeace couldn't tell. 'Was she good friends with you-know-who?'

'I doubt it,' Dapifer had said. 'The first Lady Dapifer was not a woman's woman.'

So, nothing for it but to be ready for invitations when they arrived from elsewhere—if they ever did. Hence Mme Angloss.

'Yes, I apologize for my wife's hair, madame,' Dapifer said, leaving the room. 'A sore trial. No point in hiding it, though—you know my opinion on heads. Excuse me.' He went out.

What *were* heads? And how did this female know his opinion on them?

Blast him, Makepeace thought, Mme Angloss dressed his wife.

He'd already been amazingly casual on this matter. 'What's wrong with the Yellow Room?'

'It was hers.'

'We'll have it changed then.'

Immediately there was Signor D'Amelia, tall, sinuous and, it appeared, to rooms what Mme Angloss was to fashion.

'What is your inclination, dear lady?' Not, his expression added, that it mattered; he was the artist.

She was lost. 'Clean, I guess, and no fleas.'

She could have said nothing better, it seemed. Signor D'Amelia was much diverted and spread the word that the second Lady Dapifer was a wit. His conversation revealed that he, too, had worked for Catty Dapifer.

'He'll think you're stacking up wives to employ him.'

Her husband shrugged. 'I understand he's the best in his trade. She had a gift for finding the best. And the most expensive.'

He couldn't see why Makepeace should mind employing the excellent also. Considering it sensibly, neither did she—yet she did; she might have no style herself but she'd be damned if she'd have it thought she was aping Catty Dapifer's.

Luckily, Signor D'Amelia and Mme Angloss were prepared to create one for her.

D'Amelia's sketches for the bedroom and its ante-chamber were lovely in themselves; the gold carpet remained but around it was a restrained freshness of pearl-grey plaster panels picked out in white, unfrilled, gold-threaded white hangings to the bed, and white pieces by Sheraton. 'I see purity, purity, *purity*, lady, only the colour of your hair to blaze it.'

Dapifer said: 'Very nun-like. I'll feel like a ravisher in it.' He handed the sketches back to her. 'I can hardly wait.'

However, the one most appreciative of Signor D'Amelia's art was Josh. The boy hung over the drawings and kept stroking the paintbrushes with which D'Amelia made alterations as if they were alive until he was allowed a sheet of paper and a brush to himself.

Mme Angloss was seeing purity as well. The room frothed with

white, greys, creams, drabs, all the colours of a storm-tossed sea
except green. 'Line,' she said, pointing at Makepeace but addressing
Susan, 'line is everysing. We follow client, not fashion—I spit me
of fashion. *La mode* is what I say it is. What is it we 'ave here?'

'Hair?' ventured Susan.

Mme Angloss made a 'taa' with her teeth; hair was obvious.
'Skin,' she said, dragging Makepeace's bodice down, *'boules de neige.'*
She patted Makepeace's head: 'Height.' Then Makepeace's cheek:
'Voici la dame posée, bien sérieusement. Not a furbelow will I have,
no *falbalas.'* She snatched a luscious sample of ruching from Make-
peace's reluctant hand and stamped on it. 'Nothing *jolie* for zis one.
Pretty? I spit on it.'

'You're absolutely right, madame,' said Susan. Makepeace
sighed.

The preliminary sketches, which Mme Angloss scrawled in
chalks on a drawing board rested on the seamstress's back, were
of breathtaking, simple, sweeping elegance.

Low, uncluttered necklines, tight sleeves over a plain cuff instead of the usual shower of lace, less emphasis on pannier hips
and more on the bustle—'I create a new 'oop for the world.'

If it was obvious how Mme Angloss earned her reputation, it
was equally obvious how she made her fortune; Makepeace would
require morning dresses, afternoon dresses, evening gowns, ball
gowns, nightwear, wraps, coats—each one requiring a different fan,
gloves or mittens—peignoirs, hoods, shoes, boots, slippers, stockings, on all of which Mme Angloss took a commission.

Oatmeals, greys, donkeys, olives and fawns highlighted the
cream-white chalk with which Mme Angloss represented Makepeace's skin. Caps—the 'heads'—were almost an insult to the word,
tiny strips or mere filets on a simple chignon.

'For ze daytime. For ze evenings, zees . . .' Deep, grape-dark
purples, leonine tawny, bronzes—a stand-up-and-fight challenge to
an era of pastels.

'You . . . I'll be *noticed*,' protested Makepeace.

For the first time, Mme Angloss addressed her directly. 'Madame, you are in a situation zat is noticeable all ways. Be ze mouse

and zey laugh, ha-ha. Show panache and zey are angry, ooh-hoo, but I tell you, madame . . . I, Jeanne-Marie Angloss, tell you . . . wiz zees creations in two months all ladies scream to wear what you wear.'

This from the woman who'd dressed the exquisite dresser. Makepeace looked at her carefully. '*All* ladies?'

Mme Angloss's lips curved very slightly. 'All.'

'Go ahead.'

They had a scuffle over the riding-habit.

'I cain't ride.' Apart from days bumping along on a mule behind her mother during her father's excursions into the wilderness, Makepeace had been glad to be too poor for equestrianism. In her view, horses stung people.

'And what has that to do wiz it? Brewer, fetch ze 'abit we take to Marchioness Londonderry.'

'I ain't dressing for a horse that ain't there.'

'Ze horse does not 'ave to be zere.' Mme Angloss's point was that a riding-habit enabled Makepeace to wear black, a colour otherwise reserved for funerals. 'An' zat hair was made for black.'

So much was apparent when Makepeace, still protesting, was put in the Marchioness's habit and looked at herself in the pier-glass.

There was a silence, then Susan said: 'Guess you better take up riding.'

Makepeace released her breath. 'Guess I had.'

The sound of wheels stopping at the house took her and Susan to the window. A closed, unmarked carriage had drawn up at the steps and a man was being bowed out of it.

'D'you know him?'

'Wish I did.'

Mme Angloss from behind them said: 'It is Lord Rockingham.'

'He . . . but he . . .'

'Indeed,' said Mme Angloss, markedly unimpressed, 'I dress 'is lady.'

For a moment, it madly crossed Makepeace's mind that this man, who had replaced the dreadful Grenville as Prime Minister, had come seeking Mme Angloss; it was barely less astonishing that he was calling on—not summoning, but *calling on*—her husband.

'Now, madame, may I recommend one to create ze *parfum* for you, M. Goodbody—frangipane, per'aps—and for the hair M. L'Estoret . . . '

By this time, Makepeace would have agreed to Torquemada and the consultation continued until a footman appeared to say her husband required her presence downstairs. She was still in the Marchioness's riding-habit and, if she must meet a great man, not displeased to be seen in it. Susan went with her as far as Dapifer's office door. 'Shoulders soft now, small steps, curtsey like I showed you. First it's "my lord marquis" and after that "your lordship".'

Susan had been with Mme Angloss a week and was a quick learner.

Dapifer wet his lips on seeing his wife. They exchanged a glance of private, sexual glee. 'Where's the horse?'

'Left it in the parlour.'

'Your lordship, may I present my wife? Makepeace, the Marquis of Rockingham.'

'The pleasure is mine, Lady Dapifer.' He made it sound as if it were. 'I am sorry to delay your ride.'

He was surprisingly young, mid-thirtyish, and with all the attraction of power, riches and a good tailor. Dapifer had said of him that he was on the side of the angels, which meant that he was a Whig and a liberal Whig.

'You have no objection, Sir Philip, to my questioning your wife?'

'Just don't ask her to marry you, Charles, she gets violent.'

They sat down.

'You want something to drink, your lordship?' Makepeace asked, trying hard. 'Tea? Brandy?' She explained kindly: 'The footman gets it.'

'Thank you, no. This is a flying and very surreptitious visit. Lady Dapifer, as an American your views on the situation in our esteemed colony would be valuable. Your husband tells me nobody is better informed on the thinking of the . . . er . . . man in the Boston street. You believe the Stamp Act should be repealed?'

'It surely should.'

'So do I. There are . . . shall we say, *elements*, however, who will oppose a repeal tooth and nail, thinking it would be regarded as weakness.'

'Ain't weakness to admit a mistake, that's strength.' She liked Rockingham; he didn't really want her opinion—she thought that he'd merely requested it out of courtesy to her husband. But she saw appreciation in his dark eyes—definitely, she must wear a riding-habit a *lot*—and an opportunity to do something for decent Americans.

She leaned forward to tap his knee. 'Your lordship, you're ruling us from three thousand miles away. Ain't easy for you. Harder for us. We was doing fine but then all your acts come in, taking away our work, taxing us, telling us what to do in our own land.'

She would never forgive Sugar Bart Stubbs, never, but she understood the situation that had given rise to bastards like him.

'See, your lordship, we got "elements" too and you gave 'em their chance to turn nasty. You want to keep ruling? Ease off the rein. Treat us like we was adult people. We'd trade with you happy enough iffen you just stop telling us how.'

It occurred to her, too late, that real society ladies weren't supposed to lecture Prime Ministers on politics. She thought her husband, watching Rockingham, seemed amused. Well, he'd asked her opinion and she'd given it.

The Marquis said: 'And Sam Adams?'

She was enchanted that he knew the name, and smiled. 'You listen to Sam Adams more and a darn sight less to Lieutenant-Governor Hutchinson and we'll all do just fine.'

Dazzled, Rockingham asked: 'And *iffen* we don't?'

Her smile faded. 'You got a revolution on your hands. It's war. And I don't see how you can win—not against a whole continent.'

'I don't either.' He got up, his face suddenly older. Perhaps he really had wanted to know what she thought and she'd confirmed a lot of other confirmations for him. 'Thank you, Lady Dapifer.'

'You're welcome.'

Rockingham turned to Dapifer: 'And how is young Ffoulkes?'

'Stoical.' The day after their arrival in England, Dapifer had travelled to Eton to see his ward. 'He will be spending the holidays with us in Hertfordshire.'

On the way out the Marquis kissed her hand. To Dapifer, he said: 'Well, Pip, your sybil is not only beautiful, she is honest and wise.'

'Thank you, Charles. I know.'

They stood together on the steps to watch the carriage pull away. '*Sybil?*' Makepeace said. 'Ain't good on names, is he?'

'Oh, I think he'll remember yours.'

The purpose of the call had been to ask Dapifer to go secretly to Bath, there to persuade Mr William Pitt to attend the House of Commons and speak for the repeal of the Stamp Act.

'Pretty speaker, is he, this Mr Pitt?' Makepeace asked.

'Very. If anybody can magic the House and the country into seeing sense, he can.'

'Hokey. Why's he need persuading? And why you?' Her husband had tried to give Makepeace insight into the politics of England but she had ended up confused; it had been more clear-cut in Boston. Grenville—who'd lost office—was a Whig. Lord Rockingham—who'd gained it—was a Whig. She said: 'Most everybody in Government's a Whig and nobody agrees with anybody, lessen they agree with the Tories.'

'Exactly.'

'But why you? You ain't in Parliament.'

'I am what I believe Aaron's friends in the theatre would call a behind-the-scenes man. Rockingham knows that Mr Pitt, though gouty and sulking in his tent at the moment, trusts me. And I am a very persuasive fellow.'

'Don't I know it.' She was proud of him. It kept surprising her that this unremarkable, gloomy-seeming man with whom she shared a bed should not only be *not* overlooked by this showy world—for grandeur of dress and manner, Rockingham, all velvet and lace, had put him in the shade, even *Hutchinson* back in Boston had put him in the shade—but be valued by it.

She said fondly: 'I don't know why *you* ain't a marquis.'

'Like Mr Pitt, I don't relish a peerage. I accepted the baronetcy only to please the first Lady Dapifer.'

Makepeace never commented when he said things like that; it wasn't her place to run the woman down. However, she could exult that big guns were being lined up on their side that could blow the exquisite one's boat out of the water.

Mistress Catty ain't got a Prime Minister in hers, she thought.

Dapifer was to be away at least a week. Since Susan would be following the peripatetic Mme Angloss about her business and Aaron, to his joy, was about to join a London acting company in which Dapifer had procured a place for him, it meant that Makepeace must be left in authority at Dapifer House without allies other than Betty, Josh and Tantaquidgeon.

Robert was accompanying his master, which was a relief; she'd be free of his exaggerated fawning at least. The kindness the valet had shown to Aaron and herself on the *Lord Percy*, she decided, had been partly because he had a quick sympathy for wounded creatures but also because she and Dapifer had been estranged. Now, once again, her position in his master's affection was making him jealous.

Word that she'd taught Mrs Peplow a lesson had spread and the servants now treated her civilly, if with a coldness that stopped just short of insolence. Their resentment, she saw, wasn't because she was an interloper but because she was an interloper of no higher class than their own. Catty Dapifer had been a capricious employer, sometimes over-generous, sometimes cruel, but they had expected nothing else from her—she was quality. Makepeace was not. Cruel or kind, she would never make the grade that the tortuous snobbery of London servants demanded.

Given a free hand, she would have dismissed the lot and hired a new household with which she could have rapport, but the Dapifers were an old and traditionalist family, their servants were nearly all men and women who'd inherited their post from a mother or father who had inherited theirs. Makepeace considered it a system that had led to laziness and corruption, but Dapifer refused to let her change it. 'Leave things alone. When my great-great-great-grandfather was killed at the battle of Marston Moor the soldier who tended him while he was dying was Jack's great-great-grandfather.'

Jack was the decrepit senior footman and Makepeace privately thought that, if blood ran true, his ancestor had plundered the corpse.

She'd been studying household accounts that were alarming. Jack had already retired on a Dapifer pension but, returning to work, now received pension *and* wages plus two new uniforms a year. His was the most glaring example of Dapifer lenity but the case of other servants ran it close.

'Yes, but why's he need a powder allowance? His hair's white already.'

'Procrustes, if you wish to make economies, do. But we've trouble enough with America without you stirring up revolution at home.'

Indulgence, she decided, was her husband's weakness. With less concern for others' welfare and more for his own, he would not, for instance, have spared his first wife the indignity of bringing her before the English courts as an adulteress—and look what that had led to.

On the other hand, it had led him to the Roaring Meg. Fate was a mighty funny thing. She'd have to do what she could.

When Dapifer had gone, she began to do it, poring over the accounts with Betty. Makepeace had hoped her old nurse could assume her former occupation in the Dapifer kitchens but Betty had taken one look at the enormous charcoal range, the wet and dry larders, copper fountains, ice moulds, dripper, hastener, mills, had studied the menus of previous banquets—'A man-of-war made of pasteboard to float on a great charger in a sea of salt to have trains of gunpowder to fire at eggshell boats filled with confection and rosewater'—and confessed herself beaten. 'That ain't cookin',' she said, 'that's archi'ture and I cain't do it.'

What Betty didn't say—it was Joshua who told Makepeace—

was that the hostility of the cook and her staff would have rendered even cleaning the floors miserable. 'She said she di'n't want Ma's dirty black carcase in her kitchen.'

Raging, Makepeace had set off but Betty pulled her back. 'Leave it, gal. Sir Pip's got troubles enough. Let's bide our time, bide our time.'

'All right, but they ain't swilling like hogs while we're biding. Those wasters are getting through more and better in a week than the taproom ate in a month. Look here, three dozen larks. You eaten a lark since we been here? I ain't.'

It wasn't that Dapifer couldn't afford it, but he was being robbed by his own people. Waste was something Makepeace couldn't abide and this was brazen squander.

At least she could put Betty in charge of victualling the household—and did. Butchers, grocers and wine merchants who had supplied the Dapifers for generations suddenly found their bills questioned. If the answers were not satisfactory, Betty, doing the round of the markets, found new tradesmen who were eager to supply Dapifer House at more competitive rates. Menus were studied and altered towards what was, both gastronomically and financially, a healthier regime.

The new stringency led to a formidable deputation of protest consisting of Mrs Peplow and the cook, Mrs Francanelli, waving defiance and the new menus in the faces of Makepeace and Betty.

'When His late Majesty visited unexpected in 'fifty-nine,' Mrs Francanelli declared, 'I had the wherewithal to serve dinner as'd suit a emperor, squab *à la soleil*, moulded lamb, duck with a calf's foot jelly shore . . . twenty dishes a course, finishin' with my special fantasy, Transparent Puddin' with Silver Webb—'

'Famous, Mrs Francanelli's fantasies are,' Mrs Peplow interjected.

'Ain't they just,' Makepeace said. The woman had been overordering and selling off the surplus. 'Well, the new King ain't calling, ladies, so get used to it.'

'An' we're cuttin' down on linen an' all, Mrs Peplow,' Betty said. 'We got enough to bed England as it is.' She made similar swathes in purchases of candles, soap, beeswax polish, charcoal, coal and hair powder that could have supplied a small country.

Household frigidity increased but the bills went down.

With Betty busily employed, Makepeace took on a personal maid—Catty Dapifer had taken hers with her. She promoted young Fanny Cobb from the scullery because she liked the look of her: she didn't sneer. Dapifer had discovered the child begging on the streets and broken with tradition by giving her a place in the household where, though she suffered as an outsider, she did it on a full belly.

Fanny's two years in the scullery had given her no reason to feel loyalty for the rest of the staff but she had a great deal for her master and new mistress: much of Makepeace's acquaintance with the corruption below stairs was supplied by Fanny. Her knowledge of toiletry was negligible but, by using her Cockney acumen and poring over illustrations in *The Ladies' Pocket Book*, she began to hook her mistress into her clothes more or less correctly—it couldn't be done by the wearer alone—and make a passable job of dressing her hair.

'I'll get better though,' she said, 'I'm pickin' up hints on lady-maidin' from Carmelita at Lady Judd's.'

Strangely, the only American who fitted a niche in Dapifer House was Tantaquidgeon. Blacks were common in London, Red Indians were not, and the servants, finding him alien and sinister, treated him with superstitious respect.

He'd taken a liking to a wall-hanging embroidered with dragons in the Yellow dressing room and wore it in place of his blanket. In this, a pair of breeches, and smeared with a pomade Dapifer had given him to replace the bear's grease, he'd begun to stand on the back of the carriage when Dapifer went out and about. Dapifer said he discouraged footpads.

Soon there was to be an excursion to collect Lord Ffoulkes's young son from school and take him to the Dapifers' ancestral manor in Hertfordshire for the Christmas holidays. 'I think you'll like Hertfordshire,' Dapifer said.

Makepeace was prepared to, but would it like her? So far her

English record was of servants who despised her and a female aristocracy that shunned her. She was ready to mother the orphaned little baron for whom her husband was now responsible, had looked forward to it—she got on well with small boys—but perhaps this child too would find her unacceptable.

She had time to dwell on these depressing matters. There was no one to visit or be visited by. Dapifer was engaged in seeing his lawyer, assisting Lord Rockingham behind the scenes and finding friends for the repeal of the Stamp Act. With no work other than to check the accounts and make herself pretty, Makepeace found herself idle for the first time in her life.

Every morning her shutters were opened and her curtains drawn by a maid, another brought her breakfast, Fanny helped her dress and did her hair. Any attempt to do these things for herself resulted in a look of disgust or reproach. If she attempted to poke the fire, a footman descended to snatch the poker from her hand and do it for her.

The first Lady Dapifer's card tables and harpsichord lay closed for lack of someone capable of playing on them, and a selection of novels Makepeace had no interest in reading remained on the otherwise sober shelves of the library. She wandered her beautiful house, envying the activity behind the door to the service quarters, her hands twitching for gainful occupation.

She and Betty took to going for walks in Hyde Park with Josh. For one who had experienced the limitless forests of America, it was tempting to sneer at Londoners' tendency to ascribe all the virtues of the great outdoors to these tamed sylvan acres. But the place was pretty and, indeed, once you'd passed the gallows at Tyburn, walked the avenue of walnut trees into Cumberland Gate and bypassed the Ring where the fashionable circulated in their carriages, the noise of town faded into birdsong and there were red deer beneath the trees.

There was always something new to discover: a little wooden lodge of a Cake House where they bought cheesecake or a mince-pie and washed it down with a mug of milk warm from the cow.

There were skiffs on the Serpentine and an engine house where horses turned the mill that pumped water to Chelsea.

Once, in early morning, they were stopped from approaching too close to a clearing in an oak grove by a gentleman who told them there was a duel in progress. As they walked away, they heard shots. The wounded—if there were wounded—were carried away, unseen, in another direction.

On another occasion they had to run out of the way of a four-in-hand, driven by a hatless man with a pretty female passenger, which came careering towards them across the grass. The woman's shout floated back to them: 'Faster, faster, Sidney. Make 'em jump.' They'd heard the voice before.

'That was her, wa'n't it?' asked Betty, brushing herself down. 'She tryin' to kill you?'

But Makepeace was watching Catty Dapifer encourage her driver to veer his carriage towards another group of people in order to make them scatter. 'She didn't know it was me; she don't care who she kills.'

'Democratic, I'll give her that.'

Whether the poor needed a licence to trade in the park or whether they were merely unwelcome to richer Londoners, who regarded it as their preserve, Makepeace couldn't tell. There was an elderly and malodorous woman who set up an apple stall every morning and who, with equal regularity, was ejected every afternoon, swearing loudly, when the park's beadles made their rounds. Another thorn in the side of the beadles was the sellers of pamphlets and scandal sheets, but they were quicker than the old apple woman and usually collapsed their tables and ran for it at the first glimpse of authority in the distance.

Makepeace was acquainted with political pamphlets—they'd been a powerful weapon in the hands of Sam Adams—but scandal sheets were new to her. She bought one, which seemed both political and scandalous, and carried it home to Dapifer. 'Are they allowed to write this about Lord Bute and the Princess Dowager? 'Tis very rude.'

He was working on some papers and laid down his pen to look at it. 'Ah yes, the *North Briton*. An old copy. You should read issue number forty-five, which attacked the King for constantly acting on Bute's advice—which he still does, incidentally. That was burned by the public hangman.'

She avoided another harangue on the King and Lord Bute's Tory politics which, according to her husband, belonged in the Stone Age; what she found shocking was the explicitness of the attack on Bute's—and royalty's—sexuality.

'Yes, but him and the Princess Dowager. Do they . . . ?'

'Probably not. Wilkes is an irreverent rake who enjoys stinging his opponents any way he can and writes most of his pieces while he's in bed with a doxy. Oh, come on, Procrustes—even you must have heard of John Wilkes.'

' "Wilkes and Liberty"? That trouble the other day?' There had been riots over the import of foreign silks that was ruining London weavers and the cry had been loud enough to reach even Dapifer House.

'That's the one. Actually Wilkes is in France, saying that the establishment is trying to kill him, but his name has become synonymous with protest against the Government.'

'*Are* they trying to kill Wilkes?'

'I wouldn't put it past them. They've handled the matter like the dolts they are, issuing general warrants to arrest him, denouncing his bawdiness . . . Good God, they should look to their own debauchery. Our virtuous Earl of Halifax was the first one to prosecute Wilkes in 'sixty-three and he's sired at least two children on his daughter's governess . . .'

The mention of general warrants did it; their use by the Customs and Excise in Boston had imprisoned too many of Makepeace's friends among small traders. She was prepared to overlook a bit of bawdiness in a man if he was fighting general warrants. 'Is he against the Stamp Tax?'

'He is.'

She left the room a Wilkes supporter.

She thought, when they set out for Hyde Park the next morning, that she'd remember the day because it was the first occasion on which she wore one of Mme Angloss's designs outdoors.

She was to remember it, but not for that.

It was a walking dress, almost a coat, of dark blue velvet with white linen peeping from deep, masculine revers and cuffs. As Mme Angloss had promised, the emphasis was less on the hips and more on the rear of the skirt that curved down in heavy folds from a nipped waist, its hem slightly higher at the front to display the enormous steel buckles on Makepeace's shoes. The brim of her matching hat swept up daringly over one ear.

Fashions in the park were still fussy, the only change of the season belonging to the head, where hair was rising like dough in an adornment of feathers and lace. The severity of her own ensemble, by comparison, would command attention. And deserves to, she thought, looking in the pier-glass.

But as she and Betty went out of the front door, her nerve failed and she ran back inside to take up a thin, hooded cloak. 'In case it rains,' she apologized to Betty, who was in new, red brocade and had no intention of hiding it.

They would have attracted attention today in any case because Tantaquidgeon, either fascinated by their splendour or, perhaps, sensing that it made them vulnerable, stalked after them and would not be sent back.

It was a grey misty autumn day. A fine drizzle, while not sufficient to make them surrender their walk, was enough to excuse Makepeace's use of her cloak.

Even Tantaquidgeon attracted few stares as they went into Hyde Park today because their entrance coincided with the exit from it of the man with the umbrella. He was one of the sights of the West End, though they never discovered his name; he was just the Man with the Umbrella and provided value because he was invariably accompanied by a fascinated crowd which, deciding he must be a foreigner and therefore probably homosexual, minced along behind him. He had the moral courage not to abandon what Makepeace, who hadn't seen an umbrella before either, thought a strange but sensible precaution against English weather.

She and Betty hung on their heels to watch the entertainment as the man passed the hostile, fist-shaking coachmen and sedan chairmen waiting for custom in their Cumberland Gate rank. 'Here, Froggy, can't you take a bloody coach?'

Betty shook her head in satisfaction. '*London,*' she said.

Passing the stall where she'd bought the *North Briton* the previous day, Makepeace looked on the young pamphlet-seller behind it more kindly. He was not a prepossessing object, being pasty-faced, slouched, badly dressed and scowling. However, she awarded him a we-Wilkesites-must-stick-together smile and moved on, without receiving one in return.

There were fewer people about today. The season was drawing to a close and such as had them were preparing to leave for their estates in the country. Fallen leaves sent up the pleasing smell of damp earth as their feet kicked through them.

They had reached the duelling grove when a grunt from Tantaquidgeon made them look behind.

A figure was running towards them. It was hampered by a board under one arm and a sack in the other hand; in any case, it ran badly, its feet hitting the ground flat and without spring, as if unused to the exercise.

'That paper fella, ain't it?' Betty said.

It was—and frightened; this was not a man hastening to an appointment. As they watched, he dropped his table and ran on, still clutching the sack, still heading to where they stood among the oaks.

And now they could hear the pursuit—'. . . in the name of the Law'—and just see through the mist the figures that were giving chase. Official figures, running faster than their quarry.

It was Boston again, excise men after innocent smuggler. Makepeace's hand had signalled the man to come in her direction before she could stop it. As one woman, she and Betty moved together, their backs close to one of the trees. She pulled Tantaquidgeon into line beside them; with his blanket, Betty's girth and her skirt, they made a formidable screen. 'Over here!'

The young man looked behind him, calculated for a second, ran on for another, then doubled back, crouching, and hurled himself and his sack among the tree roots behind Makepeace like a rabbit into its burrow. Scared as he was, it was a sensible manoeuvre; with luck, mist and the shade of the oak branches, the pursuers might only have seen him keep to the main direction of his flight, not his return.

Makepeace felt the back of her skirt lift; the man had crawled underneath it. She could feel him trembling against her stockings. Unpleasant, but she could do little about it now. 'Keep still, blast you.' She pushed back her cloak so that the excisemen could see the quality of her dress and hat.

There were two of them. 'Where'd he go, ma'am?'

She pointed deeper into the grove. 'That way.'

'West Gate, Bill.'

She shouted after them: 'What'd he do?'

'Libel.'

Court bailiffs, then, not excise. But all the same. All against liberty. Satisfied with her blow for freedom, she waited until the sound of running feet had diminished to nothing, then moved forward and round in order to receive the young man's tearful thanks.

He wasn't proffering any. Horrified, she saw that instead of crouching beneath her skirt he had crawled in face up. He still lay on his back, blinking. 'Never saw a red quim before,' he said.

For a moment, she couldn't think that she'd heard what she'd heard. He'd . . . Holy God, he'd looked up her petticoats. She'd saved him and all the time he'd been lying there, studying her private parts.

'You dirty little shite-hawk.' She kicked him in the side and he rolled over, whimpering. 'You worm, you peeper.' Kicked him again. 'I'll cut out your liver and cook it, I'll teach you to insult a lady, I'll lace your eyes on skewers, so I will, and make you chew 'em. Betty, call the bailiffs back.'

Tantaquidgeon, seeing her anger, placed his moccasined foot on the young man's none-too-clean neck.

'Ow! Get that heaving great Huron off me.'

Makepeace teetered in the act of kicking. 'How'd you know he's a Huron?'

'He's got the haircut. Right feather, too.'

'All right, let him up.' As the youth sat rubbing his neck, she asked: 'You American?'

'Nyah.' He said it contemptuously, but he seemed to say everything with contempt. 'Bigwigs ain't got a monopoly on education.' He got to his feet. 'You are, though, from the sound of it.'

'And a good job for you I am, you sneaking little turd. I saved your fat from frying, Hokey knows why. What's your name?'

'John Beasley. What's yours?'

'Cut off, John Beasley. I ever see you again, I'll have you charged.'

Betty had been picking up the sack and some of the papers that had spilled out of it. 'Better see this first, girl.'

Makepeace took the printed sheet. Its top half was devoted to a cartoon in which two crudely drawn women with enormous and elaborate headdresses were battling on the ground next to a street sign bearing the legend 'Grosvenor Square'. One of the figures held a raised tomahawk with a banner streaming from her mouth reading: 'He's MY husband, Lady Dapifer.' The other was saying: 'Help! Help! MY husband, Lady Dapifer.' A diminished male in the background wrung his hands.

Below the drawing was an article which she was too appalled to read. Betty's hand held a fistful of sheets, all of them the same. 'Oh God. That's *me*.' This filth was being circulated, people would see it, laugh at it.

'Is it?' Beasley looked over her shoulder, interested. 'You Lady Dapifer then?'

'Who printed this?'

'Me.' He was proud of it. 'My new paper, I'm calling it *The Passenger*. To be read on coaches and such. What d'you think?'

'Who told you about this?'

'Sorry. I can't reveal my sources. It's in the public domain anyway. If that's *you*'—he put a long-nailed and grubby finger on the female with the tomahawk—'*she's* just started an action in the church courts against *him* for aggravated adultery. That's bigamy in case you didn't know.'

For the first time Makepeace saw the full extent of what was to come. Oh my dear, she thought, oh my poor Pip. This nightmare beside her had not only looked up her skirt, he was lifting it, showing her and Dapifer naked for the public's amusement. Their affection had become fairground entertainment.

She felt very tired all of a sudden and closed her eyes.

Beasley said: 'You want to publish your version of it?'

She shook her head. 'Go away.'

'Ought to, you know. Important, the printed word. I'll call, shall I?'

Her eyes flicked open. 'Call?'

He was addressing Betty and Tantaquidgeon. 'If she don't know the power of the press, the other one does. Anyone as can swear like this 'un needs preserving for a national treasure. Tell her she ought to talk to me.'

'Young fella,' Betty said, 'you come near us again an' this here Indian's goin' to take your scalp off an' wear it.'

Beasley nodded and took the sack from her, stuffing his papers back in it. As he went, he fished a dog-eared piece of cardboard from inside his jacket and thrust it into Makepeace's hand. 'My card,' he said.

They watched him slouch away, picking up his table as he went.

Had Makepeace known it, another big gun had just been added to her future armoury.

At that moment, however, she'd have shot him with it.

Another outcome of that day was that she ordered Mme Angloss to design something which neither she nor, as far as she knew, any woman had worn before: a pair of short pantaloons to encase the thighs and the part between.

Mme Angloss did so, under protest. She regarded the garment as unhealthy and indecent. 'Ze privities should be free to ze air.'

Makepeace didn't like it much either, but there were greater indecencies.

Just before they left for Hertfordshire, Dapifer took her down to Wapping to await the arrival of a ship bringing a gift he had ordered for her. 'I trust you'll approve.'

'I'll love it. What is it?'

'Wait and see.'

They sat on the rickety balcony of the Anchor. An empty gibbet stood in the Thames silt a little further along to their right where the corpses of executed pirates were hung until the tide had covered them three times. An easterly wind brought the smell of sea from the estuary. Boats circumvented the tangle of hulls to land sailors and goods ashore, while others took apparently identical loads out to ships waiting to sail. Grubby Newcastle wherries, carrying their cargoes to the coal quays, slipped between the gilded figureheads of vast East Indiamen.

'Miss it?' Dapifer asked.

'A bit.' She didn't want to tell him how much. At that moment she'd have sold her soul to be on the jetty of the Roaring Meg about to step into her rowing boat. 'Pip, there's the *Lord Percy*.'

'She's returning to the West Indies. Calling in at Boston first.'

'Can we row out and say hello?'

'In a while, if you want to. Makepeace, may I present Captain Dobbs? He's brought you your present.'

She thanked a middle-aged naval captain, though he appeared empty-handed. 'Mighty kind of you, sir.'

'A pleasure, ma'am.' Captain Dobbs glanced wryly at Dapifer. 'Also a relief.' He moved to the rail of the balcony. 'If you look down there, Lady Dapifer, my jolly is about to unload it.'

A boatload of sailors, wearing the divided calico petticoat of ratings, was clambering up a ladder to the dockside. Some carried a ditty bag. One had a birdcage.

'A parrot,' she said.

'Not exactly.'

A marine sergeant gave a brusque order and the men shuffled into a sullen line. 'They don't look happy,' Makepeace said.

'They'll be happier in a minute,' Captain Dobbs said, 'when I tell 'em they're discharged and going home. Perhaps *you*'d like to tell them, ma'am.'

And then she knew what the present was.

Matthew Bell—he was the least changed—Laurie Crumpacker, the Sayward brothers, Jerry Batson, little Billy Kidder . . . all the *Gideon*'s crew. And there he was, the gaily fluttering ribbons on his hat unsuitable to the granite dignity his face had always kept and still did.

The familiarity of the figures pierced her, as if she'd glimpsed her own children, aged, in a foreign land.

Captain Dobbs was saying to Dapifer: ' . . . a fine seaman, Busgutt, but I'm not sorry to be rid of him. Always admonishing me as if I were a heathen. Let's hope the volunteers you've given me to replace this lot will be a little less mindful of the Lord's commands and a little more of the Admiralty's.'

'Do you want go down, Makepeace?'

She managed to shake her head. What could she say to him?

Captain Dobbs gave an order and for a moment the ribboned hats tilted as the Bostonians looked up to see where it came from. Their eyes slipped over the elegant woman on the balcony without recognition. Next minute they were being transferred to the tender from the *Lord Percy*.

The tears plopping onto her face dried cold in the wind as she watched them scramble up the nets over the *Percy*'s side. Did they know yet they were going home? Somebody would tell them. She'd like to have seen that.

She felt for her husband's hand and clutched it against her cheek. It was warm on her skin. 'Thank you,' she said.

'Wish you were going with them?'

'No,' she said, 'I'm already home.'

Chapter Nine

IT was a landscape out of Brueghel, brown figures following a plough, white earth livid against a bleak, grey sky. The excitement of winter was in the busy, cawing rooks circling above the bare branches of elms.

Two men clearing a ditch along a common doffed their caps and waved.

The horses' hooves made muffled squeaks on the snow as the coach turned to go through an ancient archway and ploughed along a village street, a track serving a row of thick-walled, deep-thatched cottages.

They turned in through open ironwork gates to begin the drag uphill between two lines of sweet chestnut trees, past a small church and cemetery, to the top and the manor called Dapifers.

Had Makepeace not known it already, the first glimpse of the house as she craned her neck out of the coach window would have told her the Dapifers were not a family to alter things. Add on, yes; change, no.

The modest keep Eudo Dapifer, steward to Henry I, had built for himself on this Hertfordshire hilltop had been patched and re-crenellated for the War of the Roses and again when Roundheads and Royalists battled across the surrounding countryside. It was still there, ivy-covered but serviceable. A fifteenth-century Dapifer had attached a hall to which an Elizabethan descendant had added a turret with a cupola. His Jacobean heir had waded in with an Italian garden and a stable block.

Queen Anne's era had passed it by, so had Palladianism. The house spread along the crest of its hill as artless and untidy as the River Drift meandering through the valley below it.

Catty Dapifer had disliked the place; too bucolic.

That day, with its firelit windows and the snow rounding its roofs, it blinked down at Makepeace like a line of huddled, wide-eyed owls on a branch, and she loved it.

To her relief, most of the Grosvenor Square servants had been left behind in London; only two footmen, both of them Hertfordshire men, were travelling with Fanny Cobb, Tantaquidgeon and the luggage in the covered cart. Robert had been given the holiday to go and visit his mother.

Betty was to be integrated into the manor's staff as assistant to its resident cook and housekeeper—a woman of advanced years and, according to Dapifer, benign disposition. Aaron and Susan were to join them in a day or two. Makepeace was to be surrounded by her friends.

She had a presentiment of joy; this was deep, deep countryside, biting air tinged with earth and manure, the Middle Ages of her ancestors. But she looked doubtfully across at the child on the seat opposite her. 'I hope it won't be too quiet here for you, my lord.'

During the journey from London she'd tended to fawn on the boy, partly investing him in her mind with the sophistication and ease with wealth his father must have had, partly out of pity for his orphaned state. His mother, a commoner from Ireland and reputedly beautiful, had died giving birth to him.

Lord Ffoulkes said with some energy: 'I hope not, ma'am.' It was the first time he had roused himself to be other than polite in her company. He was a round-faced, sturdy little boy with lamentably ginger hair.

His courteous but non-commital manner on being introduced to her and his apparently unsurprised acceptance of the fact that he was sharing the coach not only with Makepeace and Dapifer but two black people—Betty and Josh—argued either total self-possession or misery.

She'd hoped that, since Josh and he were of an age, they would be company for each other; so far neither had exchanged a glance.

'Don't worry, Andrew,' Dapifer said. 'My wife's from New England where they mark the Lord's birth in a round of riotous Bible-reading. At Dapifers we celebrate Yuletide until it surrenders. We shall *not* be quiet.'

Makepeace suppressed an 'Oh dear'. Popish practices.

As it turned out, Christmas at Dapifers was not Popish, it was pagan, as much to do with ancient invocations for the return of the sun as it was with Christ made flesh. And Makepeace was too busy with the preparations to worry about it.

Even with the addition of the footmen, the staff kept at the manor was insufficient for the entertainment to be extended from Christmas Eve to Plough Monday. A list of her duties compiled by the aged, benign but authoritarian Mrs Bygrave, Dapifers's housekeeper, was mountainous.

Makepeace went to challenge her husband with it. 'Thirty-eight silver spoons? Where'm I going to find thirty-eight silver spoons, and why?'

'Pattons of Hertford makes them for us.' Dapifer was reading some papers, his feet up on a battered escritoire in his turret room. 'Each adult on the demesne gets one every Christmas. Tradition. Gratitude for saving their Dapifer lord in the Stephen and Matilda war.'

'When was that?'

'During the eleven forties. And don't forget the bean in the plum cake for the Lord of Misrule. Oh, and the wassail bowl is kept in the church vestry, tell Simmonds to get it out. The orchard needs to be thoroughly wassailed or the apples won't grow next year.'

She groaned. 'Goody Busgutt would report us to the magistrates.'

'She should see us burying the Corn Dolly. Have the dinner invitations gone out?'

'Yes.' She looked at her list. '*Two* cows? Who're we feeding? The whole damn county?'

'Just this part of it.'

'Pip,' she said, 'suppose they won't come because of me? All that food wasted.' The guests invited to the Christmas feast were, as far as she could tell, mostly shire folk but, being so, they probably disapproved of divorce even more strongly than did the peerage.

'They'll come. Around here you don't offend a Dapifer, however many wives he's got. Sir Toby, for instance, is the local Member of Parliament, a Whig—his seat's in my pocket and he does what I tell him. He likes Forc'd Cabbage Surprise with his meat.'

Sir Toby and Lady Tyler. Top table. 'I know. Mrs Bygrave said. The surprise is how long it takes to bloody make.' She leaned across the escritoire. 'You're doing this deliberately, ain't you?' She pushed his legs off the escritoire so that his chair skidded on the floor.

'You said you lacked employment,' he said, sadly. 'I'm giving you employment. Lock the door.'

'I ain't got time.'

'Lock the damn door.'

They made love on the threadbare Persian carpet in front of the fire. Later, when she discovered she was pregnant, she ascribed it to that morning in the high, circular room with winter sun coming through the lancets onto piles of dilapidated books, the scent of burning apple logs and ancient stone, somebody whistling down in the courtyard.

'Confess you're having the time of your life,' he said, nuzzling her hair. 'I understand they refer to you as "missus". A compliment.'

'What did they call *her*?'

' "My lady".'

She despaired of keeping rooms warm and floors clean. It was as if the old, oaken manor was an extension of the countryside, tramped and sledged with offerings of holly and ivy, a tree trunk of Yule log, pots of honey—the bees had to be thanked for it—vegetables, herbs. The hall echoed with calls from ladders as the greenery was hung, the back yard with the bellows of animals unappreciative of having their throats cut in a good cause. The blur of work parted now and then to imprint other images.

One morning, in the huge, noisy and medieval kitchen, she found Sam the pigman having the blood from his nose stanched by Fanny Cobb and the blacksmith, Edgar Croft.

'What's happened here?'

'Only lifted Betty's petticoats, didn't he,' Fanny told her.

'Wanted to see if she were liquorice all a way down, tha's all,' Sam said.

Betty, up to her elbows in pastry, was grinning. 'Felt my liquorice fist instead.'

'Goin' to put her up agin Battlin' Bob in the prizefights next,' Edgar said.

There was a general air of relaxation. The village faces had a stoniness which, Makepeace was learning, in Hertfordshire passed for laughing.

She took in a breath of relief. They'd melded. 'Am I the only bugger working around here? I don't get that pig quartered in five more minutes, Sam, I'll roast you in its place.'

'All right, missus.'

On her way out, she nudged Betty. 'Told you to wear drawers.'

Two days later, Makepeace, furious because she'd been frightened, faced two small, shivering, blanketed boys. 'You varmints. I *told* you the ice wasn't thick enough, didn't I tell you? I've a mind to tan your arses. Suppose Tantaquidgeon hadn't been watching? We'd've lost you both. You stay off that damn lake till I say it's safe—I know about water.'

'Yes, Miss 'Peace.' That was Josh.

Lord Ffoulkes stared her out. 'Josh says you can sail a boat.'

'And you're sailing to bed this minute.'

But there was something there and when she'd stopped shaking she went up to his room. He was curled like a foetus among the bedclothes. She put her hand on his forehead; warm but no fever.

She lay down next to him, carefully staring up at the ceiling. 'What's this about sailing?' At least his father's death hadn't given him a horror of the sea.

'I want to learn. I want to sail to America.'

'Surely. I'll teach you. But why?'

'My father's there.'

She wished Dapifer wasn't out; he'd know how to cope with this. She said quietly: 'You know he drowned, Andrew. You went to his memorial service.' Dapifer said the child had stood it like a guardsman and answered the King's condolences with dignity.

She watched his grubby little hand tighten on the sheet. ' . . . goodbye.'

'What?' She leaned over him.

'I didn't say goodbye.'

Perhaps a goodbye couldn't be said in Westminster Abbey among pomp and dignitaries and bloody incense.

She clenched her teeth against an old, childhood agony; they hadn't let her say goodbye to her mother, either; they'd taken her away when Temperance Burke went into labour with Aaron. By the time the neighbours returned Makepeace home, Temperance was already buried.

Lord, let me help him. All she could do was tell him what she'd once told Dapifer, how quick it must have been . . .

She ended: 'But that's one good thing, it was the same sea. Same sea the Thames goes into, same sea that little Drift out there gets to in the end. Souls don't have any difficulty navigating the Atlantic. How about when we get back to London you and me sail down the Thames to the estuary and give it some flowers for your pa?'

She'd done the same thing when her father died, to help float his soul back to Ireland. Goody Busgutt had called her a heathen.

'Will he see them?'

'He surely will.' She added with difficulty: 'No need to say goodbye, neither. You and him ain't finished just because he drowned.'

The boy turned to her and she put her arms round him and they sobbed together.

Aaron and Susan arrived from London on the day before the dinner at Dapifers for the local dignitaries. They brought with them a copy of the latest scandal sheet, *Picknicks*.

'Susan didn't want you to see it,' Aaron said, 'but I reckoned you'd better. The item's short but it's dirty.'

The woman Sir Philip Dapifer now parades as his wife is reported lately to have been found serving ale to sailors in New England. A tavern wench, Sir Pip? The original Lady Dapifer has entered a suit in the Court of Arches against him, alleging his criminal conversation with this person. These columns promise to report all the interesting scenes fully, minutely and circumstantially displayed by the forthcoming trial.

It was a peculiar sensation. She wasn't in Dapifers' parlour at all but back in Boston, in the bay, and standing not on the Roaring Meg's jetty but on a hulk, drawn through the water on a long chain attached to a cutter. A target. Often she'd watched the puffs of smoke and the spout of water as the cannons fired their practice shots. Now she was the target itself and bracketed, to right, to left, waiting for the shot that would hurl her into the air in disintegrating spars.

Catty Dapifer was finding her range.

Dapifer pulled the paper from her hand. 'Is this your friend John Beasley?' He squinted at the small print bearing the proprietor's name. 'Apparently not.' He threw the sheet in the fire. 'Trash. Not worth bothering with.'

'Excuse me, but I think it is.' Aaron, usually in agreement with his brother-in-law's every word, was standing up to him. 'This needs action, Pip. People are ingesting this poison. You've *got* to counter it.'

Susan said: 'And forgive me, Sir Pip, but we all know who's doing the poisoning. Wherever me and Mme Angloss go, it's the talk of the drawing rooms; chatter, chatter, gossip, gossip—makes you nauseous.'

The parlour re-formed itself around Makepeace. She thought: *Tavern wench.* Therefore a trollop. Lord, that's a smart bitch—the judge will come to the case with his mind bent, whether he knows it or not.

'I appreciate your concern, my dears,' Dapifer said, 'but if it's a libel suit you're after, it would merely compound the frenzy. And now excuse me, I have more important business to attend to. Lord Ffoulkes, Josh and I have an appointment to build a snowman.'

The three of them watched him go like parents remembering their own innocence. 'Too good for this wicked world,' Aaron said.

Makepeace thought how old her brother had become. Whether the tarring had done it, or whether it was exposure to the raffish sophistication of the theatre, he had been catapulted into middle-aged maturity. She was comforted that he looked well on it. She was suddenly combative again.

'Well, I ain't,' she said. 'I'll give that Jezebel "tavern wench". She ain't the only one can use Grub Street. Me and my friend John Beasley, we'll splatter her over the sidewalk.' A sudden alarm made her grimace. 'Was it on sale in Hertford?'

Aaron nodded. 'We picked it up at the stage inn.'

It was apparent the next night that copies of *Picknicks* had circulated with speed among the manors and farms of Hertfordshire. A few invitees daringly sent their regrets to Dapifer—a sudden emergency at home. But most were too politically beholden to him not to come and dutifully trampled their moral repulsion under boots of self-interest and curiosity.

Makepeace, standing with her husband in the great hall, could see snow-bespattered cloaks being flung without regard onto the poor footmen in the screen passage as their owners' eyes hunted for the first glimpse of Sir Philip's tavern wench.

Some, hoping for a harlot in full garish fig, showed disappointment as they lighted on her. Others, equally expectant, rejected her as improbable and hunted elsewhere. Still others looked relieved—and these she marked down as people bearing goodwill to the House of Dapifer.

Susan had dressed her carefully for the occasion. 'We don't want to blind 'em, but on the other hand we want 'em to see we're quality.'

In the end they went for simplicity, a closed, olive-green velvet gown, its bodice trimmed round the wide neck with gold-embroidered white linen that ran to a point over the stomacher, matching her cap. Her only jewellery was a cameo of herself that Dapifer had given her on a gold-silk neckband. Receiving an incoming tide of ruffled, ribboned satins, hired jewellery, rising hair fronts and plunging décolletages—some of them over unsuitable bosoms—as prescribed by the latest issue of *Lady's Magazine*, she was a statement of restraint.

Guests with an eye for cloth and cut were not fooled but Sir Toby Tyler MP, guest of honour, was deceived into thinking her ensemble unsophisticated and, from the kindness of his heart, reassured her.

'See, my dear'—this was to his wife during their introduction—'Lady Dapifer has no need to run after the vogue to look pretty, nor to cost her husband a fortune in pursuit of it. Be modest, dear maid, and let those who will be fashionable, eh, Lady Dapifer?'

'I'm going to kill him,' muttered Makepeace.

'You'll have to stand in line behind Lady Tyler,' Dapifer muttered back.

She had splurged on candles in an effort to warm the hall, with little effect; outside the direct radius of heat from the great fireplace it was arctic and she conceived an admiration for the sturdiness of her guests, especially those with bared shoulders, in not complaining of frostbite.

On the other hand, at dinner the tables sparkled with reflecting crystal and silver as brightly as the guests' eyes at the food.

The footmen—Edgar and Sam had also been co-opted into livery and floured wigs—trotted like horses on a training rein in an endless ovoid between kitchen and hall with covered chargers of dishes: turkey, capon, roast beef, mutton, pork, stews with dumplings and wild boar pie. Makepeace had thought a hundred stomachs could not accommodate so much meat. She was wrong. Vegetable dishes had to be served individually, there being no room for them on the board. Wine sank in the glasses like water into sand and needed replenishing within minutes.

Sir Toby on her right hand amazed her with his capacity for Forc'd Cabbage Surprise as well as everything else and she agreed docilely that Americans were a troublesome people but deserved to have the Stamp Tax rescinded as long as they behaved themselves in future. Not having asked her opinion once, at the end of the meal he congratulated her on her sagacity.

When the tables were cleared, the small orchestra hired for the occasion came down from the minstrels' gallery where it had been playing softly and took up its position on the dais for the dancing.

And here was Sir Toby again, wonderful man, bowing, puffing and indefatigable, asking her to lead the first set with him. It had been anticipated that he would and the orchestra had instructions to begin with a gavotte, which was as far as Makepeace's dancing lessons had yet taken her.

She managed to prance through the quadruple metres before escaping to devote herself to those sitting out. There were still icicles to be thawed, especially among the elderly.

Assisting the relict of a cloth merchant to a glass of mulled punch, she was told acidly: 'I suppose you're used to serving drink, young woman.' Mrs Higgs, who now ran her dead husband's company herself, had once met Queen Anne and therefore considered herself entitled to speak her mind.

'I surely am. Being a tavern-owner, I didn't expect my staff to do what I couldn't. As a businesswoman yourself, Mrs Higgs, you'll understand that.'

'Oh, you *owned* the tavern.'

That was better. It wouldn't have done for the nobility but it warmed the representatives of a society interlinked with trade. Mrs Higgs was later heard to remark that Makepeace Dapifer might not have breeding 'like t'other one, but she's more our style, for all she's foreign. A good, plain girl with a head on her shoulders.'

She was invited to dance again, this time by Dapifer's agent, Peter Little.

'Is this a gavotte?' Makepeace had a tin ear for music.

'A minuet, I believe.'

'Ain't learned that one yet.' She looked around; the festivities had achieved their own impetus, she wouldn't be missed for a minute or two. 'Let's get acquainted.'

They went up to the minstrels' gallery and leaned on the fretted balcony to watch the swirl below. Peter Little looked down on it, frowning. Makepeace eased off her slippers. 'See,' she said, 'I need to go round the place, learn about it.'

'Would you really like to? *Really?*' He was pleased; obviously, the previous Lady Dapifer had shown little interest in the estate.

'Surely.' She was a woman who liked to understand how things worked; she wanted to grapple the manor closer to her. What did the land grow? What rents did it pay? Were men like Sam the pigman given a wage or was their job a condition of tenancy? There were other Dapifer estates, how did they produce the wealth on which she lived?

'Do you hunt, Lady Dapifer?'

'No.'

'Perhaps . . . There's a meet after Christmas. While everyone else is chasing the fox, perhaps you would accompany me in the trap and we could do the rounds.'

They stayed on a while; the scene in the hall was worth lingering over: a blazing tableau of light and colour. Susan was dancing with Sir Toby, Dapifer, sad-faced, with the vicar's wife and making her laugh, Aaron with Mrs Higgs, a gallant little Lord Ffoulkes with tall Lady Tyler. Aldermanic stomachs bounced, breasts bobbed, sweat ran, wigs and coiffures uncurled. In a moment Makepeace must lead the way into the dining room where a buffet supper had been prepared by her poor kitchen staff. And these already bestuffed people would actually eat it.

Heat created by energetic bodies rose up to the gallery and Makepeace found herself oddly moved, as if she had opened an interior door of an unwelcoming house and been confronted by the glow of a good fire. How irritating these people were and how unexpected. Observed from across the Atlantic, England appeared as lofty as the Dover cliffs and as little concerned with what it looked out on, a view confirmed by her reception here. But the men and women below had a rough humanity their ruling class did not; their indifference was more a lack of deliberation, or an innocence. So sure were they of their own fair play, they were surprised that other peoples were not in accord with them. Here, in its greed and good humour, was the England that built empires.

She had encountered the same breed in Boston.

'Better wrap up well,' Peter Little said, 'for our trip, Lady Dapifer. Better wrap up warmly.'

'Oh. Yes,' she said. 'Yes, I surely will.'

She and Dapifer stood in the doorway for the farewells, invitations to cards, to suppers, to balls, falling on them like the snowflakes which blurred the light spilling out into the speckled darkness.

As the lanterns of the last carriages disappeared among the ghostly trees of the drive, Dapifer said: 'Well done, Procrustes.'

She grunted, stepped out of her slippers and limped to the kitchen to congratulate the bodies that lay slumped among its debris.

They hailed the Yule Log. They obeyed the Lord of Misrule. They buried the Corn Dolly in earth too frozen to be ploughed into more than a shallow furrow. They went through night-time orchards carrying flares that lit lichened boughs and faces pale with cold. Toast soaked in cider was lifted on a stick to a little boy seated in a fork of a tree, a fiddle struck up and they sang:

> *Old Apple-tree, Old Apple-tree,*
> *We wassail thee, hoping thou wilt bear,*
> *For the Lord doth know where we shall be*
> *When apples come another year,*
> *So merry let us be . . .*

They discharged a volley from their flintlocks to waken the god of the apple-tree from winter slumber and went back to the house and drank lamb's-wool from the wassail bowl so that, when they cheered 'Sir Pip and his lady', their misted breath came to her smelling of ale and spices and roasted apples.

Popish, pagan, polytheist, whatever it was, as she knelt in the freezing little church next to the cross-legged effigy of a crusading

Dapifer, Makepeace knew she was as close to the stable in Beth-lehem as she ever had been or probably would be. Usually her periods were as regular as the moon; now, for the first time since puberty, she had missed one.

The shire turned out again for the meet, greeting her like an old friend, splendid in hunting pink and black, the horses jostling on the manor's front apron and so big she had to stand on tiptoe to present the stirrup cup to their riders. Hounds coloured like the weather flowed between the hooves, their tails wagging as if pro-viding their means of propulsion.

Susan had decided to risk going and had a groom with her in case she wanted to retire early. She looked pretty on her sidesaddle, but precarious. 'Sure about this?' Makepeace asked.

'No.'

Lord Ffoulkes bounced on his pony, impatient to start, watched by a wistful Josh. It was the first time the boys had been parted since arriving at Dapifers. Josh was going skating with Aaron, who couldn't ride either. He troubled Makepeace because she didn't know what to do about the child. Though she was as ignorant of art as she was of music, it was obvious the boy was gifted beyond his years in drawing and she was reluctant to betray his talent by subsuming it in domestic service. On the other hand, who'd ever heard of a black artist? For the time being, she'd hired Rev Botley, the incumbent of Dapifers's church, to teach him his letters.

So many villagers had come to pursue the hunt on foot, she called up to Dapifer on his bay: 'Do they get liquor as well?'

'The question's never come up.' He resumed a more important discussion on scent with the master of hounds.

Feudal, she thought. He's gone feudal. She sent to the kitchen for more mulled wine and made sure everyone had some.

It was bitterly cold. Sam the pigman knuckled his forehead: 'Kind of you, missus,' but on the whole the lower classes, too, were more concerned with scent and coverts than with democracy.

They tantivied away and the air was left to the cawing of rooks.

Makepeace went inside and wrapped herself in cloaks and tied a velvet scarf round her ears under her beaver hat.

Peter Little drew up in his trap. He'd lined its floor with straw, providing his dog for her to rest her feet on and had borrowed a puppy to put inside her sheepskin muff as a hand-warmer.

They set off eastwards down the valley. The air was bitingly clear and ahead of them the next in the range of hills which undulated across this part of Hertfordshire was outlined against the blue sky as if it were pipe-clayed. Top-heavy snow on the hedges had frozen in the act of overbalancing and formed a curving frieze that sparkled in the sun.

Makepeace was shown the village's strip fields, pigsties, cow byres, sheepfolds, most of them emptied by the annual winter slaughter.

Peter Little shook his head over them. 'It's inefficient, that's what it is,' he said. 'Given a free hand, I could be using new methods, keeping the beasts alive during the winter with root crops, not slaughtering them every Michaelmas because we can't feed them. I could double our production of wheat as well.'

'How?'

He swung his hand in a generous arc. 'Enclosure. Those woods should be cleared and the common should be fenced for arable land.'

New as Makepeace was to the country, the subject of enclosure had become familiar to her; it was the talk of the day. Some of the neighbouring landowners had already applied to Parliament for the passing of an act that would allow them to fence in their common land. To them, as to Peter Little, it meant efficiency, better production that would, in the end, benefit the country by cheaper corn, fresh meat all the year round and general stability of the food market. And themselves, of course.

But she'd also listened to villagers, the people who pastured their cow or goat on the common, fished its streams, used its firewood, eking out their livelihood through its use. To them enclosure meant dispossession. Already processions of displaced families were leaving homes they had occupied for centuries to seek work in the towns. No more orchard wassail, no goats on the green, no sun to tempt back from the darkness. It was the passing of an age. She said so.

'And Dapifers will pass as well,' Little said. 'I tell you, Lady Dapifer, we either advance or go under. We must compete in this new world. Remain in the Middle Ages, and your children's children will have nothing to inherit.'

She was alive to that now; the words went through to her belly where a child lay. 'What does Sir Pip say?' she asked.

Little blew out his cheeks, eschewing criticism of his master to the master's lady. 'Sir Pip has a great sense of tradition,' he said, carefully. 'He says the villagers have the same rights to the land that he has, they've been on it as long.'

'He would.' It was typical, lovable, of her husband that he should hold fast to his people and the ancient, ramshackle economy that kept their lives turning. It was also irritating. Her business instinct recoiled at inefficiency. If she were running the estate . . . Her ancestors had left England so that their children wouldn't have to live in the Middle Ages. *And I'm damned if I'm going to have mine return to it.* Sad that people had to be uprooted but there was always a price for progress.

She broached the subject a few days later as she and Dapifer took a walk down the avenue through trees as still and as white as statuary. There had been more snow.

'Peter Little's been putting his hobby horse through its paces, has he?' Dapifer said.

'He just said the big estates either enclose or go under.'

'I know.' He surprised her. '*Fugit inreparabile tempus.* Irretrievable time is flying.' He looked towards the village hidden behind the park wall, the smoke from its chimneys rising as straight as if it was being pulled by the cold, dry air. 'Herewith the last of the Georgics,' he said, sadly.

'New George on the throne now,' Makepeace said, 'and we don't want it to be the last of the Dapifers.'

'I know,' he said again. They turned to follow the stream that fed the lake. 'But we'd be taking the land my people, *those* people, have occupied for six hundred years. We'd have to compensate them hugely, then there's the investment necessary for the new cultivation.'

'I thought you was rich,' Makepeace said. 'It's why I married you.'

'I wondered what the reason was. But the wealth arises from income, not capital. I shall need such capital as I've got.' He hesitated and then said: 'I meant to tell you. I've decided to pay off the first Lady Dapifer. She's agreed to drop the case if I pay her another hundred thousand.'

Makepeace stopped, appalled. 'There ain't that much money in the world.'

'If I'm any judge it will barely cover her gambling debts. So you see, enclosure is out of the question, even if I were inclined to it.'

'Why?' She clutched at him. 'Pip, you doing this for *me*?'

'Procrustes, I didn't bring you from America in order to see you dragged through arse-wipes like *Picknicks*, let alone the courts, for the amusement of the rabble.'

She let him go. She thought: He wants to spare me, he wants to spare his villagers. I'll be damned if he spares her too. 'Would you pay her if it wasn't for me?'

He didn't answer.

She said: 'Don't do it. Sticks and stones may break our bones but words can never hurt *us*, not you and me. We'll fight her, Pip, you agreed. She hurt you enough in the past without mortgaging our future as well.'

From a branch overhanging the stream, a kingfisher dived into the twirling, icy water and came up with a wriggling arc of silver in its beak.

'Can you face it?' he asked.

'I can if you can.'

He sighed. 'Very well.'

As a reward, she told him he was to become a father and watched the future unroll before him as if a curtain had been raised. It was almost painful; she'd never seen his face as naked.

The phrase 'halcyon days' had always brought an image of summer to Makepeace's mind but from that day, and in all the years that followed, it was replaced by the image of a blue-tan kingfisher flickering into a winter stream and out again, in the last hour of a dream.

Chapter Ten

On her return from Hertfordshire in March, Makepeace went immediately to see the family solicitor in Lincoln's Inn. It was more usual for gentry to insist that their lawyers come to them but she enjoyed any excuse to walk in London, unsafe though its streets had become.

The poor harvest of the previous year had put up the price of bread which, in turn, had led to greater numbers of beggars and cut-purses. There were already riots in the Thames Valley where the destitute saw corn in barges passing their door on its way to be sold abroad and make large profits for its dealers and growers. Dapifer had advised Rockingham to put an embargo on grain exports in order to bring down the price but the Marquis, struggling to keep together his coalition government, had not seen to it.

Makepeace, an inveterate early riser, held to the belief that beggars, cut-purses, and probably rioters as well, were in the sinful habit of sleeping late, and that therefore even London streets were safe of a morning. However, like a respectable woman, she took Fanny Cobb with her. Betty had stayed behind in Hertfordshire with Josh. At Dapifer's insistence—he'd become very protective of her—Tom, the most reliable and muscular of the footmen, accompanied her in the place of Tantaquidgeon who, Dapifer said, was too noticeable and likely to attract brickbats.

After a severe winter, this chill but sunny March morning with a green mist of buds forming on the trees was a tonic. So was Fanny Cobb, an authority on London and happy to inform.

They passed Brooke Street where Dr Baines was now success-fully installed, and the house where Handel had lived. Eastwards, the elegant houses of music and medicine gave way to dingy courts.

'Shockin' murder there,' said Fanny. 'See that door? Carried her out of it in bits, they did. Often wonder if she was my ma, poor thing.'

Fanny, a foundling, spent much of her time speculating on whether newsworthy women of a certain age and of whatever class could be her mother. She wasn't wistful about it but it was a con-stant theme. Makepeace, wondering what it was like to float in the world without an anchor, found the girl's unvarying cheerfulness admirable.

London was extraordinary. Having negotiated a narrow, urine-scented, turnstiled passage, they were confronted by the hidden, breath-taking surprise of space, trees and Inigo Jones frontages that was Lincoln's Inn Fields.

The chambers of James and Hackbutt, Solicitors, when they eventually found them, were like the Law itself: dark, fusty and forbidding.

Mr Hackbutt, on the other hand, was another surprise, with the appearance of a middle-aged country squire come in from a shoot. His cheeks were ruddy, his coat fustian and cut away to reveal a comfortable velvet waistcoat with bulging pockets. He had clum-pish boots and open-air manners; he hailed Makepeace as if he'd sighted her fifty yards off in a greenwood.

But he was still a lawyer. 'You do realize, Lady Dapifer, that even to you I can reveal nothing of Sir Pip's affairs without his permission.'

'He's very busy just now, Mr Hackbutt.' Makepeace held out the letter Dapifer had written to say that she was in his confidence. 'The Stamp Tax debate's coming up.' Dapifer had gone to Bath to remind Mr Pitt, once more struck down with gout, of his promise to speak for the repeal in the House of Commons.

'These colonials,' Mr Hackbutt said, resignedly, then remembered. 'But of course, Lady Dapifer, you yourself are from the colonies.' He bowed to one of Mme Angloss's most attractive walking dresses, 'One would never guess, if I may say so. How may I help you?'

She hoped he was a better lawyer than he was a diplomat. 'This case my husband's first wife's bringing against us. We're going to fight.'

'Sir Pip's not settling then? Splendid, splendid.'

'How much damage can she do?'

'She will be a difficult bird to bring down.' Mr Hackbutt aimed an imaginary gun. 'I will not hide from you, Lady Dapifer, that from the first I advised Sir Pip against seeking an American divorce as treading unknown territory in more ways than one. He did not take that advice and we are now presented with a situation that is unusual, not to say unique.'

He settled himself in a chair and crossed his legs. 'As you know, in Massachusetts, even in Scotland, to obtain a divorce, is considerably easier . . .'

'And cheaper?' asked Makepeace.

'Cheaper, of course,' said Mr Hackbutt. His tone suggested that so were war-paint and woad, 'Since in England divorce can only be procured by an Act of Parliament, it is confined to . . .'

'The rich?'

'Let us say, those to whom it matters. The lower orders have more lax ways of solving their marital difficulties.'

Divorce by Act of Parliament was a long process, Mr Hackbutt said. It had to begin with a successful civil action for 'criminal conversation' against the accomplice in adultery. 'But that, Lady Dapifer, can only be brought by the husband, not the wife. The husband can sue his wife's lover because, as you know, in legal terms a wife is the property of her husband. A wife has no property in her husband and therefore she has no grounds for suing any woman with whom he has sexual intercourse.'

'But she's suing us.'

'Ah.' Mr Hackbutt rubbed his hands, as if presented with a particularly good pork pie. 'She is suing not simply for adultery but *aggravated* adultery, a course open to you ladies. That is, adultery aggravated by some circumstance such as bigamy, incest or, forgive the word, Lady Dapifer, sodomy.'

'It ain't bigamy,' said Makepeace wearily. 'Sir Pip divorced her. We're married.'

'Therein lies our defence to her action. But we are on untrodden ground, Lady Dapifer. Will an English court recognize a divorce decreed in Massachusetts and therefore a subsequent marriage?'

'Will it?'

'Impossible to say. The case may very well have to go to the House of Lords for a decision. We'll be making legal history, Lady Dapifer.'

It was a *marvellous* pork pie.

'Expensive legal history?'

'It won't be cheap, it won't be cheap. However, we hope, not as costly as the settlement the first Lady Dapifer is demanding as her price in order not to proceed with the matter. It is of considerable importance to you because in the event of Sir Philip's death . . .' He saw her flinch and went on more gently: 'In the *unlikely* event of Sir Philip's early death, his estates pass to his wife or, of course, a subsequent legitimate child. They are not entailed, he has no near male relatives and on his first marriage, he made the first Lady Dapifer his heir. He has since changed his will, leaving everything to you and any children you may have instead.'

Makepeace shook her head; she couldn't cope with that. 'I don't want to think about it.'

'Let us hope you don't have to.' Mr Hackbutt stopped and became shifty, as if the words were being forced from him. 'There's another cost, of course.'

'The scandal rags,' said Makepeace, flatly.

'Are you prepared? In human terms the price may be high.'

Suddenly she liked him. 'Not as high as paying blackmail.'

'You're sure?'

She grinned and stood up. 'I'm an American, Mr Hackbutt, I ain't prepared to be taxed.'

He helped her on with her cloak. 'If Parliament had met you, Lady Dapifer, it wouldn't even have tried.' As she and Fanny and Tom crossed the grass of Lincoln's Inn Fields, Mr Hackbutt leaned out of his window and waved them on. 'Tally-ho!'

'What's that about?' Fanny asked.

'He's scented fees,' said Makepeace. 'Nice man, though. For a lawyer.'

But the cost of fighting Catty had already gone up.

They were wandering back home through Clare Market. Fanny was speculating on the late and celebrated actress, Mrs Bracegirdle, who'd frequented the area. 'She might have been my grandma. Could have—' She stopped in mid sentence to point to a newspaper on a stationer's stall. 'That bloody *Picknicks*'s at it again.'

Makepeace snatched up a copy. There she was, front page, a travesty of herself, tomahawk aloft, chasing caricatures of Rockingham and Dapifer, their names written across their back, both of them with rabbit's ears, into the House of Commons. The balloon issuing from her mouth read: 'Repeal the Stamp Tax!' Underneath was a caption: 'The American Wife.'

She grabbed the stallholder by the throat. 'Who prints this shite? Who *prints* it?'

'Don't think he'll say, missus,' Fanny said, happily, 'you're throttlin' him.'

Makepeace still had a rower's hands. She let the man go; he was a boy, anyway, no more than fifteen. 'Who publishes this?'

'Not me,' he said, rubbing his neck. 'I jus' stand in for Mr Grout when he's sick.'

'Tell Mr Grout he's going to be sicker,' Makepeace promised.

'Here,' the boy shouted after her, 'what'm I going to do with this lot?' Makepeace, in leaving, had swept all his papers to instant ruin on the mud-splattered, well-manured market cobbles.

'Wipe your arse with 'em,' was Fanny's Parthian shot. She caught up and proffered a handkerchief for the tears of fury spurting from Makepeace's eyes. 'That's where they'll be tomorrow,' she said, consolingly, 'hangin' from a hook in everyone's shit-house.'

In the meantime, half the House of Commons would have read them. Catty was ensuring she'd get her price from Dapifer by making Rockingham pay it too.

'Where's Great Russell Street?'

'Bloomsbury.' Fanny looked startled. 'Here, you're never goin' to—'

'Oh yes, I am. Where's Tom?'

'Arguin' with the beadle.'

'Tell him to find me a cab. We're going right away.'

'Oh, missus.' Fanny was torn between alarm and admiration. 'She won't be up. She never got out of bed afore midday.'

'She will today.'

Face-to-face confrontation was what Makepeace understood, not these far-ranging attacks designed less to hurt her than others. If there was to be a battle, she had to be clear on the rules of engagement—and so must Catty. But before it came to that, before she declared war, her religion and her own conscience made it necessary to make a last try for peace.

It was a short journey. The village of Bloomsbury lay to the north of town, separated from Holborn by farms and open land, crossed by milkmaids and other early risers; some boys were flying a kite in the gusty March breeze; a man was making a sketch of the countryside from a perch in a churchyard.

Great Russell Street came up suddenly, a wide road bounded by tall, handsome houses with steps up to a portico. A maid polishing a brass knocker pointed out the house belonging to Lady Dapifer. Its curtains were drawn.

Makepeace told Fanny and Tom to wait in the cab.

The footman who opened the door to her was puzzled. 'Did you say Lady *Dapifer*, madam?'

'Lady Dapifer,' said Makepeace firmly.

She was helped out of her cloak and shown into a hallway with medallions picked out in white on its ochre walls, to be seated on an uncomfortable gilded chair. She had expected the footman to have to fetch Catty from upstairs but instead he opened the double doors of a room leading off the hallway, exposing candlelight and letting out stale air. She heard her title announced. There was silence, an outbreak of incredulous questioning, then a loud shout of laughter.

Oh Lord, she's got company. What's she got company for this hour of the morning?

Then it struck her: Catty hadn't gone to bed. Some gathering had extended through the night and was still in progress. If Makepeace had needed confirmation of her enemy's depravity, she had it now. Decent people did not carouse into the next day.

'This way, please, madam.'

She sat where she was for a moment, daunted. This wasn't going to be the tête-à-tête she had envisaged. Then she thought: 'I have put my trust in God and will not fear what flesh can do unto me.' It was too long since she'd turned to the psalms; she was calmer now that she had.

She stood in the doorway while twenty or so beautifully dressed people looked at her with amused hostility. Some of them had been sleeping in chairs and had only just woken up. One man had made himself a bed on the floor, his head pillowed on a cushion. A few of the women were adjusting their clothing, one deliberately tittered behind her fan. A group of men with salacious eyes commented to each other out of the corner of their mouths.

Shaded candles cast downward light on a large table in the centre of the room and smaller ones round its sides; cards lay everywhere alongside scraps of paper and piled coins.

They'd been having breakfast as they played—or perhaps it was the remains of last night's supper. A chicken carcase lay on a Chinese rug; some biscuits spilled caviare onto a cloth; decanters, bottles and glasses were everywhere. Heat from a banked coal fire heightened the smell of wine, pomade, tobacco smoke and sweat-stained satin.

'But how nice.' Catty Dapifer came forward, arms held out. 'How nice of you to come uninvited. I am *delighted* to see you. Ladies, gentlemen, may I present my husband's Red Indian, Make

Peace? Make Peace, my dear, this is the Countess of . . . No, no, *so* unfair to belabour you with titles; we mustn't make you feel outclassed, we'll take the introductions as said.'

She belonged on her own mantelshelf, a Meissen figurine, rigid hoops at her hips exaggerating the little waist, porcelain skin interrupted by dark blue eyes, the rose of the mouth and two small, brown half-moons where the aureola of her nipples just showed above a stiff, pearled bodice. Her guests might be jaded, but their hostess was wide awake, with a febrility that belonged to audiences in places where animals were killed for entertainment.

'Can we talk alone?' Makepeace said, keeping her voice down. 'I've come to make peace.' The phrase sounded dull; Catty had preempted it.

'Oh, she *has*.' Even the shout was pretty, it rang out in arpeggios. 'My dears, there's actually to be a pow-wow. Christopher darling, your pipe. We do need a peace pipe, don't we? Do we smoke one each, Make Peace? Or do we pass one back and forth between us?'

She snatched an ostrich fan from one of the women, pulled out a feather and stuck it in her hair. Then she sat down on the floor, her hoops rising to the level of her elbows like the arms of a chair, her feet in their little gold slippers sticking out in front of her.

One of the men gave her his pipe. Another, bowing, offered his to Makepeace, then took it away when she didn't move.

Outside this heavy, candlelit room there was fresh air; she wanted to run back to it. *I don't know what to do*. The animosity around her was more than an effort to make her feel foolish; it was almost physical, like being stoned with jeers. She had to force herself not to cower. She *was* outclassed.

Another man moved forward from the circle that had formed about them, put his arms under the first Lady Dapifer's armpits and lifted her up. 'Now, now, Catty.'

She struggled. 'Put me down, Sidney. I want to play.'

'I know, me dear. But it's got to be *fair* play.' Still in a sitting position, Catty Dapifer was carried to a sofa and set on it. The man turned to Makepeace, took her gently by the arm and led her to the other end of the sofa. She sat down. He bowed to her. 'Major Sidney Conyers, ma'am. First Regiment of Foot Guards.'

He wasn't in uniform and at the time the name was merely sound. Much later, when figures other than Catty's solidified in her memory of that ante-chamber to Hell, Makepeace was able to recall who he was and be surprised at how un-villainous he appeared. She'd thought of Catty Dapifer's lover as sensual-lipped and dark, like the portrait of Charles II, not this still-boyish, pleasant-faced man.

But, thinking back, she knew two more things about him with absolute assurance: that his courtesy to her was automatic, the skin-deep veneer of breeding and public school, and that even while he could estimate Catty Dapifer's faults to the uttermost farthing, he was helpless, enslaved to her body and soul. He showed solicitude for the woman his paramour was tormenting but if Catty had stabbed Makepeace there and then, he would have wiped the knife and hidden the body without pause for thought.

As it was, he took the pipe from Catty's hand and shooed the other people away to the far end of the room so that the two women could talk in comparative privacy.

The feather had curled over to hang above Catty's nose; what would have looked ridiculous in anyone else gave her the appearance of a child. She protruded her lower lip to blow the feather upwards. 'Well?'

Makepeace had prepared a speech in the cab; now she couldn't remember a word. What had she been going to say? Something about their situation being foolish.

'Our situation's silly,' she said. 'I wanted you to know. You've had a settlement, and there'll be no more. You fight, I'll fight. We fight each other, we'll hurt each other. The lawyers . . .' That was it. 'The lawyers'll be the only ones to profit.'

The sentences were lumpen, not the graceful phrases she'd rehearsed in her impatience to get here.

Catty blew at her feather again and turned to her audience. 'It seems the situation's silly,' she reported. 'She's worried about the expense.'

'Don't do it,' Makepeace pleaded. 'There's no money in it, I swear. Let him be. He's been hurt enough. Let's all of us live in peace, I'm asking you.'

Catty told the room: 'Apparently I've hurt my husband enough. What a saintly savage it is—for a bigamist.'

She leaned forward so that the feather tickled Makepeace's forehead; her hair smelled of bluebells, her breath of alcohol. She whispered: 'Hurt him? I haven't even begun.'

'Why d'you hate him?'

'I'm going to destroy him.' The pupils of her eyes were enormous, a night-hunting creature's. 'And you, my dear. *And* you.'

The gloves came off. 'We don't destroy easy,' Makepeace whispered back, 'we love each other.' And was appalled to suspect that this was the reason she'd come: to say this. There'd never been a prospect of peace.

'You fucking bitch,' hissed Catty.

The venom puffing from the woman's lips into Makepeace's nostrils was infectious. It was irresistible luxury to spit back: 'And I'm carrying his son.'

If she could have recalled the words, in that minute she would have. The little face close to hers withered. The effect was dreadful, like watching a healthy apple shrivel within seconds. 'Oh, don't,' Makepeace said; she'd not intended this. 'Don't.'

The man Conyers was beside them. 'Time for bye-byes, me dear.' He assisted Makepeace to her feet and hustled her into the hallway.

The footman opened the front door, letting in the damp, refreshing breeze.

Conyers said: 'Have you a conveyance?'

She looked around and pointed. The cab had moved to the end of the street so that its horse could drink from a trough.

Fanny was beside it, dabbling her hand in the water, talking to Tom and the driver. When Conyers hailed them the cabman led his horse around to bring it to the house, Fanny and Tom following.

Conyers went sideways down the steps, one hand held towards Makepeace to assist her to the level of the street.

She heard him shout, 'No!'

A push against her back tumbled her down the steps.

As she lay in the mud, face-up, she saw Catty Dapifer standing in the doorway, hands still outstretched, shaking. Then Conyers bent over her and his face blocked her view.

He was all anxiety. 'Are you hurt? Damn steps are lethal. Slipped on 'em meself only yesterday. Nasty accident, that. Say you're not hurt, I pray you.' But the worry in his eyes, she could tell, was not for her.

For a moment Makepeace lay where she'd fallen, concentrating on an internal examination of baby Procrustes. He seemed to have survived; there was no pain there, only her wrist hurt where she'd tried to grab the steps' rail, and an ankle was stinging. Yes, she felt sick, but that was not from the fall, heavy though it had been.

She tried to kill the baby.

Fanny and the footman were running towards her. Conyers was helping her up, talking, offering brandy, to take her to a doctor, to escort her home, but all the time determinedly pushing her towards the cab to get her away.

Makepeace kept inclining her head to see round him to the figure in the doorway, still incredulous. *She tried to kill the baby. Not me, it was the baby. She tried to kill my baby.* The words repeated in her head, so abominable that they took away her capacity to utter them. She could only gawp with shock.

'What happened, missus?' Fanny and Tom were beside her, quivering with concern, listening to Conyers's explanation of 'accident, accident', looking towards where Makepeace was pointing. But the doorway was empty.

'Didn't you see?'

'What, missus? Let's get you home.'

The blank face of the cab-driver indicated that he, too, had seen nothing of her fall.

She was in the cab, Conyers settling her cloak so that it didn't impede shutting the door. Their eyes met, his pleading, hers astounded.

'She *pushed* me,' Makepeace said.

'Very shaken,' he said, nodding to Fanny like a doctor to a presiding nurse, 'but she seems to have taken no harm. I'll have the steps seen to. Take her home quickly.'

As she was borne away, Makepeace leaned out of the window to look back. Conyers didn't wait to see her out of sight but ran up the steps into the house to the woman who concerned him more.

Shock kept Makepeace silent on the way home; the fall had been frightening in itself but a deal more frightening was the re-alization that nobody would believe her if she tried to tell them that a lady of quality had just attempted murder.

When she confessed, on Dapifer's return to Grosvenor Square, to what she'd done, he could barely talk to her for rage. 'I see,' he said, 'another wife I can't control,' and left her sitting miserably in the drawing room nursing her sprained wrist.

She heard him leave the house. Tom came in to tell her that Sir Pip had gone to his club; she was not to wait up.

She could hardly blame him; in view of what had happened her venture seemed ludicrous, and she was forced to re-examine her own motives for making it at all. What she'd impulsively thought of at the time as an attempt to protect him, present Catty with good New England common-sense and stop her press campaign, now revealed itself to be a jumble of unworthy motives that had nearly brought Baby Procrustes to disaster.

She jumped as the doors slammed open and her husband reap-peared. 'The bloody club can wait,' he said, 'I'm going to tell you what you're fit for.' He looked ill but not as white as he had when she'd first told him.

His list of her sins, which he enumerated as he strode the room, coincided very nearly with her own. She was an arrogant, head-strong Yankee, a whited sepulchre of a Puritan, pretending a lofty soul with a Christian mission to take peace and light into darkness when in truth she'd been meddling in matters none of her business and making him look a hag-ridden fool before a vicious and delighted audience. 'I can't wait to see the cartoon they'll make of this.'

'I'm truly sorry,' she said, and meant it.

'You flaunted yourself, didn't you? Trumpeted *our* happiness, *your* fecundity in her face.'

Makepeace felt the edges of her mouth tug into a momentary grin—'I sure did'—before she could compose them again.

'Knowing she has no children? Seems incapable of having any? What did you expect?'

She shouted: 'I didn't expect her to try and kill the baby!'

'And you,' he said, quietly. 'Christ, she could have killed you.'

It was the ultimate reassurance. Makepeace got up and crossed the room to him. Holding him, she felt an almost agonizing contentment.

After a little, he said: 'I should have told you she was insane.'

'Don't talk about her.'

'It's important.'

She saw that it was. He pulled up a chair so that they could sit facing each other and hold hands.

He said: 'You must understand that she can't help it. She needs protection from herself and I couldn't give it. God forgive me, I couldn't stand madness. It was cowardice, Procrustes, not kindness, not *noblesse oblige*; when I went to New England to divorce her, I wasn't sparing her, I was deserting. That day Ffoulkes and I discovered her with Conyers, do you know what I felt? I felt relief; she'd given me an excuse to be rid of her, she was somebody else's responsibility.'

He was leading her into the innermost centre of a mental labyrinth for which she had no clue. She couldn't follow him. She said: 'You *had* to leave her, she's wicked.'

He shook his head. He said: 'You realize, don't you, for all his faults Conyers is the better man?'

'He's a *bad* man. He betrayed you.'

'He loves that afflicted soul, poor devil that he is.'

He was talking to himself, making forays in a land of greys that an irritated Makepeace could only see in black and white.

'She ain't *afflicted*. She slept with your friend, she wants money for doing it and she tried to kill your baby. She's evil.'

Dapifer came back from wherever he'd been. 'I don't believe in evil.'

'Yes, you do.' Makepeace was on home ground. ' "He maketh his sun to rise on the evil and on the good". It's how God set the world up. If there wasn't evil, we couldn't know the good. Simple. Come to bed.'

He wondered if she knew she was paraphrasing Milton. Probably not; it was her creed, the clarity of an uncluttered soul. She knew the good and held to it, *had* held to it, knowing it was to her disadvantage, when she rescued him not only from Boston harbour but from much else. For all her narrow, single-minded Puritanism, she was health, the only health he had.

What would she say if he told her that he didn't believe in God either, but that the nearer he approached death the more he trusted in the personal salvation Makepeace Burke Dapifer continued to offer him?

She'd be shocked, he thought. He took her to bed instead.

Chapter Eleven

GRUB Street was more than an unsavoury lane in an unsavoury area of London; it had become a swear word describing everything cheap and scurrilous in the writing profession.

Originally a hiding place for seventeenth-century dissenters with their printing presses—Oliver Cromwell lived there for a while—over the previous hundred years it had become home to hacks, scandal-sellers, ballad-mongers, poets, political scribblers and dictionary-compilers eking out their existence in the shabby upper rooms rented to them in return for their output by the booksellers who owned the shops below.

It was also a battlefield for the irreverent and dispossessed versus the establishment, its gunfire the clack of printing presses in its basements. Occasionally an outraged government sequestered one of them, only to have its fly-by-night owner establish another somewhere else. Makepeace on her visits became used to seeing one inhabitant or another escaping from a window as magistrates' bailiffs or debt-collectors broke down his door.

As usual, when visiting the ungodly, she went early. Apart from Grub Street itself, the district of Moorfields in north-east London contained nearly every other species of person and activity she most disliked: brothels, soldiers—the Honourable Artillery Company had its headquarters and ranges there—dicing hells and Roman Catholics.

This morning she didn't bother to knock on the decrepit door in one of Grub Street's alleys but, with Fanny, went straight in via the cellar where a sleepy printer's devil was already at work. He nodded to them as they walked through to the winding staircase that climbed past the bookseller's apartment to the first floor. Here they knocked. Last time they'd walked in on Beasley in bed with a woman.

There was no reply today and, when they gave up and went in, no woman either. He was asleep, his bare backside protruding from frowsty bedcovers. Fanny lifted the corner of a blanket between finger and thumb and covered the protrusion before she and Makepeace started clearing up. They never knew why they did this, the place was past tidying, but no female of character could be presented with it and not try.

It was a largish room made claustrophobic by the number of books it contained. They were stacked in untidy piles against the walls, on the floor, on the window bench; they made up the missing leg of a table; they formed a dusty, mouse-nibbled frieze around the bed. Even if Beasley spent all his income on literature, which, to judge from the state of his clothes and person, he did, there was no accounting for the vastness of his library. The flyleaves Makepeace peeked at showed they were *ex libris* other people, probably stolen.

An air of piety was lent to the room by a framed and embroidered text over the bed which, on closer examination, proved to be the 'princes' error from the Printer's Bible: 'Printers have persecuted me without cause.' Some cupped wallflowers fought a losing battle with the overpowering fug of ageing paper and a full chamber pot.

Once they'd pushed open the window from its worm-eaten frame, picked up and folded the clothes on the floor and cleared quills, paper and ink pots from the table, Makepeace set out some fresh bread and cheese and a can of steaming coffee she'd bought in Clare Market.

'Breakfast,' she said. 'Get up.'

The bed swore. An eye opened; a hand gestured towards Fanny: 'Want to fuck?'

'With *you*? When pigs fly.' She held out a shirt she'd laundered, the only fresh thing in the room apart from herself and Makepeace.

They averted their eyes as he squirmed, grumbling, out of bed, put on the shirt and struggled into a pair of breeches that Makepeace proffered sideways on a pair of tongs. Slurping coffee through a mouthful of bread and cheese, he managed to spill some on his clean shirt.

Makepeace shook her head in wonderment at herself. Here was her ally, her *chosen* ally, in the fight against Catty.

After her disastrous foray to Bloomsbury, there had been no let-up in the ammunition Catty had supplied for *Picknicks* to fire at her; indeed, the articles and cartoons had increased.

It has come to our ears that the female claiming to be the second wife of Sir Philip Dapifer was recently to be seen in Bloomsbury pleading with her predecessor not to pursue the case which cites her supposed marriage to Sir Philip as bigamous. Money was mentioned but the lady was ejected by Lady Dapifer's indignant footman.

The paragraph was accompanied by a drawing showing Catty as Britannia, with 'Lady Dapifer' inscribed on her sash, standing on a plinth and brandishing her trident at a female figure crawling at its base. The caption read: 'Begone, Bigamist!'

Dapifer had refused to look at the piece when she tried to show it to him. Nor would he contemplate libel proceedings against the paper, saying it would be a descent into mud which would, in any case, merely smear it over a wider area.

But if he chose to ignore it, Makepeace knew others did not. Susan told her that *Picknicks* was being handed around in the salons which she and Mme Angloss visited and was read with frowning disapproval by Rockingham Whigs and with glee by his opponents.

She became frightened by how vulnerable her husband's decency made him. He was the real target of the filth Catty was throwing and it was damaging not only his position in society but his health. She'd had to summon Dr Baines to him one evening when he'd come back short of breath after a difficult political meeting. Baines said it was exhaustion and recommended rest although, with the imminence of the Stamp Tax debate, there could be none.

Something had to be done. Appealing to Catty had been a mistake; there was no treaty to be made with that enemy. On the other hand, to receive broadside after broadside from her guns would sink them. Makepeace had lived nearer to the earth of humanity than her husband. Yes, they could fight Catty through the courts, but by that time they would already be defeated; there wouldn't be a judge in England whose mind wouldn't already have been contaminated against them.

Something had to be *done*.

She'd unearthed the dog-eared card the man called John Beasley had given her in Hyde Park and sought him out. At first it was with the idea of finding the publisher of the tormenting *Picknicks* and either cajoling, threatening or bribing him into silence. Which, as Beasley said when she found him, showed how little she knew about the press. 'If there's someone as'll read it, there's someone as'll print it.'

'It's not you?' He had, after all, been responsible for the first cartoon, the one which had shown her and Catty fighting in Grosvenor Square.

'Nyah. That was against both of you bloody nobs. This'—he flicked the copy of *Picknicks* with a dirty fingernail—'is one-sided. *This* is a campaign.'

'Who is it, then?'

He shrugged. 'Don't know. Don't matter. I tell you, if there's someone as'll read it . . .' Papers like *Picknicks* flourished and withered. *The Passenger*, his own attempt at publishing, had failed, but that, he said, was because 'bigwigs' had considered it too liberal and outspoken and had conspired against it. He saw conspiracy in everything.

Disappointed, she'd been preparing to leave when he said, with meaning: 'Shit sticks if you don't fling it back.'

Her own sentiments exactly.

She and Beasley went into partnership. She saw no reason to tell Dapifer about it, though it made her uneasy that she acted behind his back. But if his sense of honour prevented him retaliating against Catty's guns, Makepeace's did not.

John Beasley was everything that should disgust her: he was gauche to the point of barbarism, opinionated, morbid, rabidly anti-religious; if you named it he was against it, yet she . . . *liked* wasn't the right word . . . felt friendship for him.

It was peculiar; when he wasn't outraging every Puritan principle she still held and exasperating her beyond bearing, she could confide in him as to nobody else and . . . this was the thing . . . know he would keep the confidence. He was fanatically loyal to the few, very few, people whom he admired, and on that day in Hyde Park the previous autumn she had won not only his gratitude by saving him from the pursuing bailiffs but his admiration, partly by her ability to swear and partly as an American, a nation he identified with because the government bullied it.

His first nervous question when he'd answered her knock had been: 'Where's the one in the Park, where's Madam Midnight?'

'In Hertfordshire.'

That he was frightened of Betty was somehow endearing. And he didn't like Catty Dapifer, neither her adultery—though despising the institution of marriage, he was censorious of those who betrayed it—nor her habit of aiming her carriage at pedestrians in the park. 'Nearly winged me once, arrogant bitch.'

'How'd you know who she was?' Makepeace had asked.

'Bigwigs ain't got a monopoly on who's who. Nor gossip neither.' He knew everything, or pretended to, and sulked if he was caught out in an error.

He picked up and sold his information in the political and literary coffee clubs. Makepeace imagined him sitting, glowering, in a corner, but discovered that this was not so; somehow he'd inveigled himself into the world of the arts and boasted of his conversations with 'Sam Johnson' or 'Davey Garrick' or 'Josh Reynolds' or 'Ollie Goldsmith' or 'Charlie Fox'.

Makepeace had to take his word for it that they were influential men. They sounded raffish to her; the eccentric Beasley would suit their company.

'This Josh . . .' she said wistfully.

'Reynolds.'

'Painter, you said. D'you think he'd teach *my* Josh?'

'Don't see why not.'

That was the lovely thing about John Beasley, he had no concept of limitation. He invested in hopeless causes, tilted at impossible windmills, saw insult everywhere, not only to himself but to others—big white Joshua would be reviled if he did not help black little Joshua.

But his ranting could be tiresome; he was permanently angry, with God, with Man and especially with Barnabas Fulke—'Fulke the Fucker'—who was his printer and his landlord and who exploited him.

'You can't hate everybody,' she said.

'Yes, I can.'

Unsuspected in so loutish a young man was the delicacy with which he began conducting Makepeace's campaign, selling titbits of information to the more respectable organs that gazetted the comings and goings of Society or cooed gentle gossip about the fashionable into a thousand boudoirs.

London Magazine: *Sir Philip Dapifer and his New England bride are frequently to be seen in the company of the Marquis of Rockingham. Lady Dapifer is a Bostonian and therefore particularly fitted to give her opinion and advice to his lordship on the American question.*

'Lord's sake, don't put that in. It was a private conversation.'

'Well, *I* knew about it.'

The Ladies' Diary: *It is forecast that the articulated hoop may have had its day; we happen to know that Mme Angloss, that most exclusive adviser to the* ton, *is dressing Lady Dapifer, wife to Sir Philip, more nearly to her natural and excellent figure.*

Gradually, gently, Makepeace's image was rehabilitated from that of bigamous, low-class trollop to dignified second wife, the pure bosom on which Sir Philip Dapifer had lain his wronged head.

His vilification of Catty was less gentle. He showed her today's piece.

The Coach Commissioners would do well to look to what use is made of their conveyances before licensing hackney coaches; we have heard of a liaison which took place in one such last Sunday between the Hon. Percy Cavendish and the former Lady Dapifer, divorced wife of Sir Philip, when the blinds were down. No doubt the undulating motion of the vehicle, with pretty little occasional jolts, contributed greatly to enhance the pleasure of the critical moment . . .

Makepeace was horrified. 'You can't print this.'

'Why not? Nice little gobbet—*bon ton*'ll love it. And it's true— the driver peeked. It's a topic of conversation among the *cognoscenti* already. Don't look so mimsy; she'd have told the town crier if you'd done it.'

The thing was, Makepeace had—she and Dapifer, one rainy Sunday, on their way to Eton to see young Ffoulkes. Beasley was right about the undulating motion of a coach.

But we're married, she thought. Catty isn't even faithful to poor Conyers.

She felt her womb churn as if Baby Procrustes had flinched and she fell into a panic of disgust with herself, with Beasley, with a trade that paraded people's frailty for the delectation of others. What sort of air was she feeding to the child in her womb? How had she become enmeshed in the grubby toils of this trade?

He was watching her; he had an almost feminine ability to pick up what she was feeling—and a masculine inclination to jeer at it. 'Ain't got the stomach for this?'

'No.'

'I found out something else yesterday. Want to know who's feeding the poison to *Picknicks*?'

She was all attention. 'Yes.'

'Only Major Sidney Conyers, First Fucking Regiment of Foot Guards.'

She said dully: 'He was nice to me.'

'He was nice to Sir Pigwig an' all, weren't he?' Beasley always sneered when he talked of Dapifer, as he did when he mentioned any member of the establishment. 'All my-dear-schoolchum-and-I'll-fuck-your-wife, wasn't he? He's a precious viper, that one, gambles like a lord but his pockets is marked To Let. I wouldn't go anywhere lonely with him after dark. He wants a colonelcy, he'd like to buy his regiment—Jesus, what sort of army is it that promotes officers with no experience of battle just because they're rich . . .'

Makepeace had listened to Beasley's strictures on the British Army's purchase system before. 'You sure it's him behind *Picknicks*?'

'I tell you, he's a black-hearted bastard. His men fawn on him because he lets 'em loot. There's more than one highwayman carries a percentage of his takings back to Major Robbing Conyers and calls him "sir".'

'You're making it up,' Makepeace said. Conyers's class might sleep with other men's wives but it didn't go in for criminality.

'Am I? When are you going to learn about bigwigs? They're fucking your home country and you think they're nice? They're all robbers. Conyers ain't doing it on a big enough scale yet, but he will. Look at the enclosures. If Fanny here, or me, stole a sheep we'd be swinging in chains. The bigwigs steal a thousand acres and call it an act of fucking Parliament.'

He interpreted her wince of guilt as disbelief. 'I tell you, he's your rat. I tracked down *Picknicks*'s proprietor, fellow called Grout, and got him drunk—that's a guinea you owe me, incidentally—and he told me.'

She paid him his guineas. She was scrupulous not to lay out housekeeping money on Beasley's expenses, but instead used cash from the hundred guineas Dapifer had given her for saving his life. She regarded that as her own.

Beasley had become sullen. As she got up to go, he said: 'And if you want nice little pieces in the paper about your doings, you'll have to *do* something. What d'you want me to write? The Duchess of Dunghill's ball was graced by the absence of the lovely Lady Dapifer? You don't *go* anywhere.'

'Don't know why we bother with that little noserag,' Fanny said as they went home.

'I don't either.' She did really; her visits to Beasley were as much to ensure he stayed out of prison and had enough to eat as they were concerned with her campaign. She noticed that Fanny, even while he aggravated her, tended to mother the young man; anyone so inept at survival commanded an infuriated solicitude.

Yet this morning's visit had been unsettling; she'd known Conyers for a bad man but for such viciousness to underlie so pleasant an exterior was as if Nature itself had allied with him in trickery. But Beasley was rarely mistaken; his cobweb to catch information spread from coffee houses to the criminal rookeries, taking in servants' gossip on the way.

And the little noserag was right about something else—she *didn't* go anywhere. Unwilling to face a scornful London society, doubly so since *Picknicks*'s calumnies, she preferred to shelter in company with which she felt confident.

Blast, she thought, I've got to become one of the damn *ton*.

No need to blacken Catty's reputation—Catty could do that for herself—if she could enhance her own.

London Gazette: *Sir Philip and Lady Dapifer yesterday accompanied Lord Ffoulkes to the Royal Naval Hospital at Greenwich for the unveiling of a plaque to the young lord's late father, a patron of the hospital. Lt. Governor Boys was in attendance at the ceremony. Afterwards Sir Philip, who is Lord Ffoulkes's guardian, and Lady Dapifer, an accomplished oarswoman, took their charge rowing on the river.*

Pensioners lining the terrace of the hospital bared their heads and saluted as they rowed downriver.

Once they were out of sight, Dapifer took off his hat and held Andrew's for him as the child dropped the wreath onto the surface and stood watching until it passed out of sight beyond the river's bend. Then they rowed back, returned to the carriage and, with Tantaquidgeon standing on its backboard, took the road for Eton.

Holding Makepeace's hand, the boy was silent for most of the journey. She knew he was grateful to have said a personal goodbye to his father but, inevitably, he was suffering.

As they approached Windsor through a spring-scented dusk, he asked if their goodbyes could be made in the carriage. 'May Tantaquidgeon take me in?'

Dapifer said: 'It was nice of Lieutenant-Governor Boys to attend. Andrew, did your father ever tell you about him?'

'No.'

'It was when he was a youngster. He and seven others survived the sinking of the *Luxborough Galley* on a passage home from the West Indies by eating the bodies of their shipmates.'

'Pip!' Makepeace remonstrated.

'Oh, *joy*,' Andrew said, 'a Red Indian and a cannibal all in one day. *Won't* the fellows be green?'

Sitting in the carriage, they watched him go through the school's arch, his legs trying to stretch to the pace of the tall Huron stalking beside him.

'Thought he needed cheering up,' Dapifer said, smugly.

'I guess I'll never understand men.' She pressed her hip suggestively against his. 'Shame we ain't in a coach.'

London Evening Post: *Among those in the Strangers' Gallery for the House of Commons debate on the Stamp Tax were Sir Philip and Lady Dapifer . . .*

Ladies' Diary: *We glimpsed Lady Dapifer among the crowd in the Strangers' Gallery and attribute much sense to her for not indulging the current fashion for high heads which would otherwise have obscured the view of those behind her . . .*

The carriage took them back through the night from Westminster to Grosvenor Square with Susan, exhilarated by the debate, shouting: 'We won! We won! We won!' over a clamour of church bells ringing out the news that the Stamp Act was repealed, rioting Americans would now return to being loyal citizens, merchants were once more in business . . .

Makepeace was pleased, though less excited than Susan; the repeal was not only a triumph for liberty and the America of Sam Adams, it was also victory for the men who had tarred and feathered Aaron. Aaron himself had refused to come to the House of Commons at all. Nevertheless . . .

She turned to Dapifer and mouthed: 'Well done, my boy.'

He shook his head, whether in modesty or because conversation was impossible. He'd been busy lobbying for two days, not even returning home the previous night, and in the light of the flares his skin looked deathly.

In anticipation, she'd ordered Mrs Francanelli to prepare a celebratory dinner. Once they'd sat down, she lifted her glass to her husband. 'To Liberty and all them as sail in her.'

'To Auntie's windows.' Susan lifted hers. 'As won't get broken any more.'

Dapifer didn't respond. 'I don't think so,' he said.

'We *won*,' Susan said. 'Mr Pitt was fireworks—I didn't understand a word he said, but it had me cheering.' Looking back on Boston from the other side of the Atlantic had changed her political perspective, or perhaps her original Toryism had been altered by attendance on too many English ladies of fashion.

Dapifer said: 'What you heard tonight was the repeal of the Stamp Act. What you didn't hear was the reading of the Declaratory Bill yesterday.'

'Bad?' asked Makepeace, watching him.

'Bad.' He leaned back in his chair, closed his eyes and chanted, like a schoolchild repeating a primer:

' ". . . the King's majesty, lords and commons etc, to have full power and authority to make laws and statutes of sufficient force and validity to bind the colonies and people of America subjects of the crown of Great Britain in all cases whatsoever." '

He opened his eyes on the silent room. 'Yes, I know. As a

matter of fact, only two weeks ago the French King made a similar assertion of his rights to his own troublemakers. Oh God.' He closed his eyes again. 'I've lived to see us keep step with bloody Louis XV.'

The footman was serving *foie gras* but for a moment, for Makepeace, the redolence was cut through by a smell of tar and rope and open seas. It seemed to her that they came crowding into the room so that the marble eyes of the statuary in its niches stared sightlessly into other eyes creased around from searching long horizons: Americans, men mostly, some women like Susan's auntie, people who sold things, grew things, made things, sailed ships. Grown-up men and women, their mouths open, shouting, shouting: ' . . . and that shout will be heard from end to the distant end of this Continent and across the oceans.'

She realized Dapifer, shockingly, was apologizing to her, to them. 'Rockingham couldn't have pushed through the repeal otherwise. The oligarchs had to save face. No, more than save face, save *themselves*. Allow the colonies to have a say in what laws are passed and our own people at home will start shouting: "No Taxation Without Representation." Wilkes already is.'

Sam Adams knew, she thought. There'll be no liberty unless there's war first.

London Magazine: *Lord Rockingham's musical evening to celebrate the birth of the late Mr George Handel commanded a large audience among whom their Graces of Grafton and Portland, Sir Philip and Lady Dapifer, Mr and Mrs Dowdeswell . . .*

In the early days of their marriage, Dapifer had arranged for Charles Burney, a doctor of music and a friend of his, to try and bridge what he called 'the chasm between my wife and the great composers'. It hadn't worked. Makepeace was tone deaf. Burney'd confessed to Dapifer: 'I'd do better shovelling snow. Of the two your wife would prefer the mooing of a cow to Monteverdi—that's if she could tell the difference.'

Tonight she sat in clanging boredom, making laundry lists,

counting the chandeliers, watching a tiny spider weave a web on the padding in the towering hair of the Duchess of Portland in front of her and wondering if the clocks had stopped.

If this were a dance it would be different: she enjoyed dancing— a ball was one of the few Society entertainments she *did* enjoy. She could keep to a rhythm even if she couldn't hold a tune, and under the tuition of M. Herriot, her Huguenot dancing master, was learning to cut an acceptable figure on the various ballroom floors.

Thanks to the example of the Marquis of Rockingham, who made sure that the Dapifers were included among the guests at any event of which he was the host, invitations were now being sent to the house in Grosvenor Square. It couldn't be said that the nobility clasped Makepeace to its bosom, however. Catty might be scandalous but she had breeding, she was still *Us*. Makepeace wasn't even English *Them*. The more rigid Whigs, especially the women, looked askance at Rockingham for shepherding this redheaded American into their society. (Reference was always made to her hair, as if it were an affront, a revolutionary flag, though there were other heads among the nobility nearly as flagrant.) Typical of Rockingham, where would his mania for reform take him next? However, he *was* Prime Minister and, after all, Sir Philip's family *had* come over with the Conqueror, so one supposed one had to bow to the inevitable . . . Gradually, very gradually, Makepeace was being absorbed into the fashionable world as other shameful oddities, like actresses who had married well, had been absorbed before her.

Something marvellous was happening; the noise was over, people were clapping. The Duchess of Portland turned round: 'My dears, was not that sublime? Is not the players' execution perfect?'

'Would be,' muttered Makepeace, 'if it hadn't stopped short of hanging the swine. Is that the end?'

'No. This is an interval.'

'Oh, *Lord*.'

The Old Maid: *A little bird has chirruped in our ear that Lady Dapifer is to be in the audience at Goodman's Fields tomorrow night to watch her brother make his acting debut.*

This was better than the opera. Less exalted, more shameful—holy *Hokey*, what would her mother have said?—but jolly. She stopped laughing long enough to gasp: 'I didn't know King Lear had funny dogs.'

'I don't think Shakespeare did either,' Dapifer said grimly.

For this, his first performance, Aaron was playing a knight attendant on Cordelia. He had five lines in Act I, Scene IV. It may not have helped that Makepeace clapped his entrance, a solitary firecracker of sound echoing round the crowded, rickety auditorium before Dapifer could grab her hands, but it's doubtful if he heard her. His eyes fixed on the audience like a sheep's on the knife and stayed there.

' "Where's my fool, ho?" ' Lear asked him, ' "I think the world's asleep. How now! where's that mongrel?" '

Silence. Aaron stared at the audience, the limelight emphasizing his ghastly pallor. The audience stared back.

' "How now!" ' repeated King Lear, ' "where's that mongrel?" '

There was an audible hiss from the prompt corner: *'He says, my lord, your daughter is not well.'*

Further silence broken by some booing.

'I *expect*,' said King Lear, 'he reports that my daughter is not well. "Why came not the slave back to me, when I called him?" '

'What?' said King Lear, sweating as the booing began. 'Thou whisperest that he would not?'

Eventually, the Earl of Kent got Aaron off by grabbing an arm and dragging him.

After the performance they found him in the green room, still vomiting.

King Lear, who owned the company, reassured an anxious Makepeace that Aaron's career in the theatre was safe. 'No, no, dear lady, I prophesy a successful future for your brother. Stage fright afflicts the best of us. The late lamented Colley Cibber also was unable to speak one line on his first appearance yet did he not end up as Poet Laureate?'

'Did he?' Makepeace was grateful. 'Oh, and I liked the jugglers and I'm glad the play ended so happy. I was feared it wouldn't.'

King Lear bowed. 'Madam, we aim to please.'

*   *   *

Makepeace had neither the art nor the inclination to deliberately mould herself to the set she was now in; it would be useless in any case—she was being accepted on sufferance and she knew it. But, inevitably, contact with its pumice began to smooth her rougher edges so that she fitted it better, almost without her realizing what was happening.

Her coiffure rose as her Puritanism declined. Unconsciously, her accent modified and her grammar improved. On Sundays she no longer attended the small Presbyterian chapel in Farringdon Street but, with Dapifer, joined the rest of the *beau monde* in the Wren splendour of St James's, Piccadilly.

Fewer pennies were given to street beggars; she rarely saw any as she was borne by sedan chair to charitable Society functions, to balls, to soirées, to concerts. She and Dapifer entertained.

On the last occasion that she risked being seen in the area of Grub Street, John Beasley accused her of joining 'the fucking bigwigs'. They quarrelled. Anyway, she now had no need of him; the fashionable press had taken her up—America was news—and gave her publicity that had its own impetus. Her quaint sayings were reported, so was the perfume 'Yankee Flowers' created for her by M. Floret and the emphasis put on her bustle by Mme Angloss.

Such bile as Catty and Conyers introduced to the scandal sheets became stale and was overridden by the more outré doings of the Duchess of Newcastle; in any case, it merely spread Makepeace's name and underlined the fact that she was famous for being famous.

Lady Judd was one of those who bowed to the inevitable. Living next door, it was impossible not to see the quality of the visitors now being ushered into Dapifer House. In any case, the woman had rescued a Judd child in danger of falling from the tree that overhung the Dapifer garden . . . 'Climbed the branches like a monkey, my dear, despite her condition,' Lady Judd told her friends, apologetically. 'Oh yes, an Amazon but a good-hearted Amazon. What can one do? Invitations have been exchanged and accepted. Well, what *can* one do? And Sir Benjamin dotes on her . . .'

Most men did. Her pregnancy was late in becoming apparent but its bloom suited her; she had become beautiful. Those who sat next to her at dinners found her conversation sometimes startling but generally more entertaining than that of the usual run of females. Not exactly *comme il faut*, of course, but perhaps Pip Dapifer hadn't done so badly for himself second time around.

She got on well with Sir Benjamin Judd. He was occasionally pompous but, like herself, an outsider, one of a new breed that the establishment was having to accommodate into its ranks. He'd begun life as a Black Country nailer but, acute enough to realize the possibilities of coke-smelting, had ended up with a vast foundry producing boilers and cylinders. That Makepeace didn't hide the fact she'd been a tavern-keeper delighted him. 'Mowst young ladies look down on trade. But mowst young ladies yowse their heads just to put their hat on,' he said. 'Business, that's what makes this owld world turn. Yow and me, we understand that.'

He put her up for the ladies' section of his club, Almack's, the gaming establishment in St James's.

At first she refused. 'Don't approve of gambling, Sir Ben.'

'Noither do I, Lady Dapifer, noither do I. Not with cards and dice, any old road. But yow don't go for the play, yow go to keep up with the new politics and such. Very forward-looking, Almack's. Bright young woman like yow should know who's who, what's what, where the bodies is buried.'

She wasn't interested in interment, either, but, surprisingly, Dapifer agreed with Sir Benjamin. He was a member of Almack's himself but rarely had the leisure to go. 'You need not play but, since you're embarking on the high life, you may as well join a club and Almack's is a respectable Whig stronghold. Lady Rockingham's a member of the ladies' section, I believe.'

Town and Country Magazine: *Lady Dapifer is the latest recruit of the many-headed hydra that is St James's. She has been elected a member to Almack's, known for its depravity in permitting gaming to both sexes.*

Makepeace was not so far gone in high living that she didn't hear the moan from her mother's grave as she and Dapifer attended their first function together at the club—a reception given by the ladies' section to the gentlemen's. She persuaded herself that for Temperance Burke the term 'gaming club' had conjured up the hells of Cable Lane, not a tasteful suite of rooms hung with good portraits, crystal chandeliers and satin curtaining.

'Gambling,' groaned Temperance. 'They cast dice for the garments of thy Lord at the foot of His cross.'

'I shan't play, Mother.'

'Thy father said the same.'

Almack's was unique among gaming clubs, not only for having a ladies' section in the first place, but in its balloting system; men voted for or against the women who were put up for membership, women for or against the men. It was made obvious fairly quickly to Makepeace that, had each sex voted for its own, she would have been blackballed.

She and Lady Judd were visiting the ladies' 'retiring room', a carpeted chamber with pier-glasses, dressing-tables and discreet, curtained stools of easement. A small group of women were already in there, conversing in tones more generally used to strike terror into foxes in the next county. Makepeace recognized the Duchess of Grafton and the type of the others: elderly Whig autocrats, a fearless breed of Valkyrie who regretted that the fine old custom of drawing and quartering trespassers had fallen into abeyance. She'd encountered them before. Catty supporters.

Twittering, Lady Judd tried to introduce her to the Duchess of Barnet: 'Your grace, I don't think you've met our new member, Lady Dapifer . . .'

She was dismissed by the wave of a fan. 'I do not recognize *usurpers*.'

Makepeace gritted her teeth. For the sake of the sinking Lady Judd she would say nothing.

Lady Rockingham came hurrying out of one of the closets to the rescue. 'They'll be calling supper, ladies.'

Makepeace turned to go but was hailed back by Lady Brandon, another of the coterie. 'You,' she brayed, 'what's-your-name. Dapifer. You might as well know that *I* wouldn't have voted for you. I don't believe in elevating colonials.'

Too much. Makepeace nodded to her over her shoulder. 'I wouldn't have voted for you either. Only way we colonials elevate old witches is by hanging 'em.'

Outside, she apologized to Lady Rockingham and a tottering Lady Judd. 'But they ain't chasing *me* out.'

'My dear, you were glorious,' the Marchioness said. 'Wait 'til I tell Rockingham. They're trying to chase him out too.' The Prime Minister's efforts to conciliate America and other colonies was proving distasteful to the school that believed in parliamentary supremacy over the empire. His administration was crumbling as its ministers resigned; the Duke of Grafton was one of those helping to crumble it.

'I gather blood's been spilt in the ladies' room,' Dapifer said, taking her into supper.

'Where do they get their manners—the hogsty?'

'Just think of them as a lot of blue-blooded Goody Busgutts.'

The thought comforted Makepeace through supper, though Goody Busgutt had never attacked the bottle with quite the frequency and gusto of these old women. Nor would even she have forced a pretty niece's head down onto the table in order to display the fact that her thin hair was reinforced by padding, as Lady Brandon did during the meal. The girl's humiliation was painful to watch.

Makepeace prepared herself for battles ahead—and not just with the old guard. Through the dining-room door she had glimpsed gaming tables for the first time. She had not intended to enter the salon; she would stand aloof, 'I do not play', an American Puritan in the midst of suzerain depravity.

But there was a smell . . . from heated baize table-tops like emerald lawns under the blazing chandeliers, from packs of cards being set out by the footmen, from the leather of dice-boxes. It settled in her nostrils like the scent of clothes belonging to a forgotten but exciting and dangerous lover. She'd never smelled it before but somebody had smelled it for her.

Ancestral addiction. Oh God, she was her father's daughter.

It was impossible to remain in the dining room after supper; the men had reached the port, politics and vulgarity stage; they wanted women gone. She left Dapifer to it and followed Lady Judd into the salon, trying to make her walk casual and less like an iron filing drawn to a magnet. The heavy gamblers had gone in already, putting on leather sleeves to protect the lace of their cuffs, trying to attract the Goddess of Fortune to their side with propitiations. Some of the men were wearing their coats inside out; the Earl of Orme had on a lucky hat adorned with buttercups. Lady Emily Sturt had donned a mask.

'*Wickedness.*'

'Yes, Mother.' And felt the sinful champagne fizz in her veins.

The whist tables Makepeace found uninteresting; the game was unknown to her, depended on skill and, anyway, seemed protracted. It was hazard that drew her, raw gambling. Lady Judd took two minutes to explain it. Makepeace understood within one.

' 'Tis the most bewitching of games with dice,' Lady Judd said. 'Sir Benjamin has forbidden me, for when one begins to play one doesn't know how to leave off.'

It was the biggest table in the room. The air round it vibrated with concentration; there was an intensity and accompanying little noises irresistibly reminiscent of the sexual act. Players whispered the calls of their mains, murmured the laying and taking of odds.

Dapifer was standing next to her. 'I *said*, are you all right?'

'Yes.'

'Grafton and I are going to take a turn round the park for half an hour or so to clear our heads. I'm trying to persuade him not to resign. Do you want to take the carriage and go home?'

'No, I'll wait for you.'

'I've persuaded Lady Brandon not to run you through.'

'Good.'

He turned her face to his. 'You look like Odysseus tied to the mast. Blow me down, Procrustes, *you want to play.*'

She said: 'I don't play.'

When he'd gone, she retied herself to the mast, looking askance through her mother's eyes at the towers of guineas by each player, hearing her father's siren song: *Just once, just once. For that soul-clutching moment when the scales tremble.*

Around midnight, there was a rowdy entrance by a young man bringing with him the scent of night air, alcohol—and Catty Dapifer.

The two of them began circulating the room, noisily greeting friends. The man was unsteady on his feet. Almack's' owner, William Macall, watched them from the door like a man whose house had just been invaded by exuberant untrained puppies worried for his carpet.

The first thing Makepeace had done before agreeing to join the club was to make sure that Catty hadn't. This was planned humiliation. The woman was already dividing the room into two camps: one embarrassed; the other settling down in happy anticipation of the confrontation to come.

Withdraw? Makepeace thought. That's what she wants; send me running. No, by the Lord. I ran from Boston. Here's where I stand.

She kept her eyes on the hazard game, listening to Catty's trills as she moved from table to table, gathering her forces, coming closer.

I wish Pip was here. *No, I don't.*

Makepeace was always to remember that none of those in the room whom she knew came to stand next to her.

She waited.

A charming voice said: 'Oh my goodness, there's my husband's Indian. What *is* it doing here? They told me it stood on the back of his carriage.'

A low Scottish mumble from Macall, who'd come up.

The voice again. 'But I *am* a member, Mr Macall. It said so in the papers, "Lady Dapifer," it said. "Elected to Almack's," it said. How *nice*, I thought. *Such* a surprise.'

Scots mumble.

'Let me get this clear, *dear* Mr Macall. You are permitting squaws to play, but not respectable wives?'

At the word 'respectable' Makepeace turned and looked straight in Catty's eyes.

Catty fluttered her lashes. 'Then I shall circulate. Come with me, Henry.'

The young man said: 'Goin' to try my luck here, Catty.'

'Very well. Now, where *is* that husband of mine?' She moved off, to the applause and embraces of Lady Brandon and the Duchess of Barnet at a nearby whist table.

The boy she'd called Henry was arguing with the club-owner. Macall spoke more clearly; he was on firmer ground now. 'I'm no saying ye're not entitled to play, Mr Headington, I'm saying ye *should* not. I understand ye've already lost too much tonight elsewhere.'

'Got the stake here.' Headington waved a piece of paper to which a ribboned seal was attached. 'Deed of property. Good as guineas any day.'

'Only coin of the realm at Almack's tonight, I fear, Mr Headington.'

'But the lady's relented,' Headington said. 'Lady Fortune's relented, can feel the warmth of her smile.' He began to go round the hazard players, pushing the document at them. 'Worth it,' he kept saying. 'Good bit of land, this. Thousand or more acres. Fowl an' fish an' . . . oh, all sortsa things. Scenery. Who'll sport me a monkey on it?'

There was a general shaking of heads. 'Go home, Henry.'

One of the players said: 'Where is it?'

'North'mberland.' Headington waved his arm towards the window as if Northumberland was located somewhere in the region of Highgate.

There was general laughter. 'A thousand acres of damn all. Suggest you go and live on it, Henry. Healthier for you than Mayfair.'

Desperately, the young man staggered towards Makepeace. 'You've a kind face, ma'am. You'll sport me a miserable monkey, eh? Here's m'security. Nice little property? Got an inn on it, I believe.'

Close to, he radiated an ill health caused by neglect. His flushed skin fell in beneath the cheekbones, he vibrated as if from fever and his linen, while fine, smelled rancid. His eyes were terrified.

'You go home,' said Makepeace, gently. 'Have a nice sleep.'

'No, no. M'luck's turned, ma'am. The goddess is smiling at last, I can feel it.' He pushed the paper at her. 'Jus' a monkey.'

'A monkey' was one of the few pieces of slang Boston and London had in common. Five hundred pounds.

She was shaking her head when a pretty voice called out: 'Don't bargain with a Yankee, Henry. Americans won't even pay their taxes.'

Makepeace looked up. Catty's eyes were sapphire chips. A challenge, pure and simple.

Through the cackling of the old guard, Makepeace heard a voice say: 'I'll play you for it.' It was hers.

Headington brightened. 'Straight game? My land against your monkey?'

Catty applied the goad. 'It's my husband's money at risk. Do he and I want a piece of Northumberland heath, I wonder?'

'Seventy guineas,' said Makepeace, desperately. It was all she had left from saving Dapifer's life, the rest had gone on buying him a fob watch for his birthday and on Beasley's expenses. 'My own money. I earned it.'

'I expect she did, darlings,' Catty announced reasonably, 'in a tavern.'

More laughter. Somebody shouted: 'Seventy guineas for a thousand acres? Damn cheap even for Northumberland.'

People were leaving the other tables and closing in.

'Are you satisfied by this, Sir Pip?' Macall asked.

Dapifer had come through the crowd. He put his arm around Makepeace's shoulders. 'Of course. It's my wife's own money and honestly gained, I'm proud to say.' Quietly he said: 'Don't do this, Procrustes. The lad's possessed. He's been wagering property all over London.'

'I can't back out now.' Headington was an inconsequence. She was duelling with Catty as sure as if they stood in the dawn with pistols pointing at the other's head.

They both saw Catty indicating them from the other side of the table and making Lady Brandon laugh. Dapifer tightened his grip round his wife's shoulders, kissed her and raised his voice. 'May the best woman win.'

'Seventy guineas it is, then.' Henry Headington would have played for buttons as long as he could play.

Immediately it became An Event with Procedures. This might be one of the smaller wagers of the evening but there'd been none as interesting.

The table was cleared of all other bets. A lawyer was brought from the dining room to draw up a promissory note for Makepeace in the event that she lost. She signed it with her maiden name to show that it would be paid with her personal money. A deed of transference of Headington's property from him to her, in the event that *he* lost, was also drawn up. Again, she signed with 'Makepeace Burke, formerly of Boston'.

The Earl of Orme straightened his buttercup hat. 'I shall be groom-porter for this throw. Does either caster object?'

Now that he was to placate his daemons Headington's distraction left him. Surrounded by his supporters, he prepared for battle by jogging on the spot, flexing his knees and wrists, calling for and mixing a beverage he called a 'gullet-gripper'.

'Make your sets, lady and gentleman,' said the Earl of Orme.

Headington laid his property deed on the table. Makepeace put her promissory note beside it. They shook hands.

'Call your main, Lady Dapifer.' The box holding the dice was passed to her. She could call five, six, seven, eight or nine. Her mind went blank. She could hear the dice vibrating in the box as she held it. The only number in her head was that of Creation's days. *Lord, forgive me.* 'Seven.'

Headington called five. Should either of them throw the number they'd called they'd 'nicked' it and had won outright. Makepeace had two chances of winning; if she threw eleven it also 'nicked' it.

Makepeace cast her dice. A three and a two. 'Five to seven' called the Earl of Orme. From this point on if she threw a seven she'd lose, five being her number to win.

Headington threw. Four and three. 'Seven to five.' Now the odds were in his favour; there were three ways of throwing a seven and only two of throwing five.

Around the table the betting began as spectators became players by betting on the chances of the two casters. The Duchess of Bar-net's ring-knobbled hands stacked guineas on the baize. 'Five hun-dred on young Headington, my lord.'

It don't matter, Makepeace tried telling herself, I can afford to lose.

And saw Catty's eyes. *No, I can't.*

She threw again. Eight.

Headington had a peculiar habit of rattling the dice-box before he threw, first against one ear then the other. 'England and St George,' he said.

The table cheered him. Lady Brandon hallooed: 'Go it, my boy. Let's win back those taxes.'

'Liberty,' said Makepeace, clearly, and threw. Eight.

She lost count of the throws after that. Dapifer told her later there were twenty-three. It seemed to her there were a hundred, God keeping her on the griddle for her wickedness; a winning score refused to come up for either of them.

Tension and temperature rose, so did the cheers—and bets. The Countess of Orme led an impromptu choir into 'Rule Britannia'. Somebody at the back of the crowd had found a hunting horn and was blowing the tantivy. Spots came and went on the baize like an errant disease.

The dice rolled and stopped. One of the little squares on the table showed a four, the other a one. Confused, Makepeace stared at them; she'd lost count. That had been her throw; *had* that been her throw? She looked over to Headington and saw the ravaged face assume peace. Had *he* won? But the noise had ceased. People were turning away from the table. Catty had gone.

Headington moved towards her. 'It seems America's not to be beaten. My congratulations, Lady Dapifer.' He held out the deed and its transference.

She was reluctant to take them. 'I'm sorry.'

'For this relief, much thanks.' His voice was kinder than any she'd heard that night. He took her hand and closed it over the papers. 'You must promise me not to be sorry.'

They heard next morning that he went back to the Mayfair house he'd gambled away earlier the previous day, thanked its servants, walked into his study, closed the door and shot himself.

With a blotched, desperate note, Makepeace sent the Northumberland deed back to his lawyer, begging him to return it to whomsoever inherited his estate.

A letter from Lord Braybourne, Headington's next of kin, returned it to her.

Madam, you are distinguished in being the only creditor of my unfortunate young cousin to cancel one of his debts. I cannot allow that this, the last and least of the properties he gambled away— one, moreover, that was fairly won—should place me under the burden of so rare a generosity. Luckily, I have no need of it. Here it is back again.

From that day on she kept the deed in her pocket wherever she went, in the way that a medieval sinner wore a hair shirt to remind himself of his need for salvation.

As things turned out, it was to be hers.

Chapter Twelve

IN July the Marquis of Rockingham lost office and was replaced as Prime Minister by the Duke of Grafton who, in turn, appointed as his Chancellor of the Exchequer Charles Townshend, a man whose solution to the American problem was the reassertion of British authority by the imposition of more customs duties.

It was a relief to leave London. Makepeace and Dapifer spent two weeks with young Andrew Ffoulkes on his estate in Kent and then repaired with him to Hertfordshire for the rest of the summer.

The weather was not good. There was trouble getting in the hay.

It can't be said that Makepeace laid Headington's ghost to rest. *For this relief, much thanks*; the words haunted her. On her knees in the little church at Dapifers she prayed that in death he'd maintained the peace which had settled on his poor, living face at the last; she begged forgiveness for giving way to Catty's goading and her own lust to gamble. 'Never again, Lord.'

Penance, however, took time and there was much to do: accompanying the villagers to St Alban's Fair and having to stop time and again for flocks of sheep on their way to provide roast lamb for Londoners; St John's Day, dressing the apple-trees with ribbons; cricket: Dapifers v. Tewinge, young Josh the highest scoring batsman; Lammas and well-dressing.

On St Swithin's Day it rained and therefore, they told her, would continue to do so for the next forty days. She wasn't to remember whether it did or didn't, only that the month passed in a sort of languorous busyness, a self-imposed, pleasing bustle of cleaning and tidying that Betty called 'gettin' the nest ready for the egg'.

She was becoming big now, adopting a waddle that made Dapifer laugh. The village women patted her belly for luck and Sam the pigman said she were 'good breeding stock from the look of ye', which he meant as a compliment and which she accepted as such.

She took gentle rides with Tantaquidgeon in the trap to pay courtesy calls through a landscape suddenly teeming with men mowing and women gathering sheaves for tying. Dapifer took off his coat and drove a wagon back and forth between the field and the yard where young Andrew and Josh were being taught the art of rick-building. Everybody but her was called in to help with the harvest. She was her own harvest.

Despite the weather, all corn was in by the beginning of September.

The letter came two days later.

Robert brought it to them at breakfast, fanning his nose with it and sniffing. 'That nice Mr Little brought it up. He called in at Mrs Yates's this morning.' Mrs Yates kept the shop on the Great North Road a mile and a half away where local letters and parcels were deposited by the passing Royal Mail coach to await collection. 'And we know who it's from, don't we?'

Dapifer slit the seal. '*Thank* you, Robert.'

'Oh, don't think *I'm* interested.' The valet flounced out.

'What is it?' Makepeace asked.

'A white flag, I think.' Dapifer handed it to Makepeace.

The letter smelled of bluebells, was unsigned and very short, *Pip, dear hart, I am in Town this month. Please recieve me that we may discuss matters.*

'She wants you to go to London?'

'I may as well. It's time to return Andrew to school in any case.' There was a groan from behind a platter piled with kidneys and kedgeree. 'And I can bring Baines back with me.'

Makepeace had been content to let Betty be the attendant at baby Procrustes's birth but Dapifer wouldn't rest easy unless Dr Baines was standing by.

'What's she want, d'you think?'

'Terms, I imagine.'

'Don't give her any. She's had one settlement, that's enough.' Makepeace feared for her husband's generosity; she could imagine how pitiful in defeat Catty would make herself. They would be alone together.

'Take Peter with you,' she said.

'Thank you, I am perfectly capable of conducting negotiations without Peter Little.'

'You'll be back for Harvest Home?' she asked, anxiously. It was the biggest festival of the year. Next Monday the household of Dapifers, the village and people from outlying farms would attend church and then a feast in the Great Barn afterwards. Preparations were already under way.

'What's today? Tuesday? If we set off now I can be back on Saturday. Pack your traps, Andrew.'

After Dapifer had gone to order Thompson the driver to ready the coach, Andrew said: 'Can't I stay for the feast?'

'I wish you could.' The two of them had become very close. 'But you'll be back in a month. Remind Pip to ask your headmaster for leave of absence for the christening.' The boy was to be god-father to baby Procrustes, along with the Marquis of Rockingham.

She and Betty filled the Ffoulkes' tuck box with cakes, apples, a ham and stone bottles of cider.

'I'll take Robert with me,' Dapifer said. 'Tantaquidgeon can stay with you, in case of emergency.' He set great store by the Indian.

'There ain't going to be an emergency,' Makepeace said, 'Betty says another three weeks.'

'Let's hope she's right.' Dapifer addressed his wife's stomach: 'Stay in there until I get back, my son.'

She kissed him and Andrew, told Robert to look after them, and stood at the manor door, waving, as the coach rocked down the yellowing chestnut avenue. The moist air was punctuated with the sound of popping from the cornfields where men were shooting rabbits.

That was Tuesday. Dapifer had hoped to return on Saturday night but Makepeace was not worried when he didn't. He had a lot to do in the time: take young Andrew to Eton; attend to various business matters; conduct the negotiation with Catty. Quite possibly, the coach hadn't been able to reach London in one day, the roads were still muddy . . .

She had a great deal to do herself. The church must be decorated with fruit, sheaves and berries for the service, so must the Great Barn for the supper. Chutneys had to be made, fruit preserved, apples stored . . .

She was more concerned when he hadn't arrived by Sunday night but allowed herself to be reassured. Bad day for travelling, Sunday; there'd be difficulty getting fresh horses—he'd have stayed the night at Barnet, probably. He'd be here tomorrow, he'd be back for Harvest Home.

On Monday afternoon, she decided to take a stroll and meet the coach returning as it surely must; he'd said he'd be back for Harvest Home. Betty wanted her to go by trap if she had to go out at all. 'Suppose he don't come 'til tonight, you got too much babby in you to climb back up that hill.'

'I need to walk.' She was restless; she was fixed on the moment when Dapifer's coach came along the road; she could get in, hear the news of Catty, have a few moments alone with him before they were embroiled in harvest celebrations.

As she set off down the avenue, she heard the pad of moccasined feet behind her. Betty wasn't letting her go alone; she'd sent Tantaquidgeon.

Well, he could sit on the coach roof. Robert too.

The village street was quiet. Dust and the sound of flails came from the threshing floors, the smell of cooking apples and spice from the open doors of the cottages.

Old Mrs Nash sat on her threshold making corn dollies. 'Don't you go far now, missus. That looks like rain.'

Wisps of straw garnished lanes where, only a few days before, harvest carts had gone frantically back and forth. Children were blackberrying along the hedgerows.

Any minute she'd see the coach roof in the distance . . . round the next bend . . . the next. She waddled on. Unseen behind her the sky blackened.

By the time she emerged from Dapifers Lane into the Great North Road the first drops of rain were hitting its surface in plump spatters. Even here there was little traffic today; the farming world was staying home to store the harvest. Northwards, to her left, the toll-booth waited for travellers, the smoke from its chimney ragged in the squall of the sudden breeze. A horseman jogged past her, hurriedly raising his hat.

Southwards lay the hill down which Dapifer's coach would be coming. Makepeace turned right and walked towards it, making a long diagonal across the ruts of the road to Mrs Yates's shop, a solitary cottage with beetle-browed thatch frowning over its windows. 'I'm waiting for Sir Pip to come back from London, Mrs Yates. Can I watch for him here?' The shop had a tiny glazed peep-window in its south wall; she could see the hill from it.

Mrs Yates set a chair, exclaiming at Makepeace's long walk in her condition and such weather, then jumping as if she'd been goosed as Tantaquidgeon's long shadow fell over the threshold.

Having offered Makepeace a cup of herbal tea and seen that she was in no mood for conversation, Mrs Yates said: 'In the middle of making coughdrops I was, I'll get back to 'em if 'ee don't mind.' She stole on tiptoe past Tantaquidgeon to her kitchen.

The front door had to be shut against the rain and the shop was dark, its elderly stock of almost everything just massed and varied shapes. The rain slanted past Makepeace's window in gusts that blurred her view of the hill. The smell of wintergreen from the kitchen mingled with that of cheese and damp. Makepeace shivered. An ache was developing in her back.

In a sudden, slashing downpour she thought she saw the coach and ran to the door, pushing Tantaquidgeon out of the way. The hill was empty.

'There now,' said Mrs Yates, coming in as the wind slammed

the door back shut. 'Forget my own head next. There was a letter came Saturday and I meant to send it up but I been that busy with apples . . .' She dabbed her hands among dark pigeonholes. 'Here 'tis . . .' As Makepeace snatched it from her: 'Tisn't Sir Pip's hand, I know that.'

> My dear Lady Dapifer,
>   I beg you to remember your condition and not to be overly anxious but you should know that Sir Pip has been taken ill. In the event that it has slipped the mind of those looking after him to inform you, I thought it best to write. I entreat you not to flurry yourself. A doctor has been called and all is being done for him. In haste,
>   your friend and neighbour, Emily Judd

The date was Friday's.

Get to him, get to him. Board a coach here? No. No, no, no, *think*. The stage wouldn't pass until evening. The mail even later. Back to the house. Get the trap, Peter Little would drive her, or one of the men. Get to him.

Mrs Yates was hanging onto her arm. 'You're never goin' out in this, missus?'

She threw the woman off and lumbered into the deserted road, Tantaquidgeon behind her.

And *now* the coach was coming. Suddenly the hill was busy: vehicles, horsemen and, unmistakably, the Dapifer coach with Thompson driving.

She sobbed with relief; he was all right, he'd come home. She stood where she was, waving her arms.

The coach slowed as Thompson saw her and pulled on the reins so that the horses slithered to a halt in spraying mud. Two riders in military, rain-blackened cloaks drew their mounts up on either side. She began picking her way through the mud.

A head peered out of the coach window, facing in Makepeace's direction to see what was causing the delay. After a moment it said something she couldn't catch over the noise of the rain. One of the horsemen saluted and then called to Thompson, 'You heard the major. Drive on.' He put his hand under his cloak as if to draw a sword. 'Drive *on*.'

The reins were shaken. She saw Thompson's face, wet, beseeching, turned to hers, as the coach went past her.

Two more outriders accompanied the conveyance that had been held up behind the coach. It was a funeral cart drawn by four black-plumed horses, the rain drooping the feathers down over their ears in a way that reminded Makepeace of Catty as she sat on the floor of her house in Bloomsbury, a bit of fan tickling her nose.

The hooded driver took it past her, gleaming black mahogany with a brass rail round its sides. Rain bounced on the lid of the coffin.

She didn't move. It wasn't him.

The cortège turned left, into Dapifers Lane.

She said quite brightly: 'Well, what's all *that* about, I wonder?' And began to run.

Peter Little, coming to find her in the trap, met her at the bridge. 'Oh dear God, are you all right?'

Tantaquidgeon was helping her along as she struggled to walk through a contraction. 'Get me home.' Tantaquidgeon lifted her in.

'Lady Dapifer . . .'

'It isn't him,' she said.

'We don't know who it is, they've shut the gates.' It was so dark he'd hung a lantern from the whip-holder and in its light his eyes were pale and staring.

Words didn't associate with their meaning or things with what they were. She said: 'It isn't him.'

He turned the trap with difficulty. Leaves driven by the rain plastered themselves against her face as they went up the hill.

Half the village stood by the gates in groups hunched over lanterns which illuminated patches of glistening rain and faces distorted by upthrown light so that they were unrecognizable.

The world had come loose. No moment flowed into another; instead static, vividly drawn tableaux presented themselves and were washed away by the rain to make way for the next.

An outline had Fanny's shape. 'Oh, missus, they say he's dead. Oh, missus.'

Josh knuckling tears from his eyes.

Another shape enfolded her and spoke in Betty's voice. 'You gotta be strong now, girl. You gotta mind that babby. They gone an' turfed us out.'

The gates were high; she had never seen them closed before, their wrought iron was angular and coldly wet against her hands. One of the coach's outriders stood behind them; she could see the white cross of webbing under his cape and the gleam of a bayonet.

'Let me in. I'm Lady Dapifer. I live here.'

'Sorry, miss. No admittance.' A neutral voice, not unkind, not sympathetic. The patterned shadow of the gate blacked out one of his eyes.

'Let me in.' She broke. '*Pip*. I'm here, Pip.' Once she'd begun shouting for him she couldn't stop. 'Pip, they're not letting me in.'

The rain wouldn't accept the sound she made, earthing it into the mud, so she shouted louder.

A light sprang up in the churchyard on the hill; there was movement.

The soldier turned to somebody she couldn't see. 'Better fetch the Major.'

Someone behind her put an arm across her shoulders. She shook it off, rattling the gates, shrieking like an imprisoned animal.

Conyers was at the gate with two more soldiers. 'This is unseemly, madam. I must ask you to desist and go away.'

She didn't understand. 'This man won't let me in.'

He didn't move. The same shadow that had fallen on the soldier's eye obliterated one of his.

He didn't understand, she realized. She was a maenad to him, wet hair plastered to her face, unrecognizable. She said with relief: 'You know me, I'm Makepeace Dapifer. We met. Please let me in, I must go to Pip.'

'I do *not* know you, madam.'

He gestured to the soldier with the lantern to raise it so that its light shone on his face. He shouted: 'People of Dapifers, I regret to inform you that Sir Philip died three days ago in London. His wife was with him. We are about to bury him.'

Somebody screamed. A man's voice yelled: 'We're comin' in. We needs to see 'un. Why you stoppin' us?'

'I am Major Sidney Conyers, Lady Dapifer's champion. On her authority I am seizing this property and all Sir Pip's properties back to her, his lawful wife.'

'His wife's yere.' A female voice.

'That woman's an interloper, as will shortly be proved in a court of law. The true Lady Dapifer is once more in possession of her husband's land and my men here will see to it that order is kept. There will be a magistrate here in the morning: don't make it necessary for him to read the Riot Act.' The strain went out of Conyers's face and it became kindly. 'Go home, good people. Mourn our dear Sir Philip as I shall. Let his lady bury him in peace.'

The stilted phrases sliced the air into neat pieces.

Peter Little called out: 'This isn't right, major,' and somebody else said uncertainly: 'No, it ain't. You open they gates. Let's rush 'em, lads.'

But words of power had been spoken in an educated voice. Lawful. Magistrate. Major. Riot Act. Order. Authority. The lantern gleamed on bayonets.

Conyers nodded and went away.

Nobody rushed the gates. Only a mud-spattered, hysterical woman shook them and went on shaking them, hour after hour, as if there was any hope of them opening.

People buzzed around her, trying to draw her away. She clung on to the bars like a monkey.

From the house came a file of glow-worms. Rain and darkness took away distance and depth so that the beetle-lights seemed to creep down a flat, immense blackboard.

The file reached the avenue. Its shine against the trees restored perspective. Not glow-worms, but a train of flares and lanterns; those carrying them blended into the darkness so that they seemed to carry themselves. People in black. Too far away to make out, too flickered by the waving branches. Heading for the church. Clustering in the graveyard.

'It isn't him,' she said again and began screaming, pulling at the gate, kicking it, vomiting sound, commanding, begging, promising any abasement, only let me see him. It's not him. I can save him. You're burying him alive. He's alive. Let me save him. I saved him before. It's not him.

The lights broke away from each other, re-formed into their file to crawl back up the hill until the house swallowed them, one by one, and there was nothing.

They raised Makepeace out of the mud but couldn't dislodge her hands from the ironwork. Eventually, when they saw that the baby was coming, they forced her fingers back and carried her away. Part of her, the best of her, stayed at the gate.

Baby Procrustes was born an hour later in Peter Little's house. Makepeace bore the labour almost without interest, as if it had no validity of its own but was merely a physical manifestation of the greater agony.

Anyway, it was a girl.

Chapter Thirteen

'WHERE is she?'

Betty walked with him along the village street. The weather had cleared but underfoot it remained muddy. The air smelled of leaves and cow-pats. In the fields seagulls followed the ploughs like a ragged train of lace blowing in the breeze. A blast of heat and the clang of hammering came from the smithy as they passed it.

Something should have stopped, Aaron thought. Everywhere there was occupation, and people avoiding his eye.

They reached the vast, iron embroideries that were the gates to Dapifer House. Plumed and blanketed, Tantaquidgeon looked outlandish against them. A figure was sitting at his feet, its head drooped into its lap like an exhausted beggar. Fanny Cobb stood helplessly beside it.

'Three days, Aaron,' Betty sobbed. 'She keep comin' back. You make her come away. You tell her.'

'Makepeace? *Makepeace?*' Aaron threw himself on the gates and rattled them. 'Open up.'

A soldier shouldering a musket ambled out of a makeshift sentry box standing just within the grounds. 'What now?'

'I'm Lady Dapifer's brother. Open these gates at once and let her in.'

'Go home,' said the soldier, wearily. 'And tell the Indian if he tries to get her in round the back again, we'll shoot the bugger. No trespassers.'

'It's my sister's house, there's a law against this.'

'Take her home, son,' the soldier said, gently. 'Looks like she's ill.'

At his side, Betty said: 'Ain't no good, Aaron, we tried and tried.'

Aaron knelt down and smoothed the hair back from his sister's face. Was this broken thing Makepeace, feared landlady of the Roaring Meg, his surrogate mother, arbiter, lifelong prop? 'Come away, 'Peace. Just for now.'

''Aaron?'

'I'm here, 'Peace. I'm here now.'

''Pip's in there,' she said, 'but they won't let me go to him.'

'We'll make them, 'Peace. I promise. We'll have the law on 'em.'

He got her to her feet and put one of her arms round his shoulder and the other round Betty's so that she could walk. With Tantaquidgeon following, they went back down the street. Over his sister's head, Aaron said to Betty: 'They can't do this.'

'They's gentry. They's doin' it.'

As they passed the forge, Edgar the blacksmith came out to them. 'How is she, poor soul?'

Aaron shouted: 'How d'you think she is? And what are you people doing about it?'

Next day, taking Peter Little's advice and his horse, he set off to appeal to the Lord Lieutenant of Hertfordshire. 'Soon get this cleared up,' he said. He was still sufficiently American to believe that it could be.

'Civil matter,' the Lord Lieutenant told him. 'Nothing I can do.'

Aaron pointed out that he was appealing to the head of the county's magistracy. 'My sister, Lady Dapifer, is being denied access to her property by armed intruders and I want militia or bailiffs, or whatever arm of the law you use, sent to expel them.'

'Young man, in this country we're civilized, we don't send in troops, we prefer legal methods.'

'My sister has been evicted from her house, how legal's that?'

But the Lord Lieutenant was acquainted with the situation through his reading of the newspapers and knew that the late Sir Philip Dapifer's second marriage was questionable. He was a blunt man and made no bones about his and his wife's friendship with the first Lady Dapifer ' . . . who may well be repossessin' property that was rightfully hers in the first place. It's a civil matter. Get your sister a lawyer and fight it out in the courts, not in my county. I wish ye good morning.'

Over the shoulders of the two footmen escorting him out, Aaron shouted: 'You weren't too bloody civilized to send in troops to Boston.'

But he was frightened. It was his first encounter with the invisible ranks which the aristocratic English held closed against outsiders.

Sir Toby Tyler MP was more courteous but pronounced himself equally hamstrung. 'Matter for the courts, my boy.' He also used a phrase that was to become hideously familiar. 'I'm afraid that possession is nine points of the law.'

'How many points the law got?' Aaron demanded.

Sir Toby blinked. 'Ten, I imagine. And the first Lady Dapifer's just taken nine of 'em.'

There was another phrase Aaron was to become sick of. Sir Toby said it. 'Inform me if there's anything I can do,' he said.

'Anything', however, Aaron noticed, did not extend to taking Makepeace and her child into his home nor prosecuting their cause—the first indication that possession had not only nine legal points but all ten of the status quo.

On his way home, a low autumnal sun poured honeyed richness onto grass banks, the harlequin-coloured leaves of trees, clusters of thatch and a great house on a hill, as if the countryside were flirting with him and trying to make him oblivious to the concrete in which it was set.

He swore at it and heard his American curses dissipate, absorbed into English birdsong.

Back at Peter Little's house, Mrs Little opened the door to him.

A nice, worn-looking woman, Mrs Little, whose love for her own husband had put her into an agony on Makepeace's behalf. She'd had to farm her children out to villagers in order to accommodate them all.

'Peter's been called to the big house,' she said, 'but that Robert, Sir Pip's man, is here. Perhaps he can persuade her poor Sir Pip is really dead.'

Aaron followed her into her scrubbed, sparse little parlour. Dapifer's valet was kneeling on the floor, weeping into Makepeace's skirt.

Betty stood protectively over her mistress; she'd never liked 'that nan-boy'.

Makepeace's eyes were directed out of the window. 'They killed him,' she said.

Despairingly, Robert looked up. 'Oh, tell her,' he said. 'We weren't *well*. We looked poorly by the time we reached London. I said to him: "You're not well, my dear. Let *me* take Lord Ffoulkes back to school," but, oh no, we had to stir ourselves and do it. Then *they* came. Thursday, that was. We didn't want the Major in the house, you could see that, but didn't we *always* have to listen to everybody? So in the Major comes *and* her, bold as a miller's shirt the both of them.'

Robert sat up, wiping his eyes on Makepeace's petticoat. 'I tell you now, I was at the door. Not to make out the words, but they weren't going to stop me listening. Talk, talk, talk, her voice mostly, sometimes the Major's, ours once or twice, very quiet. And then *crash*. And her scream. Well, I didn't care, I ran in. We were on the floor, bless him, breathing like . . . well, *snorting* really.'

'They killed him,' said Makepeace, still looking out of the window.

Almost regretfully, the valet said: 'They weren't nowhere near him.'

'Didn't have to be, did they?' Betty said. 'They bothered him to death.'

Robert closed his eyes.

Outside the wavered, greenish glass of the parlour window, a thrush was singing in an apple tree, punctuating the stresses of the valet's falsetto as it recounted the death of a beloved.

At first, he said, Dapifer's repetition of 'Heart, heart' had been received as an indication of where the pain lay. Only Robert recognized that his master was demanding to be taken to Hertfordshire. 'It was "Hert . . . Hert . . . Hert . . ." with him, and "Crust" over and over.'

In a sudden return of the old jealousy he pulled away from Makepeace's knees. 'Yes, *yes*, we meant *Procrustes*. He wanted *you*.'

The man turned to Aaron. 'I *said*. Shall we send for her? I said. I told them fair and square, he wants *her*, I said. But nothing was done.' His shoulders sagged. 'Anyway, she couldn't have got there in time.'

Sir Finlay Robertson, a doctor resident on the other side of the square, had been called in. '*Very* important,' Robert said, perking up for a moment. 'Attends royalty and I don't know what-all.'

Dapifer was carried to his bed, leeches had been applied. There'd been a consultation between the doctor and Conyers which Robert didn't hear, 'but you could see Sir Finlay didn't have hope.'

Catty, he said, had been hysterical and had confined herself to another room. The valet's voice became higher and more mincing. ' "Can't bear to see poor Pip like this." Well, who could? But I wasn't going to leave him and I didn't, never let go of his dear hand.'

The doctor had been back and forth; Conyers had left the house and come back again.

Everything had been provided for the patient's relief. 'But you could see it wasn't going to be any good. Our breathing . . . oh bless us.'

The noise of it had filled every room, Robert said. It had gone on grinding, on and on like a millwheel, all night until—and Robert had lost track of time—the house was suddenly silent.

So, now, was the Littles' parlour, except for the thrush's careless twittering and the creak of a windlass as, further away, someone drew water from the village well.

It hadn't seemed unreasonable, Robert said after a while, to take the body back to Hertfordshire for burial. It was the Dapifer ancestral home, the family tomb was there. 'And *she* was there.' He nodded his head towards Makepeace; there seemed no point in addressing her directly.

The haste with which transport was arranged, and that Dapifer's important friends were not invited to accompany it as mourners, might have struck him as strange but he was, he said, too distressed to have his wits about him. He was only glad to be given a place in the coach. And to have an escort of Conyers's soldiers seemed only proper.

Every time the cortège stopped, the Major and Catty moved away to talk secretly and with calculation. 'Whisper, whisper,' Robert said. He'd thought they were discussing arrangements for the funeral.

Once at Dapifers, he'd stayed with the coffin like a dog at its dead master's side, followed it to the graveyard, heard the stone grate back over the tomb . . .

The song of the thrush in the apple-tree mingled with Robert's weeping.

From upstairs, where Fanny was looking after the baby, came the sound of crying. 'Time for that chil's feed,' said Betty.

They were trying to interest Makepeace in her daughter, at least to choose its name. The vicar on the estate was too careful for his benefice to perform the christening but Peter Little had found a priest in Hertford prepared to do it.

Once she'd taken Makepeace upstairs and seen the baby begin sucking, Betty left them both to Fanny and joined the two men and Mrs Little in the garden. Evening was bringing out scent from an overcrowded herbaceous border where transparent pods of honesty glowed like moon-pennies.

Mrs Little shaded her eyes to where the sun was setting behind Dapifers. 'I wonder where Peter's got to.'

'Mebbe we can shift her now,' Betty said. 'Where we goin' to go, Aaron? We cain't stay here.'

'London. Her lawyer.'

'When do we set off?' Robert asked. At Betty's and Aaron's stare, he said: 'Well, I ain't staying with *them*, am I? She's got the right of it that far—they done him in. It was them upsetting him as done for us.' Tears began again. 'I'm still his man, I'll always be his man and he didn't want *her*—' a wave of his hand towards Dapifers—'he wanted *her*'—his thumb jerked towards the parlour window.

Aaron warmed to him; but it was going to be hard to support his sister and the others, let alone take on another mouth to feed. He said so.

'No money at *all*?' Robert said.

'She got a pearl brooch on her as *he* give her,' Betty told him, 'an' that goes to pawn tomorrow.'

'I've a hand with ladies' hair,' he said, 'I could set up for a hairdresser.'

'What with?'

They'd defeated him and were sorry; behind the irritating posturing lay a breaking, loyal heart and a rare sense of honour. Aaron nodded towards the big house: 'Keep you on, will they?'

He gave a dreary shrug. 'Expect so. I used to do her hair, she said I was better with it than anybody.'

'Stay with 'em.' Aaron took his limp hand. 'We need someone behind enemy lines.'

'A *spy*.' He was cheered. 'My dear, you shall know what I know as soon as I know it. I'll get a black cloak. We can use a *code*.'

They watched him prance back to the house along the village street on his high heels, the long feather nodding in his hat. 'He look like a titmouse strayed into a farmyard,' Betty said, wiping her eyes.

Peter Little came slouching back. He could hardly bear to tell them. The call to the big house had been to inform him that if 'the troublemakers' were not promptly evicted from his house, indeed from the village, he and his family would be—it was Dapifer property.

He said: 'They're maintaining the will Sir Pip made that left everything to the first Lady Dapifer is the only one valid because she's his only wife. It'll be a matter for the civil courts. What can I do?'

Betty patted his bowed shoulder. 'Ain't your fault, you got to think for your childer.' And to Aaron she said: 'Ain't the villagers', neither. Chattels cain't choose who owns 'em. Slavery taught me that much.'

They couldn't have stayed in the house any longer, anyway; four people, having learned separately of Dapifer's death from the *London Gazette*, immediately and coincidentally boarded the same coach to Hertfordshire, and the arrival that night of Andrew, Lord Ffoulkes, truanting from school, a distraught Susan Brewer, Dr Baines offering medical help and, astonishingly, John Beasley, surly as ever, added to the overcrowding.

At last Betty managed to strip Makepeace of the dress she'd refused to take off since Dapifer's body had been brought home. She set out a bodice, petticoats and shawl provided by Susan with which to replace it in the morning.

'You got to look decent tomorrow, no matter what,' she said firmly. 'We gettin' that chil' named afore we take the coach for London. An' we callin' her Philippa after her pa.'

There was a long silence. 'If you say so.'

Betty sagged with relief. Until now Dapifers had been the only place that held validity for Makepeace. Wicked as anything else Catty and Conyers had perpetrated against her, Betty knew, was the deprivation of her husband's death. Without watching life depart, closing the coffin lid, taking part in the obsequies and interment, for her, for all of them, it was as if he'd merely sauntered off into the mist.

She took the soiled dress down to the wash-tub. There were some neatly rolled documents in the pocket let into the skirt. She had neither time nor light to read the densely written pages and put the roll into the holdall that, along with a rush basket and baby clothes, they were having to borrow from the Littles.

The next morning, at the hasty christening in a Hertford side-chapel, the priest protested: 'All of you?'

'All.'

'Him too?'

'He's a baptized Christian,' Aaron said. 'All of us.'

Betty, Mrs Little, Susan Brewer and Fanny Cobb were pronounced godmothers to Philippa Dapifer. The ceremony also gave her seven godfathers: an estate steward, an American uncle, a small lord of the realm, an equally small black boy, a Scottish doctor, a Red Indian, and a hack scribbler who didn't believe in any of it.

'Oh yes,' Mr Hackbutt said, 'he changed his will right enough. "To my beloved wife, formerly Makepeace Burke of Boston . . ." She's entitled to everything, bar annuities to the servants. But we have to prove to probate that she *is* his wife against the first Lady Dapifer's assertion that she is not. Did you manage to safeguard his deed box?'

'Deed box?' Aaron looked at Betty.

Betty put her face close to Makepeace's, speaking as if to the deaf. 'Where's Sir Pip's deed box?' The response was a tired shrug.

Mr Hackbutt was displeased. 'You've let the vixen go to earth,' he said. 'A merry job we'll have diggin' her out now. The divorce decree's in it, and the ship's marriage certificate, I saw them myself. Without those, we'll have to send to Boston for a copy of the decree nisi, get hold of the sea captain who married them . . .'

'Grosvenor Square,' said Makepeace wearily. 'There's a box in his office.'

'Speaking as a friend and not as a lawyer, I suggest you go and get it this minute, before our friends return from Hertfordshire and destroy its contents.' Mr Hackbutt cracked an invisible whip at his hounds.

At the door, he held Aaron back and handed him a letter. 'Young man, I would spare your poor sister this for fear of distressing her further but she must be apprised of it sooner or later. I leave the matter with you.'

The letter was from Cresswell and Partit, Solicitors. It informed Mr Hackbutt that an injunction was being taken out by their client, Major Sidney Conyers, against Mr Hackbutt's client, Makepeace

Burke, to prevent her from meeting, visiting, writing to or in any other way making contact with Lord Ffoulkes of Gosse in Kent.

'They *can't* do that. She loves that boy, he loves her.'

'I fear they can,' Mr Hackbutt told him. 'On the birth of his son, the late Lord Ffoulkes appointed his two greatest friends to be the child's guardians in the event of his death. One was Sir Philip Dapifer, the other Major Conyers. Sir Pip, as I have reason to know, attended to his duties in that respect most conscientiously, the Major rather less so. It may be that Lord Ffoulkes forgot he had appointed Conyers—certainly, the Major himself appeared to do so. Whatever the case, his lordship sailed for America having neglected to change his will.' Mr Hackbutt's mouth tightened. 'It seems our good Major has just reminded himself that he is now in sole charge of a minor with a fortune.'

Aaron handed back the letter. 'There's nothing they won't take away from her, is there?'

'Hold up,' said Mr Hackbutt. 'Possession may be nine points of the law but—'

'What the hell's the tenth?' Aaron asked, hopelessly.

'Eh? Oh, I see. There *are* only nine. Success in a law suit requires first, a good deal of money; second, a good lawyer; third, a good counsel; fourth, good witnesses; fifth, a good jury; sixth, a good judge; seventh, a good deal of money; eighth, a good cause and, ninth, good luck.'

'We've no money.'

Mr Hackbutt's smile was unexpectedly charming. 'Yes, well, we'll do what we can. I pride myself that your sister has a good lawyer, she certainly has a good cause and, well, good luck is a chancy bird. It may settle on us yet.'

Aaron had expected to find one of Conyers's troop stationed outside Grosvenor Square's Dapifer House but there was only a solitary maid, scrubbing its steps. At the sight of Makepeace, Betty and Aaron she hurriedly plopped her brush back into its bucket and disappeared.

The door was opened by a woman whose time had come. 'Yes?'

'Let us in, Mis' Peplow.'

Aaron stood back; when Betty took that tone it was best to let her have her head—or lose your own.

'I take my orders from Lady Dapifer,' said Mrs Peplow, smiling. 'No hawkers.'

The closing door wedged on Betty's boot. 'Git.'

Greek met weighty Greek but Betty was the greater. The tussle ended with the housekeeper pinned to the wall by a black fist round her neck, her cap over her eyes. 'We's goin' to the master's office,' Betty explained. 'You arguin'?'

A blink from Mrs Peplow's popping eyes indicated that she was not, but as they crossed the hall they heard her scream: 'Too late. It's all gone to Hertfordshire. You're too late.'

She was right. Catty, or more probably Conyers, had acted quickly. Dapifer's tall escritoire was empty, his deed box no longer stood on its shelf.

Idiotically, Aaron started searching the bookshelves.

Betty risked a quick foray upstairs to look for Makepeace's clothes and jewellery while Mrs Peplow stood on the outside steps, shouting for the Watch.

Dapifer's bedroom was much as usual but Makepeace's had been stripped, the top of the delicate dressing-table was cleared of creams and perfume pots, its drawers hung open. The lids of the presses in which Mme Angloss's creations had been laid away were thrown back to display empty interiors.

There was an apologetic cough behind her. Tom the muscled footman, said: 'Can't let you stay, Bet.'

She indicated the room. 'Thorough, ain't they?'

He shook his head sadly. 'They say as none of it was hers to begin with.'

She allowed herself to be escorted downstairs. Makepeace was sitting at Dapifer's escritoire, her cheek pressed against its walnut lid.

'Nothing?'

'Nothin'.'

As they raised his sister up, Aaron was thinking of a scene his father had witnessed in his youth during an expedition to the Tiwappaty Bottom on the east of the Ohio when Indians had captured a horse from the wild herds that roamed those alluvial plains.

The horse was encircled, his father had said. When it bucked, lassoes of plaited rushes flipped through the air and tightened on each pawing leg. Two more lassoes caught the rear hooves as they lashed upwards, another landed about its neck, then another from the opposite direction, until radii of rope cobwebbed the beast into immobility and it was ready to be broken.

Catty Dapifer and Sidney Conyers, Aaron thought, had nothing to learn from Indians about entrapment. Money, houses, clothes, status: everything Dapifer had given Makepeace had been taken away in one expert, audacious move. She had nowhere to turn. They'd broken her.

'Time to go, 'Peace,' he said.

Mrs Peplow's triumphant vituperation followed them as they left Dapifer House for the last time.

BOOK THREE

Newcastle

Chapter Fourteen

PHILIPPA Dapifer made her stage debut aged six and a half months in a barn at Stickney in Lincolnshire. She played Moses/e was very good.

The wind from the North Sea was moaning like a bassoon through the hayloft, a suitably mournful accompaniment to Pharaoh's daughter's soliloquy in the barn below on her father's refusal to let her marry Alphanus. Draught guttered the candles nailed into the earth floor for footlights and shifted the distant turrets of Pharaoh's palace which, last week, had been the spires of Canterbury cathedral and, the week before that, the towers of Elsinore. They could only afford one backdrop.

The hen they'd tried to dislodge from the rafters during rehearsal started to squawk, inciting a wag in the audience—there was always one—to call out: 'That's another dang female wants to lay a egg.'

Peg Devereux knew when she was losing an audience and cut to the last of her speech. 'But soft!' she exclaimed. 'What is this that floats so gently down the Nile?'

'What?' asked the wag.

Peg glared at Makepeace, hidden in the prompt corner behind one of the upturned haywains that formed the wings. Concealed behind the other, Aaron signalled frantically to his sister to pull on the rope. Makepeace roused herself, pulled, and a rush basket slid into the stage area, causing gasps at the magic of its entrance.

'But, soft!' exclaimed Peg again. 'What is this that floats so gently down the Nile? An offering to the river god?'

'Danged if I know,' the wag said, genuinely interested.

Peg kept them waiting for a few more lines, then knelt among imaginary rushes and lifted out the basket's contents.

There was a coo from the audience. 'That's a real babby, look. Ahh.'

It had been a physical risk to go on the road as early in the year as March, when carts got bogged down in mud and actors died from exposure, but Aaron hoped that an untried travelling theatre company might survive if it could reach places where other companies had never been—and before they could get there.

'Picture an East Anglian winter,' he'd pleaded to Betty. 'Wouldn't you lay out good money on some drama after five months of looking at sheep and cabbages?'

She was reluctant. 'We ain't had enough drama?'

But *something* had to be done; the landlord of the two Holborn rooms they all shared was becoming restive for his rent. She and Fanny and Makepeace were taking in ironing in order to eke out Aaron's salary from the theatre but sometimes there wasn't enough money to light a fire to heat the iron with.

'And it'll give 'Peace an interest,' Aaron said. Makepeace was in the room with them but they talked about her in the third person.

'Maybe.' Nothing else had, not even the baby. They could see her trying to make conversation, be bright, and then her mind would drift back to whatever place it inhabited. Betty said: 'Wish I knew what that bitch-whore said to her.'

Carrying home some washing, Betty had seen the Dapifer carriage drawing away along Holborn from the front door leading to their rooms and had run after it, hurling mud and abuse at its elegantly pretty passenger. Then she'd raced back and up the stairs. 'How'd she find us? What she say?'

'She asked somebody at the theatre.' Makepeace was sitting on a stool, perfectly still, the baby in the drawer that served as its cot beside her.

'What she say?'

'Nothing.'

'She must've said *something*.'

'No.'

Whatever else Catty had done, she'd scattered some coppers on the floor for Makepeace to pick up; they were still there. The old Makepeace would have rammed them down her throat.

So Betty had said, yes, they would join Aaron's touring company. 'But we ain't *actin'*, we ain't fallen that far.' It would be a living of sorts, Aaron said it would be a fine one, and maybe, maybe, it would bring Makepeace back from the dead.

The money for three carts and the mules to draw them came from Susan Brewer, who'd been saving the tips given her by Mme Angloss's aristocratic clients. 'Oh, Lord's sakes,' she said, when Aaron worried about taking it, 'Pip helped *me* enough.'

She'd had the opportunity denied to the rest of them of watching the reception given to Makepeace's downfall by the best drawing rooms. Mainly it had been one of amusement and a vague relief, even by those who had received Makepeace while Dapifer was alive. *Yes, yes, how naughty of Catty and how typical, a stroke worthy of her grandfather—you remember old Lord Falworth? Recaptured his ship singlehanded from the mutineers? Hanged every man jack of 'em?*

An interloper had been taught a lesson, the old order restored, the rightness of things-as-they-should-be now flowed seamlessly over the rift.

'Just you make a fortune,' Susan said, 'so that we can all go back to Boston where we belong. I'll form a whole new force called the Daughters of Liberty and its aim will be to cut any female throat with blue blood in it. Aaron, these people are *foul*. For two pins, I'd come with you.'

But the prospective touring company had too many nonprofessionals on its books already, it couldn't support more; its actor-manager was looking for performers with theatrical experience— and desperation.

He didn't need to look far; there were enough of the outworn and the broken-down to choose from in the area of Goodman's Fields itself.

Peg Devereux joined because she was thirty-seven and saw the chance in a ramshackle company like Aaron's to continue playing the romantic lead, as well as staying one step ahead of her pursuing creditors. Aaron welcomed her, partly because she was a good actress but mostly because her lover, Frederick Tortini, was a talented musician and he came with her.

Tom Capper was another addition escaping a debtor's prison, a comedian of genius, who could roll an audience on the floor with one twitch of his eyebrow. The difficulty, as Aaron found, was to stop him doing his own floor-rolling in the nearest ale house.

At first it didn't occur to Aaron to ask Mr and Mrs Hartley Witney to join him; they were too grand and, well, too old. Between them they'd appeared with everybody who was anybody in the established theatre, including James Quin, the last of the great Restoration actors, on whose declamatory style Mr Witney modelled his own, so that a simple 'Pass the salt' thundered like an edict from the gods. Aaron, an aficionado of Garrick's naturalistic acting, had passed them over. But so, it appeared, had the established theatre; they'd been asked to retire to make way for younger luminaries.

'It'll be hard going,' Aaron said, doubtfully, when they applied to him.

'We have supped too long from the flesh-pots of Egypt, my dear boy,' Hartley Witney said. 'It is time for us to take our art to the untaught, to awaken bucolic souls to a glory beyond them.'

Or, as Penthesilea Witney put it, 'We'd rather drop in harness than be put out to grass.'

Mr Burke's Touring Company was complete.

Before it set out, John Beasley shambled into the Holborn attic and looked shiftily at Betty. 'Where's that youngling of yours?' He never said 'hello'.

'Runnin' errands.' There was an emphatic bang of the smoothing iron. 'Earnin' his keep.' Betty could never believe that people who merely wrote things were earning theirs. Nor could she see that the newspaper campaign Beasley was conducting against Catty and Conyers and their usurpation of Makepeace's property was doing any good. She admired his loyalty but was easily offended by him.

'The boy still want to paint?'

'How you know that?' She was defensive, she found her son's love of art mystifying and a touch effeminate, as if he showed a propensity to play with dolls.

'*She* told me.' He nodded towards the other side of the ironing table where Makepeace, having smiled brightly at him, had returned drearily to her goffering. 'Only, you want to bring him to Leicester Fields with me? There's a place going in Josh Reynolds's house. Might suit him.'

'Who he?'

'He's a painter.'

'He earn money for that?'

'A hundred guineas for a full-length portrait.'

A whistle escaped Betty's teeth.

'And for your information, Leicester Fields is full of royal residences. Not that our dear King'd patronize a good liberal like Josh Reynolds.'

'He goin' to teach the boy? Or do he just want a little black servant?'

'He wants a little black servant—at least, *he* don't, his sister does. She keeps house for him. But Reynolds says he'll let the boy mix paint, do jobs around the studio.' Beasley became grumpy. 'He'll learn more'n he will watching you two take in ironing.'

It was a job at least. Josh was found, washed, brushed and lectured: 'I think there's any nanny-boying round that house an' you comin' straight home, paint or no paint.'

The three of them went off together, Betty suspecting every step of the way that her son was about to be plunged into a pool of homosexuality.

She came back reassured. Mr Reynolds had been charming—in a manly way—and allowed Josh a peek into the great octagonal room where he worked, watching the boy—in a manly way—as he explored it.

He hadn't seemed surprised that a black child should be interested in art. 'See him sniff the paints for their bouquet? He may be a natural, ma'am. If he shows promise, I shall bring him on, yes, bring him on.'

As for the sister, who would be Josh's real employer: 'Reckon that Miss Fanny's a fuss-budget,' Betty said, 'but she kindly, she goin' to take the boy to church every Sunday. Mr Reynolds, he don't go, but she do.'

It was wonderful yet heartbreaking. There was no room for Betty in the Reynolds' household and if she stayed on in London to be near it she would descend to a level of poverty below even the one she endured with Makepeace. But Josh had lived his entire life among those who loved him.

Makepeace managed to say: 'Certain sure this is what you want, Josh? We can't be with you for a while.'

He nodded through tears. 'I want it.'

As she held him, Makepeace thought: He's being brave. He don't want to be a burden on us, that's why he's going. And felt the advance of an agony she couldn't afford, so she thought: But it's his opportunity. He's got to go.

They saw him settled in the house at Leicester Fields. When they said goodbye, he was being led off to be fitted for his livery.

The next day the new company was gathering in Holborn to load the carts before setting off when another young boy presented himself. '*There* you are. I've had the devil's own job finding you. I wish you'd tell a fellow your address.' Lord Ffoulkes's round, freckled face was aggrieved and desperate. 'I've run away from school. I'm coming with you.'

Gently, Makepeace kissed him goodbye and walked away from him. As she climbed the stairs to the attic she heard Aaron begin the explanation: 'Andrew, you can't. The injunction—'

'I don't care about the injunction . . . They're pigs . . .'

She shut the door of the attic to keep the voices out, to stop hurt from piercing the dullness. No chink through which the pain thrashing outside could seep in. Don't feel.

Betty came up, sobbing: 'First his pa, then Sir Pip, now you.

Ain't nothin' those whoresons'll spare that boy. Take his fortune now, I wouldn't wonder.'

'Has he gone?'

Betty rubbed the window. 'He goin'. He cryin' but he goin'.'

Makepeace picked up her daughter and looked around the attic. 'We're off, then.'

Betty turned on her. '*When* you goin' to get mad?' But she had to follow Makepeace down the stairs unanswered.

Aaron had been right. Avoiding urban centres like Norwich, where there were established theatres, they took themselves to the barns, inns and booths of small towns and villages. The people of rural Norfolk, and then of Lincolnshire, had come in droves—or at least small flocks—lured by Aaron's playbills which, no matter what the play, always promised an endangered virgin.

Everybody had to hand out playbills. They were an expensive item but the larger the area of distribution the greater the subsequent audiences.

Letting Tom Capper wander off delivering on his own, however, was not efficient. After three successive days on which he was brought back, comatose and in the cart of a concerned, admiring labourer, Aaron was forced to send Tantaquidgeon with him as his sobriety-enforcer.

The sight of a six-foot Red Indian in a market square intrigued the local populace as much as the posters did.

'Your amiable friend is a phenomenon to these poor bucolics,' Hartley Witney pointed out. 'Use him.'

They already used him as cart-unpacker and loader, scene-shifter and mule-driver. However, the next night, Tantaquidgeon was given a spear to carry during the last act of *Amanta in the West Indies*. Unmoving, unspeaking, he nevertheless attracted hoots of admiration. After that the bills for every play, whether set in Verona or Scotland, gave him an ethnic background to suit all tastes and featured 'that Illustrious Noble Savage, Chief Hassan, own grandson to famed Pocahontas.'

But the greatest home-grown phenomenon was Fanny Cobb. Perhaps the late Mrs Bracegirdle had been numbered among her ancestry after all. The whiff of make-up sticks and footlight candles came to the girl's nostrils like the scent of ocean to a stranded seal. She badgered the cast until Penthesilea Witney, always kind, taught her Polly's songs from *The Beggar's Opera*.

Fanny's voice was pleasant enough, nothing special, and she could hold a tune but . . . 'I want you to hear her,' Penthesilea told Aaron.

'Over the Hills and Far Away' was not a particularly bawdy song but the way Fanny sang it was. She was not consciously seductive; merely by opening her mouth the girl released a contagious joyousness that was as sexual as it was unaware.

'God bless us,' said Aaron with feeling.

The next night Fanny was the musical entre'acte. 'She'll bring the magistrates on us,' Peg Devereux said, jealously.

'She'll bring the house down first.'

She was singing again, now, in order to cover an unplanned hiatus in *The Pharaoh's Daughter* caused by Tom Capper's disappearance to the Red Lion down the lane. Aaron and Tantaquidgeon had gone to fetch him. The audience, apparently, was finding no incongruity in the sudden leap from Biblical drama to Cockney street songs just as, on Capper's return, they would accept cruel Pharaoh's comic knockabout with his clown. All part of the magic.

And it *was* magic, Makepeace could see that. The panic was magical. The elderly Hartley Witneys behind her, hastily reshuffling the sequence of the play, were magical. Fanny singing, Aaron tearing his hair out and loving it, Capper reducing his audience to helplessness . . . all magical. They jerked and postured in gyrations that were wonderful and inexplicable, as if she were watching from too far away to understand why they made them.

She was the marionette, not them. For them the dreadful journeyings were an adventure at the end of which they could perform behind six candles stuck in a dirt floor. She just got into a cart, stayed in it, got out, moving on strings, a wooden thing among the living.

'*Prompt.*'

Peg Devereux was glaring again. The entr'acte was over, so was the comic scene. They had reached Act III without the prompter noticing. Makepeace turned her pages. 'One child of Israel you shall not kill cruel father for . . .'

'One child of Israel you *shall* not kill, cruel Father, for he is safely hidden.'

The play went on. In the wings the safely hidden Moses began to whimper. Makepeace handed the script to Fred Tortini and carried the basket through to the green room, a flapping tent attached to the barn's side door.

Betty was counting the night's takings. ' . . . an' sixpence and a ha'pence and I don't know what this is but it ain't coin of the realm.' She looked up. 'Two pound, four shilling an' sixpence ha'penny, a duck, two hens, a basket of bread, clutch of eggs an' a pot of somethin' as looks like someone been sick in it.'

'Very good,' said Makepeace politely.

'Ain't bad. We all eat tomorrow, any rate.' She produced a small jar from the region of her bosom where it had been kept warm. Makepeace took it and began spooning its contents into Philippa's mouth. Her milk had dried up three weeks before and the baby was on solid food—much too early in Betty's opinion.

'How'd she do as Moses?'

'Very well.'

'Very *well*.' The magic of theatre escaped Betty. 'Half a year old an' *actin*'. That Sir Pip's daughter we talkin' about. What'd he think, his chil' raised with painted Jezebels?' She didn't approve of Peg Devereux either.

'I don't know what else to do.'

It was no use for Betty to employ the child's vulnerability in order to provoke her into a reaction, a plan or anger—she was incapable of those things; they washed around like wreckage of the woman she'd once been, flotsam in a sea kept at bay by wooden walls.

The only vulnerable sound in the world was not a baby's crying, it was a man's voice calling for his wife as he died among those who wanted him dead.

The odd thing was that her mind didn't, couldn't yet, accuse Catty or Conyers. That blame, too, circled in the sea outside, a leviathan. The real guilt was within the walls. God had presented her with the loveliest of His gifts and she had not protected it. She hadn't seen how ill he was, hadn't wanted to see.

And sometimes she blamed him for his complicity in abandoning her to this awful place where he didn't exist. Catty wanted you dead—*and you obeyed her.*

Mr Burke's Touring Company made its way slowly into Yorkshire, keeping ahead of its rivals by going always northwards so that it seemed to be keeping pace with winter while at the same time promising spring to snow-fatigued villages.

At Thornton-le-Dale, as she got out of her cart, Makepeace stumbled and couldn't get up again.

The company extended its stay—'By Popular Demand!'—until she was over the pneumonia and audiences were reduced to a trickle. Even then, she was still too weak to travel.

'We'll have to go on, that's all the money we've got.' Aaron pressed what there was into Betty's hand. 'And somebody paid with a goat. I'll leave it with the innkeeper, it should give her milk. We'll be at Fylingdale and then Whitby, which is on the map. Somebody's sure to give you a lift.'

He paused. 'I suppose we can't take Philippa with us? Fanny'd look after her . . . Oh, all right, all *right.* She's a draw, that's all, I wanted her for *Caroline's Secret.*'

Betty watched them go from the inn's upper window, Tantaquidgeon striding forward at the mules' heads, the painted, canvas-hooped carts garish against the sweep of the moor.

'*Caroline's Secret,*' she said, bitterly. '*Caroline's Noah's Ark* more like.' She turned on the figure in the bed. 'You goin' to live.'

'I suppose so.'

'Ain't a question. I'm tellin' you. We ain't goin' on like this.'

She told Aaron the same when they caught up with the com-

pany and found him arranging its accommodation in two fisher-
men's cottages rented for the purpose.

He was busy and irritated. The Whitby justice of the peace,
having Puritan objections to the theatre in general and actors in
particular, had invoked the 1737 Licensing Act which made strolling
companies illegal and refused them permission to perform. Penthesilea Witney had gone to see the man—a visit from that awe-
somely respectable woman usually changed the magisterial mind.
But if it didn't, Aaron was going to have to turn the entire script
of *Pharaoh's Daughter* into vaguely rhyming couplets, insert some
songs and call it a 'burletta'. Burlettas were not classified as drama
and could be played anywhere.

It was difficult for him to comprehend that a way of life he
found all-consuming and all-satisfying, hand-to-mouth though it
was, was in fact helping to keep Makepeace in her limbo. 'For God's
sake,' he said to Betty, impatiently, 'it's a living. And it keeps her
busy.' Privately, he was beginning to think that it didn't matter
what course was chosen for Makepeace; she was too broken.

Betty knew she wasn't. 'She need to catch up with herself. She
been pushed down too far too quick; she need time to get over
the grievin' an' take in what those shites done to her. *Then* she get
mad. *Then* she do somethin'.'

'What? *What* can she do?' Aaron was stung by his own failure
to avenge his sister. His request to Conyers to meet him in a duel
had been dismissed with a note: *Major Conyers is obliged to Mr Burke
but would point out that, for their sake, he does not accept a challenge
from his inferiors.*

Aaron had raved but a weasely relief stopped him pursuing the
matter; he wasn't a good shot and, while he could fence nobly
enough on stage, an experienced swordsman like Conyers would
cut him into portions. Another death in the family would be of no
help to Makepeace.

'She do *somethin'*.' Betty was steadfast. 'She jus' need to be still
for a bit.'

'I'd set her up somewhere, you know I would, but there's no
money. We're only getting by as it is.'

'You been a good brother to that chil',' Betty said, soothingly. 'Maybe she set herself up. I found this.'

Makepeace's enforced convalescence in the little inn at Thornton-le-Dale had given Betty the opportunity to carry out what life on the road had not: a spring-cleaning of their travelling kit. The pitifully few clothes they possessed had been washed and darned, some of Philippa's dresses sacrificed to enlarge the others, boots patched and oiled—and the bulging holdall they had borrowed from Peter Little, which contained everything, had been turned inside out to be brushed.

This had inveigled itself behind a rip in the holdall's lining, stuffed away by Betty and then forgotten in the haste of the eviction from Hertfordshire.

'I asked her what is it an' she don't remember, then she say it jus' property an' throw it away, like she don't want to remember.'

'*Property?*'

Betty held out the squashed documents. 'You look 'em over, Aaron. I kin read or'nary but I ain't up to scriv'nin'.'

He took them to the window. ' "Manor of Raby in the County of Northumberland . . . held in fee simple"—*Lord*, this is old—"four hundred and two virgates . . ." '

'What's a virgate?'

Aaron squeezed his education for a clue. 'About thirty acres, I think. A lot, anyway. "Préciput"—I don't know what that is— "messuage"—Hell and high water, Betty, that's a dwelling-house— "fishing rights, brew-house, forest . . ." This is an estate!'

'We can sell it?'

'She can't live there, for sure. It's in Northumberland.' Aaron had been a Bostonian and was now a Londoner, a townsman heart and soul; he was prepared to exploit the poor savages who lived north of Potters Bar but be damned if he took up residence among them. 'That's about as far north as you can go without painting yourself with woad.'

'You sure she own it?'

'Seems to. There's a deed of transference from the owner to Makepeace Burke that looks legal enough. Wonder why she used her maiden name? It's dated only last year. Still, there it is, she's got property. Should buy her a nice little place in Chelsea.'

Or a tavern on the river, a second Roaring Meg, not too far from Josh. Betty's imagination was soaring. But in Betty's book one didn't sell a pig in a poke without examining it, any more than buy one. 'We better go see this Raby. Quick.'

Chapter Fifteen

'GAN a step doon the lonnon passin' the stob an' ye're hyem,' the wagoner said. 'Aa'd tyek ye but Aa'm queer.' He flicked his whip and they watched the wagon lumber away northwards.

'What he say?'

'I don't know. Maybe Tantaquidgeon scared him.'

To the east, on their right, there was a path that meandered to where the land petered out in sand-hills and sea; against darkening clouds they could see gulls and a white smudge of smoke from hidden habitation.

But the wagoner's whip had indicated a track that led west, into moorland deserted by everything but sheep. The air held miles and miles of unpopulated silence, broken only by curlews and a slight clank in the breeze from a gibbet.

Betty nodded at the bones in the gibbet. 'Trampled in the crush, I guess. Well, let's git.' She was regretting bitterly her insistence that they investigate the Raby estate. Her image of a manor house had petered down to a shepherd's hut—if they were lucky.

Newcastle upon Tyne had proved to be a town of unexpected prosperity and they'd seen industry as they travelled the road leading from it, but the further north they went the greater sense they had of approaching the space at the end of the world.

'Should've waited for Aaron to come with us,' Betty told herself. However, Newcastle had been avid for entertainment and prepared to pay in hard cash for seats under canvas in a timber yard; it would not have done to interrupt the company's run.

Fanny had loyally, if reluctantly, offered to come along as well but Aaron couldn't spare her; a large, admiring, male clique attended every performance on her account.

So here they were, three of them with a child, trudging along ruts that showed no sign of recent traffic, presumably already on Raby land.

Should've brought vittles, Betty thought. Have to butcher a sheep an' cook it. I'm too old for this-all.

She had watched those around her become impatient of Makepeace's grief and was herself at last wearying of the burden it put on her; she had done nothing since Dapifer's death but make vast decisions. Ain't my place, she thought self-pityingly, old nigra woman like me; time *she* was doin' the orderin'.

But Betty still held to the belief that the motive behind this expedition was good. The bustle of other people's activity left Makepeace rudderless; she must be forced to take the tiller, run her own tavern again, assume responsibility for her daughter. The discovery that she had something to sell whereby all these good things could be achieved had seemed God-sent—and now didn't. Who'd want to buy bare moorland?

'How much you wager to win this place?'

Makepeace didn't want the memory. 'Seventy guineas, maybe.'

'Cheaper if you lost the bet.'

They hustled on in failing light to keep ahead of the rainclouds behind them, the two women taking turns to carry Philippa, who was becoming heavy, Tantaquidgeon with the holdall on his shoulder.

You let pirates board my chil's boat, Lord, an' you ain't doin' nothin' to save her. *Nothin'*.

The rain caught up with them. They sheltered under some wizened trees but were forced out by encroaching darkness, afraid they'd soon be unable to see their way. Despite the joggling, Philippa slept under Makepeace's cloak like the good child she was.

'Whatever it is they gone pulled it down,' Betty panted. Even a shepherd's hut had become desirable. She and Makepeace were stumbling now, unable to see where they were going. They kept their eyes on Tantaquidgeon's feather floating ahead, trusting to the Indian's cat's eyes.

He stopped. They'd breasted a hill. Below them, in a dip, was a light.

Praise the Lord.

They went down towards it, slithering on the muddy incline. Not a hut but an ugly house, its shape wetly black against the lesser darkness of the moor. A glimmer from a downstairs window showed a yard, dilapidated outhouses, more mud and a woodpile with an axe in one of the logs. They picked their way through. Betty rapped on the window.

There was movement, the glow faded from the window, more movement and a man's voice: 'Howay, ye porvorse sod, git back.' A sound of fumbling at a door to their right and a grumble: 'Wha's aboot this sneck? If it's gaugers Ah'll push your bloody fyesses in.'

Betty had the presence of mind to shove Makepeace ahead in case the door, once opened, shut again. Visiting black women and Red Indians were probably rare in these hills.

The door scraped against flooring as it opened. 'It's daft to be out on such a neet.' A rushlight was held up. A furious-looking man in shirtsleeves stood in the doorway, a plaid round his shoulders. As his light illuminated Makepeace's face beneath her dripping hood, the anger faded. After a moment, he said: 'Howay, pet. Coom in.'

He cut short Betty's apologies and explanations and hurried them in. There was a donkey in the passage behind him, as well as a pig and several hens. He shooed them away, telling his visitors to step carefully over the manure. 'Ah've had no time to mend the hemmel, d'ye see.'

They were in a room that was dark except for a small coal fire. He shut the door to keep the animals out and busied himself lighting candles. 'Thought you might be the gaugers.' He caught Betty's look of incomprehension. 'The excise, pet. There's no peace from the sods wi' candles dutiable.'

He was a grim-looking man, of medium height, though his width of chest and shoulder made him seem squat, like a pugilist—an impression enforced by a powerful neck and a broken nose. He had black eyebrows and dark hair, grizzled at the sides and cut brutally short.

The room was clean but bare and too high and too narrow, like the house. He'd been reading, a book lay on a stool beside a grandfather chair with a bootlace to mark his place. There was no other furniture.

Betty was led to the chair, a chaff mattress was fetched and curved against the wall for Makepeace to sit on, the stool offered to Tantaquidgeon, who ignored it.

The man introduced himself. 'Andra Hedley, the factor of this place. Gi' us those wet clothes.'

The divestment of their cloaks revealed Philippa. He knelt down to her. 'What cheer, wheen-love. Hoongry? Shall us see what's in the yettlins?' He held out his hand, Philippa took it and toddled with him to the door. They could hear him talking to her as he lifted her down the passage.

Betty nodded at Tantaquidgeon to go after them, just in case. It was an automatic precaution, she wasn't really concerned; whatever a yettlin was Philippa would be safe with it—and him. The man exuded power enough to split rock, but not, Betty felt, the sort dangerous to little girls, except as an energetic sea was dangerous. He hadn't asked their names or their business, nor had he batted an eye at their variety of race. On receiving them his Northumbrian dialect had ameliorated into something nearer English; he'd greeted Philippa with concern; he was offering food.

'A Christian,' Betty said, taking off her boots and putting them in the grate. She noticed that, as she did the same, Makepeace picked up the man's book to read the title. It was *Gulliver's Travels*.

Philippa marched in, chattering baby gobbledegook and holding spoons, followed by the men with wooden bowls and a cooking pot that Hedley hung over the fire. 'Carlins,' he said. 'Grey peas.'

It was only courteous to state their business before they accepted his meal, however unappetizing. As Makepeace wasn't saying anything, Betty asked: 'This Raby we're at?'

When he nodded, she felt in the holdall and brought out the documents. He took the papers and held them close to a candle for examination.

It was difficult to tell how old he was from his face in concentration, anything from thirty-five upwards. When he'd greeted Philippa he'd looked younger. The hands holding the papers were criss-crossed with little blue scars; there was another across his flattened nose.

'I've been expecting these. I was sent copies from London.' He looked up. 'Mr Burke, where is he? A hard man to find.'

'*Mister* Burke?'

'Ay, Mr Makepeace Burke.'

Betty said: '*That's* Makepeace Burke. There ain't no mister.'

He went still. 'Female.'

'Yes.'

'Bought the place from the Headingtons.'

'Yes.' She looked at Makepeace through Hedley's eyes and saw a figure resembling not so much an estate owner as a woman who sold pegs door-to-door. Honesty compelled her to add: 'She sort of acquired it.'

He asked, flatly: 'She's not rich?'

Betty was getting tired of it. 'We left the jewels and gold coach at the crossroads.'

He nodded. Then he got up and walked out of the room, carefully closing the door behind him. They heard a squawk from hens and the bang of the front door. Betty hurried to the window, Makepeace with her. They cupped their eyes to the glass.

He was standing in the rain, his face lifted to a sky he was threatening with his fists. His mouth was open and glinting like a howling wolf's.

All at once he stooped to the woodpile and came up with the axe. With a roar that vibrated the window against the watchers' noses, he hurled it at an outhouse door. For a while he stood, watching it quiver, then turned back.

Hurriedly, the women resumed their places.

When he eventually returned to the room, he'd exchanged his plaid for a jacket and was carrying a jug and beakers. He served them. 'Nettle beer.' He slopped the contents of the cauldron into a frying pan and balanced it on the flames while he fetched butter, honey and rum, mixed them into the pan, poured the resultant mess into bowls and handed them round. 'Eat,' he said.

He took his own bowl to the corner furthest away from the light and ate, holding his spoon like a shovel. Anger radiated out of him as if from a furnace but he was controlling it.

The food was surprisingly good. The beer wasn't.

Makepeace broke the silence. 'What's wrong with me being a woman, may I ask?' It was the first time she'd spoken since entering the house and her first question since Dapifer's death. Betty sat up.

'Nothing, pet,' Hedley said, bitterly. 'You've the requisites as far as I can see and wi' a wheen more flesh I've no doubt you'd reduce a lad to ecstasy. But I'd have liked you wealthy, or at the least with access to wealth.'

'Me too,' Betty said, with feeling

'Why?' Makepeace asked.

But he was musing, resentfully—more to himself than them. 'I've been waiting for rich Mr Burke for over twelvemonth. Even ventured to London in quest of the man and a foul sink it were. Now, who comes tapping at my window? A benighted female.' He crashed his fist against the wall and left a dent in the plaster. 'And both of us sitting on a treasure house wi' no cash to turn the key.'

The noise woke Philippa, who'd been dozing over her bowl, and he was immediately sorry. He apologized to her. She went to sleep again.

'Treasure house?' asked Makepeace.

'Coal, pet.' He put his face in his hands. 'Just coal.'

'Oh, coal.' For a moment the word 'treasure' had conjured sunken galleons, a miser's hidden hoard, gold from an ancient burial mound.

'Coal,' he said, lifting his head, amazed at her tone. 'That in yon fire, and a' the fires in London to judge fra the smeech. Stuff as smelts iron and steel, as powers the blast furnaces, as'll take us to the machine age and free men fra drudgery . . .'

He regarded their incomprehension. 'God save us the ignorance.' He went to the grate, grabbed a lump of coal from its scuttle and pressed it into Makepeace's hand. His skin grated on hers like wood. 'How many ton o' coal were dug from the northeast last year, tell me that?'

She shook her head.

'Two million, give or take. Two *million* ton.' He grabbed the stool and sat on it so that his face was level with hers. 'Can tha take in the size of it? If Ah said a million days ago puts us back centuries before Christ, would tha realize then? You *southerners'*— it was a dirty word—'thinks that England's wealth is corn? Wool? Na, it's coal. They tell us the Lord Chancellor takes his seat on a woolsack. Wi' more sense the lad would be sittin' on a bag o' coals.'

Hedley swivelled on the stool to face Betty, who was still struggling to multiply the price of a ton of coal in London by two million. 'An' that's without wor new steam pumps. Ah tell thee, coal's but in its infancy. Who's got coal's got riches an' power an', better, he's got the future.' He got up, shaking his fist at the ceiling. 'Ah could be the new Prometheus.' He went to the window and stared into the darkness. 'An' what am Ah? Bloody Tantalus. We're standin' on the sod and can't reach it.'

Silence fell over the room as if a high wind had suddenly stopped blowing. They could hear the puff of the fire and Philippa's slight snores. 'Howay,' he said, wearily, 'no use gollarin' at the moon. Tha's not to blame. I'll light you to your beds.'

Makepeace was turning the coal in her hand so that its facets caught the light, like a black diamond. 'Why can't we?'

'Eh? Oh, equipment, pet. Pump engines, picks, wagons, rails, props. Men to dig, ponies to drag. Outlay of thousands o' pounds before the gain of ha'pence. The earth surrenders her treasure wi' parsimony.'

As he took up a candle, Makepeace, still sitting, said: 'Suppose I'd had money and could've got the coal out, it would've been my profit, not yours. How would you benefit?'

He looked back at her, grinning, suddenly vulpine. 'Half, pet. I'm the only one knows where it is.'

'Do you believe him?'

'Nyumwhaa?' Betty woke up. Her body told her it was the middle of the night and the dark of the room confirmed it. Complaining, she heaved herself onto her other side. A thin moonlight showed Makepeace standing at the window.

'Do you believe him?'

Betty yawned. 'I believe he believe it. But he ain't sane. What you doin', girl?'

Makepeace was regarding her hand, where moonlight put a sheen on a piece of coal. 'Power,' she said.

'An' fairy gold an' moonshine an' no use thinkin' about it—'

'Know what I'd do with power?'

'How 'bout sleepin'?'

'I'd crucify them.'

It should have been a moment for the Nunc Dimittis but Betty felt no inclination to say it. She was suddenly chilled. She'd wanted Makepeace angry, but this wasn't anger; it was too matter-of-fact, too quiet; this was decay, a cold malignancy that infected the carrier.

She heaved herself out of bed. 'You don' want to worry 'bout them no more,' she said. 'They get their come-uppance. Di'n't the Lord say He goin' to deal out vengeance? He got them in his sights. Sure as taxes, he'll see to 'em.'

'He won't,' Makepeace said. 'He doesn't. He just keeps letting them crucify His son.'

Betty put her arms around her. 'You git back to bed, chil', give that baby a cuddle. You well again now, this place perked you up, bless the Lord. Maybe tomorrow we see what we kin do with it, maybe it ain't so bad as it looks.'

She was embracing marble. It said: 'I'm going to crucify them. As sure as Jesus gave His blood for me, they're going to shed theirs, every last drop, for Philip Dapifer.'

She slept late next morning. The room was empty, a small dint in the pillow next to her where her child had lain. It was a cupboard bed, the higher of two that took up an entire wall—she'd had to climb up to it by ladder; Philippa had loved it—and of surprising beauty inside where the panels were carved with festoons of leaves and apples.

At one end, shelves of books held the Bible, Milton, Shakespeare, Smollett's *History of England*, Fielding's *Joseph Andrews*, a grammar and a dictionary, the library of a man educating himself; but the greater section was taken up with home-made folders of canvas, their titles neatly inked: 'Coke-smelting', 'Crucible-casting', 'Puddling and Rolling', 'Steam Atmospheric Engines', 'Drainage', 'Coal Damp', 'Circulation of Air'.

She washed with water from a ewer set on the windowsill. It was a lovely morning, laundered by last night's rain. Immediately below, the view of the yard was still unprepossessing but beyond it the hills were a palette of gentle colours and the air smelled of bracken and grass, like spring. But it was no longer spring, it was autumn.

Philippa, who was being led round the yard on a donkey by the man Hedley, caught sight of her and waved. Awkwardly, Makepeace waved back.

In the bad place she had been occupying, Philippa had demanded an energy and attention she'd found difficult to give. If the child had been the boy Dapifer had thought it to be there would have been a dearer connection in her mind between father and baby. As it was, 'It's a girl' had seemed at the time yet another betrayal of a betrayed man, the birth merely part of the loss. Mentally, if not physically, she had neglected her daughter.

The little girl mostly went to Betty when she was troubled, even to Fanny or Aaron, instinctively avoiding the invisible fence of grief that surrounded her mother. And Makepeace did not know how to bridge it.

She'd be a year old now.

Twelve months. How in hell had she survived them, in Hell with the damned? Such laceration, she'd had to crawl into the deepest part of her soul to withstand the agony. Something, God she supposed, had been stitching the wounds to preserve the patient from bleeding to death, but so haphazardly had He done it that the result of the recovery was of appalling ugliness, a lopsided, limping freak in permanent pain.

With survival, if it could be called survival, the outside world had crashed in and brought with it this flooding hatred.

It was almost amusing, Makepeace thought, that what Catty and Conyers must see as the deepest injury they'd inflicted on her was, in fact, the least. They would be rejoicing at their cleverness in stealing Dapifer's wealth, his status, his lands, and they could have had them without trouble; they'd only ever been peripheral to her. If they'd said: 'Sign over all his worldly goods and we'll allow you to attend him while he dies . . .' But they were incapable of even that grace.

Certain sure, she would kill them for it one day. But the reason she would make them suffer before they died, see them chomped alive from the feet up like fledglings being eaten by a hedgehog, was for their petty cruelty, the malice that had kept her from burying him, of separating her from Andrew Ffoulkes, not caring how they hurt the boy as long as they hurt her.

And for the visit to the attic room in Holborn, that last banal gloat Catty had found irresistible—a revenge, Makepeace supposed, for her own ill-judged expedition to Catty's house in Great Russell Street.

'*What did she say?*' Betty had asked and asked.

The thing was, she'd said nothing, just stood in the doorway and smiled: at the dingy room, at the grate's two pieces of coal, at other people's clothes on the airing horses, at the wounded thing in the middle of them.

And one day, when *you're* in the last extremity, I shall stand in your doorway. And I'll be smiling. Hear my prayer, dear Lord, for the power to put the earth back in balance by hurling her to bottomless perdition. Hear my prayer. Only that. If I have to fall in after her, Lord, hear my prayer.

She picked up the piece of coal from the windowsill and looked down again at the man who'd given it to her. He'd hoisted Philippa on his shoulders now and was trying to talk to Tantaquidgeon who stood watching.

The man had no respect; his language was foul but he was kindly enough, for all his anger. In effect, this was his house, the factor's house. He'd casually surrendered it to them last night; Headington House itself was a ruin, he'd said. He'd gone off to sleep in his workshop at what he called the but 'n' bens along the track.

She knew his type. Another one who wants power, she thought, though she was too incurious to wonder what he wanted it for. Men like him had visited the Roaring Meg; rough, capable artisans obsessed by a dream: to find El Dorado, or discover a passage to the Pacific Ocean.

'Can any good thing come out of Nazareth?'

She would go down and see.

At her approach he swung Philippa down from his shoulders. 'Off you come, Pip.'

'*Don't call her that.*'

He glanced up. His gentle 'All right, pet' told her that Betty had been talking to him.

She was irritated. 'About this coal . . .' she snapped.

They went indoors for the discussion. Betty had been busy already; the passageway that had accommodated last night's animals was swept and washed. The clank of pots and a smell of rabbit stew came from the kitchen. The fire in the parlour was newly laid with coals.

He set the chair for her and took the stool. 'You'd best sell,' he said. 'It's what I advised yon Mr Headington in wor letters. Sell, I told him, if you're not interested, sell to them as is, but the lad would never give us his attention.'

'Too busy gambling,' Makepeace said.

Hedley raised his eyebrows. 'Were that it? They were ever a porvorse family.'

He had the estate's books and accounts ready to show her, all meticulously kept. Raby had been a prosperous manor in the days of the Commonwealth but, he said, had since suffered a hundred years of neglect from being awarded to a Sir Henry Headington, an acolyte of Charles II, 'a pornicious monarch' in Hedley's opinion.

To the Headingtons Northumberland had always been here-be-dragons land; they preferred London and their vast holdings in the south, 'though they bleated quick enough if they worn't sent the rents'.

Without repair the manor house had eventually fallen down; workers had left; there had been no investment into more advanced breeding of sheep so the wool from which the Headingtons derived their income had been outclassed by that from other, better-managed estates.

They'd been fortunate in having an honest factor—Andra Hedley's grandfather, a man with a head for business, who'd begged his employers to speculate in order to accumulate.

'He quoted Francis Bacon at 'em 'til he bubbled. Money's like muck, he told 'em, no good 'less it's spread. Would they hear him? I doubt they read his letters. "Keep up the rents, Mr Hedley." So he did, canny man. He found 'em coal. Would they put money in it? "Just keep up the rents, Mr Hedley." ' He glared at Makepeace as if it were her fault. 'We dug what we could and the main seam was there, ready as a lass on a Saturday night, but she wouldn't wait for ever and she didn't.'

Makepeace shifted. Coal was not a substance she was acquainted with: it had never been used at the Roaring Meg; Mrs Peplow had refused to desecrate the Grosvenor Square chimneys with it—mineral fuel was still regarded as dirtily vulgar by the gentry's old guard—and in Hertfordshire it had been unnecessary to burn anything except logs from the estate. As for where it came from . . . she'd supposed, when she supposed at all, that it lay around in dark, wild areas where dark, wild men—not unlike this one—shovelled it into sacks.

'Can't you just find another seam?' she asked.

Hedley lowered his head and drummed his fist on his forehead. After a minute he looked up. 'Get your boots on.'

They set out along a continuation of last night's track. As Tantaquidgeon fell in behind them, Hedley asked: 'Is that lad mum fra choice?'

'Wounded,' Makepeace said, shortly. 'The talking bit of his brain got hacked away by another tribe.'

'How old is he?'

She shrugged. 'About five.'

'Pity,' Hedley said. He paused for a moment. 'What're you to be called? Mrs Burke? Lady Dapifer? What?'

Betty *had* been busy. Makepeace was suddenly at a loss; what creature was it that had been spewed out to begin another dreary round of acquaintanceships? She couldn't answer him because she truly didn't know. Lady Dapifer? She'd yet to win that title back and, anyway, having gone to ground she was reluctant to call attention to herself. And you couldn't call yourself Hate, it wasn't a name.

Hedley was striding on, either from impatience or a reluctance to witness her confusion. She hurried to catch him up, the matter unresolved.

Going upwards, the track became a green lane sunk between beeches that diffused the sun into penny-sized dapples. A path to the right led to a row of cottages but they kept straight on.

At the top of the hill two gates marked an overgrown drive to a ruin. Ravens perched on its tumble of stones, stabbing their beaks into the ivy in search of insects.

'Headington House,' Hedley said as they went by.

They came out into moorland where sheep pulled at the thin grass in soft, dry rasps, unalarmed by intrusion.

'My sheep?'

'Na,' he said, 'Wully Bolam's.' He said that after William the Conqueror had subdued Northumberland—and it had taken some doing—he'd scorched it. Huge areas, of which this moorland was part, had been described as 'waste' in the Domesday Book. 'They're still waste.'

She presumed they were heading for the Raby mine but there was no sign of slag heaps or the stark chimneys and wheels denoting a colliery such as had lined the road out of Newcastle.

However, it was a long time since she'd gone walking other than at Betty's behest or to trail behind Aaron's theatrical carts and it was not unpleasant to be suiting her own purpose for once, especially on a day like this.

Butterflies bounced along with them. Peregrines winnowed the air before disappearing in a stoop to kill; grouse whirred from under her feet. Some red deer posed as if for their portrait under a hangar of trees, then galloped away.

The moor concealed lush, steep little valleys with fast-flowing streams that had to be crossed by stepping stones. Hedley didn't offer his hand; he would turn to see that she and Tantaquidgeon were safely over, then go on. He walked in silence and with a roll of the shoulders as if he were breasting a heavy sea. Makepeace wondered if he'd been born angry or had anger thrust upon him, as hatred had been thrust on her.

They'd negotiated another valley and come to the top when he pointed. And there it was in the distance, a mound on which stood a black tangle of chimneys, frames, wheels and huts, laid out untidily against the sun like the dropped stitches and pulled wool of a child's attempt at knitting. It had the weary stillness of abandonment.

Now she got her bearings. From where she and the mine stood on the same height, the ground dropped away to the road that had brought her from Newcastle. From here it looked as if someone had drawn it through dust with a wavering finger. Beyond it was the straight, dark-blue pencil line of the sea. They had come along the upper two sides of a pentangle of which the other three were the track from the house to the road, the road itself and, presumably, a track from the road to the mine.

She'd passed the damn thing yesterday and hadn't seen it.

They walked towards it. Nettles grew around the buildings; machinery rusted quietly in the sun. Weeds were beginning to forgive a slag mound and covering it in a haze of green.

'Not but a step fra the sea's edge,' Hedley said, furiously. 'With a wagonway, we could get the coal to the staiths wi'out crossin' any land but Raby's.' He spat. 'Ah deor, words fail me.'

They didn't, though. Makepeace had no chance to find out what staiths were; now he'd begun to talk, he didn't stop, his Northumbrian accent becoming stronger and shooting the penultimate syllables of sentences upwards like grapeshot at pigeons' nests.

He removed boarding from under a rusted crane to reveal a great hole in the ground. 'Here's the main shaft.' A stone was pressed into Makepeace's hand. 'Chuck it doon.'

She leaned over the hole and let the stone drop. After what seemed a long wait she heard a tiny, echoing splash. Hedley said: 'That's watter. *Watter.* She drowned her bloody self when the roof came in.'

The shaft had been dug on his grandfather's initiative, he said, with the Headingtons reluctantly paying for only minimal equipment. After the roof fell in they'd refused to provide any at all. 'A decent pump, one decent bloody steam pump and we'd still have her dry but Headington would only afford us a horse gin.'

Still standing on the edge of the shaft, Makepeace was given a brief history of coal. Hedley said it had first made its appearance on the human stage in the thirteenth century when monks had started gathering the strange, black mineral pebbles scattered along the coast and using them for fuel. Once it was realized what enormous deposits lay around Tyne and Wear—as well as the ease of shipping them down the rivers—the great exploitation began under Elizabeth and James I. At first it was by drift mines, shallow slanting passages to get at what lay near the surface; then, as that ran out, by deep, vertical shafts like this one.

Vast fortunes had been made from coal. Newcastle and its industries—salt, glass, brewing, brick-making, the metal trades, shipping—had been built on it and were growing fast. London fires depended on it and a thousand ships ferried sea coal down the Tyne to the Thames.

'There's talk it'll run out,' Hedley said, 'but that's blethor. We'll all have to go deeper, mind. The colliery at Walker's just sunk a shaft a hundred fathoms.'

Makepeace wasn't interested in other collieries, only this one. She peered again into the depths. 'There's still coal down there?'

He thumped on the stem of the crane, making it shudder. 'Think on a wall,' he said. 'Bloody eighteen yard of coal face, smooth, hard as diamond, colossal. That's what my father and me saw down there. We were following a small seam through rock and there she was. Rich? I been down pits twenty-seven year an' never glimpsed richer. I tell you, we stood there gowfed. An' then dust started tricklin' over wor heads an' we heard the creakin' an' we knew she was comin' in. The quicker the dust trickles, the faster you run. We bloody ran. Down comes the roof behind us, followin' like a juggernaut intent on wor destruction. How we got out wi' wor lives is a bloody miracle.'

His voice changed into that of a lover mooning over an unattainable mistress. 'She's under rock and water but she's still there, black as deeth, and I know which direction she bides. Her or me, I'm havin' her.' He straightened up. 'Make us partners, we told Headingtons, invest an' we'll dig you a fortune but lug-brained louts divvn't listen.'

He jerked his thumb. 'Come on, pet, we'll go down.'

She drew back. 'Down *there?*'

He clicked his tongue at her stupidity. They moved away from the pit head and walked down the hill to a clearing hidden from it—more tumbledown huts, more nettles. 'All began here.'

She wouldn't have noticed this other entrance to the mine if he hadn't led her to it, a narrow cave overhung by ferns. It was where his grandfather had noticed that a small section of hillside had given way and exposed a stratum of coal. They'd begun the dig horizontally—'a drift, it's called'—following the coal seam as it went deeper until, at last, they had approached it more directly by sinking the shaft.

Hedley brought out various items from the bulging pockets of his coat: a tinderbox, candles, and a cap of quilted leather he told her to put on.

For a moment, as she took off her linen cap, the sun on her hair made him blink. 'That'd set off fire-damp,' he said and led the way. Almost immediately, the entrance became a tunnel little over four feet high so that they both had to stoop.

Hedley paused, looking back. 'What's doing?'

She turned to see that Tantaquidgeon wasn't following. 'Come on,' she called to him. He didn't move.

It was so unusual, she went back. 'What's the matter?'

There was no expression on the Indian's face, there never was but, looking at it, she saw the deep creases carved into the bronze of his skin.

He's got old, she thought, and I haven't noticed. Under her gaze he folded his arms and turned away.

Behind her, Hedley said: 'Don't make him.'

'He's gone into fire for me before this,' she said, defensively.

'We all have wor demons, mebbe his lies underground.'

Perhaps it did. She turned and left him, feeling naked.

The tunnel sloped downwards, turned, flattened and sloped again, never at any point rising above back-breaking level. 'High enough to get out coal,' Hedley said, his voice echoing back to her. 'Coal counts, not bodies.'

The place was a labyrinth, other tunnels gaped to right and left; she lost her sense of direction. As they went deeper they were passing among small pillars, hand-hewn four-cornered piers of jet which glistened wetly as Hedley's candle went by. 'Coal,' she called. 'Is this coal?'

'Ay. Keeps the roof up.'

She hurried to catch up with him. 'Isn't it worth something?'

'A bit.'

After a while he stopped and held the candle low so that it

shone on a black and motionless pool of water ahead covering the tunnel floor as it went on and downwards. 'Flood,' he said. 'Same watter as at the bottom of the shaft.'

There was a niche in one of the walls with a bench fixed across it. He told her to sit. He sat beside her and put the candle down. She was in his classroom—he was a teacher who believed in physical experience. 'See, pet,' he began, 'the earth doesn't appreciate being violated, she'll keep her coal if she can . . .'

'She', apparently, had terrible ways of killing the human moles who tried to rob her, sometimes crushing them, sometimes flooding their tunnels to drown them. There was a noxious fume called 'choke-damp' that took miners' breath and lives, and 'firedamp' which caused explosions so strong it could blow men's bodies hundreds of feet up vertical shafts into the open air.

'Wor Peter were killed like that at Walker's,' he said, heavily, 'me brother.'

She wasn't ready for other people's tragedies. The silence was broken only by the far-off, echoing drip of water. Around her the walls were decorated with little stalactites of mineral salts that showed whitely brilliant in the light of the candle.

'How d'you know the wall of coal you and your father saw doesn't run out further on?' she asked.

He grunted, amused, and raised the pitch of his voice into a parody of upper-class English. ' "Are you dowsers of coal, you Hedleys? Can you divine it? Surely, it's too far north to be a significant field." I saw it. She's there, I *smelled* her.'

He stretched and stood up. 'One more thing. Folk that send men down mines do it lightly. They need to know what light is— *and* dark. Don't be feored, I'm dousing the candle for a minute.'

She saw him lick his fingers, then the flame went out.

Black. It wasn't darkness like a moonless night, not mere absence of light, it was a presence that pressed upon the eyelids, it was the coffin lid coming down, the withdrawal of self, of hope, of God. In that moment she knew what death actually was; it wasn't death because she was aware but she saw the unawareness that awaited her.

She lost Dapifer then. *Is this where you are, Pip? Is this what you know?* But he didn't know anything; he was in eternal insentience.

There was the scrape of a tinderbox and a tiny waver of light as the candle lit. Hedley started to say something, then stopped, put down the candle and went to his knees beside her. 'I'm sorry, pet, I'm a clown. You seemed unafeored . . .'

She thumped on his shoulder with her fist. 'He was the most alive person I ever knew, oh *God*, and they sent him into . . . there isn't a God, I saw it, just nothingness.' The loneliness was intolerable.

He sat down, one arm around her so that she could weep onto his jacket. It smelled of coal dust and iron.

'Obliteration,' he said, after a bit. 'Whiles I thought the same.'

When her weeping grew less fierce, he withdrew his arm and produced a kerchief. She blew her nose into patches of machine oil.

'But see, bonny lass,' he said, 'the candle lit up again. Persephone comes yearly out the shadows and you'll do the same.' He retrieved his handkerchief, gave her face a couple more wipes with it and put it away. 'Give us your hand and I'll take you home.'

With her hand in one of his, the other holding the candle, he shuffled with her out of the tunnel.

Air and birdsong and the smell of bracken blasted themselves at her and for a moment she put back her head, letting sunlight wash through her. Then she was hurt by her body's surrender to physical contentment as if, like a child, it had not been paying attention to the grown-up business of mental agony. Merely being alive was a helpless betrayal of the dead.

She noticed Hedley walk up to the statue that was Tantaquidgeon and talk to him, a squat, dark shape beside the tall Indian. She experienced a sudden nausea at the intimacy he and she had shared below ground. She'd exposed her soul, her *husband*, to a damn quarryman.

Anyway, it was her job to comfort Tantaquidgeon, not his.

'Anybody could get the coal out,' she said, nastily, 'they wouldn't need you.'

'They could try, pet,' he admitted, 'but they wouldn't find her, they'd need to know where she lies.' He was dismissive, absent-minded, walking off in a hurry to be home. He'd shown her the difficulties so that she would know what she was selling and why she must sell it; she was no longer his responsibility.

She took a last look around, trying to imagine the maze beneath her feet, the stone-blocked, water-filled tunnels lying in the dark acres between here and the shaft. Damn the man, he was right; you'd need to know which direction to dig in.

As she began to trail after him on the path back, she was still shaken, prepared to blame him for momentarily extinguishing more than light. It was a terrible thing he'd done merely in order to teach her a lesson for enquiring into his trade.

Common-sense and the sweetness of being above ground gradually brought her balance back. The lesson had been well learned; she'd seen the locality, heard a little of its history, and absorbed more knowledge about the working of mines by actually being in one than if she'd attended fifty lectures.

She called out to him. 'How much money would it need to get the mine producing?'

'Ten thousand pound,' he called back. 'At least.'

She had a sudden image of the careless piles of guineas on Almack's' gaming tables. A resentful layer added itself to her stratum of hatred, this time at the sheer bloody wastefulness of those who excluded her.

When Hedley left her at the door of the ugly house, she was too preoccupied to say goodbye.

'Wife died givin' birth,' Betty said, serving rabbit stew. 'Only got the one and had him eddicated. The boy's gone for a lawyer in Newcastle. Andra said he di'n't want his chil' down a pit draggin' coal wagons at eight-year-old, like he was. Sent down to join his pa, Andra was, when work run out here. We both known slavery, Andra an' me.'

'He's a talker, I'll give him that,' Makepeace said.

'Put a spark back in you,' Betty said defiantly. 'It's nice to see you eatin'.'

'What's that got to do with it?' Another betrayal by the body—being hungry.

'It's his brother give us the coneys, tha's what. One got killed in the pit, this 'un's Jamie, lives in one o' the but 'n' bens down the track, got two childer.' Betty, also, had been absorbing local knowledge.

'What sort of man d'you reckon him, Bet?'

'Billie?'

'Andra. Clever? Or mad?'

Betty raised her eyebrows. 'You was out with him all mornin', what you reckon?' Then she said, 'Bit o' both, mebbe.'

Which wasn't helpful.

The scales of Makepeace's opinion were out of level all night, first on one side, then the other. He *couldn't* know whether the mine was worth the enormous investment of ten thousand pounds; the wall he and his father had seen might be just that: a freak seam of coal behind which was just more rock. But *if* it didn't run out, *if* it went on to form the equation: Wealth equals Power equals Ability to Harm . . . what then?

Fighting Catty through the courts would be the least of it. Makepeace'd buy newspapers and blacken the bitch's name with them. Buy politicians as well and get a certain Major thrown out of the army . . .

The cupboard bed became a bloodbath: Catty's metaphorical nose exploded as Makepeace's heel went into it; Conyers's metaphorical liver spilled onto an executioner's table. The images became more and more ridiculous as sleep continued to elude her; she knew they were ridiculous, a childish recompense to herself. *But they're all I've got.*

She got out of bed, tiptoed round the small truckle bed one of Betty's new friends had provided for Philippa, and laved her face in the ewer to start weighing the argument over again.

It all depended on the person of Andra Hedley. Prophet or crackpot? Even supposing she could procure the ten thousand pounds, he would have to be her security; she had no other.

The moon was full; usually it was a searing reminder of the

times she and Dapifer had looked at it together; but tonight it was kinder to her. It was light at least, and today she had come to value light.

Nobody was left in total blackness for ever, hadn't he said? Tapers were relit and poor old Persephone, perhaps led by a continuity of lights, from the chandeliers of Almack's to a miner's candle, staggered out of Hell's tunnel to wreak revenge on the shites who'd sent her there.

Yes, that was it.

She carried her decision back to bed like a drunk trying not to spill his tankard. Waking the next morning, she found it slopped and the whole thing began again.

Another look at Hedley might make up her mind one way or the other.

She went up the track and took the turning off it that led to the but 'n' bens, which turned out to be a row of two-roomed cottages.

Most of them were deserted but two at least were neatly kept and appeared to have been converted into one dwelling to judge from the identical paint on four pairs of shutters and one of the doorways which had been filled in with bricks. Vegetable plots were laid out along the backs and two toddlers were playing on the hill beyond them that hid the ruin of the big house. Hens pecked at feed a woman was scattering on the bare earth outside her front door. She nodded good morning at Makepeace. 'Andra?'

'How d'you do. Yes.'

'Plodgin' wi' his fire engines, end o' raa.' She indicated the last cottage in the row.

If she'd said the man was cavorting with a dragon, it would have been believable; smoke issued in strong, regular puffs from the cottage's open door and windows. Makepeace could hear clanking as if scales rubbed against each other, and the wheeze of giant breathing.

She approached carefully—into wet heat. It wasn't smoke, it was steam. Peering through it, she saw that the two rooms had been knocked into one, giving the ceiling an unfortunate pot belly.

Rough shelves held metal objects, springs, wires, tubes and God-knew-whats.

In the middle of the room, from what she could see through the steam clouds, the puffing dragon consisted of a brass cylinder on top of a washing boiler on top of a fierce fire in a bucket, the whole thing topped by a moveable beam with two vertical arms, one of which, connected to the cylinder, was going up and down, while the other, also going up and down, went into another God-knew-what beyond her view.

'Hello?' she called.

'*What*?' The figure of Andra Hedley came like a ghost out of the steam, his shirtsleeves were rolled up, and his short hair had gone into tight curls that glistened with damp. He was not pleased to see her. 'Go 'way, pet, Ah'm busy.'

She'd had her education; school was finished. He disappeared again.

She waited. In all the information he'd given her yesterday, there'd been mention of the names Savery and Newcomen, two gods who had converted fire to the pumping of water out of mines and had thereby supplanted the antiquated method of a horse-drawn gin-mill. The contraption before her, she supposed, was one such engine.

Again, she was reminded of Boston's shipyards and odd little men, like this one, who built model hulls in their parlour in order to make a marginal improvement on them, who drew better charts, conceived of better block and tackle, suggested better seamarks; men who obstinately refused to accept things as they were but had a vision of things as they could be; men who drove their wives mad and the world forward.

Eventually, the boiler ran out of steam and the contraption shuddered to a halt. Hedley approached the thing with implements in his hand, muttering something to himself about 'a separate condenser'. Cessation of noise was a relief.

'I'll find us the ten thousand pounds, Mr Hedley,' she told him. She had, she realized, made up her mind some time before.

What else was there to do? Those with nothing might as well make a throw for everything.

Hedley looked at her as if unaware of who she was. 'A valve box,' he said to himself. 'Inject steam in on *both* sides, that'd be it, thinks tha?'

'A good idea,' she said, and left him to it.

Chapter Sixteen

In order to raise the ten thousand pounds she needed to develop the Raby coal mine, Makepeace decided to approach Philip Dapifer's richest and closest friends. She felt no qualms about it, she would swallow her contempt and go to those who knew she'd been his preferred wife, playing on their sympathy and conscience. Investing in her mine would be recompense on their part to Dapifer's ghost for having allowed a woman he loathed to disinherit both his child and the woman he'd loved.

She disliked the thought of entering their world again, especially as a supplicant, but her hatred of Conyers and Catty was the stronger force. If it meant that she could take up arms against those two enemies she'd grovel to Old Nick himself.

Betty had a more jaundiced view. 'They done you wrong,' she said, 'an' nobody don't like feelin' they done a body wrong, they goin' to act like you ain't there—that's what they done so far.'

Which might or might not have been the case. But what neither Betty nor Makepeace took into consideration was that the time was right for investment. There was an excitement now, almost amounting to panic, which possessed men who saw that Britain was entering a new era. Wonderful inventions were finding practical application. Industries without ancestry were springing up at every turn. There were vast fortunes to be made through adventuring as there had not been since the reign of Elizabeth. The world was starting afresh.

Nor was it entirely greed. There was a sense that the whole country could be bettered. Britons were an *old* people but a *new* nation. The word 'new' was magical: hurry, hurry, don't leave modernity to others, join the new crusade or remain stranded in the Middle Ages.

Because Dapifer had shown no interest in the coming of the Mechanical Age, Makepeace hadn't either. But the men she was to visit during that winter of 1767, asking them almost literally for money to burn, knew better. The new Jerusalem could only be built on coal.

They might have initially granted Makepeace a hearing through guilt or compassion or even curiosity, but it's doubtful whether they'd have given her anything more—if it hadn't been for Andra Hedley.

She very nearly didn't take him with her. They were seriously at odds over their partnership contract; Makepeace wanted a controlling interest in the company to be formed if they found coal; fifty-one per cent.

Hedley refused to countenance such an agreement. 'Fifty-fifty or nothing, pet.'

'I own the damn land,' she said.

'And I'll be getting the coal out of it.'

His experience of coal-owners had not been happy; all of them 'pornicious sods' who treated their miners no better than rats and paid them crumbs for doing the most dangerous job in the world. At annual hirings the men were bonded for a year not to go on strike, and to deliver so many baskets of coal a day. For each six-hundredweight basket, they were paid five farthings—nothing, sometimes even a fine, if it contained any rock—and had to deliver one free. Few collieries gave sufficient compensation for injury or death incurred in an accident, some gave none at all.

In order to earn a living wage for the family, wives and daughters had to join their men underground and drag the baskets from the coal face to the surface. 'And I'm not having that in any pit of mine.' Hedley's colliery was going to treat its men and women as human beings should be treated.

He refused to believe that Makepeace wouldn't tolerate inhumanity either. 'I heard ducks fart before,' he said. What farting ducks had to do with it she didn't know but the message was clear enough: he didn't trust her.

Infuriatingly, he saw her as a representative of the ruling class. She might call herself Mrs Burke—the title she'd opted for—but in truth she was Lady Dapifer and *ipso facto* a persecutor of the labouring poor. All government, aristocracy, landowners and new industrialists were in a conspiracy to maintain a cheap work force.

She knew that to some extent he was right. At dinner tables with Dapifer there had always been someone to propound the theory that the illiterate poor must remain poor and illiterate or they would not want to work—and would demand higher wages if they did.

It was useless to protest that she didn't subscribe to this proposition—'I'm an American, damn your eyes'—in Hedley's book she'd betrayed the cause of Liberty by marrying one of its oppressors.

In any case, Americans beating some drums and burning a few effigies to escape a bit of tax . . . that wasn't serious protest. 'In 'sixty-five the whole bloody Tyne and Wear coalfields were out to get some food in wor children's bellies—*that* were rioting.'

He described the violence, burned houses, injured miners, injured troops who'd been sent in to put them down—and nodded at the distaste brought to her face by this reminder of what had happened in Boston.

'See, pet?' he said. 'When it comes to us poor sods fighting for wor existence, you're on the other side.'

The first visit to Raby by Aaron, who brought Fanny with him from Newcastle where their run was being extended by genuine public demand, had merely confirmed Hedley's view that here was a family with social pretensions. Introducing her brother to him, Makepeace saw that the two men were inimical. Against Hedley, whose idea of elegance was a clean shirt, Aaron looked every inch an actor, clothes a little too highly coloured, heels a little too high, gestures too grandiloquent.

'Coal?' asked Aaron, to whom sinking holes in the ground was merely a new method of boring people to death.

'It's the future,' Hedley said, shortly.

Aaron shrugged with incomprehension: 'If you're raising money, 'Peace, you couldn't do better than build a theatre for Newcastle. The demand's there.'

She grinned. 'When I've made my fortune, maybe. Not until.' She was irritated by Hedley's reaction to the two thespians, though it would once have been her own. He had all the common man's prejudice against the theatre and, while he treated the blooming and confident Fanny with his usual dogged courtesy, it was obvious he regarded her as a woman no better than she should be. He mistook Aaron's bafflement at the mining process as belonging to a man who despised those who got their hands dirty.

He might have had more understanding if Makepeace had told him what had happened to Aaron at the hands of men who dabbled in tar, but she didn't. Nor did Betty, though she had confided much else to him.

Since Aaron had healed, mentally and physically, as well as he had by pretending his scars were not there, it was not for the two women who loved him to display them to others.

In fact, that Boston had left her in sympathy with the causes for which people rioted while loathing riots themselves, was a complexity which Makepeace felt was too intimate and betrayed too much of her personal life to confide to him. Anyway, she decided, it wouldn't make any difference; she could present libertarian credentials from the Archangel Gabriel but Hedley would not be shaken in his belief that, given the chance, she would grind the faces of her employees and that he must not therefore allow her a controlling interest with which to do so.

'He's worse than John Beasley,' she fulminated to Betty. 'Thinks he's the only radical in the business. A pretty penny I'll get out of Rockingham and the others with him in tow. He's so damn rude.'

'Clever an' all,' Betty pointed out.

There was that. According to him, his adaptation of the Newcomen engine made it a more efficient pump. Makepeace had no way of judging the mechanism but she thought she could judge men and whatever else Hedley might be he was neither self-deluded nor a boaster. Furthermore, that swarthy head of his boiled with ideas for improvements to this or that mining technique.

If potential investors could disregard how uncouth he was, she might yet get her money. But she wasn't going to sign an equal partnership agreement.

In fact, on anything connected with business she and Hedley had come to conduct themselves almost like a married couple, swearing horribly and with complete freedom as each harangued the other, arguing their different positions, planning, and sharing unembarrassed silences while they contemplated.

It was, she supposed, what an honest partnership should be. On that plane they *were* intimate and she was content. On that plane. Delve deeper, return underground, descend into the coaly darkness where her grief, her very intestines, had been momentarily exposed . . . she wouldn't go there again. Her private places belonged to Dapifer and she guarded them with ferocity. Her past was forbidden territory; she might have emerged at Raby fully fledged from a long delay in some womb. It made her more comfortable with Hedley that he showed no curiosity about her history and was nearly as reticent about his own.

What was less comfortable to her was the fact that, if she took him with her, they would be travelling on their own. Aaron's players had put on a benefit performance to raise money for the journey but the takings had been only enough to provide accommodation and coaches for two. Betty and Tantaquidgeon would have to remain at Raby with Philippa.

Even in these morally easy days it was questionable for a woman to journey unchaperoned with a man not her husband or a relative. Makepeace didn't care what the people she was going to visit thought of her but she *did* need their money; they must feel no hesitation on moral grounds about giving it to her.

Yes, she would take him but, first, she gave him a lecture on behaviour. 'The men we're going to see won't lend us a farthing if you talk to them like a damn Leveller. Where'll your Ideal Colliery be then?'

He looked her straight in the eye. 'Credit me with sense, pet.'

'And don't call me "pet".' In his Northumbrian mouth the use of 'pet' was a comma, not an endearment, but she didn't want it taken as a sign of intimacy between them.

She had to hope he would behave himself and that his obvious social inferiority would acquit them both of anything other than mutual business interests in the eyes of those who saw them together. And, as they stood side by side in the glory that was Wentworth House, waiting for a footman to show them in to the presence of the Marquis of Rockingham, she was sure it would. Hedley looked as if she'd brought him along to do the plumbing.

The hall was sixty feet square and forty high. Fluted Ionic pillars in white and sienna marble supported a gallery round the whole, niches held antique marble statues, gold leaf was everywhere. It loomed over her so that she felt like a pygmy pushed into the ring of the Colosseum to amuse the crowd. But at least she looked smart. Susan Brewer had sent up a loaned wardrobe of clothes to see her through the tour, though sitting on a coach roof—they could only afford outside passenger seats—had not improved it.

Hedley's coat might have travelled the world already. It was mouse-coloured, careworn and under strain across his massive shoulders, and its pockets bulged with drawings. The most that could be said for him was that he wasn't showing anger at the riches around him. 'Grand,' he said, dismissively. 'Can't expect it to be comfortable.'

He's going to insist on being common, she thought. On the other hand, the observation was apt; the place didn't overawe her either. She'd lost the capacity to be impressed by grandeur.

The Marquis of Rockingham came to them in the hall, almost bounding. It flashed into Makepeace's mind that not only did this man own the fifteen hundred manicured acres of Yorkshire that constituted his grounds but also a large part of the county beyond them, and what he didn't own was in his political control.

This eager courtesy from such a magnate to one poor woman was either guilt on his part or, possibly, because he was a very nice man. She didn't care either way; she merely wanted his money.

'My dear, *dear* Lady Dapifer, I cannot tell you the relief of hearing your name announced . . .' But he continued to do so, detailing the enquiries he'd made for her, his worry, his distress over Dapifer's death ' . . . of all Englishmen this country could spare him the least.'

You could have found me if you'd wanted to, she thought. Wasn't he related to Catty in some way? Yes, she thought she remembered Pip mentioning that he was.

Unsmiling, she introduced Hedley. 'It's a matter of business, my lord.'

Rockingham ushered them towards his library 'so that we may be cosy'.

He looked much older now that he was out of office than he had during his Prime Ministership. Never a favourite with the King, his liberal attitude to America had earned him George's particular dislike, and Pitt, recently created Earl of Chatham, had refused to co-operate with him in keeping the administration alive. Pitt was a politician whose approach to government was to build one round his own personality.

He's missing Pip, Makepeace thought. Pip was the one who worked behind the scenes to keep them all together. Out loud, she said: 'How is Lady Rockingham?'

'Mary's taking the waters. She will be laid low again to learn that she's missed your visit, she was always so attached to you.'

Was I attached to her? I can't remember.

The Rockinghams' marriage had been that rare thing among the aristocracy, a love match, but it was barren. As if conscious that his own lack of a child must not let him ignore the fact that other people had them, he was quick to ask: 'The baby is thriving?'

Doesn't know the sex, she thought. 'Philippa is very well.'

He lowered his voice: 'And the law suit? How does that fare?'

'In abeyance until I've got funds to proceed with it.' Now he'll think I'm begging for charity.

'Cosy' was not a word she'd have chosen to describe a library sixty feet long, but firelight and walls of gold-brown books rendered it more welcoming than the hall. Coffee and sweetmeats were laid on a table by the fire, chairs drawn up.

Makepeace began by reminding Rockingham that his wife had been present at Almack's on the night of the wager between her and Headington. She explained what she'd found at Raby and stated her business.

Immediately she mentioned the word 'coal' Rockingham's expression sharpened out of its dutiful chivalry and became more truly interested: the face of an entrepreneur. Makepeace realized, almost with shock, that if he did indeed lend her money it wouldn't be from charity but because he saw the chance of profit.

He's got millions already, she thought. At the inn where she and Hedley had put up for the night, they'd been told by Rockingham's adoring villagers of the eighty-five thousand pounds he'd spent on building Wentworth's stables, a work that had employed large numbers of local men at decent wages for several years—hence the adoration.

But that was *noblesse oblige*; this was . . . what? Where had she seen the look before? *Pioneering!* Good Lord, it was the same gleam that had been in the eyes of her father and other men setting out to explore the American wilderness.

He'd turned his attention to Hedley, asking sharp questions, listening carefully to equally sharp Northumbrian answers. How thick was the seam? Hard coal, was it? How deep?

Watching them, Makepeace saw a new thing: two people from the two most distant ends of society bridging what had previously been unbridgeable.

Here was the new age. Aristocrats with forebears going back to Saxon times recognizing the worth of men with no ancestry whatever. A Hedley in a dreadful coat could say impatiently—as this one was doing now—'Na, na, it's the vessel with the steam acting on the piston has to be always as hot as the steam itself, d'you not grasp that?' And a silken, brocaded marquis could answer, humbly—as Rockingham was—'Oh yes, Mr Hedley, I see now.'

For all three of them at that moment there was something in the room representing more than ambition, profit or vengeance.

Makepeace thought: Sam Adams should see this.

The two men left the subject of pumping water from the mines and passed on to the problem of raising coal from its depths— Hedley had taken a pencil from his pocket and was drawing with it on one of the table's fine linen napkins. Makepeace heard Rockingham ask: 'Rectangular corves?' and Hedley say: 'Wheeled, d'you see. Save emptying, put 'em straight on rails. We'd stop fouling with conductors braged on opposite sides of wor shaft . . .'

Makepeace intervened. She had no idea what braged conductors were but there was no need to make Rockingham a present of them. This new age was wonderful, no doubt, but it still involved the old acquisitiveness; Yorkshire had coal reserves of its own—the Duke of Norfolk owned extensive collieries around Sheffield and for all she knew Rockingham could be planning to set up in competition with him. He damn well wasn't going to do it on *her* braged conductors. 'I'm sure we needn't waste his lordship's time on details, Mr Hedley,' she said.

Rockingham was wily. He took his guests on a carriage tour, ostensibly to show Hedley a new, improved threshing machine and for Makepeace to see the gardens, but during both these inspections, she noticed, he found an opportunity to speak first to one, then the other, alone.

He and she were by themselves in a rose garden when he gently offered to buy Raby outright at a price which, invested, would see her comfortable for the rest of her days. 'Coal production is a hard taskmaster,' he said, 'even supposing your pit proves profitable.'

Then why d'you want it? She didn't even consider the offer. He might be being kind, paying his dues to Dapifer's memory, saving her from association with an unfeminine trade—he could certainly afford these motives. But she didn't want comfort, she wanted to slake her hatred in blood and for that she needed vaster wealth than he could give her. Besides, how else was she to fill these left-over days of her life? Needlework?

'I have time to kill,' she said, and was struck by her unconscious *double entendre*. She smiled.

He saw the smile and gave up. 'What free-thinking spirits you Americans are. I told the King, we shall be forced to give America her independence one day.'

Her smile broadened. 'I don't think you will, my lord,' she said. 'We'll just take it.'

In the end she settled for a straight loan of five thousand pounds; she thought she could probably have got more but Hedley had insisted on not being beholden to one solitary investor who could thereby dictate policy or withdraw on a whim. 'It's a long-term investment,' she warned Rockingham.

'I have no doubt of it,' he said, 'but if I'm a judge of your Mr Hedley, it is a secure one.'

'Not *my* Mr Hedley,' she said quickly. 'He's merely my business partner.'

Seated in one of Wentworth House's carriages on the way back to the inn, she passed on the compliment. 'Rockingham thinks you're clever.'

'I am,' he said, smugly. 'Yon's a canny lad. Asked me to come and work for him.'

So this was the world of business, was it? You couldn't trust anybody.

'The shite,' she said.

At his foundry in Birmingham, Sir Benjamin Judd was less amiable towards Makepeace than he'd been in Grosvenor Square. Her reappearance troubled him and he was one of those who made a virtue of speaking his mind. 'I was sorry for yow,' he said, 'and so was Lady Judd, very upset she was, but yow have to consider my position.'

He'd certainly considered it himself; Catty had returned from the wilderness, not only as his immediate neighbour but as a force in Society—and Sir Benjamin had invested a great deal of time and money on consolidating his social position. He had plans to marry his sons into the nobility.

Under Makepeace's unblinking gaze he grew almost hostile.

'Yow seem to have landed on your feet, any road. Well, I'll lend you a shilling or two for old times' sake . . .'

'Lord Rockingham's investing five thousand pounds,' she said.

'Is he? *Is* he now? Easy come, easy go, I reckon. Ay, but hard coal's no use to me, my furnaces need coke and a damn job it is to get it with the state of the roads. They talk of canals though when they'll be finished . . . Any road, where's your security?'

For all his bluster, he'd been noticeably impressed by the Rockingham connection. Makepeace said: 'My security is my business partner. Talk to him.'

Sitting quietly in the background while Sir Benjamin and his foundry manager questioned Hedley, she watched the miracle happen again. The iron industry needed contrivances to raise water and turn the great wheels that operated bellows, forge hammers and rolling mills. Any improvement to the atmospheric engine would save energy at the moment going to waste. Iron-masters were prepared to invest in professors with a theory or illiterate men with an idea or anyone in between who might increase production—if they believed him. They believed Hedley. She would get her money, not so much for the Raby mine as for the future of Hedley's condenser.

Hedging it around with repayment requirements and eventual interest at the standard rate of three per cent, Sir Benjamin raised his offer to three thousand.

Makepeace took it, without thanks.

In Hertfordshire, she called on Sir Toby Tyler, MP, and let Hedley work the oracle once more—to the tune of two thousand pounds.

It had been amazingly easy.

Hedley took the next stage back to Newcastle. Makepeace stayed on; she had duties in the south of England. She wouldn't go near her old home but she received two people from it in an upstairs room at the White Hart in Hertford. One was Peter Little, its steward, and the other Robert French, her husband's—now Conyers's—valet.

Her friendship had narrowed down to the few people who'd

rallied round her at Dapifer's death; even in that time of turbulent darkness she had registered their presence. The rest, apart from her new acquaintances at Raby, could go hang themselves—just as they'd let her and her child go hang. She'd milk them if she could but they remained cattle that must roam beyond the picket fence with which she'd surrounded herself. Only Robert and the men, women and children who'd attended Philippa's christening had human faces and could be allowed in.

Even so, Peter Little found his meeting with this hard-eyed woman difficult. She enquired kindly enough after his wife and children but when he wanted to tell her how the Dapifer villagers were getting on, she stopped him. 'I'm not interested in them, Peter. Tell me what's happening at the big house.'

He pleaded for his people. 'They didn't shun you, Lady Dapifer, truly. Edgar, the rest . . . their livelihood depends on the lord of the manor, whoever he—or she—is.'

'So does yours. *You* took us in. Tell me about the big house.'

Loyalty to his present employer prevented Little from saying too much. It had been another bad harvest. No, the . . . um . . . lady of the manor had not been at Harvest Supper; she'd stayed in London.

Makepeace filled in the gaps. With its fountain-head gone, the village of Dapifers was neglected; Catty was not a woman to leave the London season in order to attend a ceremony in a country orchard or remember to put a bean in the Lord of Misrule's plum cake; nor was Conyers a man to encourage his harvesters by helping to toss the corn-sheaves onto wagons. Who, if anybody, put flowers on Dapifer's grave?

I will, Pip. One of these days.

But, of course, Robert had. On the anniversary of Dapifer's death, he'd taken French leave and travelled as an outside passenger to Hertfordshire. 'Nobody else there. Just a quiet little moment twixt him and me. The Major looked at me very old-fashioned when I got back, I can tell you.'

'Why does he keep you on?' Makepeace wanted to know.

Robert surprised her. 'Because he wants everything that was Sir

Pip's. He'd have given his eyes to be like him—oh yes he would, you didn't know him in the old days. Almost pitiful it was, trying so hard to imitate him and Lord Ffoulkes, using every wit to be what they were and not being able to and hating them for it. That's what he's doing, you know, living their lives for them. I think it's sending him mad.'

In his high, mannered voice, Robert drew sketches of Hogarthian horror: Conyers's languid ease of manner and frantic lapses; the quarrels with Catty that went through a cycle of screams, blows and eventual reconciliation in violent sex. 'They'll do it anywhere, you know, doesn't matter *which* servant's in the room.' Catty forced to come up from London to attend the ceremony of the rents, bored to distraction; Catty bored again at the Christmas feast for the county: 'Too, *too* bucolic, my darlings.'

That was something Makepeace already knew. Sir Toby Tyler had been affronted by his hostess's yawns. 'I always served the house of Dapifers well in the Commons,' he'd told Makepeace during their interview, 'but if it wants me to put forward an Enclosure Bill it'll have to show more appreciation.'

'*Are* they going to enclose?' she asked Robert now.

'Peter Little wants it, always did, but, oh dear me, she and the Major know as much about farming as I know about astronomy. And I *don't* think we've got the money.'

'They've got all mine,' said Makepeace, grimly.

'And are *spending* it, my dear, make no bones about it. Of course, a lot went in paying off debts but then there's our clothes, all our pretty new jewels, the gambling, entertainments in Town— we hired all of Ranelagh for a night on our birthday, *everybody* came. And we're buying *him* out of the army, which costs a pretty penny. Then there's the wedding . . .' Robert cocked an eye. 'You know we're getting married?'

'Not before time.' She hurried him on to what was important: 'Robert, how's Andrew?'

'Ah, *well*, Lord Ffoulkes is a disappointment. The Major's not only *in loco parentis*, he wants to *be parentis*. We've tried buying the boy's affection, we've positively *rained* gifts, but the little serpent's tooth lacks gratitude. Didn't want to come down for Christmas. The Major insisted so he came, but he would *not* enjoy himself.'

'You'll tell me if they hurt him. In any way.'

'Of *course*.' Robert began crying again. 'Didn't we love that boy?'

'Can you get a message to him for me?'

In London Makepeace stayed with Susan Brewer in the pleasant Clerkenwell apartment she was renting in Theobald's Road from a Jewish family, relatives of Mme Angloss.

'I didn't know Mme Angloss was a Jewess.'

'I didn't either,' Susan said, 'not 'til recently, not 'til I gave her notice—'

'You've left Mme Angloss?'

'Stop interrupting. I've left her in one way, not another . . . well, it became impossible, Makepeace, Catty was everywhere. Twice, once when we were fitting Lady Ormond and again at the Brandons', she came prancing in, twitting Mme Angloss about the clothes she'd designed for you and being *hideously* amusing about American taste. She didn't know me from Adam, of course, but if I saw her again I'd have stuck the scissors in her which wouldn't have done Mme Angloss's trade any good, so I gave in my notice.'

'Oh, Susan.' Makepeace was conscience-stricken; immersed by the tidal wave of Dapifer's death, she'd ignored the difficulty others might be experiencing in its undertow. Susan had lost weight and much of the rumbustiousness she'd brought from America.

'It's all right, Makepeace, really it is. Mme Angloss understood; she's a surprising woman. She said she knew what it was to hear one's race belittled in the mouths of vulgar English *aristos*—that's what she called them, vulgar *aristos*. She doesn't tell them she's Jewish, of course, or she'd lose a lot of business. I'm not even sure she's French—Spanish, I think. *Anyway*, she put me in touch with Mr and Mrs Franco, they own this house, and lots of others as well, and you'll never guess what I'm doing . . .'

'What?'

Susan went to a tallboy and opened one of the deep lower drawers to produce a hat such as the second Lady Dapifer in her heyday would have killed for. It was straw, tip-tilted back and front, it was blond, it was springtime.

'Leghorn,' said Susan, trying to be casual. 'Mr Franco trades with Tuscany, they grow some wheat or another which produces *the* most malleable straw. I draw the designs, the milliner makes them up.'

Makepeace snatched it. 'You designed this?'

'Good, isn't it? I call it the Philippa.'

'Susan.'

'Sakes, I'm one of her godmothers, ain't I? I sent a consignment to Auntie that sold out in a week. Mr Franco says he could put me in touch with importers in the Carolinas—honestly, Makepeace, the Jews are *everywhere*. They'd have advanced your ten thousand in a wink. They . . .'

Makepeace was standing in shock at the looking-glass. 'I'm too old for it. God, Susan, I'm *old*.' Something had happened to her face, not lines—there weren't any yet—but as if it had been rigid when the wind changed and was set into permanent austerity. It was not just haunted, it was haunt*ing*. She tried a smile—and wouldn't have wanted to encounter it in a dark alley.

Wearily, she took the hat off. 'What were you saying?'

Susan said: 'They . . . the Jews, Mr Franco says they're grateful to Sir Pip. When he was a young man, at the time of the "Jew Bill", something about giving them more rights or something, Pip was lobbying to get it made law. It didn't get passed, there was awful rioting against it, apparently, but . . .' Susan's voice became very gentle. ' . . . they loved him for it.'

The loss filled the room; Dapifer was everywhere in it, gloomy, funny, valuable.

After a while Makepeace said: 'They've got to pay for him, Susan, I can't live if they don't.'

And Susan said: 'He didn't have a price.'

John Beasley turned up uninvited and told Susan he was moving in for the duration, having abandoned his own rooms in Grub Street because court bailiffs were after him. 'Like old times,' he grumbled to Makepeace. 'Remember Hyde Park?' He turned to Susan. 'She let me crawl under her skirts and look up her fanny.'

Makepeace didn't rise to the bait; he was only setting it in order to enliven her, her appearance seemed to worry him. 'What have you done this time?'

He'd drawn a cartoon for *Town and Country Magazine*—and was justly pleased with it. It showed a man and a woman, both masked and armed, driving off in a coach, leaving its occupants, a mother and her baby, shivering in the snow. The name of Dapifer was writ large on the coach door and, to point it up, the corpse of a Red Indian hung partly out of one of the windows. The title read: 'Highway Robbery!'

'Major Conyers didn't like it,' Beasley said. 'No appreciation of art, that bugger. Took out an injunction against me and *Town and Country*. Too late, though, it had got round most of the clubs by then. Now the bastard's trying to sue us for libel.'

'We'll see about that.' Makepeace took the matter up with Mr Hackbutt when she went to consult him in Lincoln's Inn Fields.

It was an indication of how widely this particular edition of *Town and Country* had circulated that Mr Hackbutt had seen it and still possessed a dog-eared copy which had obviously done some circulating of its own, though, as a lawyer, he feigned disapproval.

'Ah yes, your friend Mr Beasley, a young man sailing *very* close to the wind,' he said. 'However, in this case I doubt if Major Conyers will proceed with the libel prosecution; the resultant case would be unpleasant for him. A scrawl in a scandal rag is one thing, evidence produced in court another. Evicting a recently bereaved widow and child from their home is not an act to rehabilitate him and his fiancée in the minds of respectable people, and respectability appears to be what they are after. I understand that royalty has been invited to their wedding—*she's* distantly related through the Stuart line, of course—but whether they'll attend is another kettle of fish.'

He had bad news. After chafing at the delay in receiving a copy of Dapifer's divorce papers from Boston, Mr Hackbutt had written again. 'And I have just received a reply to tell me that such confirmation was destroyed during the rioting, along with many other records.' He stopped being judicious and gave his desk a blow with his fist that slopped his inkwell. 'It seems the Boston court registrar of those days took papers home with him, kept them in his house if you'll credit it—in his *house*—and the damn building was burned down with them in it.'

Makepeace said nothing; there was nothing to say. No evidence of divorce, no means of proving the legitimacy of her and Dapifer's marriage, no case to regain his property. The stars in their courses were fighting for Catty.

Mr Hackbutt got up to thump his client encouragingly on her back. 'Now, now, we'll not give up the chase merely because the fox has a lead. I have hounds in America even now approaching the judges who heard the case. We'll have their affidavit in time and then it's "Tally-ho", eh?'

'I'm tally-ho-ing now.' Makepeace told him about Raby. From her pocket-book she brought out the proposed partnership agreement that had been drawn up in Newcastle for Andra Hedley by his son.

Master Oliver Hedley had proved to be a newly qualified young lawyer, *very* young, with arms too long for his sleeves, and, to Makepeace's surprise, tall, carrot-headed and graceful. His mother, she thought, must have been beautiful. His offices comprised one cheaply furnished room on a steep hill called the Side, inhabited more generally by Newcastle's cheesemongers—and smelling like it.

He'd suggested she take the draft he'd composed to her own lawyer. 'I shan't sign it,' Makepeace had told him, 'I want a controlling interest.'

'Dadda wants equal shares,' Master Oliver had said, smiling politely, almost lovingly, down at her.

'It's *my* land, *my* coal.'

Master Oliver had nodded affectionately. It had been like trying to push through cotton wool. 'But if you'll forgive me, ma'am, Dadda says "Find it".'

Mr Hackbutt took the document to the window. 'It's a workmanlike agreement as far as it goes, very workmanlike indeed for a provincial lawyer, but I cannot advise fifty per cent—such an arrangement invariably leads to stalemate.'

'That's what I thought,' Makepeace said, 'but it's him got us the money, not me. I'm going to sign.'

On Makepeace's last night at Theobald's Road, those who had loved Dapifer and his second wife gathered round Susan Brewer's dinner table for what was, though none of them said so, a delayed wake. Alexander Baines came to join John Beasley and so, because it was Sunday and the theatres were closed, did Aaron; Mr Burke's Company had returned to London for a winter season after its Triumphant Tour of the Provinces and was resting before setting off to delight Ireland in the spring.

Dr Baines took the opportunity to examine Aaron and declared himself well pleased. 'Ye have the constitution of an ox, young man.' He was less happy with Makepeace: 'I've seen fatter maypoles. Are ye eating, woman?'

Baines was another who'd been caught up in the undertow of Dapifer's death. Catty had spread word around Town that he was an incompetent doctor who'd ignored Dapifer's dangerous condition. It was taking time for his practice to recover from the damage; worse, Baines was flagellating himself. 'Who's to say she's no right? I told him his heart was weak, begged that he take more rest, but mebbe I should have done more than warn the dear man.'

'What *could* you have done?' Aaron was explosive. 'The hag's merely chucking dust in people's eyes so they won't look in her direction, that's all. She's the one who irked him to death at the last, her and Conyers. Bloody strumpet.'

'Oh, oh'—Susan Brewer covered her face with her hands—'why don't we all get on the next boat to Boston, or *somewhere*? I can't bear this country any more.'

'I'd come,' Beasley said. 'England's too bloody Tory for me.'

'Ay . . .' Baines was wistful. 'It's no a bad plan, that. Pandering to English nobility was naiver my idea of serving Hippocrates, mebbe I'll come with ye. What does our Makepeace say to it?'

'She says there's two people to be ruined before she can go.'

'Lass, leave vengeance to the Lord, ye're no fit for it. Look at ye.'

' "A spaniel, a woman and a walnut tree, The harder you beat them the better they be." Pip used to say that. They're beating me into being better. I'm going to bring them down.'

The two boys, Josh and Andrew Ffoulkes, arrived together into a riotous welcome. At his own suggestion, Lord Ffoulkes was having his portrait painted by Joshua Reynolds in order to keep in touch with his friend. He'd gained leave from Eton to come up to Town for a sitting and stay the night with his guardian. 'Conyers has gone to Almack's with *her*,' he told Makepeace bitterly. 'If he asks, which he won't, I'll tell him I spent the evening with friends. It's true.'

She was concerned that an eleven-year-old boy should be walking the footpad-infested streets of London at night but he said he'd commanded one of the Grosvenor Square carriages to bring him, calling for Josh on the way. 'I told Miss Reynolds Josh was the son of my old nurse—that's true too, in a way—and I was taking him to see her.'

Another of her enemies' sins: forcing a child to use deception in order to stay in touch with those who loved him. 'Are you all right?' she asked.

'Oh yes.' He was able to pass most of his holidays on his Kent estates with his servants, with whom he was happy enough. 'I don't like visiting *them* much,' he said of Catty and Conyers. 'They're very excitable, you know . . .' It was a gentleman's languid condemnation such as Dapifer might have used and it brought tears to Makepeace's eyes. ' . . . but I'm all right.' She hoped that he was; there was a reserve to him she hadn't seen before, though not with her. 'I miss you,' he said.

'I miss you too.'

She turned to Josh. 'Are *you* all right?' Betty's son had suddenly shot up, becoming lanky but with the promise of good looks. She hated the fact that he was in brightly coloured livery like any other negro servant.

'Fine, I'm doin' fine,' he told her. 'Sir Joshua's lettin' me paint some of the drapery in Andy's portrait.' But he too had become guarded.

It was Andrew who said: 'Reynolds don't let his apprentices paint much though, do he, Josh? You mostly run errands for his sister, don't you?'

'I'm all right, I'm learnin',' Josh said, staunchly.

She didn't want them brave. Not yet, not yet. The glowing patina of expectation was being rubbed off them both; the world would not, after all, be wonderful. She supposed that even while they hurt, they were more fortunate than most—she thought of Andra Hedley, down the pit at eight years old—but her arms twitched to hedge the two of them about and save what was left of their shine.

They were all happier once they'd crammed themselves around Susan's small dining table, as if they'd formed a protective circle against the dark. Jugs of porter helped, and so did Baines's contribution of a bottle of malt whisky.

Susan patronised the local shops and had provided capons, fish pie and cow pudding. 'You can never get pork round here,' she said, puzzled.

Beasley, scoffing, explained Jewish dietary laws.

He likes her, Makepeace thought. How much it was difficult to guess. And Susan liked him, though he shocked her and she had been quick to go to her landlord to procure him other accommodation nearby. No, that horse wouldn't run. Pity, it was time both of them settled down. Why hasn't Susan gone back to America? Why struggle on over here? She's got wealthy relatives. Lord, I couldn't spare her.

What about Baines? He'd be suitable. No, he still fancies he's in love with me, though he ain't at all. Just like Pentecost Pringle. Dr Baines had settled down to a contented life as a single man on the excuse of unrequited passion.

Aaron? He'd been attracted to Susan on the boat coming over, but that had faded. There's probably some actress now . . . anyway, Susan treats him like a brother.

Picking over her friends like a miser over a hoard of jewels, Makepeace felt how precious it was, this unbreakable circlet of ill-matched friendships, how freeing to be given this little holiday from hate to play with them.

It didn't stop her getting up before dawn the next morning and catching the stage coach to begin the six-day journey that would take her back to her coal mine. She had other riches in mind.

Chapter Seventeen

THEY bought a Newcomen engine and housed it, suitably adapted, in the flooded shaft—the one Hedley imaginatively called Shaft A. The machine clunked and after every clunk came the bronchial wheeze as water was raised to a wooden soakaway that ran to a stream and from there to the sea. You could hear it, *clunk-wheeze, clunk-wheeze*, from as far away as the Factor's House and the but 'n' bens.

At first it sent rooks scattering from the trees while its inexorable regularity took humans to near madness, but gradually the sound entered flesh and bone; birds ceased to take notice of it and the humans adapted so that Makepeace, walking to and from the mine, and Betty, sweeping the yard, unconsciously moved in time to its rhythm.

Another shaft—Shaft B—was sunk. Then a ventilation shaft, to let out the gas that had been accumulating in the mine since it was abandoned.

For Makepeace, keeping the books as she sat in the Factor's House parlour, now her office, pounds were escaping faster than the gas. Tunnels had to be safely propped with timber: Hedley refused to rely on the old wasteful method of leaving pillars of coal to keep the roofs up; this was to be the most up-to-date bloody mine in Northumberland. Doors had to be constructed to encourage draught along the tunnels; rails laid; wagons purchased; the staith (a pier) built at the sea's edge from which coal could be lowered into the keels (boats) to sail it to the great collier fleet on the Tyne for delivery to London. Miners hired . . .

'We're not going to have enough damn money,' screeched Makepeace.

'Have to get more then, pet,' Hedley said, and went back to work.

Grumbling, she slammed the door behind him; the early spring day was chilly. 'And not a bloody lump to put on the bloody fire.'

Spring came and went in hard work and expense.

One day in June, with the sun so hot that the arc of moorland around them stood to rigid attention while, in the east, a vacillating haze on the sea made the eyes water, Makepeace suddenly raised her head from the accounts. Betty came hurrying in from the kitchen with Philippa; they both had hands covered in flour from making patties.

The noise of the pump had changed.

'Come *on*.' Makepeace took Philippa's hand, Betty took the other, and between them they swung the child out of the yard towards the mine with Tantaquidgeon behind, keeping his unvarying pace.

Jamie Hedley, his wife Ginny, two children and a dog Makepeace had never seen before joined them, running down the track from the but 'n' bens.

Hedley was standing by his engine shaft, shrugging as if it was nothing. 'She's dry,' was all he said. But Makepeace knew him now, could sense the triumph in the very stance of his body.

Like a couple of allied generals meeting on a field of victory they shook hands. '*Now* do we get coal?'

'Got to clear the fall first, pet,' he said.

'Why not start now? Time's money.'

He ignored her. He was looking around. 'Where's that bloody dog?'

'Here, Andra.' Jamie had a ball of string leading from his hand to the neck of one of the most miserable bitches Makepeace had ever seen. 'Stray,' he told Makepeace. The dog was wearing a harness with a pocket which held a candle.

Women and children followed the men to the new wheelhouse at Shaft B where a large basket hung from a windlass over the platform beneath which was the pit.

Hedley swung the basket to the shaft platform. 'In you get, pet.' He lifted the dog in and got in himself. When Jamie tried to climb in with him, his brother pushed him away. 'Who's going to man the bloody wheel?'

'Let us coom, marra.'

'Stay here, tha bugger. Get 'em all out and when Ah'm down, howay thasself.' Leaning over the side of the basket, he pushed until it swung into the mouth of the shaft. 'Let away.'

The windlass shrieked. Makepeace, leaning over the safety rail, watched the basket and its cargo descend at speed until it was lost in the darkness. 'What's he going to do?'

'Test for fire-damp.'

A ratchet had stopped the windlass of its own accord. Jamie pulled on a lever, his eyes on the swinging chain threading down the pit. 'Howay wi' 'em, Ginny.'

His wife began shooing the other women and the children out of the shed. When she pulled at Jamie's sleeve, he shook her off and she left with the others, leading them down the hill to sit on the grass in a dip out of sight of the mine. 'Reet, bairns, who'll get most dayseyes and pittlybeds?'

As the children ran to pick flowers, Betty said: 'Why the dog?'

'Carries the candle aheed on a long lead. She drops deed or blows up, you've found fire-damp.' She wiped sweat off her forehead. 'Deor, it's het.'

'What happens then?'

'Get another bloody dog,' Ginny said and Makepeace, sitting beside her to help with the daisy chain, noticed her hands were trembling.

Hadn't he said . . . ? She asked quietly: 'Wasn't there another brother?'

'Ay. Peter. Deed in Walker's explosion. Poer sod, only nineteen. Blown up shaft an' fifty yard off, split like a herring.'

'Fire-damp?'

'Fire-damp.'

'Look, Mam.' Philippa showered daisies and dandelions into Makepeace's lap.

'Lovely, pet. Stay here a bit.' She got up and walked up the hill to the wheelhouse. Jamie Hedley was by the wheel, watching the motionless chain. 'Howay, bonny lass,' he said, not moving, 'a fireball could blow us all into etornity.'

'You go then,' she said.

'He's me brother.'

'It's my coal.'

In the quiet they could hear the new, gentler note of the pump as it kept the mine dry and the low drawn-out liquid notes of curlews on the moorland teaching their young to fly. *Hedley calls them whaups.* She thought of him following the dog with the lit candle on its harness through darkness and knowing, however long the lead between, that if it came across a large enough concentration of the silent enemy the flame would ignite it, them, the whole damn mine.

She sat down with her back against the rail. It was hot; the place smelled of machinery and warm new wood. Sun formed a wide square on the floor by the doorway, sparrows fluttered among the roof beams, the chain on the windlass didn't move.

Jamie was watching her. 'You and Andra sparkin', pet?'

'Sparking?'

'Lovers.'

'No, we're *not.*'

He nodded and turned his attention back to the rope.

Lord, these people, reducing things they didn't understand into their own little worlds. His Ginny couldn't think beyond the price of her next dinner so how could he recognize the phenomenon of a businesswoman? That's my capital down there, fellow. Why wouldn't I worry about it?

Years went by. At last the chain jerked. Jamie shouted: 'He's hoom! She's clear!'

By the time the basket was up and the two Hedleys, complete

with dog, came down the hill, Makepeace was sitting with the other two women, busily helping her daughter make a daisy chain.

Later, back at her office, she and Hedley argued. He wanted to hire miners right away.

'If we're just clearing the fall, we don't need skilled men yet,' Makepeace pointed out. 'We can shift it ourselves with a few others. We'll hire women to pull the corves, they're cheaper.'

He pounded on the table. 'Didn't I tell you no women down pit?'

'And didn't I tell you we're running out of *money?*' she screamed back. She pressed her fingers against her temples; it had been a bad day.

Hedley looked at her with his head on one side. 'Jamie said you were concerned for us.'

'I was concerned for the bloody mine,' she told him.

Here was the trouble with an equal partnership, neither had a casting vote. But she knew she was right; there was still horrific expense to be laid out when they reached coal; even now she would have to go cap in hand for more investment.

To tempt skilled miners away from other collieries would mean building accommodation for them and their families. And Hedley, damn his eyes, wanted pit ponies to drag the corves of coal to the surface, not women, not boys, which meant more outlay, stables, feed . . . They hadn't constructed the wagon-way yet, nor the staith, nor bought the wagons . . .

She shouted at him. He shouted at her.

Betty came in with a tray of nettle beer to say they'd woken Philippa.

'Will you tell this lug-headed miser she knows fuck about coal,' Hedley roared at her.

'An' you tell this ground-hog want don't mean git,' raved Makepeace, reverting to American in her rage.

Betty said: 'Ain't tellin' you two gumps nothin' 'cept quit cussin'. You forgittin' tomorrer's Sunday?' There was to be a church outing next day and she was looking forward to it.

When Betty had gone, Makepeace went to the window and threw the contents of her tankard outside. 'I can't drink this piss.'

'You don't like nettle beor?' Hedley was amazed.

'No.'

'I wor brought up on it,' he said.

'You can tell.'

She hadn't seen him laugh before; it was a loud surprise.

'Fifty-fifty, bonny lass,' he said, back in a good temper. 'We'll use women to clear the fall, temporary like, but it's men for the coal and paid enough to keep their wives at home where they should be.'

Where they should be . . . He reckons I'm a freak, she thought, but had the sense to say: 'Done.'

They shook hands and she held the front door for him. He stood for a moment on the threshold breathing in the sweet night air.

'You reckon me a freak, don't you?' she said.

He said: 'No, pet, I reckon you should be wed.'

'When pigs fly.'

The next morning, dressed in their Sunday best, the two households met in the yard and headed seawards down the track with their children and provisions on the donkey. The yellow bitch, looking considerably better than she had yesterday, slunk along behind: Andra had named her Persephone.

Instead of heading for the fishing village where a tiny church tower rose among a prickle of roofs, they turned left to a large, flat expanse of grass on the edge of the sea.

'Why aren't we going there?' Makepeace asked, pointing at the tower. According to her reading of the Raby title deeds, not only did the village belong to her but she held the advowson to the church.

'Priest lives in Morpeth,' Jamie told her. 'Don't coom often. Anyway, he cast us out, divvn't he, Andra?'

'Apostates,' Hedley said.

They were Methodists and had been ever since John Wesley had come to the north-east to spread his message of Christ's love to its unlettered masses in the 'forties. He'd stood in Sandgate, one of the roughest streets in Newcastle, and begun singing the hundredth psalm to four or five curious onlookers whose number had swelled to five hundred and then fifteen hundred as he preached. The Hedleys had been taken to hear him as boys by their grandfather.

Up to then, Andra explained, the Church of England had more or less left the labourers of the north-east in their spiritual darkness, but it became upset that Wesley, however much he professed orthodoxy, commanded huge outdoor congregations of pitmen and their families with his message that Christ loved them as sincerely as he loved the coal-owners. In consequence Raby's absentee priest had suddenly turned up in its parish church to tell them they were rebels.

'We were,' Hedley said. 'We'd seen the light.'

They were still seeing it. The field already held three or four hundred people with others still threading in—Makepeace wondered where, in this wilderness of sea and moorland, they'd all come from.

The hot sun was tempered by the nearness of the sea that fretted the edge of the field into hummocks like grassy bollards in the water. The crowd was quiet and only seagulls and the whistling of redshanks bobbing along the shore vied with the preacher's voice, except for the occasional shout of 'Je-sus' from Tantaquidgeon for whom it seemed to reawaken memories of the Boston meeting house. Whoever the preacher was, his message of a simpler Christianity was familiar to Makepeace as well, but it carried fewer threats of Hell-fire than had the Puritan pulpit-thumpers she remembered, and more hope of salvation.

'Only the free grace of God can save us without the help of good works, for by the sin of Adam all are under sin and would be damned if it were not for the free and gracious sufferings of Jesus Christ. All by prayer can obtain this free grace. But, though good works alone cannot save us, we may assure ourselves that without good works we have not the necessary faith, for good works are the evidence of our faith.'

Next to her, Philippa's little hands were squeezed tight in imitation of the Hedley children, John and Polly, as were theirs in imitation of their parents. Makepeace looked along the kneeling row to the profiles of Andra and Jamie Hedley, so similar in outline—does mining *demand* a broken nose?—so different in expression: Jamie's amiable, lacking the ferocious intelligence of his older brother; Andra's grim but momentarily at peace.

That's what he wants from my coal mine, she decided. It's his good work. Well, Lord, let it be that. But let it be *my* salvation and all; unless Philip Dapifer's score is settled there'll be no peace for me.

After the service there was chatter and exchange of news by people who met rarely. Makepeace was introduced to friends of the Hedleys as 'Mrs Burke, the new missus at Raby' and courteously greeted, but without excitement. She was recognized a woman nearly as poor as themselves; besides, while there was awareness that 'wor Andra' was reopening the Raby pit, these smallholders and agricultural workers from inland had no interest in mining operations.

Andra went off to the village to see if he could recruit corve-draggers from among its fishwives. Makepeace and the others settled themselves on a strip of blond sand to eat their provisions, paddle and build sandcastles with the children. Now that she had leisure, Makepeace tried to make friends with Ginny Hedley. The woman wasn't actually hostile but Makepeace had hoped for more fellow-feeling from a mother with children of Philippa's age. There was a reserve, sometimes amounting to covert scorn, which suggested that, like her brother-in-law, she regarded Makepeace as an escaped member of the ruling class come down in the world to exploit and then desert them.

'What's Ginny short for?' Makepeace asked.

'Ginny.'

I'll show *her*.

Further along the beach a group of village women sat apart by upturned boats, their wide-winged caps clustered in disapproval of those with leisure. Makepeace and Philippa walked along to them and stood watching knobbled hands thread mussels on catch lines ready for the men to take to sea next day. Each line had at least five hundred hooks, each hook two mussels. 'How long's that take?' Makepeace asked one of them.

The woman didn't answer. Lord, these people . . . but in this case it was probably not so much rudeness as incomprehension; they weren't speaking the same English. And, *Lord*, this was poverty: the woman looked sixty years old but had a child at her breast as she worked.

Makepeace produced a ha'penny from her pocket and pointed at an upturned rowing boat . . .

The sea trip was a success as far as the children and Jamie Hedley were concerned. 'This is grand. Where'd tha learn to row, pet?'

'Ran a waterfront inn. Kept lobster-pots.'

Ginny showed no sign of being impressed; maybe ownership of an inn was the equivalent of an earldom to someone living in a but 'n' ben.

To hell with her, Makepeace thought. It was balm to be on the water again, a user rather than an onlooker; she hadn't realized how much she'd missed the sea. Oh God, to return to the days when worry had centred on catching enough lobsters . . .

After a while her muscles began to protest. She handed over the oars to Tantaquidgeon and concentrated on helping the children dangle the hook, line and mussel that her ha'penny had also bought for each of them.

Polly caught a dab, John a flounder. Even Ginny began enjoying herself and waved at friends on the sands to point up the fact that only her family was privileged enough to be at sea that afternoon.

They arrived back to return the boat to its owners, sunburnt, fishy and happy. Hedley was waiting for them on the beach.

'She's a good waterfront lass,' Jamie told him. 'Owned an inn wi' lobsters. Rows like a bloody mermaid.'

Hedley looked at Makepeace as she tucked her untidy hair back into her cap. 'Ay, a woman of surprises,' he said.

Appraising the village women who reported for work next day, Makepeace saw that the fishing trade used all its able-bodied, male and female. The women gathered here at the pit head were the leftovers: the too-old, the too-young, the weak in head and body. Only two or three looked capable and these, she guessed, were either widowed or unmarried and had to rely on charity because they had no man with a boat to provide for them.

To her surprise, Ginny Hedley was among them. 'Left the bairns with Betty,' she said, shortly.

Makepeace had hoped for ten workers at least. Hedley had lain rails for the wagons along two tunnels. She'd reckoned two women at each site of the fall to load the stone cleared by the men, two others per tunnel taking the loaded wagons to the shaft and two more at the shaft attaching the wagons to the chains that would raise them to the surface.

The men had already gone down. Despite her protests, Hedley had hired six skilled miners, not just to help him and Jamie dig but for their expertise in shoring up tunnels. 'I'm not having her fall in again, pet.'

Winnowing out the obviously unfit and sending them away, Makepeace was left with Ginny and four others—and one of those only because the girl had pleaded. 'Ah'm stronger'n Ah look, missus, and missus, me mam's sick, please, missus.'

'What's your name?'

'Hildy, missus.'

'How old are you, Hildy?'

'Twelve, missus.'

Ten, more like, and thin as a taper. 'I suppose you'll have to do.' Makepeace felt disgust at herself; the weight of each full wagon these women would be pulling was a chaldron, the coal measure equivalent to almost a ton.

But what else was there to do? As it was, those pulling the

wagons would also have to help fill them, which would slow the work. As it was . . .

'God dammit, I'll have to come with you.' She rolled up her sleeves and saw that Ginny was smirking. *The cow doesn't think I can do it*. She clapped one of the hard leather caps Hedley had provided onto her head and stepped out of her top skirt; the petticoat underneath was not only thick, it was luckily, her oldest. She got into the corve that would take them down the shaft. 'This way, ladies, if you please.'

Grumbling all the while at their whole makeshift operation— 'Ah shudder for what they'd think of us at a proper pit.'—Hedley had trained Tantaquidgeon to use the windlass. The women dropped at a speed that left the stomach behind, only to have it jerked violently back into place as the ratchet pulled them up a foot above the tunnel floor.

They got used to work underground, though for the first week Makepeace seriously thought death would be the happier option. It was hot, limestone dust choked nostrils and throat and mixed with sweat to plaster men and women so that they looked like statues on the move. A filled wagon was so heavy it was immovable until the women learned the trick of making the sharp pull in unison that would set it sliding over the rails. Once under way, it could not be allowed to stop or it would slide back down the gradual incline, taking its pullers with it.

The harness the women wore chafed their shoulders and the strap between their legs bunched their skirts so that the folds of calico rubbed their skin raw. Makepeace said, 'To hell with it,' and got Betty to buy her a pair of boy's second-hand breeches from a pedlar, though the other women refused to countenance anything so disgraceful and kept to their petticoats.

At first their backs ached, not just from pulling but from the effort of being permanently bent under low roofs. Thirst was terrible and they took to bringing down with them a forty-eight-pint cask of water that they'd empty by the end of the day. They were in the mine by five in the morning and finished at four in the afternoon when the men did, rising up into daylight, grey and blinking.

Betty learned, as miners' wives had to do, to have the meal waiting on the table because if it was in any way delayed Makepeace fell asleep in her chair. After two days of this, Betty said: 'Give it up, chil'.'

Makepeace looked up, said, 'No,' and fell asleep again.

There were two Makepeaces, one above ground and another in the pit. In the sunshine, she steeled herself for the next descent into self-imposed slavery with the knowledge that she was approaching coal, therefore wealth, therefore the eventual destruction of Catty. That it was worth it.

Below ground, her desires narrowed down to proving to Ginny, a tireless worker, that she was as good as she was and to finishing the shift without falling down.

There was something else. Midway through the day, diggers and pullers gathered at the bottom of the shaft for 'snapture', to chew on some bread and drink more water. A month ago, if she'd been asked why a son would follow father and grandfather down the pit to its inevitable and terrible risks instead of acting like a sensible man and taking to highway robbery, she would not have known the answer. Now, listening to them, she saw Andra, Jamie and the others as men in a skilled and invaluable job, inspired to an almost fanatical loyalty to one another by their shared danger underground and the incomprehension they faced above it.

Met in the street, the men Hedley had hired were not worth a second glance; scarred and rough, they were creatures to hurry past. Wullie Fergusson, the oldest, looked a nightmare in sunlight; he was bald and misshapen, his enormous trunk tapered into thin legs so bandy from childhood rickets that a pig could have run between them. He'd been Hedley's first mentor in the mining trade and Andra introduced him to Makepeace with pride as 'my marra', the accolade pitmen accorded to those with whom they worked side by side. When she tried talking to him, he proved inarticulate to the point of rudeness. She was astounded to learn from Hedley that the man was a Methodist lay preacher.

But in the dark, during those candlelit breaks in labour, he became a giant of knowledge, advising and warning in his singsong dialect, telling tales of disaster and heroism much as his Viking ancestors had recounted the great Norse sagas.

'Where does he preach?' Makepeace asked Hedley.

'In the pits.'

She thought: We're different people when we're under the earth.

The fellow-feeling spread to the women. To the outside world they were sluts working in degradation and too-intimate a relationship with men, but they were proud of what they did. It became a matter of honour, and not just for the farthing they earned by every load they carried, to work faster—and a matter of shame to show weakness. The donkey had to carry little Hildy back to her village at the end of the day, the other women holding onto her so that she didn't fall off from fatigue, but she was at the pit head every morning ready to begin again.

It was a democratic darkness; what was important was trusting one's marra to literally pull her weight, not to let the wagon slide back, to ensure it was properly loaded and chained so that it didn't spill its contents on its way up the shaft. Ginny and Makepeace staggered home together too tired to talk but knowing that if they did it would be as equals. Now they spoke the same language—a different one from anyone else—calling light 'lowe' (pronounced 'now'), the men wielding the picks 'hewers', and themselves not loaders and pullers but 'fillers and putters'; the work-face was 'inbye', to move in the direction of the shaft was to go 'out-bye'.

The mine had its own beauty provided by the human body at work. In the barely tolerable heat, men had stripped off their flannel shirts by the end of the day and light flickered on muscles constantly moving, on the silhouette of a face, on a pose all the more vital because it was held for less than a second.

It was always noisy from the *hit-hit* of the picks, trundling wagons, shouts of conversation or instruction. When the silence came, it was eerie. Makepeace and Hildy at the shaft became aware of a loss of sound that left the pit to the quiet beating of the pump and trickling water. 'What's happened?'

Voices echoed along the tunnel and came nearer, Ginny and her marra were pushing an empty wagon, behind them were the other women and men.

'What's happened?'

'We're through, pet. Andra's sent us back.'

'*Through?*' So there was an end to the endless. She was Sisyphus being told by a forgiving god that the stone could stay at the top of the hill. She took a candle from its holder on one of the wagons. 'Let me see.'

Ginny tried to stop her as she pushed past. 'Andra says stay here.'

'To hell with that. I want to see the coal.' She hurried along to the right-hand tunnel and walked down it. The props on either side of it were like an avenue in a regulated forest. There was nobody at the face, she was looking at a wall. 'Mr Hedley?' Then she saw that she was in a cross-piece like the head of a hammer; the men had dug a narrow passage across both tunnels at right-angles.

'*Hedley.*' She turned left, into the bigger arm of the cross-piece.

His voice said: 'Howay, she's not right propped yet.'

Damned if she howayed; it was her coal. 'Where is it?'

A barely discernible figure was standing on a lump of stone with a candle held high, studying the roof.

'Is this it?' she asked. 'Where is it?'

'Look, woman.' He was impatient, still inching the light along the roof.

She turned. Behind her was a man-sized niche for a hewer to stand in and let a wagon go by. Nothing there. She turned back. All around her was the pungent smell of coal and she couldn't see it.

Then she did.

Straight in front was the wall of coal Hedley and his father had uncovered all those years ago. She'd missed it because it sucked in light and was only apparent in contrast to the reflective stone around it. At this point it looked as high as he'd said it was, but further on it narrowed down to a ribbon. 'Oh God,' she said, 'it peters out.'

'Bloody doesn't.' He was irritable and inattentive.

Of *course*. The word 'seam' was misleading, suggesting something linear; but here was a wavering layer of black jam in a cake, an enormous cake with near-endless jam; now, looking to her left, she saw it went all through the cross-piece, even on its other side at her back. 'It's good, is it?'

'It's grand if this bloody roof stays up.' He was nervous. She was chattering with excitement and he told her to shut up.

'What's that?'

'What's what?'

She heard it, a creak like the swing of a badly hung door. Hedley got down. 'Gi' us your lowe.' He took both candles and held them up so that he could see along the cross-piece. '*Fuck.*'

In the light there were downward trails of mist as dust fell from the roof further along. 'Out, pet,' he said, pushing her ahead. She stumbled forward, then he suddenly pulled her back—and the roof fell in.

Noise and shock took away her sense and she watched, almost like an uninvolved spectator, as thundering angular boulders filled her view, not so much falling as suddenly being there, bouncing and rolling into position. Dust hit her in a wave so that she had to close her eyes against it.

When she opened them, she was in a room of which one side was a heap of jagged rock from floor to ceiling. Detritus was filling its gaps, hissing like a viper.

Hedley's voice, steady now, said: 'It's all right, pet. It's not a bad one. Wullie'll get us out. Won't take long.'

She was on her knees tugging at stone, but he stopped her. 'Don't disturb the bugger.' Glancing up, she saw his eyes were directed at the room's ceiling, then they slid back to her and his teeth flashed white in the grime of his face. 'We found her, pet. She's here, we've hit gold, this is nowt but an inconvenience.' He helped her up.

She tried to copy him. 'You sure gold hasn't hit *us*? Have we got air?'

'Ay, there's always air.' He kept talking—they were rich; this fall was nothing; he explained the science of falls; made plans—as if they were in the parlour at the Factor's House instead of a small cell made of rock and coal. 'You're all right, bonny lass. Wullie'll get us out.' He said it over and over but when she would have sat down because her legs were shaking, he made her stay standing, and every so often he looked at the roof above them. She noticed he positioned her with her back to the cavity in the wall. 'You're all right, bonny lass.'

She was, but only because he was with her; without him she would have been scrabbling like a rat, squeaking, pleading to get out.

They both saw the dust falling, heard the massive crack above their heads. Their eyes met.

He leaped at her and the weight of his body pushed hers into the cavity. All light went out. The fall came at them like a thousand-strong cavalry charge. She felt Hedley jerk and groan as he was slammed closer against her by rock that tumbled on and on and on, an insane living thing walling them up until it was satisfied that it had done all it could to kill them. Gradually it settled itself. There was pattering; it hadn't finished the job, it was filling gaps, and then it was quiet.

Her back was pressed hard against rock. Hedley's body was so tight against hers it held her suspended on tiptoe; he might have been a tree she'd got stuck to while climbing it. His arms trapped her shoulders, his cheek rasped against hers, he was panting with pain. There was only darkness. 'All . . . right, pet.' His breath coming and going on her skin. 'They'll . . . ah, *fuck* . . . get us out.'

Entombed, getting smaller, God oh God oh God, not like this, nowhere, I must, I can't, a worm wriggling, it was coming in, God help, stop, she was a fossil, a smudge pressed into rock, thin, thin, they were stuffing her throat with black velvet, covering her nose . . .

She opened her mouth to scream herself into the blessed release of madness.

'*Stop* it.' Through the blackness and compression, not a voice, a jagged hook of sound. 'Breathe, you . . . silly bitch.'

'I can'tIcan'tIcan't.'

'Breathe when I breathe.'

She took in air from him, and again. I can'tIcan'tlet me out.

'Breathe.' He was her lungs. Her mind kept sliding so he nailed it to himself, whispering like a lover, terrible things. 'Breathe, fuck you . . . hear me? *Hear* me?'

'Yes.'

'Breathe . . . There's . . . air . . . Breathe it, you little bugger . . . Breathing?'

'Yes.'

'I'll not . . . let you die.'

She had no identity; like one organism they took in air together and let it out. For hours. He wasn't anybody, just her oxygen. Only his words were corporeal, less something spoken, more a rope she clung to as it pulled her through the ocean of panic.

It wasn't bad, this end of the fall, hear him? Yes. Wullie'd come, they'd clear it, hear him? Yes. You'll not die, I'll not let you go. Hear him? Yes. Any moment they'd hear the picks. Hear them? Yes.

And then she did. A needle of sound so far away, so ineffectual, the panic began again.

'*Stop* it. Breathe.'

'Yes, yes.'

'We're going to live, pet.'

'I know.'

She felt his muscles make a gigantic move to free his arm, causing him to grunt with pain. His hand was against one side of her face, his thumb smoothing her cheek. 'Good lass.'

They were separate beings now, a feminine and a masculine again, very feminine, *very* masculine.

Life oozed back and with it a lust like no other, blood-red, wriggling, salt desire. She felt a hard swell against her pelvis and if she could have inveigled herself onto this new hook she would have. Of all bloody times not to be able to move. There was no past, probably no future, but *Lord* let there be a Now. I want, I want. I want *him* . . .

The hit of the picks was nearer; somebody was shouting.

Another effort from him: 'Here, Wullie.' There was a vibration in the chest against hers; God, was he laughing? Or dying? She heard him say sleepily: 'Don't go 'way, pet.'

'I'm here.' But it was dead weight on her now, the life had gone out of him and she was shouting for the rescuers.

Somewhere there was light. When they got through and lifted him away from her, they got blood on their hands.

Jamie's voice: 'God Jesus, Wullie, is he deed?'

'Not him.' They threaded him like a baby through the hole they'd made to where other hands took him and put him on a stretcher, then they came for Makepeace. 'All right now, pet.'

'Will he be all right, Wullie?'

He grinned. 'Andra?' She'd asked a silly question, but when she wanted to follow the stretcher, he held her back.

Jamie stayed with them so she knew it was serious. 'See, lass,' he said, gently, 'the second fall . . . it spread down the tunnel a way.'

She wanted to go with Hedley. Wullie kept a grip on her arm. Jamie said: 'He'll be all right, pet, Ginny's wi' him.' He reached out a hand to pat her and then let it drop as if she was too delicate to touch. 'See, he heard the first fall an' down he coom, we tried holdin' the sod back but it were like hinderin' a bull . . . He were goin' to get to you no matter—an' the second fall tuk him.'

Who? Hedley had been with her. She didn't know what they were blethering about until they led her to the side of the tunnel and light from the candle that Jamie held fell on a broken white feather.

They'd cleared the rock off him and straightened him out. He was alive still, breathing fast and shallow.

'No,' she said, 'oh no.' She went to her knees and put her arm under Tantaquidgeon's head to raise it. 'No.'

'Don't shift him, lass,' Wullie said. He knelt beside her. 'He were still tryin' to move but a bloody great block were crushin' him, we had a job liftin' the bastard off him. Let him go easy.'

'*No.*'

The Indian's eyes were wandering; she cupped her hands round his face so that they could find hers. 'Don't go.' Her tears were plopping onto her fingers. 'What would I do without you? Oh, my dear, stay with me.' Terror was making her mouth into ugly shapes; his was as firm as ever and she tried to smile at him. 'Don't be brave, does it hurt? Stay. Oh, *no.*'

Beside her Wullie said: 'The Lord's ma shepherd, He teks care o' me. Ah lie in pastures of tranquillity . . .'

'*NO.*' She watched the light recede from the dark eyes as if they were too tired to hold it.

' . . . for His namesake the paths of righteousness Ah tread wi' soul restored, nor could care less when Deeth his shadows ower the valley crowds . . .'

'He's gone, pet,' Jamie said. His hand came over her shoulder and his thick fingers closed Tantaquidgeon's eyes with a touch like swansdown.

'Heor in the midst of dangers Ah thrive, me table strewn wi' plenty. As Ah live, me cup runs ower wi' its thankfulness that all me days your love each hour will bless . . .'

She leaned down so that her cheek was against the poor chest, feeling the warmth go out of it.

Remorselessly, quietly, Wullie Fergusson finished his psalm: ' . . . Me hairt 'n' mind ruled by a peace divine. For goodness, grace 'n' mercy will be mine, An' when my spirit flights to thee, wi' ye Ah'll dwell through all etornity.'

Tantaquidgeon was buried in the graveyard next to the ruins of Headington House. Apparently it was still sanctified, though no Headington had been interred there for seventy years.

Jamie and Ginny, with Wullie Fergusson and some of the other hewers, cleared it, weeded it and scythed the grass, while Makepeace kept vigil in the Factor's House parlour by the body on its catafalque of a trestle table.

She and Betty had washed the dragon-embroidered wall hanging that Dapifer had given him and wrapped him in it. They'd brushed his hair so that it shone like a rook's wing. When Betty had splinted the broken eagle's feather and stitched it on a new band, they put it round his head.

'Oh God, I don't know what to do for him, I don't know Huron customs.'

'Don't need 'em, chil',' Betty said. 'He's a Christian.'

Jamie came to tell them the grave was dug. 'Now, pet, are tha certain sure tha'll not have a proper priest?'

'I want Wullie to do it,' Makepeace said.

Even if they could have afforded a coffin, she wouldn't have put him in one, so Jamie and the hewers laid him on a wooden stretcher and carried him up the track on their shoulders with the sun coming through the beech leaves onto the still, bronze face.

All the hewers, the fillers and putters were there in decent black and a Huron Indian was laid to rest to the murmur of Northumbrian voices praying for his soul.

Makepeace wouldn't allow the body put into the grave until the service was over. Better to have left him in a tree in the open air than in a hole in the ground, the only thing he'd ever been afraid of. In the end she couldn't speak the word so it was Wullie who covered the face and gave the order for the stretcher to be lowered. Philippa and the two other children scattered flowers over it.

There were no hymns; instead George, one of the hewers, piped the lament for the passing of a champion.

Hedley was there, against doctor's orders. As Betty and Makepeace went by him he said: 'I'm sorry, pet.'

'Thank you,' Makepeace said. She paused. 'I'm going to London to raise more money, as we discussed. When I've done that I'll set up in Newcastle for a while, to get the business going. You can contact me through your son. I won't be living back here.'

She nodded to him and went on down the hill.

It was perfectly clear. She had betrayed her husband and his cause in lusting after that man and she had been punished by the death of her oldest friend. There was a long way still to go—she must not be deflected again.

Chapter Eighteen

IT was as if Newcastle upon Tyne had pricked its finger on a spindle and, instead of going to sleep for a hundred years, had been catapulted into a time of extreme wakefulness.

Constructionally, it still belonged to the Middle Ages. With twenty thousand busy souls constricted by walls that had been built to contain four thousand, it bulged out of its seven medieval gates like flesh wobbling through rips in a too-tight corset, tilting down to its one great thoroughfare, the River Tyne and a solitary bridge of houses and shops that were unchanged since the fourteenth century. Streets were virtual tunnels through overhanging houses and its lanes were worm-holes, most of them so steep they had to be cobbled or stepped. It smelled of lime from its kilns, salt from its pans and the sea, and sewage from the common midden of Dog Loup Stairs.

But it nursed a product and ideas that, it knew, would change everything: landscape, thinking, ways of living—and in Newcastle were already doing it. The future streamed from Tyneside, not just to London but Europe, Scandinavia and Russia, while the town itself waited for the rest of the world to catch up.

It was dirty, it was undemocratic, it was an anachronism, it was wonderful.

And it was male.

'Item Six,' said the secretary, 'a plea by Mrs Burke of Raby for permission to use the Tyne for shipment of her coals. Gentlemen, there is a drawing before you showing the location of Raby and its environs.'

There was, but not one of the ten men round the table bothered to lean forward and look at it.

An enormous painting on the far wall behind them was of the Court of the Hostmen in session during the time of Charles I. There'd been a reduction in the size of wigs and the number of ruffles since then, but both painted and living faces showed the same studied indifference; they might have been blood related— and probably were.

The fifteenth-century hall had been built to overawe. The over-mantel of its fireplace alone was so magnificent, so heavy, so carved with Biblical bas-relief, bosses and scrollwork that it seemed as if it threatened to fall on Makepeace and young Oliver Hedley as they passed beneath it to stand at the foot of the long, beautifully pol-ished conference table like the petitioners they were.

These were the hostmen, kings of the coal trade, men who had fought for monopoly of their river for centuries against kings, the Bishop of Durham, Oliver Cromwell, Stuarts and Parliament, when necessary changing tactics, sides and religion to do it.

'The vicar of Bray's got nowt on Newcastle,' Hedley had once told Makepeace. 'But you want to ship from the Tyne, you get the hostmen's permission.'

'Bit medieval, isn't it?' she'd said.

'Mebbies, but you still need their permission.'

His son now produced a lump of coal and placed it on the board, which reflected it. 'Honourable sirs, Ah am Mrs Burke's spokesman in this matter. Ah represent her, the landowner, an' t'partnership she's formed with me father, Mr Andra Hedley, to mine the coal. If tha'd care to examine this piece, gentlemen, tha'll find it of foremost quality, good as Wallsend's.'

He'd broadened his accent, Makepeace noticed. He'd told her to let him do the talking; he didn't think women were allowed to speak in the hostmen's court.

'No precedent for females usin' Tyne, 'cept to do their laundry,' one of the men said, looking straight ahead. A cauliflower wig

surrounded his large, pale face and his eyes were like slugs. Alderman Sir somebody.

And they want their washing turned black, Makepeace thought.

'Ah think tha'll find exceptions, sirs,' Oliver said—he'd anticipated the difficulty and done his research, 'Early sixteen hundreds,
Mrs Dorothy Lawson of St Anthony's—'

'She were eccentric,' said the first hostman.

'An' wealthy, and a damn Roman,' said another, 'but there
weren't nothin' foreign about Dot Lawson.'

'Ay, salt of the earth, old Dot. Proper Tynesider. I remember
we gave her a municipal funeral.'

God help us, thought Makepeace, whoever the woman was
she's been dead one hundred and fifty years, and these men refer
to her like their auntie.

'An' she were elderly. A respectable married woman.'

Now we're getting to it.

'Mrs Burke is a respectable widow . . .' protested Oliver.

'How'd she come by Raby then?' From, his tone, Makepeace
knew Alderman Sir somebody's wife stayed home and didn't go
around collecting properties like a scarlet woman.

There was a sudden burst of viciousness.

'Ah heard she got it throwin' dice.'

'Ay, who were her husband?'

Makepeace had taken enough. She leaned forward and put her
hands on the table. 'He's dead, that respectable enough for you?'

Oliver put a warning hand on her arm. 'Mrs Burke's an American, sirs—'

'I surely am. It's my land fair and square. There's a grand seam
there and I want it shipped—from the Tyne if I can, but if necessary
I'll bring keels up from Ipswich to my own waterfront and ship the
damn coal from there.' She'd been doing research of her own. 'Do
you gentlemen want my revenues or not?'

She heard Oliver issue a long sigh and slump in defeat. But the
atmosphere had altered.

'American,' a hostman said, sadly.

'Boston, Ah wouldn't wonder.'

'Red-haired.'

They'd placed her. As a good-looking woman trying to compete on their territory she was nothing, an amateur, had probably earned her land by opening her legs; she could use the Tyne when it—and Hell—froze.

But as an eccentric—and she'd just proved herself that—with some knowledge of the game they played—she'd proved that too—she might one day make a worthy successor to the formidable Dot Lawson.

They still didn't ask her to sit down, but . . .

'Pass bloody loomp along table then.'

The coal was tapped, sniffed, passed from hand to hand—most of them a good deal whiter and smoother than Makepeace's own, and nearly all beringed with the jewels of rajahs.

You frauds, she thought. You could buy the throne and put it in your pocket—you probably have. They could speak genteel English when they had to. Their determined Northumborness—*pass bloody loomp*, indeed—was a . . . what was it Pip used to call it ? . . . *a langue de guerre*. They assumed it among themselves out of pride and a contempt for those who had a contempt for them. They sent their sons to Eton, might even have been there themselves, and there were as many titles around this table as there were in the Cabinet. When did you hypocrites last go down a coal mine?

In that she did the hostmen of Newcastle an injustice. They might send their sons to Eton but they married them to the daughters of families like their own, the ones they knew to be the real power in England, the aristocracy which made the land work, not the one that merely took its rents.

And they knew coal, had known it for five hundred years.

'Ah hear Hedley's usin' rectangular corves,' one said.

'What's that he's done wi' the Newcomen?'

So they'd been aware of her and the activities at Raby all along; probably a leaf didn't bud in Northumberland without telling them first.

She heard Oliver plunge into the opening they'd given him, explaining his father's improvements and inventions and offering them free to the local collieries should the honourable gentlemen see fit to include Raby among Tyne users.

Makepeace wouldn't have done that; she and Hedley had argued about it. 'Let them invent their own braged conductors,' she'd said, 'or use 'em under patent.'

Hedley had borne her down; if his work improved coal production and made life easier and safer for miners, he worn't bloody standin' in the way.

No horse sense, that man, she thought, and battled with a treacherous languor in her body as she thought it.

Oh, but she needed the Tyne. Ipswich did indeed have boats capable of carrying coal—it had once been a serious competitor to Newcastle's keels but, like all Newcastle's competitors, was now being crushed out of the trade. And its extra distance along the coast would cost her a great deal.

God, why was she still standing? The hell with them, she wasn't a prisoner at their damn bar. There was a flunkey of sorts standing by the door and Makepeace beckoned him with a finger to bring her a chair.

Alderman Sir somebody's eyes made a slow crawl in her direction as she sat down but he said nothing.

The negotiations went on for some time. Oliver fought valiantly. For all his air of vague gentleness the young man had a sharper sense of expediency than his father (again that disgraceful sweetness). He did well.

At last. 'Howay,' said Alderman Sir somebody, 'mebbies we'll give . . .' He looked down at his agenda so that she'd know he'd forgotten her name. ' . . . Mrs Burke a temporary licence but coal's for them as understands it. There's been a fair number o' Southorners cumen and gannin on Tyne and they usual end up drownin' in it.'

I can swim, you buggers. But she said: 'Thank you, gentlemen.'

Outside on the steps, Hedley's son picked her up and swung her round. 'You'll get a metropolitan funeral yet.'

She grinned back at him. 'Let tha and me go lay some flowers on Dot Lawson's grave, pet.'

★   ★   ★

At first Makepeace rented a tiny office in Merchants Court on the quay so that she could keep an eye on the keelmen and what they did with her coal.

Oliver virtually abandoned his practice and worked with her, partly to protect her decency and even more because there was so much to do. Her lodging was a room in the Side, a weary climb at nights when she was tired. Again for respectability's sake, she had to have a female companion and so she took on her former marra, young Hildy, as attendant and maid—a good attendant, terrible maid. They went to St Nicholas's on Sundays, her foot tapping at time wasted by the lengthy and vacuous sermons, with Alderman Sir somebody—it turned out to be Atkinson—watching her with his slug eyes.

She went back to Raby as often as she could; Betty and Philippa were there. But of necessity her visits were short and infrequent.

She made sure her discussions with Andra Hedley were even shorter and more infrequent. In any case, he was as busy as she was and virtually lived in a cubicle at the pithead filled by papers, drawings, dockets and noise. With both of them stressed and exhausted, their meetings were edged with temper.

It seemed to her he was dismissive of how difficult it was to be a woman negotiating with men who displayed the amusement—and then the impatience—they'd accord to a talking beetle. Of the degradation in bartering with keelmen who were rude or lecherous, mostly both, and thought it their duty to charge her more than they would anyone else.

Of trying to join the Grand Alliance, a cartel of the big colliery-owners, who laughed her out of court. Of dealing with contractors who were slow with services but quick to present bills.

'You've no idea of my problems,' she said.

'I've got my own.'

To make the point, he walked her round the pit head, pointing out engines that broke down and had to be adapted, ventilation doors that warped, the necessity of a viaduct to correct the wagonway's gradient, the damage to the staith by a violent wave that had taken away part of its foundations.

All she saw was money draining out. More investment had been needed; this time she'd raised it in London, from Susan's willing Jews. 'And what are you wasting it on?' She pointed. 'Luxury bloody houses.'

At the moment their miners were being accommodated in tents but from this hilltop she and Hedley looked down on a rising village of sturdy, slate-roofed cottages, two up, two down, with gardens and pigeon lofts. With Northumbrian logic the village was already referred to as 'Collory Raa', though in fact the houses were not a row at all but would eventually form neat squares around a school.

'They'll lodge better than I do,' she said, resentfully.

'And me,' he said. He still lived in the but 'n' bens. 'But we're not the poor sods riskin' wor lives hewing coal. I'll have decent conditions here or you'll find yourself another partner.'

'Don't think I can't.'

It was a lovely autumn day. Some terns were squabbling out at sea where the damaged staith's drunken shape was perfectly reflected in the water. Suddenly she wanted nothing so much as to be out in a boat.

'Oh, Mr Hedley,' she said wearily, 'what are we doing here?'

His arm shifted as if he would put it round her but instead he smiled. 'We're having the time of our lives, pet,' he said.

The next year Raby went into full production. The year after it sank another shaft and began tunnelling under the seashore. A steady river of coal began an uninterrupted journey down the wagonways to the staith, to the Tyne, to the Thames, into the voracious fires and furnaces of London.

And as coal flowed out, money began to flow in.

Aaron heard his sister's voice through the screech of the cranes loading and unloading the keels further along the quay, the rattle of coals pouring into holds, the shouts of dockers and sailors.

' . . . ye knacky-kneed donnart, ballast tha bloody keel wi' this muck again an' Ah'll skelp yer arse . . .'

She was standing on the deck of a boat moored to the quay,

shaking her fist at a salt-stained, coal-pigmented seaman who was shuffling his feet and listening to her with abashed admiration. Men loading nearby had stopped work and, as Aaron opened his mouth to call her, one of them nudged him. 'Whisht, sor, when the Missus's seein' reed 'tis a privorlege t'hear her.'

' . . . Ship it again, yer scarecraa, an' Ah'll swing thee fra nearest stob and God hev mercy on yer sowl, ye divvil.' She waved her fist one last time under the seaman's nose, turned and strode down the gangplank.

'Hello, Mrs Burke,' Aaron said.

She flung herself on him. 'When did you arrive?'

'Just now. What has that unfortunate gentleman done?'

She got angry again. 'Brought rubbish as ballast on the voyage back from the Thames. If I've told him once . . . I want good china clay, we've started a pottery business beyond Close Gate. What's the point unless I can make a profit going *and* coming?'

'What indeed?'

She held him at arms' length to admire him for a second. The showiness had gone; he was dressed with taste. Among the detritus of the quay he stood out slim and sleek—like a clean young carrot, she thought. She tucked her arm under his. 'Come to the office while I finish.' The dockers whistled at them as they went off and she grinned at them: 'Howay, ye whaups, he's me brothor.'

'I see you speak the language.'

'Only one they understand.'

The brass plaque on the door in Merchants Court read simply: 'Burke and Hedley'. She'd extended the premises since he'd last seen them, its ancient woodwork was freshly oiled and there were boxes of pale geraniums in its windows. The noise from a shed next door was ear-shattering.

'What's that?'

'What? Oh, that's Mr Palmer's shop . . . Evening, Mr Palmer . . . he's invented a new form of anchor. Doing very well.'

'Can't he do it somewhere else?'

'Hasn't got time to find new premises, too busy making a profit.'

That's Newcastle all over, Aaron thought. Everywhere he'd passed, ancient frontages decorated with gargoyles were, in fact, producing up-to-date manufacture; the town had no street lighting but there was no need of it when everywhere was illuminated by the flame of furnaces.

Inside the offices clerks were busy writing at high desks and stood up politely as Makepeace entered. 'You look well,' she said.

'So do you, but what on earth are you wearing?' She was in widow's weeds of differing black, the skirt dusty from hem to hock, her hair entirely hidden by a scarf underneath a battered, greenly aged tricorn. The mobile face, which had now lost years rather than gained them, peering out from such elderly swaddling added to the scarecrow effect.

She looked down at herself. 'It's not Mme Angloss exactly, but . . . well, I'm playing a *character*, I'm not supposed to be fashionable.'

'You're not supposed to be an eyesore. Haven't you anything else?'

'Only my best. I haven't got time . . .'

He made her close up the office and hustled her to Middle Street where, he remembered, there were some decent drapery shops— or as decent as drapery went in Newcastle—to buy her a made-up bodice and skirt to go with the lawn shawl he'd bought her from Dublin, where his company had been playing to packed houses. He scandalized the girl assistants by scrutinizing every item and rubbing it between his fingers for quality. Newcastle men didn't do that.

'Whisht,' she said, 'they'll think you're a puff.'

He smiled. 'They'd be wrong.'

She loved his poise. Mr Burke's Touring Company was gaining a reputation for excellence and had staged a private performance of Goldsmith's *The Good-Natured Man* before Their Majesties. In the gossip newspapers his name was constantly linked with beautiful women, several of them titled. She'd offered to set him up a theatre in Newcastle now that she had money to fund one but he'd said his future was in London and Dublin—he was finished with the provinces.

She was renting an apartment in the Side to live in, larger but not much more comfortable than her original room. After completing their purchases they set off towards it. 'For Heaven's sake,' he panted as they climbed the hill, 'it smells of cheese round here.'

'It's handy though. Near enough to the office and the right side of town for Raby. Hildy looks after it, I only sleep in it.'

Once inside, Aaron saw that Makepeace extended the indifference she showed towards her personal appearance to the furnishing of her home, which was good but sparse, and lacking ornaments. It reminded him of the Roaring Meg but without the cheer and fellowship; it smelled of lye soap, like the cottages of the cleanly poor. His own fashionable rooms in London were scented with beeswax and pot-pourri.

'Oh, I leave all that to Hildy,' she said.

'Where's the kitchen?'

'There's only a scullery. We get food from the tavern down the hill.'

God, Aaron thought, even the Roaring Meg had lobsters. So when she'd dressed in her new clothes, they went to dine at the Pilgrim's Inn in a private room. He noticed that she took pains to introduce him to its landlord as 'my brother'.

'Can't afford gossip,' she said, 'not in Newcastle.'

The meal was good but, again, an anachronism. There was caviare brought in by ice-boats from the Baltic, but for the Pilgrim Inn, as with the rest of Newcastle, the potato had yet to make its debut.

Aaron was relieved to find that she had at least not cut herself off from London. Andrew Ffoulkes visited on his way to friends in Edinburgh, so did Dr Baines. She was in touch with Susan through the Jews—though her correspondence was more with the Jews than Susan.

Her most surprising visitor, she told him, had been John Beasley. She'd taken him to Raby, shown him the colliery, sent him down one of the mines, introduced him to her people—and watched in amazement as he and Hedley became friends.

'Of all men I can't think of two more different,' she said. But

Beasley was always attracted by the clever and unpretentious while Hedley, she presumed, saw in Beasley whatever it was that endeared the journalist to his coffee house acquaintances like Joshua Reynolds.

'They've come to some arrangement to get Mr Hedley's rectangular corves and braged conductors registered with the Patent Office, though they're both very rude about the place. Beasley says they're "inefficient fuckers" and Hedley says they're "porvorse sods".'

Aaron saw her delight and saw, too, that she forced herself away from it. She began to talk of coal.

'We've paid off the original debt,' she said. 'Now we can pick and choose our investors—we have to fight 'em off.'

'Are you making a personal profit, though?'

'A lot,' she said, 'I just don't have time to count it.'

She bored him with accounts of negotiations with recalcitrant fellow coal-owners, bloody-minded miners, porvorse sods of keelmen, her new pottery business, contacts with Birmingham, Manchester . . .

He interrupted her. 'What are you doing all this *for*?'

'To become rich, of course.'

'You *are* rich. 'Peace, they left you sobbing at their gates, *your* gates, and cast you into the wilderness, *this* wilderness.'

'I haven't forgotten,' she said.

'Isn't it time you came back? You're Lady Dapifer, not Mrs Burke. God, it distresses me to see you standing on a coal barge, swearing like a fishwife *and* dressed like one. I thought we'd finished with docksides.'

This one hasn't done badly by you, she thought. Her coal had bought him proper scenery, more players and better travelling. But she didn't say so; she remembered what a Boston dockside had cost him.

'*She* was in the audience the other day,' he said, 'Mrs Conyers as is. We were doing *Cleone*. I think she's completely forgotten you had an actor brother; she's probably forgotten *you*, probably thinks you're dead. Blasted harpy chatted to her friends through the whole damned performance.'

'I don't suppose *she* looked an eyesore, did she?'

'No,' he said, grimly, 'she didn't. She . . . glowed.'

Makepeace said: 'I happen to know she's glowing on borrowed money.' She leaned across the table and patted her brother's cheek. 'I have it in hand, Aaron.'

'Oh, 'Peace, it isn't the getting back at them so much—though, Lord knows, I'd like *him* spitted on the end of a toasting fork—it's knowing what Pip would say to you having to live and work in this squalor, what he'd say to me for letting you do it. It's what he took you away from . . .'

She was grateful to see his tears. There were few to cry for her husband nowadays. 'You loved him, didn't you?'

'I've never met anyone better.'

'Nor have I.'

The next day they set off early in her carriage—an equipage more sturdy than smart, like its horse; he wondered if she bothered with anything that wasn't strictly functional—to see Betty and Philippa. But as they came to the colliery track she turned into it, going under the bridge formed by the wagonway viaduct. 'You won't recognize it,' she said.

They passed by a small village where the sound of chanting came from a schoolhouse and mass washing was spread on bushes nearby. 'They have to watch the wind,' she said. 'If it changes they run out and put it in another field or it gets covered with coal soot.'

A man was walking what Aaron took to be a dog along a stretch of moorland; nearer, the animal on the lead turned out to be a not unhandsome fighting cock. 'Favourite sport round here,' his sister said, 'that and pigeon-racing. Good morning, Joe.'

'Mornin', missus.'

Further up, the landscape became a mass of chimneys, wheels, blackened buildings and rails. New mountains of slag were rising out of the earth to disfigure it.

It seemed to Aaron that everything he saw either moved, made a noise or was filthy, mostly all three. A huge wheel turned above one hut which was disgorging a band of fiends from hell: black shapes with gleaming white eyes and teeth.

'Night shift,' Makepeace said. 'Wha' cheor, lads.'

'Mornin', missus.'

There were imps among the fiends, swaggering and shouting incomprehensibly in high voices. 'We don't use as many boys as other pits,' his sister said, 'Mr Hedley won't have it. Ponies do the pulling. Much more costly, of course, but he doesn't care for that.'

There was something in her voice that Aaron couldn't analyse.

He was relieved when she turned the trap and the two of them were trotted away, even more relieved to find that Headington House was being rebuilt for her. One wing had been finished and the wilderness around it was being returned to garden. Even here, Aaron thought, there was lack of attention. The site was lovely but the finished wing promised that the eventual whole would be over-heavy and graceless.

'Why didn't you bring in Robert Adam?' he asked. 'Build something classical?'

'I just wanted it restored,' she said, 'I haven't got time to fuss about with architects. It's mainly for Betty and Philippa to live in anyway.'

After a rapturous reunion with Betty in the kitchen, and a meal—also taken in the kitchen—brother and sister walked across the moor to meet Philippa from school. 'Hasn't she got a governess?' Aaron asked.

'Mr Hedley found an excellent teacher for the school,' she said, 'so she goes there with the rest. She seems to have brains, she's very mathematical.'

'What about her music? Dancing? Elocution?'

'Oh well,' she said, 'I'll see to that when I have time.' She put her arm through his. 'We weren't even allowed to dance round a maypole, remember?'

He didn't answer. Three children were coming towards them chattering in Northumbrian dialect.

One of them, the neatest of the three, had shoes but they were laced together over her shoulder and her prehensile little feet trod the tough grass and heather with apparent imperviousness. She ran towards him: 'Uncle Aaron!'

She introduced her companions nicely enough: 'This is Polly, this is John. Polly, John, my uncle Aaron.'

'Ginny and Jamie's children,' said Makepeace. 'They're in the Factor's House now.'

Philippa turned to her mother. 'Mam, Johnny says there's greet monsters doon the lonnen, wi' reet sharp teeth an' waarts, but tha's blaa, in't it, Mam?'

'Blaa,' nodded Makepeace. 'Howay now, pet. We'll be in when we've said hello to Tantaquidgeon.'

Aaron kept his silence until after the visit to the grave but when she would have returned to the house, he took his sister's arm and sat her on a tombstone. 'In the name of God, Makepeace, what are you doing?'

'What?'

'Leave aside that you're content to live as a vagabond, you cannot, you can *not* bring up Philippa like this, like . . . some gypsy whelp.'

She looked up at him. 'Is it the shoes? We went without shoes . . .'

'Yes, we did. But she's not the child of a shiftless, drunken Irishman, she's the daughter of Sir Philip Dapifer. Look at her . . .'

From this edge of the graveyard it was possible to see down the hill to the but 'n' bens, where the children were talking through the window to someone inside. A door was flung open and Hedley came out, growling like a bear, to chase the three as they fled before him. When he caught them he gathered them up. Their laughter was like seagulls' cries.

'Look at her, *hear* her, for the sake of God! Are you so occupied steeping yourself in this northern sinkhole that you haven't noticed what she's become? Walking along just now I couldn't tell her from the pit brats.'

'There's *time*, Aaron,' Makepeace protested. 'When I—'

'You haven't got time—you keep telling me. But time's a-wasting, 'Peace, you just haven't noticed. What is she now? Five? Nearly six? And I wouldn't dare lead her into a decent drawing room.'

At the shock on his sister's face, he sat down beside her and took her hand. 'I'm sorry, my dear, but you must see. Who's she to marry? Some burly, black-faced miner who'll beat her and drink her money? You say she's clever but that's not good enough, she must be cultured.'

He was becoming moved by his own rhetoric, tears again not far off. 'Pip was the most cultured man I ever knew. What would he say to what you're doing to his child? What would he say to *me* for letting you do it? After all he did for me? Dear God, he'd think I'd betrayed him.'

It was as if he'd taken a broom to her mind and swept away everything except memories.

The call of whaups from the moor and the distant pounding of the colliery pulled at the sleeve of her attention like insistent, nagging children. She shrugged them off.

Procrustes? It was her husband's voice.

'Makepeace?' It was Aaron's.

She turned to her brother. 'You're right,' she said. 'But you haven't betrayed him. I have.'

Hedley caught up with her as she climbed the Side, her boots slipping on its cobbles. The rain found its way down the hill's depressions in grey, vitreous-looking rivulets and dulled the light of the candles in the cheese shops, which were anyway closing up for the night.

She felt his hand grasp her elbow and lift her along.

'I want to talk to you, lass.'

'I'm tired,' she protested.

'You'll be tireder when I've finished.'

A side door led to the staircase to her rooms. The day had been bright enough when she set out that morning but the rain made everything so dark she had to fumble in the candle cupboard for tinderbox and fungus before they had light by which to move.

Upstairs smelled damp. She put the candle on the mantelshelf. 'There's no food.'

'Drink'll do.'

By the time she'd found the brandy bottle and glasses, he'd taken off his sopping cloak and hat and was lighting the fire. His hair had curled tight as it always did in damp, the flames reflected on tiny shreds of grey. He stood up and looked around the comfortless room but made no comment. 'Where's Hildy?'

'I sent her home for a day or two. Her mother's ill again.' She braced herself. 'What do you want?'

'Sit down.' He set two chairs by the fire facing each other. Brusque movements indicative of anger. Any moment now he'll howl like a wolf, she thought.

He tossed the brandy down his throat and sat down opposite her. 'Betty says you're taking her and the bairn away.'

'Yes.'

'To live in London.'

'Yes.'

He sat back in his chair. 'Why?'

'It's time Philippa took up her position as her father's daughter. I can afford it now.'

'Isn't she her father's daughter at Raby?'

Makepeace sidestepped. 'Anyway, I have business in London that must be attended to.'

'Would that be wor famous revenge?' He nodded at her. 'John Beasley told us. Canny lad, that.'

She tried to become angry. 'It's none of your business.'

'Mebbies not, but young Philippa is. I've affection for that bonny lass and she's affection for me. That apart, she's warm and bound in a tight community. What for d'you want to take her from it to that ugly town o' yours?'

Now she was angry. She leaned forward. '*You're* not her father.'

He leaned too, so that their noses almost touched. '*Damnation,*' he shouted, '*but Ah'm the next best thing.*'

They stayed where they were for a second or two, their eyes fixed on each other, then he got up and poured them both another glass of brandy. 'Medicinal purposes,' he said, handing one over.

She gulped it, more to stay resolved than because she liked it. The cessation of their shouting emphasized the lesser sounds: rain drumming on the skylight in her attic; a sudden spit from the fire. She got up and went to the window to a view of the wet, grey, descending roofs of the hill. Well, she thought, drearily, it's going to be easy to leave.

She heard him say gently. 'I'm the next best thing, pet.'

She looked round. He was leaning against the mantelshelf, watching her. He said: 'We've been that busy, the day never came. But it's come now. I need you to make an honest man o' me.'

'*What?*' she screeched.

'I've been compromised, pet.' He sounded aggrieved. 'Down in t'pit, when roof caved in. You took advantage of me.'

She said warily: 'I don't know what you're talking about.'

'Yes, you do. Very compromising position, forced against a female body. Not the plainest I've ever seen, neither. Let's face it, bonny lass, it was a matter of who came first, bloody rescuers or you and me.'

She bit her lip, trying not to laugh, then she gave way.

He grinned back. The candlestick fell over and went out as he lunged for her. 'Where's bloody bedroom?' They were returned to darkness, this time his arms right around her, forcing her back and back, down and down, and she was scrabbling to help him get them both undressed.

There was no comparison because there was no memory; no room for it; he possessed her mind and body; here was greed, violent and no holds barred. No flight to the stars but a desperate, grinding wrestle in sexual mud, go on, go on, until its groaning conclusion with both of them winners.

Peace fell on them like the rain on the window. She lay with her nose buried in his chest, breathing him in, wondering where she was, when it was. She was suffused with physical gratitude from the top of her head to her toes. She turned her cheek so that she could rub it against his skin. It was all she had the strength to do.

Flames from the steel plant down the hill made a sub-fusc square out of her window.

He said something. Dreamily, she cupped her hands round his face and moved her lips across his. 'What?'

'I was hungry for you.'

'I don't feel guilt for this, I was starving too, Andra Hedley.'

He sounded surprised. 'Guilt never entered my mind.'

She looked down at their entangled legs, hers very white in the dimness, his very dark. 'It'd enter a lot of people's if they saw us now.'

'Porvorse sods,' he said. 'No idea of ecstasy.'

She settled her head into his shoulder and wrapped her arms round him; he was luxury, satisfaction, humour; she wanted to anoint him with compliments. She felt surprisingly chatty.

'I think I was shipwrecked,' she said. 'Struggling to stay afloat for years—difficult, I'm tired of difficulties—and you're the island I've bumped into in the night, all warm and dark and safe . . .' Her voice trailed off; this wasn't her at all, though it was what she felt.

'An island,' he said. 'I'd hoped for a bloody continent.'

'Nothing wrong with islands.'

' 'Cept you get off 'em eventually.'

She said: 'I've *got* to go to London, Andra, I've a score to settle.'

'Tell us.'

She told him everything. Here was mental release after the physical; an orgasm of pain and wrongs, explanation, confession. She knew she was exposing her soul to this man as she had to nobody outside her circle—but, Hell, she'd exposed everything else.

'I've been watching them these years.' She told him about Robert as well. 'When I go to London he keeps me up with what they're doing. He makes it . . . vivid . . . It's like sitting in the dark at a theatre watching clowns on the stage. You wonder at them: so evil and at the same time so bloody *silly*. There's no understanding them. They've no conception of earning, or even paying their way. He owes his bootmaker nine hundred-odd pounds. Nearly a *thousand pounds*, just on boots. He'll ruin the man. Money spurts out of their fingers like taps: gambling, entertaining, doing nothing valuable. Everything's impermanent with them, as if they haven't long to live.'

'No bairns?' he asked.

'No bairns. She's barren. You could be sorry for them; sometimes I almost am, and then I think: That's Philippa's money, you're not sorry for her. They wouldn't even let me in to bury him. Oh God, Andra, they wouldn't let me say goodbye.'

He held her tight until she'd cried herself into a hiccuping stillness.

'Clay, pet,' he said. 'They've come from clay and they'll return to it.'

'Indeed they will.' She sat up, sniffing and wiping her nose on the back of her hand. 'And I'm sending 'em. That's what I've been doing—buying their debts. Susan's Jew's been collecting them for me. Nearly every penny of my profit's gone on financing Mr and Mrs Conyers—and at a very pretty interest. Next year, oh-ho, *next* year the price of coal goes up and so does mine.'

She held up her hand so that he could see it against the square of window and curled it into a fist.

'*Then* I've got them. *Then* I send in the bailiffs. The Fleet, I think—King's Bench is for gentry. The Fleet'll hurt bad.' She looked down at him. 'Did you know that when you can't pay you need permission from every single one of your creditors to get out of debtors' prison? Well, you do. One creditor to say no, one creditor to keep them in for life. Just one.'

'You,' he said.

'Me.'

He watched her watching her own fingers gripe, stretching and clawing like a cat's. 'Know what I'll do then? I'll dress in my very, very bloody best and I'll walk into that prison, just to the door, and I'll stand there and smile at her. And then I'll walk away.'

'Smile,' he repeated, flatly.

'She smiled at me once.'

She felt his chest rise in a deep breath. 'You've gone to a lot o' work for one smile, lass.'

'A lot.'

'And a lot of blaa,' he said. 'You'd have done it anyway. I saw it. One sniff o' that coal and you woke to what you are—as good a businessman as ever came over the Atlantic. No need to make that trash the excuse, pet—I shudder to think o' their minds. Leave 'em to the Hell they've made for their own selves. You and me, bonny lass, the earners and makers, we're blessed wi' building things that matter.'

He reached for her. 'Furthermore, you've breasts a man could drown his soul in.'

'Oh,' she said, 'oh, *Andra*.'

When she woke up, the window had gained light, though rain still pattered softly against the glass. 'It's morning,' she said, stretching. 'What?' He was muttering something.

He yawned. 'I said you'll have to marry me now.'

Makepeace sat up. 'Marry? I can't *marry*.'

'Have to, pet. I've been led astray.' He turned over and went back to sleep.

She peered at him closely. She saw a curly-headed man with grey beginning in his hair, a blue cut across his broken nose.

Have to, pet. It panicked her. I can't marry you, I can't marry anybody. I've been alone too long, I can't be owned now. Not by you. I don't belong to you. I'm an independent woman. What she spent her money on, how she earned it—if she earned any at all— who she left it to, these things would be at this man's command.

She looked around, desperate, and her husband came into the room, not vulnerable as he'd been these past years, not the victim who'd died calling for her. Here was the essential Dapifer: laconic, elegant, amused and suddenly so vivid she could smell his skin.

And here she was, nauseatingly naked in a bed with a man marked by coal. Hurriedly, she got up and wrapped herself in a petticoat, took the ghost with her into the sitting room and, at once, they were back at the Roaring Meg, the narrow encompassment from which he'd rescued her.

He asked: 'And where is Captain Busgutt and his improved mizen now?' It was typical of him to say nothing to any purpose.

Captain Busgutt, she thought tenderly. How long ago.

'Let me tell you, *Mister* Dapifer,' she said, smiling, 'Captain Busgutt's sermon on the Lord's scourging of the Amorites caused some in the congregation to cry out and others to fall down in a fit.'

'Pity I missed it.'

'Who's Captain Busgutt?' said a Northumbrian voice.

The tall image gave way to a living, stocky man in the doorway pulling up his breeks.

Another unsuitable man I was saved from marrying, she thought. Her husband haunted for a reason; she saw it now. How could she not have seen it before?

In a rush she said: 'I'm marrying nobody.' It was only fair to tell him; she had slept with him, after all, *and* enjoyed it, God help her. 'We're partners, Mr Hedley, that must be enough for us.'

He stroked his chin. It rasped. 'Partners,' he said.

'Yes.'

'Still going to London?'

'Yes.'

'Still taking Philippa away?'

'Yes.'

He jerked his thumb over his shoulder at the bedroom. 'And you and me in there, what o' that?'

She said timidly, because there were long years of starvation ahead: 'I'll keep the rooms on, I'll have to come back now and then—I'm not leaving the business.' She couldn't rule out hunger.

'By *Christ*,' he said, slowly. 'What do you think o' me?'

He made her flinch. 'I think highly of you, I truly do. Don't look at me like that.'

He said: 'You've lived too long among gentry, pet. What am I? Some prick-peddler comes round every year to render his bloody services?'

'No, I . . . Oh, go away.'

He dragged her hands from her face and shook her so that she had to look at him. 'I'm a marryin' man, lass, what's wrong wi' that?'

'Nothing. *Yes*. You see . . .' She grimaced at him, baring her teeth. 'I've a duty to my husband. He was a very special man.'

'I heard. But I'm special too, pet. And *he's* dead.'

She didn't say anything and he dropped her hands. She watched him go to the bedroom to pick up the rest of his clothes. For the first time she saw the deep scars on his back where his body had protected hers from the roof fall. When he came out he was putting on his coat.

At the door to the stairs he looked back. 'Tha's to be pitied, missus. We could have had wor bit share o' happiness, thee and me.'

She heard him go down the stairs, heard the side door slam behind him.

After a long while she raised her head. The candlestick Hedley had knocked over was still on the floor. She picked it up and put it back on the mantelshelf, took their two glasses and the brandy bottle to the scullery, came back again, put the chairs back in their place. There had to be some order to counteract the chaos in which so many people were ashamed of so much for so many different reasons. Aaron ashamed of her, Pip ashamed of her, Hedley; even Temperance Burke was adding a far-off toll of condemnation to a slut. 'Thee offered thyself outside marriage? To a good man? Are thee lost, daughter?'

It evens out, Mother, she thought wearily. I was ashamed of him and he shamed me.

There was no further resurrection. She sat for most of the morning in a tidy, unhaunted room, apologizing for the fine mess she'd made in it.

The only ghost that came was female. It turned up around midday. It stood exquisitely in the doorway and smiled at her.

Makepeace welcomed it like an old friend. 'Howay, wor Catty.'

He was wrong; this was the object for which she'd raised money, and fought the hostmen and keelmen. This had been her purpose: the downfall of this woman. She just hadn't been attending to it properly.

But now . . . here was simple, clean hate, flags fluttering; here was an enemy to clear the mind and decks for. Here, at least, was a defined thing still to be done. Here was unfinished business.

Chapter Nineteen

As part of London's Twelfth Night celebrations in 1772, distinguished actors, singers and musicians came together at Drury Lane Theatre to give a concert to benefit the Foundlings' Hospital. An invited audience included the Duke of Cumberland as well as lesser royalty, peers, a member or two of the Cabinet and distinguished commoners, among them that well-known couple-about-town Major and Mrs Sidney Conyers.

One of the dramatic offerings was a burletta, *The Pillar of Fire*, set in early Troy before its troubles with Greece. It told the story of a kindly, mythical king, Philippus, whose wife, Katerina, betrays him with his brother, Sidneus and plots his overthrow. This achieved, and with the King dead, the evil couple banish his second, faithful wife and her child to a barren island where they are left to starve. The goddess Athene, however, taking pity on the exiles, transforms them into a pillar of fire with the ability to haunt those who've wronged them. It is seen flickering through the castle and its ramparts, sending the wicked King and Queen mad before eventually consuming them in its flames.

Mercifully, because it wasn't very good, the burletta was short and doubtless would have remained in the common memory for no longer than it took to perform if it hadn't been for three events.

One was that, during the first scene, Major and Mrs Conyers angrily left the theatre. The second was that, at the burletta's close, its cast lined up on the stage to curtsey and bow, first to His Grace of Cumberland and then to a neighbouring private box in which sat a woman with red hair.

Thirdly, one of the burletta's songs, the best of them, which was sung in her famous Cockney style by Miss Fanny Cobb as the good Queen's cheeky, faithful servant, became popular. It was called 'Playing with Fire' and its chorus ran: 'Them as filch what they ain't earned Shall have their naughty fingers burned.' Not deathless lyrics, perhaps, but the tune was catchy and it hymned the fate of all dispossessed: the Enclosure Acts were creating a lot of those. Overnight, it was being sung in taverns and whistled everywhere on the streets.

Following an appeal by Major Conyers to the Lord Chamberlain, wrath was called down on the heads of the actors responsible but, since they had packed their bags and departed for a tour of Ireland immediately after the curtain fell at Drury Lane, it missed. The burletta was banned from any future performance.

The song, however, proved harder to suppress, and those who heard it were reminded by some well-placed articles in the scandal sheets that it referred to the forgotten plight of a real woman. 'Where is she now, that unhappy lady?' was the question. 'Has she returned to haunt her persecutors?' For it was being rumoured that a certain Mrs Burke, a wealthy widow, had lately been seen in London and that she bore a remarkable resemblance to the person who had once described herself as Lady Dapifer.

The house near Hatton Garden had a dusty front door behind which was a spartan office. Both were deceptive. Makepeace had to stand in the street until the clerk identified her through the door's grille.

She was welcomed and led up a tiny, creaking flight of stairs hidden behind a cupboard to a room warm with the wealth that a man of Mr Franco's race and occupation dare not display to the outside world. Its hangings came from Arras, the carpets from Isfahan and the excellent coffee was served in cups of frail, blue-green porcelain. The place had a dry, oriental scent which Makepeace, having never seen one, associated with the desert. Its plump, middle-aged owner, on the other hand, was dressed as if for the Stock Exchange, though such jobbing as he did there was conducted under the colonnade known as 'Jew's Walk' and without a licence.

'How is Miss Susan?' asked Mr Franco.

'Very well.'

'The hat trade, that goes well too?'

'You won't believe this, Mr Franco, but we're now selling to Russia.'

Mr Franco pretended to hit his forehead with the heel of his hand. 'I should not have let the Leghorns go, no, no, nor Miss *Susan* should I have let go. But what can a poor man do against you? If there were more women of business such as yourself, we men would have to stay home and suckle our children.'

Makepeace smiled at him. 'You're not doing so badly, Mr Franco.'

'Not badly, no. But I am not Raby coal, I cannot even burn Raby coal in my poor hearth, only His Majesty can afford it.' He laced his ten fingers and waggled them at her. 'When may I invest my few shekels?'

'We're over-subscribed at the moment, Mr Franco, but I do bear you in mind, I promise.' It was a ritual; they'd held virtually the same opening conversation for months—they both enjoyed it.

Mr Franco heaved himself up and went to a bell pull. A clerk came up from the depths like a genie from a bottle, bringing a file of papers. 'Yes, yes, I was summoned to Grosvenor Square again, Mrs Burke.'

'Good. How much this time?'

Mr Franco waited until his clerk had gone downstairs. 'Fourteen thousand?' He scanned a page; he was summoned to lots of houses. 'Yes, fourteen thousand. I gather the lady and gentleman in question have been once more unlucky at Mr Almack's gaming tables.'

Makepeace shook her head. 'Why do they *do* it?' She could never get over the fact that they made things so easy for her.

Mr Franco reached out and pulled aside a curtain on the wall near him. Behind it were eight cheap prints, superbly framed, of *The Rake's Progress*.

'Every day I show those pictures to my son,' said Mr Franco. ' "Regard the last two and pay your bills on time," I tell him, "for here is what happens to men who do not." Mr Hogarth painted from life, I tell him. "Sir Thomas Lowther, Lord Hoby, the King of Corsica, great men in their day, you are looking at them all."

'It is so with your friends,' Mr Franco went on, 'it is the usual thing. They chase the rainbow and think it can be pocketed. They invest in bubbles that promise a return of two thousand per cent, they mortgage their homes against a win at the tables which never comes, they dress well and keep fine horseflesh because the further they drop the less it must appear that they are falling.'

'What security did they offer this time?' she asked.

'Some forest in Kent.' Mr Franco consulted his papers again. 'Yes, yes, Barton Wood. Five hundred and forty-two acres of prime oak. Good security—the navy is always eager for oak.'

'Barton Wood? Are you sure?'

'Yes, yes. Here is the valuation. As always, I temporize. I must consult my hard-hearted associate before I can advance more, I tell them. They appreciate such things, it confirms their opinion that I am a perfidious Jew wishing only to keep them on the rack.'

Mr Franco was of the Sephardim: he knew about racking; he still had relatives locked in the Spanish cells of the Inquisition. 'The Major called me a reptile in his light-hearted way. Do you agree the loan?'

'Not this time, no. May I borrow that valuation?'

Mr Franco raised his thick eyebrows. 'You know something? Very well. Then they are nearly done. Unless they have a friend rich enough, or unwise enough, to cover such a debt you should soon be in a position to execute a warrant for their arrest.'

Mr Franco didn't smile but he breathed in satisfaction like incense. His charge of forty per cent—lower than many of his colleagues'—had not covered all the names Major Conyers had seen fit to call him.

'There are promissory notes as well,' he said. 'Most bills find their way to us reptiles sooner or later. Yes, yes, here they are. These as well?'

'If you please, Mr Franco.'

'Also, you remember, you asked me to keep an eye open for those of other ladies and gentlemen. Now, where . . . ? Ah here, yes, yes.'

The column of names on the page he handed over was a long one and might have been culled from a list of the peerage. Half the English gentry was exposed on it as being in debt to greater or lesser extent.

Again, wonderingly, Makepeace shook her head. 'How *can* they?'

'Mrs Burke, do not question it. Where would we poor money-lenders be if it were not for the British aristocracy?'

Before he showed her out, Mr Franco asked: 'You are well guarded as you go abroad, Mrs Burke?'

'Why?'

Mr Franco shrugged. 'Major Conyers is a good soldier and therefore a bad man. He does not know of your . . . interest . . . in his affairs, of course, but the word among my people is that your presence in Town annoys him.'

While she waited for Robert in the upstairs room of The Spaniards, Makepeace asked for paper, ink and pen.

Dear Mr Hackbutt [she wrote],

   Today a money-lender showed me this valuation (enclosed) on a property in Kent offered to him as security on a loan by Major Conyers now I know it is not part of the Dapifer estate and I believe it to be part of the inheritance of Ld Ffoulkes and therefore Major Conyers is using land that is not his but belongs to his ward. Andrew is travelling in Italy and cannot have given his permission. You will know what to do send it to Lord Ffoulkes' lawyers and tell them what is toward.

   Yrs respctfly, Makepeace Dapifer

There was a quick triple knock on the door and then two slower ones. Makepeace sighed. 'Come in.'

A muffled figure slouched in. 'You should've asked who it was, you naughty thing.'

'I knew who it was.'

'Well, *I* think we ought to have a password.' Robert crossed to the window and pulled the shutters to. His cloak covered the lower part of his face. He's probably got a dagger as well, Makepeace thought.

She'd ordered a meal for him: one of The Spaniards's famous hams, some pickles and a bottle of wine; he didn't like ale. He could have come to her home and eaten there—they were very close to her house—but he liked to believe he was being followed. It cost little enough to indulge his affection for subterfuge in return for his information. In any case life was becoming harder for him as his employers' debts mounted and more and more servants left them.

But these sessions made her uneasy; Robert could evoke a scene between Conyers and Catty so exactly that it was like eavesdropping.

But how the hell else can I know what they're up to?

Robert ate ravenously. 'No food at home,' he said, 'nothing to eat it off, neither. Our bootmaker finally lost his patience and sent in the bums. They took the silver plate in payment.'

Philippa's silver plate.

'And the grocer's took the epergne. And what we'll pawn next I don't know because the place is empty, completely *stripped*. We'd like to sell the Hertfordshire manor but it's mortgaged to the hilt.'

'I know,' Makepeace said.

Robert eyed her over his plate. 'Oh-ho, *you've* got it, have you, little sly-boots?'

'What do they plan to do?'

'Well, if I were *us*, I'd flee the country, but we still think we can recoup with a lucky win at the tables.'

It astounded her that both her enemies could look to gambling, which had been their downfall, for their salvation. A disease, she could only suppose, that they had recognized in each other and, instead of repelling, had bonded them together in a desperate form of mutual suicide.

'Why Macall puts up with it, I can't think,' Robert said. 'We must owe him *thousands*. I suppose he's afraid the Major will run him through if he excludes us. *She's* going to Almack's again tonight, some little do of Lady Brandon's.'

'I know. Macall told me.' The Scotsman was now one of her investors.

Robert was quick. 'Are you planning something?'

'I might be.'

'You be careful. I know you think I've got a bee in my bonnet, but you're *haunting* them and that's dangerous. He was at his window the other morning and heard the coalman whistling "Playing with Fire" as he delivered to the other side of the square. Well, *out* comes the riding whip, *out* comes the Major—still in his *nightcap*, my dear—and gives the poor fellow such a lashing as I feared would *kill* him. The blood . . .' Robert shook his head. 'I wish you'd make your move, I really do, and put us out of our misery.'

As he swung his cloak around him before setting out into the night, he said gently: 'Don't be too hard on them.'

She was incredulous. 'Hard on them? Hard on *them*?'

'I know.' He tapped her cheek with his forefinger. 'What they did . . . they're awful, awful. But she's deranged, oh completely. Did I tell you about the dog?'

'That dog's watching me, Siddy.'

'Darling, how can she be? Poor Bracken's blind as a mole, I ought to have her put down but she's been a faithful old thing.'

'She's got the Squaw's eyes, Siddy.'

'No, my dear. The red-headed bitch has blue eyes, Bracken's are brown.'

'She's watching me, Siddy.'

And two days later . . . 'What the hell's that noise?'

'I think it's the dog, Major. Madam's got it in there with her.'

'Catty. Open the door. Catty!'

'I don't know what she'd done to the poor creature, he wouldn't let us see,' Robert said, 'but he buried it that afternoon.'

'And you don't want me to be hard on her? She's *evil*.'

Robert shook his head. 'Mad and getting madder. Sir Pip understood.'

As her carriage took her home, Makepeace nursed a headache and a longing for Newcastle, that smoke-grimed repository of everything clean. She must go up again soon—on business, of course. The Grand Alliance wanted to restrict production in order to put up the price again . . .

Oh God, she thought with an attack of honesty, I just want to *be* there.

'We're home, ma'am.'

'Yes. Thank you, Sanders. I shall need you again tonight. The coach, I think.' She was handed down from the carriage. Light flowed across the portico as a footman with a branched candlestick opened the door to her.

It was a nice house, in the highest and most prestigious part of Highgate, not modern but graceful, designed by Roger Pratt circa 1650, a comfortable version of English Palladian. She'd bought it, complete with furniture and servants, from Lord Braybourne's widow after his death because it hadn't needed alteration and its situation was healthy while still being close to London.

Lady Braybourne had returned to her native Ireland immediately after the sale so the other great advantage of the house was that Society had not yet become aware that Makepeace was living in it.

As she passed the footman, she said: 'Tell Hildy to lay out the gold satin, if you please.'

'Going out again, ma'am?'

'Yes.'

She went through to the Grand Saloon.

Pip would approve of this room, she thought. Certainly, Aaron had: 'This is more like it, 'Peace. A cut above the Roaring Meg, eh?' Yet she felt no sense of ownership; it was to the Braybournes' excellent taste she owed every piece of furniture within the rosesilk walls; theirs were the white wainscoting and doors, the marble fireplace, the delicate plaster ceiling.

Even the paintings had been picked for her—by young Josh: a Reynolds portrait of her and Philippa and Betty, a Gainsborough and a large, alarming 'Raising of Lazarus' by van Haarlem.

Susan and Betty sat by the window in a concentration of candles, Susan doing her embroidery, Betty knitting. 'Is Philippa in bed?'

'She got tired waitin',' Betty said. 'Thought you'd be home afore this.'

'There were things to do.' The more she entangled Catty and Conyers in her web the less inclined she felt to talk about it. She added: 'And I've got to go out again later on.'

Betty sucked her teeth.

Susan followed her up to her room and stood in the doorway, her hands pleating her skirt. 'I think it's time I went home to see Auntie, 'Peace.'

Makepeace looked up. '*Boston*, do you mean?'

'Yes. She isn't getting any younger and I can help with her business.'

'You're a help with mine.' The export of Leghorns didn't compare financially with the other pies Makepeace had her fingers in, but its purpose had been to provide Susan with a good income while working from the home they shared—which it did. Miss Brewer might well look shifty.

Oh damn, this was going to require manipulation. 'My dear, what would I do without you? What would *Philippa* do without you?'

And, actually, what would you do without Philippa? she thought. It had been a happy arrangement to buy this house for them all and, while she was in Newcastle, to leave her daughter in the care of Susan and Betty. The child was the apple of Susan's eye and she devoted a good deal more time in attending to Philippa than she did to creating hats; the embroidery downstairs was putting little stitched sea-shells onto one of Philippa's dresses.

Miss Brewer looked shiftier, then squared her shoulders. 'I was wondering, Makepeace . . . I wondered if you might allow Philippa to come with me—just for a visit. Cousin Bart has a large farm in Concorde, his children just run wild there—she'd love the freedom.' At Makepeace's look she said: 'Well, sakes, she *is* half an American.'

Makepeace was astonished and amused. 'Susan, it's good of you, but I really think Philippa's visit to the Americas must wait 'til I have time to go with her.' She went back to her dressing.

'When's *that* going to be?' It was a rhetorical question; Susan was already on her way downstairs.

Some members are paying their gambling bills even if Catty isn't, Makepeace thought as she went up Almack's staircase. The club looked even more luxurious than it had, with more chandeliers, more excellent hangings, deeper carpets. Macall was standing at the head of the stairs talking to the Earl of Orme. Catching sight of Makepeace he bowed, then excused himself and moved away—he was going to stay out of this. The Earl just stared. 'Good God!'

She passed him with a nod.

As she went by the entrance to the gaming tables the scent of heated baize table-tops came out to her, the wink of dice and jewels, the almost tangible, sexual hush. They didn't tempt her now; there were too many flushed young men in the room and they all resembled Headington.

She didn't go in but proceeded on along the gallery to the open door of a smaller room in which other people were gathered around green tables. The footman on its threshold bowed. 'May I announce you, ma'am?'

'Lady Dapifer,' Makepeace said.

He turned. 'La-*dee* Dapifer.'

There was immediate silence. Every head in the room turned to her like a field of sunflowers. She let them look; she was in splendour and she knew it—gold suited her. *I'm the ghost of your past come back to haunt you.*

Then she thought: No, I'm the ghost of their future. I'm the new age, me and Hedley.

After a moment she heard Catty's voice break the silence: 'It's the Squaw, my dears. I thought it was dead but I see they've gilded it.'

Given the circumstances, Makepeace thought she did well.

Another footman came hurrying over, very flurried. 'I'm sorry, madam, but Lady Brandon says this reception is by invitation only.'

'I know,' Makepeace said. She put a piece of paper in his hand. 'This is my invitation.'

Lady Brandon advanced on her. 'What does this mean?'

'It's a bill, madam, a note promising to pay, one of several signed by you which I have bought off those to whom you owe money. I can show the others to your husband if you'd prefer.'

Catty came dancing up. 'Is it being a nuisance, Prissie? Dispose of it.'

The rouge on Lady Brandon's cheeks formed garish circles against skin that had turned grey.

'Prissie? What is it?'

Lady Brandon remained silent.

'Prissie!' Catty turned to Makepeace almost in appeal. 'What are you *doing*?'

'I'm being invited to play,' Makepeace said. 'Aren't I, Lady Brandon?'

She watched Catty's hands scrabble at her friend's sleeve. *Do you see them? Did you see my hands clawing at closed gates?*

'She's got to go, Prissie. Send her *away*.' It was a plea.

Lady Brandon opened her mouth, then closed it.

'I see,' Catty said. Makepeace was surprised at her sudden control—until she saw her eyes. 'You will pay, you know.'

'I already have.'

Lady Brandon's hand came out as Catty swept past her out of the door, and then fell back to her side.

Makepeace waited until the sound of clicking heels had faded before she said: 'Thank you, Lady Brandon, but I'm afraid I must refuse. I don't gamble.'

On the way back to Highgate in the coach, she took in deep breaths of satisfaction. It had been a pleasure. The first hand-to-hand engagement of the war—petty, perhaps, even unchristian, but, whatever else happened, the memory of that little skirmish could be laid away with battle honours.

She was pleased to see that there was still light in the Grand Saloon. Betty had waited up for her. 'Wait 'til I tell you—' she said.

'I'm a-goin' with Susan,' Betty said.

'What?'

'Boston. I'm goin' home.'

It developed into the worst quarrel they'd ever had.

'How *can* you be lonely? You've got Susan and Philippa. You see Josh nearly every week; Aaron's not far away.'

Betty's lower lip protruded dangerously. 'Don't like it here.'

'Oh, for God's sake.' Makepeace looked around the room, then reined in her temper; this had to be dealt with. She tried syrup. 'This is your home, Bet. I'm here as much as I can be. You know I'd be lost without you, you're my mainstay, always were. And you're Philippa's.'

'That chil' need to come with us, she ain't happy here neither. She don't fit in; she ain't got friends.'

'Of course she does. Susan has the Mansfield children in to play with her. She's got a pony, a governess. It's everything Pip would have wanted for her. Dammit, you didn't like it when we were hauling her around in a basket with Aaron's troupe—you said it wasn't suitable for Sir Pip's daughter, remember?'

Betty shifted her ground, an infuriating habit of hers. 'They all Tories round here. You want her growin' up Tory? She need a place where they ain't ashamed 'cos their money come from trade.'

'I suppose you think she was better off at Raby?' It had taken long enough to rid the child of her Northumbrian accent.

'She surely was. An' you too. Should've married Andra.'

'Don't you dare say that to me. Marry a . . . a fellow like that? Don't you remember who I *was* married to?'

They were shrieking now.

'You 'memberin' he's dead? Sir Pip's dead?'

'Not to me.'

'Then he oughta be.'

'You bitch, you *bitch*. Get out of my sight.'

There was a rustle of Betty's silk petticoats as she lumbered from the room.

It took a long time for Makepeace's hands to stop shaking. She felt ill; they'd never rowed like this, never. She strode up and down the length of the Aubusson carpet, her pace gradually slowing as the seriousness of the situation became more apparent.

She ain't lonely, how can she be lonely? The matter with her is she's had her nose put out of joint because she ain't with me every second nowadays. She's too bloody old to cross the Atlantic and she knows it. What she wants is me to give it up . . . stupid old baggage . . . *now we're almost there.*

Wallowing, Makepeace thought of what it had cost her to reach this position; labouring in the mine, fighting the hostmen, every second given to clambering up the ladder. She'd bought houses, dressed her family in silk, provided for those who'd helped her, given money to the damn poor. And she hadn't done all that by sitting at home to keep company with a fat old black woman.

Oh, *Betty.*

She left the saloon and went up the double staircase that curved the hall in white, balustraded, festooned wings.

Betty's bedroom was red, her favourite shade, with a state bed once occupied by a Venetian ambassador. It was unlit. A bulky shape sat slumped in a gilded chair by the open window, it didn't turn at Makepeace's approach.

'Don't leave me, Bet.' She knelt down and rested her forehead on the old woman's knees.

'Ain't me as is leavin'.'

'We're so close, almost *there*. I've nearly got 'em, girl. Only a little while more and we'll settle the score, then we'll go any place you want.'

Betty said nothing. The moonlight reflected on wet runnels down her cheeks but her face was set.

Makepeace crossed the room to fetch another chair. 'Look at this bed, will you? Remember the ones at the Roaring Meg? Pip said mine was what Procrustes tortured people on. He always called me Procrustes after that.'

Betty remained unmoved. 'You ain't doin' this for him. You ain't even doin' it for you. You like one of them pit wagons, the rails is there an' you jus' runnin' away on 'em. You likely crush your own child whilst you doin' it. Not me, you ain't crushin' me too. Susan goes, I go.'

The argument went on for an hour, gently on Makepeace's part, obdurately on Betty's. Only once did her voice waver: 'I miss that smelly ol' Indian.'

'So do I. Oh, so do I.' All the time.

She evoked every memory she could bear to, every cause of gratitude for both of them; she piped but Betty would not dance.

'Susan goes, I go.' It was her final word.

In bed that night, it came to Makepeace that Betty was passing the judgement of Solomon on Philippa. You love this child enough to give up your revenge for her? Or do I cut her in half?

For, sure as taxes, Philippa would be cut in half by Betty's departure. Without that big, black buoy, the one fixture to which she had always been attached, she would be lost and unhappy—like I'd have been at her age, Makepeace thought, if the blasted woman hadn't been there.

Which could Philippa least afford to lose? Betty the constant? Or a mother who was travelling elsewhere for eight-tenths of her time?

It comes to this: Do I love my daughter enough to abandon everything I've strived for these last years and be a better companion and mother to her?

She heard her groan break the silence of the room. 'Lord forgive me, I don't.' It was, literally, a physical impossibility; she knew her own physique, she would be eaten away by a disease called unfinished business.

Next morning, she called her daughter into the saloon. 'Now, Philippa, I don't know if your aunt Susan has told you, but she intends to go to America for a visit to her relatives. She wants to know if you would like to go with her.'

I sound like a schoolmarm, she thought. I can talk on equal terms with a Wullie Fergusson and a Marquis of Rockingham, but I'm stilted with my own flesh and blood.

Makepeace watched her daughter consider. The child had her father's long face, his sallow skin and hair, without in any other way resembling him. Her habitual expression possessed none of the mock-gloom and humour that had made Philip Dapifer so attractive; it was merely grave. She looked like a small, studious camel.

'Philippa?' prompted Makepeace.

'Would you be coming too, Mama?'

'No. I have things to do in England. I must go up North again soon.'

Was the girl disappointed? It was difficult to tell. Oh God, she's guarded—so young and guarded. My fault, I uprooted her; I haven't considered her feelings enough and she's learned to hide them.

Makepeace became irritated by her own accusation. Wasn't I bloody uprooted? I'd been dragged over half America by the time I was her age—*and* lost my mother. *And* I was running errands to earn money so Aaron didn't starve. Didn't do me any harm; she's got nothing to complain about.

The thing was, Philippa did not complain. She never has, not to me. Makepeace said gently: 'Betty thinks she would like to go with Auntie Susan.'

Was it panic, that shift of the child's eyes? Makepeace added: 'But I don't think she means it. If you'd like to stay here, I'm sure she'd stay too.'

'Are you going to be busy again, Mama?'

'Only for a little while longer.'

'Could I go on with my mathematics?'

Makepeace blinked. 'I'm sure you can.' Susan had found a tutor for the child.

Philippa said, thoughtfully: 'The Professor of Mathematics at the Royal Academy at Woolwich is the son of a pitman from Newcastle.'

'Is he?'

'Yes. Uncle Andra told me. Are there more Indians in America? Like Tantaquidgeon?'

Makepeace smiled. 'There was never another soul like Tantaquidgeon but, yes, there are Indians.'

'Could I see the Roaring Meg?'

What *had* Betty been telling her? 'If Auntie Susan thinks it suitable.'

'I think I should like to go. Just for a visit.'

Don't go. Stay here. 'Are you sure?'

'Yes.'

Is this how she feels every time I leave *her*? Awkwardly, Makepeace reached for her daughter. 'I'll come and fetch you back, you know. If you like America, we might even stay there together.'

The small body resisted. It was the worst moment of the interview; Philippa didn't believe her.

The fact that Philippa was prepared to go wasn't the end of the battle. Betty no more wanted to return to America than visit the moon; her strategy was to make Makepeace give up her career of revenging angel; Makepeace's was for Betty to capitulate unconditionally and stay in England.

It was Josh who called the bluff of them both. He turned up one morning on the Highgate doorstep, having walked from Leicester Fields, with an air of defiance and a pack from which stuck out some paintbrushes. 'I've run away.'

Makepeace hauled him into the saloon. Betty arrived in it at the gallop. 'You git back there, boy.' She still marvelled at the fact that it was Josh who'd painted the hands and drapery in the portrait Makepeace had commissioned from his master.

'No.' His face was set—he had become handsome. 'I ain't saying Sir Josh ain't a great man in his way, but it's *his* way. "Got to do it like this, not like that." Mam, there's a thousand ways of painting, and he won't let us try any of 'em. He's got apprentices higher up the ladder'n I am an' they're as frustrated as me. I ain't a-goin' back.'

'What are you going to do?' Makepeace asked.

'Work my passage to Boston. Ain't no Royal Academy in America to tell a man how an' what to paint.'

Two combatants looked past him at each other in helplessness and despair. Now Betty would be forced to leave. She must go with Josh; separation from her son at her time of life could be permanent. Makepeace saw her concede defeat and conceded her own; the very thing neither wanted had been taken out of their hands to become a reality.

In a fury that she had to do it at all, she began making the arrangements. Since she was killing birds she'd use one stone; the ship that would take them was to be the *Lord Percy*, the same frigate that had carried them all to England seven years before. Makepeace had been corresponding with its captain.

In September, subject to wind and tide, the *Percy* would dock at Deptford after an Atlantic crossing. Along with the usual dispatches, Captain Strang was bringing the papers Mr Hackbutt needed to begin the case against Catty. *Lord Percy* was a sound craft, her captain trustworthy; Makepeace could take possession of the papers and wish her people Godspeed at the same time.

The drive to Deptford was awful. Josh chattered brightly, Susan and Makepeace tried to, Betty and Philippa didn't say a word.

The *Lord Percy* was anchored in midstream, sails neatly furled, the scrollwork on her aft cabin, where Dapifer had proposed marriage, newly gilded.

Dinner was worse than the drive down. Makepeace had ordered fresh salmon and champagne but only Captain Strang and Josh enjoyed the meal. Makepeace needed constant reassurance that Boston was safe.

Captain Strang gave her assurance along with her documents. 'No, no, ma'am,' he said, 'all's quiet. Your compatriots are once again loyal subjects of King George, more loyal than those at home if what I hear about Mr Wilkes and his supporters be true. And, of course, we keep them on a looser rein than we did. We should have hanged the Rhode Island smugglers when they burned a revenue cutter last year but, no, the government merely demanded an investigatory committee to look into the matter.'

The goodbyes were stiff, partly because they had to be made as Captain Strang stood by, waiting for them to accompany him in his pinnace to the ship.

Betty was unyielding to the end. 'Best get off, I spect's you got work to do.'

'I will then.' The *Lord Percy* wasn't sailing until the early hours— and she *did* have work to do. 'Don't stay away too long or I'll come and fetch you.' She said it to all of them. Only Josh smiled.

'You come anyway,' he said, 'I don't reckon I'll be back.'

As she held Philippa, she felt the child's hands tighten around her neck and then make the effort to let go. The little face was expressionless and Makepeace didn't know if the gesture indicated grief or whether it was being interpreted as such by her own agony.

Susan said carefully, as if she'd been rehearsing over dinner: 'I love her like my own but I know she's yours. I'll keep her safe for you.'

'My dear, I know you will. I don't deserve you, either of you.' She had neglected them both.

The knowledge that she had failed all of them in different ways, even Josh—she should have enquired into his disillusion earlier— was too overwhelming to be borne and she took the coward's way out, not even waiting to see the pinnace reach the ship.

'London,' she told Sanders, 'at the bloody gallop.'

Usually, when she travelled by coach, she took Hildy with her, but there'd been no spare room on the journey down so she was able to give way to a fit of crying like no other she could remember. Whatever else Betty-Solomon's judgement had done, it had cut her in two. One half persisted in screaming at her to turn round and bring them all back. The other, no less painful, knew a hideous relief at being free of emotional ropes.

As the coach entered the City, she put her face to the window so that air blowing on her eyes could reduce their swelling. A muffin man was whistling 'Playing With Fire' as he pushed his cart along Aldgate.

Oh well, it wouldn't be for ever. In the meantime, she'd cleared the decks. Now she could run out her guns. *Now*, by the living God, she would deal with Major and Mrs Conyers.

She leaned up and opened the little trap with which enabled her to speak to her coachman. 'Straight to Lincoln's Inn Fields, Sanders.'

Mr Hackbutt sorted through the documents. 'Marriage certificate from the ship, properly signed and sealed, excellent, excellent. Sir Pip's decree—I have to say, Lady Dapifer, that with your fellow-countrymen behaving themselves and in view of our government's present conciliation towards them, there has never been a better time to ask their lordships to recognize an American divorce and acknowledge your right to Sir Pip's property. We shall hope for the Lord Chief Justice to hear the matter, a most enlightened man.'

'Oh, I think he will,' Makepeace said. 'Lord Mansfield's a neighbour of mine.'

Hackbutt cocked an eye at her. 'Shooting high, Lady Dapifer?'

'Using cannon now, Mr Hackbutt. In the meantime, what have you done about Barton Wood?'

'I informed Lord Ffoulkes's lawyers immediately, of course. They were as appalled as myself and have informed Major Conyers that any further attempt to defraud will result in prosecution.'

Hackbutt had been more shocked by Conyers's attempt to bargain with some of Andrew Ffoulkes's land than he had by her own eviction from Dapifer property. There had, she supposed, been rags of legality attached to her dispossession but none at all to a guardian stealing from his ward.

He went on: 'I did not tell them whence my information came and we can only hope the Major does not guess. You are tweaking his nose, Lady Dapifer, and he is a dangerous man.'

'I'm a dangerous woman, Mr Hackbutt.'

The lawyer nodded; she could see he didn't like her as much as he once had. Nobody does, she thought. 'Have you made out the other documents I asked you for?'

He counted them into her hand. 'And here's your opening

salvo—a warrant ready for your signature. It can be executed at a moment's notice, the bailiffs are standing by.'

The thought of returning to a house empty of everyone but servants was daunting. She needed a friend to talk to—where was the nearest of the few she had left?

'Grub Street, Sanders.'

Out of a perverse superiority, Beasley had refused to leave Grub Street, though, once his debts were paid and he had some money coming in from the investments Makepeace made for him, he'd bought the house of his old landlord. It still looked as if it had been drawn onto the rocks by wreckers. The only seats were two stools paddling in a tide of books round an ashy, empty grate.

He himself was nearly as comfortless. 'You going armed?'

'As a matter of fact, I am,' Makepeace said and called out of the window: 'Sanders, fetch the gun case.'

'That's very good,' John Beasley said. ' "One moment, Major, before you shoot me. I've a gun of my own—I'll just send Sanders to fetch it." Very useful. The sooner that man's committed the better. Why not execute the warrant now?'

'He's not going to shoot me. He doesn't know I hold most of his debts.'

'Doesn't have to. The songsheets are selling like hot cakes, I'm happy to say.' Beasley had written the lyrics for 'Playing with Fire', Frederick Tortini the tune. 'And if he don't, *she* certainly will after the Almack's incident. Take a drink, Sanders?'

'No thank you, sir. I'd as well return to the coach.'

'Better. They take the wheels off round here.'

Makepeace balanced the case on her knee and opened it. The two weapons inside were smaller than the average duelling pistol, chased and inlaid with ivory. 'Nice, aren't they? Sir Benjamin Judd had them made for me—he's started up an armaments factory.'

'You're mad, woman, I was joking. What are you going to do, shoot Conyers before he shoots you?'

'No, these are for drilling highwaymen. I've been practising.'

Like most people forced to travel a great deal, Makepeace had fallen foul of highway robbers, once on the way to Newcastle and again on the way back—both times without physical harm, but she'd resented the loss of jewellery and time. 'Watch out, they're loaded.'

Beasley, a self-acknowledged coward, hastily put the guns back in the case. 'You do realize you've become insane.'

'I have not.'

'Yes, you have. When it comes to the point of having to carry guns, the game's no longer worth the bloody candle. Give it up. I'm serious.'

'Not yet.'

'When? You're a hundred times richer than they are, you're hounding them into Bedlam. Ain't your revenge wreaked yet?'

'There've only been little wreaks so far.'

'What are you going to do after the final wreak?'

'Smile.'

'Smile at what?' Beasley leaned forward and poked his finger into her sternum. 'There won't be anything there, woman. Madam Midnight's gone, your kid's gone, Susan's gone, Josh . . . Aaron's had to run for it to Ireland. Where's young Ffoulkes?'

She said: 'Conyers sent him on a Grand Tour.'

'That's it, isn't it? That's nearly all of us. You're scorching your own earth, you madwoman.'

She'd let down her guard, exposed her triumph, thinking she could relax with a friend. She began gathering her wraps. Her head was aching. She said: 'Your breath stinks.'

He sat back, nursing his knee. 'Andra's in Town, did you know?'

Makepeace closed her gun case carefully. 'How is Mr Hedley?'

That was the trouble with John Beasley, he clawed like an animal and then, as you bled, came a reminder of what a true ally he was. Not once but three times in the last few years he'd arrived in Newcastle, cold and furious from his long perch on top of a stagecoach, to make sure she was prospering. She was still bewildered by the cross-fertilization of ideas that had taken place between him and Hedley at Raby to make them such good friends.

'Another bugger intent on suicide, like you,' Beasley told her.

'Nearly blew himself up the other day experimenting with fire-damp. He's come to London to try and find someone either to neutralize the bloody gas or invent a miner's lantern that don't set off a gas explosion. How you can have a flame that doesn't burn, I don't know, but he thinks you can. I've put him in touch with a couple of chemists I know. What's the matter?'

Blast him. She wiped her hands hard down her skirt to get rid of their sudden perspiration. 'It's just that it's . . . a terrible thing, fire-damp. A spark can set it off. But you can't dig coal in perfect darkness.' She tried smiling. 'Sometimes our lads take rotten fish down with them so they can work by the glow of phosphorescence.'

'Hell, I'd prefer fire-damp.'

'You wouldn't,' she said. 'I was in Newcastle when the pit at Gerrards blew up, ten miles away. The ground shook; I thought it was an earthquake. Thirty-five killed.'

She hadn't known any of them but she knew people like them—Wullie Fergusson, Jamie—and had grieved for the loss of such men. Hedley *had* known them, most of them. Of course he'd be experimenting. Of course it was suicide. *Blast him.* And it probably would.

Beasley hated being caught out in lack of knowledge. 'I introduced him to Johnson as well,' he said, altering course.

'And what did Dr Johnson think of Mr Hedley?' asked Makepeace, idly.

Beasley crunched himself up like a bear and lowered his voice an octave: ' "Andra Hedley is an ingenious, hard-working descendant of *homo sapiens*." He liked him.'

'Well, I must be going, I've some wreaking to do.'

Beasley didn't move from the stool; he let people see themselves out. 'From the look of you, you could do with a bit of ingenious hard-working *homo sapiens* yourself. When'd you last have a fuck?'

'Oh, shut up,' Makepeace said, and went.

It was late. There was light in the windows of the still-grubbing grubbers of Grub Street and the night clacked with protest and scandal from their printing presses. Once beyond it, however, the alleys to its north were empty and dark and lit only by the coach's own lanterns, enabling Sanders, an excellent coachman, to take short-cuts that would have been too obstructed to negotiate by day.

They'd reached the open, deserted, cobbled space of Clare Market when Makepeace heard an extra clatter of hooves approaching fast on the coach's right-hand side. She saw a pistol-barrel appear at her window and then a flame as whoever held the gun pulled its trigger.

Chapter Twenty

WHAT saved Makepeace's life was her headache.

She'd taken off her hat to ease the constriction on her forehead and hung it on the seat opposite hers by stuffing its ribbons behind the coach upholstery. Then she'd sunk into her corner, put her elbow on the arm-rest and cradled one temple against her gloved hand.

The hat, one of Susan's Leghorns, hung flat and downwards. It was of undyed straw and its pallor, in the darkness, misled the attacker into thinking he fired into the flesh of a face: the bullet smashed through the middle of its crown.

She sat and stared at it. Somebody was shaking her arm. She turned her head. Sanders was leaning into the coach, his face as pale as the hat, his mouth making shapes but no sound.

'What?' she asked and couldn't hear her own voice either. The report of the pistol in the confined space had been literally deafening.

He pointed behind him. She would have got out but he pressed her back in her seat, shaking his head. She peered past him. The market was empty apart from some stacked trestles and beaten cabbage leaves. In the direction Sanders pointed an alley led off to the west—the coachman's thick gesticulating hands indicated her assailant had gone that way and should he go after him?

She forced a 'No'. She wanted to say there was no point, the attacker was on horseback and a mile away by now and, if he wasn't, pursuit by one man was too dangerous. She tried, but it was difficult to go into explanations one couldn't hear oneself make.

She touched her ears so that Sanders could understand what had happened to her and was relieved that her fingers came away without blood on them.

She was too frightened to face the journey through darkness to the lonely house in Highgate. Probably Sanders was as well, poor man; he looked in a terrible taking.

Where then? She needed a brandy and a friend as she'd never needed either. Clare Market was equidistant between Baines's house and Beasley's. Baines's was tempting, she'd like a doctor for her ears, but he was frequently out on call at nights and she couldn't, she really could *not*, stand in a street knocking on a door that wouldn't open.

'Back,' she told Sanders, exaggeratedly formulating her mouth. 'G-rub S-t-reet.'

He nodded and disappeared. She felt the shake of the coach as he turned the horses around.

At which point logical thought left her.

Sanders was supporting her up Beasley's staircase. The two men were engaged in animated conversation, she could just hear their voices though not what they were saying. Sanders had brought her hat with him and kept pointing to it. Me, she thought, pay attention to *me*. And began to cry.

She was seated on one of the stools by the unlit fire. Beasley was actually lighting it. Unheard of. A dirty glass containing brandy was in her hand, Sanders was sitting on the floor, a chipped beaker in his.

Now Beasley was shouting at her, his voice reaching her from a muffled distance. 'Where's the bloody warrant?'

'What?'

'The warrant for the Conyers's arrest. For debt. You showed it to me.'

She pointed to her reticule and watched without interest as he scrabbled through it. He found the document, laid it on her knee, fetched a book to rest it on and presented her with a quill and inkpot.

He wants me to sign it.

Shock made her slow, she just stared at the pen Beasley forced into her hand.

'Oh, for Christ's sake,' he shouted, 'he tried to kill you.'

She nodded agreeably; that was a given. There'd been no demand for money, it had been attempted assassination. But to sign was to precipitate the end of a long, long stratagem; she'd wanted to linger over this final act, lick her lips, make a ceremony of it.

'And he might try again. Sign the bloody thing. Get him put away.'

She signed, with difficulty, on the line left for the complainant, and he snatched it from her. 'Sanders'll take me to the magistrates, we'll set on the bailiffs immediate.' He was miming as he shouted, pointing to the door, pressing his wrists together to indicate handcuffs . . .

She nodded.

'Stay here. I'll put a couple of men downstairs to guard you.'

She nodded again.

The unnatural silence, so heavy that it was almost noise, enfolded her as the men left. Makepeace huddled over the fire, unable to get warm or stop shaking.

He tried to kill me.

Sanders had left her hat on the other stool. The pretty brim was untouched but blackened strands of straw made a jagged surround to the hole in the crown. Mentally, she transposed her face to it. The bullet would have smashed her nose and ploughed on to the brain.

Had he, perhaps, merely tried to frighten her? Shot at the hat as a warning? No, there'd been no time for him to distinguish between hat and living head. He'd meant to kill her.

She shook so hard she had to hold her glass with two hands to stop it slopping.

She began to sob; what she needed was someone to cuddle her, tell her she'd been brave—which she hadn't—listen to the story again and again; analyse, discuss, discuss, be appalled.

Betty. I want Betty.

But you let her go. And Susan. And Philippa. And Josh. Aaron's gone, Andrew . . . She'd allowed all the people whom she loved, and who loved her, to slip away.

She clutched at anger. I was *right* to go for revenge no matter what. God damn their two souls to hell, look what they did to me, to us; they wouldn't stop hurting, wouldn't stop even at murder. Oh please, the scales *had* to be balanced.

And now they had been. She took in a deep breath, then another swig of brandy. If Beasley and the warrant did their job, Major and Mrs Conyers were even at this moment being hustled out of the house in Grosvenor Square and into the closed cart that would take them to the Fleet Prison.

And there they would stay. *For the rest of their lives.*

Thousands of pounds, nearly a hundred thousand, well spent in procuring this happy outcome, almost all her profit from the mine. Hedley had ploughed his into improvements, inventions, into creating things. Hers had gone to stopping every hole by which the foxes might escape her.

She had bought her own property back—virtually the entire Dapifer estate was mortgaged to her—in order to foreclose on it.

The law of debt, capital's revenge on those who did not pay their bills. As their creditor, only her word could open the door of the prison which, by now, Catty and Conyers were entering.

She had spent pleasant hours of leisure envisaging their years of hopelessness and now, to regain a sense of control, she did it again. Conyers's hair was greyed to the colour of the walls around him; wrinkles glazed Catty's face. She watched them wither into dust like two forgotten apples in a store cupboard.

And they'd know how hopeless it was. From the first, they would know. She'd ordered the dress she would wear to the prison from Mme Angloss. She'd decided on primrose: her summer, their winter. Catty had worn primrose in Grosvenor Square at their first encounter; she would reflect it back at her for their last.

The times, thinking about it, her mouth had curved into the smile that would pronounce their life sentence. They would see the exaction she was making for Dapifer, for Philippa, for humiliation, poverty, pain. She curved it again. Payment in full.

Oh yes, she was in control now. She was the victor.

Shock was receding; she had comforted herself with a stroll along a path she had taken a hundred times before. In a sense she'd been sucking her thumb.

Now she became fully awake and found herself cold. The fire was going out. This was victory, was it? Alone, drinking inferior brandy in a dreary room?

Beasley and Sanders were away some hours. For Makepeace the time was spent in travelling the landscape of her life from the harsh spring of a Boston shoreline into the summer of Dapifer country and on to this chilly, urban winter in which she found herself. With newly appraising eyes she reread fingerposts, saw her wrong turnings and the shocking inclines down which, willy-nilly, she'd been precipitated.

You're scorching your own earth, you madwoman.

You ain't doin' this for him. You ain't even doin' it for you. You like one of them pit wagons, the rails is there an' you jus' runnin' away on 'em.

And truest signpost of all: *You'd have done it anyway. I saw it. One sniff o' that coal and you woke to what you are—as good a businessman as ever come over the Atlantic.*

That, then, was where she should have settled. Newcastle. Would it have made a difference if she'd known that the mountain she'd clawed her way up in order to reach down her enemies had, in fact, been of itself her journey's end? No need to go further.

Probably not. She'd have made no better mother nor friend, but in recognizing herself for what she was, for what Hedley had known she was, she'd have been less of an ache in everyone's arse, her own included.

Hedley was right—he'd always been right. The years in Northumberland had been the time of her life. Not because she'd made money with which to destroy two souls, not at all . . . that had merely been the goad, almost the excuse to do what Makepeace Burke was good at doing.

As Lady Dapifer she'd been blessed with an exceptional husband but she hadn't suited his life nor had his suited her. The year she'd spent in Society had been astonishing, but only because she'd spent it with him; after a while the endless round of giving and receiving entertainment would have palled and she would have itched for gainful employment, which her position as Lady Dapifer would not have allowed.

They had loved each other. In one way she had been good for him, but not, perhaps, good enough; he had suffered continual pinpricks from those who'd disliked her and always would. She had not advanced his career because she hadn't known how; she'd held him back even, unable to manipulate behind the scenes as good political wives did. She'd been his health, he'd said, but in the end she hadn't been able to invest him with enough to stay alive.

Oh Pip. My dear. You married a square peg that didn't fit into anything so well as the shaft of a Northumberland coal mine.

There, at least, had been achievement. Whatever else she'd done or hadn't done, enabling Raby to become a working colliery, creating employment for one hundred men, making a village where their families could live in dignity, that was a labour she could show to St Peter with pride when she arrived at the gates of Heaven.

When John Beasley came back, it was to a woman who'd drunk a lot of brandy and yet was more sober with self-knowledge than she'd ever been in her life.

'Is it done?'

'It's done.' He looked haggard. 'They're taking them to the Fleet. I didn't wait. She was screaming.'

'I'm going back to Newcastle tomorrow,' she said.

'You're going back to Highgate tonight,' he said, ushering her out of the door and down to the coach, 'and I'm damn well coming too. I'm not staying here. You realize that bastard must have been watching this place, waiting for you to leave. Supposing it wasn't him, supposing it was a fucking assassin he'd hired—Sanders says the sod was masked. He might try again. Jesus, he could shoot *me* by mistake.'

And Makepeace laughed.

She woke up the next morning to be surprised at how assuaged she felt. Well, she'd escaped death and trampled her enemies underfoot—good reasons as any for a sense of peace.

But it wasn't that alone; the battle of the past years hadn't just been with Catty and Conyers, it had been against herself. That, too, was over. At some point during the previous night she'd made terms with Makepeace Burke.

Mrs Burke, it turned out, was not a Society woman, nor even a family woman; she had failed in both capacities. Instead she was a trader, a doer, a money-maker, a woman of business.

Society, she thought, blinds itself to females like me, but we're there: Susan's auntie, Susan herself, flower-sellers, weavers, shop-keepers, landladies of inns and taverns; all earning our living by our own efforts.

She sat up as another idea attacked her. There's Philippa, bless her; with her bent for mathematics: she's not going to fit into Society's idea of womanhood either. Well, Society will just have to make room for her because I'll bloody well see that it does. I'm blazing the trail for her.

I'm a businesswoman, she thought. I'm the New Age.

Now that she was sitting up she could see the ormolu clock on the mantel at the far side of her bedroom. Seven o'clock.

It's early. What's it doing *early*? I should be sleeping in, I've had a nasty experience.

There was movement and rustling in her dressing room. She pulled back the side curtains of the bed. 'What are you doing, Hildy?'

'Packin', missus. Sanders is gettin' the horses ready. We're off hoom.'

So we are.

She lay back. Hildy was never so happy as when they were going home. Me too, she thought.

She said: 'Sanders'll be tired. Tell him to bring Smith as assistant driver. And Hildy, try not to crumple *too* much.' A horrible packer, Hildy.

She sat up. 'Last night . . . did I tell you to pack?'

'No, missus, tha was duzzy stannin' up. Tha jus' craaled to yer bed. It was Mr Beasley told me. He's doonstair havin' his breakfast. An', missus'—Hildy's pleased, narrow little face peered round the door—'there's a surprise wi' him.'

Joy flooded through her. 'It's a nice day, Hildy.'

'Drizzlin', missus.'

'It's nice. Smallest hoop since we're travelling. Oh, and the black cardinal.'

'Reet y'are.'

They'd finished breakfast by the time she swept into the dining room, looking her best. It was the part of the house she liked most: a white, unfussy room picked out in blue, with long windows giving on to the gardens. This morning they were open, letting in moist air and a scent of new-cut grass to mingle with the smell of ham and toasted muffins.

'Good morning, John. Good morning, Mr Hedley.'

They were both reading, Beasley a newspaper, leaning back in his chair, his boots on her delicate Irish tablecloth to show he was a true revolutionary, Andra pencilling notes in the margins of a learned-looking publication. He got up at her entrance, which Beasley did not, and then returned to his journal. 'Morning, missus.' He was as polite, even affable, as he always was nowadays when they met—nothing more.

Makepeace considered him. An extra pencil was stuck behind his ear. Despite better cloth and a smarter cut to his coat, he'd ruined its shape with too many documents in the pockets. He still managed to look like the man who'd come to do the plumbing.

'While I was risking my damn neck on your errands last night, I rousted Hedley out,' Beasley said. 'He says he'll travel back north with you. Bloody sight more than I'd do.' He was truculent from lack of sleep. 'Why didn't you use those vaunted pistols of yours, woman? Save all the trouble.'

'I was keeping them for men who put their boots on my table-cloth. Thank you, Mr Hedley. I have to make two calls in the City first, perhaps we could go on from there.'

'Where?' demanded Beasley.

'The Fleet.'

'God, Andra, she's going to smile. Lord save us from vengeful women.'

'I thought you wanted me to shoot him,' she said.

'Better than smiling at the poor sod.'

The source of the Fleet was the Hampstead Ponds nearby. The river began life as an eager little rivulet that leaped down the hill to London, gathering less pleasant waters as it went until it became a reluctant sewer flowing under the reclaimed ground called Fleet Market. Here it followed the line of Farringdon Street, a wide, well-favoured thoroughfare, made less impressive by the stink of the gaol that ran along most of its length.

The Great Fire of London had destroyed the original Fleet prison but it had been such a profitable enterprise for the previous five hundred years that its keepers, royal appointees, hadn't wanted to kill a golden goose by altering it, and rebuilt the place virtually unchanged.

Up again went the long wall of miniature brick with its arched doorway and the grille through which prisoners could beg for alms from passers-by. Up again went four storeys of wards and cubicles for the better-off inmates. In again went the Master's Side with its spacious and comfortable rooms for the very richest. Down again went the cellar known as Bartholomew Fair where those with no money at all lived—and died. And back came the centuries-old smell of too many people in too small a space with too few facilities looked after by too-greedy, too-lazy warders.

Common criminals incarcerated in it were either hanged, or

released after serving their sentence. Debtors, on the other hand, the majority of the prison's population, were in for life unless their creditors relented. And for their sake there was one delicate addition to the new Fleet: the figure 'nine' was placed above the entrance gates so that they could write and receive letters under the euphemism of '9, Fleet Market'.

Makepeace's coach drew up on the other side of the road and its three occupants peered across at the immense wall opposite.

Her business with Mr Hackbutt had taken longer than she'd expected—it would be late now before they reached Barnet.

'Aw, dear me,' said Hildy, 'is there poer creeters enough to fill it?'

Sanders had opened the door and let down the step.

'Howay,' wailed Hildy, 'I'm feored o' goin' in.'

'You're not coming,' Makepeace said.

'Best not go in alone,' Hedley said, following her out.

'Sanders is coming with me.'

He stood and watched her as she picked her way through the mud of the road, refusing Sanders's proffered hand.

She was surprised at how busy the entrance to the prison had become, with people going in and out, wearing everyday expressions as if it was the usual thing.

A woman squatting on a stool was doing a good trade in orange pomanders at the gate. 'Keep off infection, ladies, gents.'

On the other side of the entrance, hands were reaching through the grille; the one stretching through the largest aperture had a hat in it. A babble of voices echoed the words carved round its arch: 'Pray Remember Poor Debtors Having No Allowance'.

Makepeace bought two pomanders, one for her, one for Sanders. 'Is this a good trade?'

The woman was instantly suspicious. 'Keeps me an' the young 'uns, what's it to you?'

Makepeace gave her double the price. 'Another businesswoman,' she explained to Sanders.

A tipstaff took them to the office of Mr Amos Middleton,

Assistant Keeper, a well-dressed man with spectacles. 'Ah yes, madam. They came in last night. Your complaint, I understand. A high-spirited couple, very debonair, very humorous.'

So Catty had stopped screaming and put on a show. You had to admire her.

Makepeace told Mr Middleton what she wanted and signed several documents to effect it. It was an expensive procedure; virtually every activity in the Fleet had a price to be paid by inmates or their visitors—she'd even been charged for coming through the gate—the money going into the pocket of Mr Middleton and his superiors.

When it was all done, Mr Middleton took off his spectacles and tapped them on his desk, like a doctor about to deliver an opinion. 'We do receive creditors as visitors, of course,' he said, 'but I always advise them not to enter the room of the debtor alone. Ah, you have a manservant with you—good. Our clients have the right to inspect the warrant, you see, so they know who has sent them here. You may find Major Conyers keeps himself well in hand—alternatively, he may not.'

There was a fee for being led along the passages and climbing urine-scented stairs. 'Sixpence in advance is the usual, ma'am,' her turnkey escort told her, holding out his hand. 'Shillin' if you want me to wait.'

'D'you charge for breathing?' Makepeace asked as she paid him.

'Air's free,' he said, cheerfully. 'Diseases extra.' He was a jolly man and proud of his prison.

Despite the law forbidding spirits to be sold in prisons, there was a taproom on both second and third floors offering, so Makepeace's trained nose told her, rum and gin as well as ale. Vomit along the passageway outside suggested trade was brisk.

A child inmate—there were several around ('Proper family prison, this')—was trotting ahead of them, carefully balancing a tray on which was a Dutch bottle and glasses. She was about Philippa's age. Makepeace watched her go into one of the wards shouting: 'Here we are, Papa.'

There was a skittles alley, a meeting-room, a food hall ('Best hot-pot and dumplings in London'), a chapel where a wedding was in progress . . .

Sanders was impressed and resentful. 'It's a ruddy villains' palace.'

'This part's for nobs,' the turnkey told him. 'You ain't seen the cellars.' As they reached the top floor, he slapped his leg with his keys: 'Number Four, o' *course*. I remember *them*. Come in last night, lady pretty, gentleman humorous. Ordered visitin' cards to be printed immediate with this address. Got to admire 'em.'

There was a quarrel in progress at Number Three where two women were screaming at each other while some men traded half-hearted pushes. 'Keep it down now,' the turnkey told them mildly, 'we got visitors.'

Number Four was quiet, its door closed.

'Nice room this,' the turnkey said. 'They ain't purchased any pieces yet, but lovely view.' He raised a circular disk attached by a nail to the door and peered through the hole behind it, then nodded to Makepeace to take his place. 'Nice 'n' quiet.'

Conyers sat on the bare boards of a truckle bed, both arms round Catty who was leaning against his shoulder, her eyes closed. As Makepeace watched, he pulled a handkerchief from his pocket and wiped the spittle from her mouth.

When he heard the door opening, he disengaged himself and laid Catty gently on the bed, standing carefully in front of her. His face went blank on seeing Makepeace, then he smiled. 'I missed, did I?'

'You did.'

'Ah well.' He turned, eased Catty nearer the wall and sat himself on the edge of the bed so that her head was hidden behind him.

Surprisingly, it *was* a nice room—somewhat cold and with flaking plaster, an empty grate, but the ceiling sloped down to enclose an open dormer window beyond which Makepeace could see the masts of small trading boats in the Fleet inlet. A seagull had perched on the outside sill. She was reminded of the Roaring Meg.

'Close that window, will you?' Conyers said. 'It's chilly in here.'

Makepeace closed it. The turnkey brought her a stool to sit on and returned to join Sanders in the passage outside, leaving the door open.

Conyers brushed some dust off his knee. 'Well,' he said, 'that brings us to Plan Two. We sell Grosvenor Square.'

'No.' Makepeace reached into her reticule for her account book. 'You passed that alternative on . . . March the twenty-second. The loans and interest overtook the value.'

'Nice house,' Conyers said, persuasively.

'I know. I lived in it.'

'So you did. One forgets.'

The row next door had ceased and was replaced by the sound of someone screaming on the floor below. Sanders and the turnkey had lit their pipes and were chatting quietly.

She'd forgotten what a pleasant face Conyers had; apart from the wide eyes, which seemed to stretch round the corner to his temples, it was trustworthy, not too handsome, not plain, very English.

As much a mask, she thought, as the one he'd worn last night when he tried to kill her.

'Did you buy *all* the debts?' he asked after a moment.

'Yes.' She consulted her book again. 'Except the shirtmaker, he wants to come after you himself.'

'Coal trade must be profitable.'

'Very.'

'Couldn't spare a few lumps, I suppose?' He laughed a little shyly because he meant it. He got up, took off his coat and laid it tenderly over the unmoving Catty. Rubbing his upper arms, he sat down again. 'That rather brings us to Plan Three. We recognize your marriage as legal.'

Makepeace shook her head. 'You can if you like, but I'm advised I'll win the case anyway. My estate marches with that of the Chief Justice.'

'Well, well, the *nouveau riche*.' Conyers examined his fingernails. 'Plan Four then.' He leaned forward suddenly so that his face was near hers. She smelled sweat. 'Cancel the debts, set my wife free and I confess—before witnesses—to attempting to murder you.' He sat back. 'My final offer.'

It was love of a sort. Hadn't Dapifer once said Conyers was the better man?

No he ain't, Pip. The man was acting, not for her, but to some unseen audience applauding in his mind: old schoolfellows, university cronies, regimental officers, fellow-gamblers, playing to a conception of honour that precluded the paying of bills and murder.

She shook her head. 'I doubt you'd hang and there'd be a term to your sentence. This way you're both in for life.'

Should've put on the black cap, she thought, it's death for him; he'd rather hang. He'd make a good end, too: the gallows for a stage, brave, a debonair speech to win the crowd.

She watched the long eyes flicker towards the doorway and assess the chances of gouging out her windpipe before Sanders and the turnkey could stop him, and saw the regretful rejection.

Suddenly she placed him. He'd always confused her but, of course, he was a pirate. He didn't belong; he'd been born to the wrong society in the wrong time—the golden years of piracy were over. Pip and Ffoulkes had mistaken him for one as enlightened as themselves, whereas the man should have been striding the deck of robber ships, adventuring across the seas, his ruthlessness subsumed in the legends that would have grown around a short, dramatic life. He had no business in the Mechanical Age.

She said: 'That's what I *intended*.'

He leaped at the past tense. 'You changed your mind?'

She reached into her reticule for papers tied together with black ribbon. She took them with her to the window and pointed.

'Sooner or later,' she said, 'there will be a schooner in the Pool out there. Her captain will be handed some money you can survive on for a while when you reach your destination. *If* you two will be aboard her when she sets sail, and *if* you sign these papers now, I won't pursue the debt.'

'Where's she bound?'

'The Carolinas.'

He laughed; you had to admire him. 'Kill us now.'

'Oh, I don't know,' she said. 'Other criminals have prospered over there. I'm sure you will.'

'And what are the papers?'

They damned him. There was an acknowledgement that Major and Mrs Conyers owed Lady Dapifer, otherwise known as Mrs Makepeace Burke, the sum of £190,000 exclusive of interest, the debt to be pursued if they returned to England. Another acknowledgement by Major and Mrs Conyers that they had committed adultery while Mrs Conyers had been married to Sir Philip Dapifer and a recognition of Sir Philip's subsequent divorce. That Sir Philip's second marriage had been legal and that his daughter, Philippa, by this second marriage was therefore the true owner of all his estates.

'They're hers by default now anyway,' Makepeace pointed out, helpfully.

The last document was the one he balked at. 'I'm not signing this.' It was a confession that he had attempted to defraud his ward, Lord Ffoulkes, of moneys from the property known as Barton Wood.

'Then you can rot,' Makepeace said without heat.

He was blustering; he had to sign and they both knew it. There were men and women in the Fleet who had served twenty years for a debt of a few pounds and would serve another twenty unless their creditors relented—and they lived so long.

'Do you intend to publish these?'

'Only if you come back.'

Odd, she thought, that he should bridle at the admission of a crime involving considerably less money and hurt than that committed against her and Philippa. But young Andrew was of his own set; it was the one offence his audience would not forgive.

They waited for the turnkey to bring pen and ink. Conyers, showing agitation for the first time, left the bed to pace the room, leaving Catty exposed.

Makepeace looked and then looked away. The woman's eyes

were half open but fixed on a point in the ceiling; saliva came from the corner of her mouth.

Don't pity her; she didn't pity you. Yet to see the damn woman vulnerable was like watching a wolf limping. We've hated each other too long; we're fixtures in each other's mind.

She said gently: 'Let me get her a doctor.'

Conyers turned and Sanders came forward from the doorway in case he attacked. 'How dare you,' he said. 'How *dare* you. She's merely tired. And you're not fit to lick her shoes.'

The turnkey came back and, with Sanders, witnessed Conyers's scribbled signatures. When he'd finished, he threw the pen on the floor.

Makepeace put the papers in her reticule; they were as watertight as Mr Hackbutt had been able to make them in the time. She was also putting her trust in the two tipstaffs and Mr Hackbutt himself who were to take the transportees on board when the ship came, only leaving it themselves as it passed Tilbury for the open sea.

She'd promised herself she wouldn't say it but she did. She said: 'Did you ever wonder what happened to us when you turned us out? Did you care at *all*?'

He was calm again. He considered it. 'Do you know,' he said, thoughtfully, 'I don't think I did. Somehow one doesn't attribute feelings of any depth to the lower classes.'

As she readied herself to leave, Conyers said, idly: 'What made you change your mind?'

He doesn't want me to go, she thought. He loathes me but I'm still an audience; when I leave he won't have one.

Mr Hackbutt had asked her the same question that very morning. Why had she decided to let her catch off the hook?

There'd been so many reasons. Because revenge was not, after all, a dish better eaten cold; it palled. Because she had personally lost so much in pursuing it. Because she had found a completion in herself that this diminished couple before her would never know. Because she knew what love was. Because Jesus would have forgiven them—and so would Pip Dapifer.

She searched now for explanations that would hurt—she wasn't that much of a Christian—while at the same time being true.

She shrugged and made for the door. 'Actually, you did me a good turn. If you hadn't robbed me, I'd never've found out how clever I was at making money.'

Did that sting? Well, here's another. 'And Pip found you pitiable. Even when he caught you swiving his wife, he pitied you both.'

'God,' he said, 'you're a barbarian, aren't you? Sheer gutter-slush. What did he ever see in you?'

She whipped round. 'What did he ever see in you?'

He was shaking but he smiled. 'It's called style.'

'It's called shit,' she said, and left.

Hedley was waiting for her in the street and, with unspoken consent, they walked together down to the mouth of the Fleet to breathe the clean, cool air coming upriver from the estuary.

'Did you smile?'

'I meant to,' she said wearily. 'But there wasn't much to smile about.'

'Relieved at the thought of Carolina, were they?'

'Not much.' She blew out her cheeks. 'The money they've cost me. It'll be the most expensive voyage in history—I should send 'em steerage.'

'But you won't.'

'No.'

He nodded and turned away to look at the shipping.

Not just the money, she thought. They've cost me everything. Or *I've* cost me everything.

A voice behind them said: 'We won't make Barnet 'less we go now, missus.'

Six days to Newcastle—five, if the going was good.

'All right, Sanders. Just one more delay tomorrow.' To Hedley, she said: 'There's somebody I must say goodbye to.'

'As you please,' he said.

It was no better in the coach; he was pleasant and unapproachable, talking mostly in dialect to Hildy, who adored him. Ever since he'd once told her she was named for St Hilda, the girl had thought better of herself. 'Tha's followin' in t'line o' grand Northumbrian women,' he'd said.

Watching them, Makepeace became irritated. *Why do you get everything right all the time?*

Because, she supposed, unlike her he'd always been at peace with himself—and remained so. Even now, with all his wealth, he'd hardly changed his way of living—too busy setting up miners' benevolent funds, pensions, societies for the betterment of this and the prevention of that. His one luxury, which he regarded as an essential, had been to turn the but 'n' bens at Raby into one of the best-equipped metallurgical laboratories in England.

'Tell me about your fire-damp experiments, Mr Hedley,' she said.

Immediately the coach interior became a Leyden jar of energy. If we'd got fire-damp in here, she thought, he'd explode it all by himself, he wouldn't need a candle. As it did when he was in the grip of emotion, his speech became increasingly Northumbrian.

'Blowers are no bloody good, nor steel mills, it was a steel mill set off Gerrards. And I'd bray the bugger as left the ventilation door open except he blew hisself up wi' the rest.' He was pounding the coach seat so that little Hildy, beside him, bounced up and down. 'But Ah tell thee, pet, it don't go off every time. Ah know. Ah've tried. Singed wor eyebrows once or twice, nothin' more. There's a mystery to yon bloody gas and 'lessen we solve the sod it'll continue to slay good men.'

He glared at Makepeace as if she'd contradicted him. 'An' bloody coal-owners are wussun useless—"Why fret, Andra? It's coal that matters, not the poer yakkors as hew it." ' He gave another thump to the upholstery. 'Porvorse sods.'

It would have been useless to point out that he was a coal-owner himself, he could never ally himself with the overlords.

And that's why I love him.

She said: 'You're bloody-minded enough to make a good American.'

He didn't rise to it; he wasn't going to ally himself with her either. 'I met another o' them, t'other day,' he said. 'Young Beasley introduced us. 'Benjamin Franklin. Know him?'

She shook her head.

'Born in Boston, so he said. I've read his papers on electricity. I was telling him about fire-damp, very interesting conversation.'

Makepeace fell asleep; there seemed nothing else to do.

They dined at Barnet, went to their separate beds and set off again next morning, smoothly over the turnpike stretches, of which there were few, horribly over those still in the care of their parishes.

At Hatfield, she told Sanders to stay on the Great North Road instead of making for Hertford, where they usually stayed and changed horses. 'I'll tell you when to turn.'

She was tense now, as if what was to come was a confrontation. Hedley and Hildy were watching her fidget. She stopped the coach, got out, ordered Smith onto the roof and clambered up beside Sanders.

Evening was drawing in; they were encountering wagons carrying corn, bales of straw and tired men and women. She realized with a shock that in London she had lost track of the seasons—in the years since Dapifer's death, she'd been too busy to relate that September to this.

The weather was more chilly, though drier, than it had been then; it looked as if it was another poor harvest. She thought: That'll put the price of coal up, and grimaced at herself for thinking it.

Mrs Yates's shop at the bottom of the hill, where she'd waited for Dapifer to come back to her, had been pulled down and a new inn stood in its place.

'Next turning left, Sanders.'

The lanes seemed narrower than she remembered, at some points brambles scratched the sides of the coach.

'Gawd help we don't meet summat coming the other way,' Sanders said.

This was neglect: they hadn't been trimming the hedges. She experienced irritation, as if at an insult. Conyers might have had no idea how to run an estate but, for God's sake, Dapifer's people should have kept it tidy in his memory.

By the time they'd gone through the splash and were heading uphill to the village, it was becoming difficult to see into the fields but light from the carriage lamps fell on a broken gate and thick colonies of willowherb obstructing the little stream that ran down the track's right-hand side.

At the Littles' house she made the introductions then cut the family's welcome short. 'I've foreclosed on the place, Peter. I'm the new owner.'

She was too strung up to give explanations or hear out his effusions of thankfulness. 'I'll leave my party here for a while if I may. Are the gates open?'

'Let me run up and tell Mrs Bygrave you're coming,' Mrs Little said. 'She'll be that pleased, but there's only her and Minnie there now and they'll needs get the beds aired.'

It hadn't occurred to Makepeace that they'd be expected to stay at the Big House. For a moment she was at a loss. *I can't.* There was no reason why she shouldn't, it belonged to her now, but she knew she couldn't. The place wasn't really hers, never had been; the time in it with Dapifer had been a lovely idyll—she saw it now as one of Aaron's entre'actes, a happy but illusory pause in which she'd been allowed to play a comic shepherdess. She was too altered to learn the lines again, too . . . different. Anyway, the stage set had gone dark.

She gathered her wits; they had to stay somewhere. 'Sanders, go back to that inn on the main road. See if they'll take us for the night.'

Without a look at Hedley, she left him and the others to the care of Mrs Little and set off along the village street. Peter walked with her, carrying keys and a lantern.

'What happened?' Some of the cottages were empty.

'They didn't have any interest in the place,' he said. 'Absent most of the time. Took the rents but didn't pay the wages. Freeholders have mostly gone—Edgar went to Birmingham to work in a factory, doing well so I hear. Young Bill Nash took his family to

Luton, gone into the hat trade all of 'em. They'd have starved here else.'

'We'll enclose now,' she said, 'I want you to see to it.'

'Good.'

The gates were locked. She'd been dreading them. They'd lost their massivity and looked rusty. Weeds grew around the bolt that secured one of them to the ground, the other squealed as Peter pushed it open. 'Hasn't been coach nor carriage up here in a year,' he explained. 'Wagons generally use the back way.'

'You go back now,' she said.

'You'll need the key.' He handed it to her; he knew where she was going. 'May be a bit stiff but the lock's been oiled.' He paused. 'We keep it nice.'

'I knew you would.'

He was reluctant to leave her. 'There's not much candle left in the lantern.'

'I won't be long.'

The elegant leaves of the sweet chestnuts showed yellow and pale in the light of the lantern as she made her way up the avenue. A barn owl, disturbed at her approach, launched from a branch and made her jump as it flapped heavily away.

Taking the path to the church, she left the avenue behind her, glad of the lantern; cloud kept covering the moon, which was anyway on the wane. The lych gate made an entrance to a tunnel between yews which had provided longbows for the archers who'd accompanied a fifteenth-century Dapifer to Agincourt.

In the churchyard she dithered for a moment before she remembered where it was that Dapifer had taken her once to meet his ancestors. She went towards it and hit her foot against the tiny, half-hidden gravestone of a child.

At the door of the vault she had to put the lantern on the ground and struggled with both hands to turn the huge key in its escutcheoned lock. The door was eight inches thick and solid iron— God Almighty, did they expect tomb robbers?—and she had to lean backwards to pull it open.

She picked up the lantern and went carefully down the steps.

One relief; the place smelled merely of fungi. The candlelight fell on shelves filled with coffins, coffins of stone like sarcophagi, coffins of ancient, cracked wood, funerary urns. She raised the lantern up and down, looking.

They have taken my Lord, and I know not where they have laid him.

But, of course, it was the newest. She found it at the vault's far end next to that of his mother. She'd been expecting simplicity, something constructed quickly—they'd had so little time. But this . . . oh God, they'd found some London undertaker to provide a monstrosity of lead funerary wreaths and eye-hiding cherubs to acquit their conscience and satisfy the audience they played to.

Did you laugh at it, Pip? Of course you did.

The only thing of dignity was the plaque bearing the family motto: *'Dapifer Aquillifer'.* 'Dapifer the standard-bearer'. He'd said it was the shortest and most meaningless of all mottoes, but she'd liked it—it suited him. She put her fingers to her lips, kissed them, touched the plaque . . . and waited. There were so many things to tell him and she couldn't think of any of them.

After a while, the cold of the stone penetrated her feet and she went back to sit on a corner of the steps, packing her skirt underneath her bottom to cushion it.

The coffins breathed mushrooms at her to mingle with the smell of autumn grass from the churchyard. Beside her, the lantern guttered and went out, leaving her in the dark—though not the blackness she'd experienced in the Raby drift; the moon came and went, casting a weak path through the door behind her that ended on her shoes.

What had she expected? Confrontation? Reunion? Instead, she was sending love and gratitude into nothing—but not a vacuum, a *space.* He'd gone on to wherever he was going and left her to go on to wherever she wanted to go. *'Oh Pip,'* she said.

A figure in the doorway interrupted the light from outside. 'Where are you? You all right? You've been a long time. I were worried.'

She said, crying: 'He's gone, he's not here.'

'I am,' Hedley said.

She reached up and touched his boot. He came down the steps and sat beside her, proffering a handkerchief so that she could blow her nose. It still smelled of engine oil.

'Shall we go, pet?'

'Yes.'

Once they were outside, she took his arm. 'Do we *have* to be married?'

'I'm not fathering bastards, I can tell you that.'

She stopped. 'You want *children*?'

'My brains and my looks,' he said, 'they'll be grand. And we'll have young Philippa home. Ben Franklin reckons it's not so quiet over there as it looks. I told him: I know Americans, I said, red-haired, mule-headed, bound to cause trouble.'

'Porvorse sods,' she said, happily.

A CATCH OF CONSEQUENCE

By Diana Norman

ক্ষ্য

INTRODUCTION

From the moment Makepeace Burke fishes Englishman Sir Philip Dapifer out of the Charles River in pre–Revolutionary War Boston, saving his life, her own is forever changed. Suddenly finding herself ranked a traitor for rescuing a member of the English aristocracy, Makepeace is forced to leave her home and set out on a journey that will steer her in directions of which she could never have dreamed.

A Catch of Consequence is at once a vivid historical novel, a haunting love story, and an unforgettable portrait of a remarkable woman. Diana Norman has crafted another richly textured tale of passion, loss, and courage—and of the power and the pain wrought from being true to oneself against all odds.

PRAISE FOR THE WORK OF DIANA NORMAN

"Drama, passion, intrigue . . . I loved it and didn't want it to end ever."
—*Sunday Times* (London)

"She captures the feel of the period with wit, verve and emotion."
—*Woman's Own*

"Quite simply, splendid."
—Frank Delaney, author of *At Ruby's*

ABOUT DIANA NORMAN

Having worked on local newspapers in Devon and the East End of London, Diana Norman became, at twenty, the youngest reporter in what used to be Fleet Street. Now the author of biographies as well as historical novels, she is married to film critic Barry Norman, with whom she settled in Hertfordshire. They have two daughters.

1. Early on, Makepeace and her brother, Aaron, stand on opposite sides of the politics of the day, i.e., colonial autonomy vs. British rule. Yet even when they "were back on their ancient battlefield," it is made "more bitter by the knowledge that both had truth on their side." What is meant by this? Are they both, in fact, right, in their differing views, and if so, how?

2. After Makepeace learns that Captain Busgutt and his crew aboard the *Gideon* have been *pressed*—when she at first feared the news would be that they were dead—"the word tolled through the kitchen like a passing bell. It was almost as dreadful, it was almost the same." Why? What did it mean for an American sailor to be pressed? Why is it that this news causes Makepeace to "come to terms with an altered future"?

3. Dapifer first calls Makepeace "Procrustes" in her bedroom at the Roaring Meg. How did this nickname evolve, and what does it come to mean between them as their relationship deepens? Although Dapifer "set[s] her blood fizzing," why does Makepeace reject his offer to accompany him to England—even though "she'd cherish it for the rest of her life"? Why, at this point in time, does the thought of marriage occur to neither Makepeace nor Dapifer?

4. Betty and Tantaquidgeon—besides Aaron—are Makepeace's family, her greatest supporters, her dearest friends. They are also both her servants and people of color. Do their differences in class and color ever cause conflict for any of them? Why is Makepeace devoted to Betty? To Tantaquidgeon? How do Makepeace's and Betty's views of their relationship differ? Do you see Betty's ultimate decision to return to Boston as a defection?

5. After Susan Brewer assists her with a requested makeover aboard the *Lord Percy*, Makepeace experiences the revelation at dinner that "men responded to the wrapping, not the content." Why does Makepeace bother getting rouged up and corseted? Was she trying, despite the fact that since boarding the ship she had "fallen out of love with him," to woo Dapifer? She had been aware of Dr. Baines's desire to propose; did she suspect, subconsciously, that Dapifer too had marriage in mind—and that she was, in fact, still in love? Why does Makepeace feel that "their relationship was now alienated beyond repair" and that "she was a burden to him"? Do you think this was Dapifer's view, at any point?

6. When Catty and Makepeace first meet at Grosvenor Square, Catty greets Dapifer with, "Husband, welcome home," despite the fact that he has procured a divorce from her in America. Is this foreshadowing of the brutal battle Catty is about to wage? How serious does it appear at this stage—did you imagine Catty's greed and desire for vengeance could reach such colossal heights? How is it that, although "Makepeace knew she'd been born to hate her," and even as Catty spews cruel declarations—from insulting Makepeace's dress to calling Tantaquidgeon a "totem pole" and Betty's son Josh "a little picaninny"—the term *exquisite* remains the *mot juste* to describe Catty? What is exquisite about Catty? Is it merely her petiteness and delicacy? What does her "animal quickness with a smile of tiny, white, backward-sloping teeth" signal about Catty's character?

7. Had Dapifer not chosen to journey all the way to America to obtain a divorce, Catty wouldn't have had any grounds for her accusation of bigamy. What does Dapifer's—eventually fatal—decision in the divorce matter say about him? Do you believe he truly had no idea that a divorce acquired outside his native country might not be honored within its borders? What does her opinion of her husband's choices tell us about Makepeace?

8. At Hertfordshire, as she considers her guests contrasted with her kitchen staff, Makepeace thinks: "How irritating these people were and how unexpected. Observed from across the Atlantic, England appeared as lofty as the Dover cliffs and as little concerned with what it looked out on, a view confirmed by her reception here. But the men and women below had a rough humanity their ruling class did not; their indifference was more a lack of deliberation, or an innocence. So sure were they of their own fair play, they were surprised that other peoples were not in accord with them. Here, in its greed and good humor, was the England that built empires. She had encountered the same breed in Boston."

Discuss the effects of British rule in the early days of New England colonization, and the resultant reverberations of class distinction. Was Makepeace ever truly accepted into upper-class English society? Was the issue of class very different from the way it is today, in America? In England?

9. Makepeace lived for years on her plan to exact revenge on Catty and Conyers. How did her quest for reprisal impact her life?

Did her campaign to settle the score shape who she became to those who loved her? How did Betty take Makepeace's grim crusade? What effect did it have on Philippa?

10. The coal-lined netherworld that Makepeace descends into with Andra Hedley is a metaphor for death: pitch-black darkness, like "the coffin lid coming down, the withdrawal of self, of hope, of God. In that moment she knew what death actually was . . . She lost Dapifer then." Hedley tells her, "Persephone comes yearly out the shadows and you'll do the same." This is both belated acknowledgment of reality and our earliest glimmer that Makepeace might recover from Dapifer's death. Is there yet more underlying this encounter? Do you see, at this stage, any sign that her relationship with Hedley might symbolize something beyond a means to the wealth she requires to carry out her revenge? Does it seem unlikely, here, that she could have an intimate relationship with a man who is Dapifer's antithesis? Does Makepeace entertain the idea at all?

11. Relatively late in life—although she is young yet—Makepeace discovers the satisfaction of female bonding, beyond the rich relationship she has long shared with Betty, in her friendship with Susan Brewer. Do you think Makepeace's relationships with the women whom she employs in the mines are significant in her discovering who she really is? As a hard-nosed, goal-driven businesswoman whose sole ambition is to settle a grudge, how great is Makepeace's capacity to appreciate her female helpers and colleagues?

12. When Makepeace and Hedley become trapped in the mine and share their near-death/sexual experience, does it seem like a fluke—a freakish representation of what can happen during times of crisis, when life is threatened? Is it merely Makepeace's release after such prolonged and intense grieving? Does it seem plausible that she can feel for a man after losing one "for whom there was no comparison"? In what direction, at this critical moment, do you think Makepeace's life will head?